SHADOW OF THE SOLSTICE

ALSO BY ANNE HILLERMAN

SHADOW OF THE SOLSTICE

A Leaphorn, Chee & Manuelito Novel

ANNE HILLERMAN

HARPER

An Imprint of HarperCollinsPublishers

SHADOW OF THE SOLSTICE. Copyright © 2025 by Anne Hillerman. All rights reserved. Printed in the United States of America. No part of this book may be used or reproduced in any manner whatsoever without written permission except in the case of brief quotations embodied in critical articles and reviews. For information, address HarperCollins Publishers, 195 Broadway, New York, NY 10007.

Designed by Michele Cameron

ISBN 978-0-06-334485-3

For Kevin, Carrie, Sean, and Brandon with love

SHADOW OF THE SOLSTICE

Chapter 1

He noticed the body in the place where he'd been told never to go because of leetso, also known as uranium, the monster of yellow earth.

He had been running for the past few days on the land just outside the fence, taking a slightly different route each morning. The fence and the warning signs were designed to keep people like him away from the radioactive material disposal site. Then, this morning, he found the new opening, the place where someone had cut through the links.

He jogged through the opening, happy to run a different route.

He had stopped to catch his breath when he saw the hat, a newish brown cowboy hat with a handsome silver hatband.

And in the flash of an eye, he realized it wasn't just a hat, but a head. Then he saw the rest of the man. An odd place to sleep, he thought. The person wasn't dressed the way you would expect someone sleeping rough to be, and he had a handsome ring with some turquoise on his left hand.

Then, in less time than it took to look away, he saw the battered face, the congealed blood.

He was staring at a dead man. Leetso had claimed another life.

Shock and terror began to fill him from the tips of his toes to the crown of his head. He had never seen a real dead person before.

He ran away from the dead one as fast as he could, wishing that there was school today to distract him from the terrible image that seared itself into his memory.

No more drinking for him. It was time to get out of that place, and get out fast.

Chapter 2

Bernadette Manuelito was dressed for her morning jog.

She smiled as she glanced at the clock. She had plenty of time to cook breakfast before the day grew too hot. Her aged mother had moved from the house she had shared with Bernie's younger sister, Darleen, into Bernie and Chee's home. They had adjusted their work schedules to make sure that someone was always there with Mama.

But because life happened, especially in their mutual world of Navajo law enforcement, they often needed Darleen's help, and she did what she could while juggling her new job as a health aide and her college assignments. Today Darleen was working with Mrs. Raymond, one of her favorite clients, so they were lucky that Officer Harold Bigman's bilagáana wife could also pitch in.

That morning Mrs. Briana Bigman was coming over with her little boy. Bernie would be able to go for a run, do essential errands, and then meet retired lieutenant Joe Leaphorn, her mentor and adopted uncle, for iced tea and conversation.

She was looking forward to a day off.

Mama needed advance notice to handle transitions, and the more

warning she had, the more smoothly things went. But if Bernie told
her too soon that Mrs. Bigman was coming, Mama would forget.
Bernie sat on the couch with Mama and looked at her lined face, her
gray hair still in the braid Bernie had created for her yesterday. Her
mother had once been taller than Bernie, almost as tall as Darleen,
but age and gravity had shortened her. While she had never been fat,
now she edged toward too thin. Bernie took Mama's hand in her own,
noticing that despite the day's warmth, her skin felt cool.

Bernie called up some inner calm before she spoke. "Today is the
day Mrs. Bigman will be here to visit with you. I have to leave for a
while, and then I'll be back."

Mama stayed focused on the television.

Bernie tried again. "Mama, I'm fixing breakfast for you now.
After that, someone you like is coming today."

Mama nodded. "That's good. Why?"

"I have to leave for a little while."

Mama nodded again. "Do you have to go to school?"

"I have a lot to learn." Bernie said it with conviction.

"OK then." Mama frowned. "Where is your sister?"

"Oh, she's not here now, but I know she will eat her breakfast."

"Good." Mama patted Bernie's hand. "I already had my breakfast.
Watch this show with me."

They sat together and watched some old movie for a minute.
Then Bernie rose to fix the breakfast of scrambled eggs, toast, and
coffee her mother imagined that she'd already eaten. Bernie shared
the coffee and put her own eggs into a burrito to eat after she ran.

So far the morning had been smooth, and for that she was grateful. She cleaned the kitchen and helped Mama get dressed. They were
down to the socks and shoes when Bernie heard a vehicle approach.
She left Mama and went to the door. She expected Mrs. Bigman and
her two-year-old son, even though it was early, but instead the rookie
cop, Roper Black, stood there, embarrassment all over his face.

"Hey Roper. What's up?"

"Hey Bernie. The captain tried to call, but your phone is off. He told me to tell you to . . ." Roper hesitated. "He said you need to keep your phone on all the time in case of emergency."

"Right. I know. I screwed up."

Bernie remembered that when Mama finally fell asleep, around 2:00 a.m., she had shut down her phone and neglected to restart it.

"The captain needs you to report ASAP. Something about a big shot coming to Shiprock. It's a mandatory meeting."

"Really? On my day off?" She felt her eyebrows rise. She named the Navajo Nation president. "Is that the hotshot?"

"I don't think so. I'm the rookie, remember, the last guy to learn anything. When I asked what was up, all he said was 'I'll explain at the meeting. Go get Manuelito.' " Roper looked at the camping trailer parked next to their home. "You guys planning on a vacation?"

"My mother is living with us. We needed some privacy, and that seemed like a good solution for now, so Chee and I are sleeping in there." That had been the plan, at least, but Mama's nighttime restlessness meant that one of them usually slept on the sofa in the living room, in case of a crisis.

Roper smiled. "If you get tired of your husband, you and your mother can climb in there and head out into the sunset."

"I'll have Mama send you a postcard." Bernie heard the squeak of a walker, and then Mama herself stood in the doorway. She looked at Bernie, and then her gaze switched to Roper in his uniform.

"Officer, what is the problem?" Mama spoke in Navajo.

Roper responded slowly, in good Navajo, politely sidestepping the question and instead introducing himself with his clans.

Mama's deeply instilled habit of graciousness kicked in, and she reciprocated. After that, she opened the door and motioned to Roper to come inside. "That one doesn't have manners." She pointed toward Bernie with her chin. "It's time for lunch, and we are hungry."

Roper looked at the ground a moment before he responded. Bernie knew it would be rude for him to ignore the offer or to point out that breakfast had just passed.

Roper proved wiser than his twenty-some-odd years would suggest. "Oh, my grandmother, I would like that very much. I need to talk to your daughter a bit more, first. About things where we work."

Mama frowned at both of them. Bernie hoped she wouldn't lose her temper. "Policeman, OK. I need to eat now. You come to my house tomorrow."

Bernie spoke softly. "Mama, I left some applesauce and a cookie for you on the counter. Try those, and I will be in soon." Mama must have already forgotten that she had eaten breakfast.

Roper nodded. Mama turned in her walker, and they heard the squeak as she headed inside. Bernie stood a bit straighter. "Thanks for coming by. Tell the captain I'll get to the station as soon as I can."

She expected Roper to head off, but she noticed him watching Mama through the open door.

"You know, my wife gets lonely some days with just our baby girl for company. I could talk to her about spending time with your mother." He adjusted his hat as he spoke. "My wife's mother is making things difficult for her and, well, for all of us, because she wants us to do everything her way. It would be good for Hannah to get out of the house for a while. If you say yes, you'd be doing us a favor."

"So your wife's mother lives with you, too?"

"No. Actually we live with her."

Bernie understood. "Ask Hannah to call me, and we'll talk. Mama might enjoy someone new to visit with." And she and Chee welcomed all the help they could find as Mama grew more challenging.

Roper walked to his unit, and Bernie went inside. She unobtrusively checked on Mama, who was watching a game show on TV. So much for her day's plan. She sent an apologetic cancellation message to Leaphorn, and then headed to the back of the little house to dress for work.

The sudden mandatory meeting made her curious. Usually Chee stayed on top of things like this and shared what he could with her. He knew that Mama's presence gave her less flexibility at work. If the captain needed her to work all day, Bernie had a conflict. Mrs. Bigman planned to stay for only three hours. Maybe Darleen could help after that. She knew her sister wouldn't mind having Mama all to herself, but she didn't remember Darleen's school schedule for the day. She texted her sister and then called the station and left a voicemail for Captain Texas Adakai, to let him know that she would be there as soon as she could.

Then she called Chee's cell phone. He answered right away. "Hello beautiful. How is your morning going?"

His voice always lifted her spirits. "Oh, more interesting than usual," Bernie said. "Roper Black was just here. I left my phone off and the captain sent him to tell me to come in this morning for a meeting. Even though it's my day off. What's going on?"

"Only rumors at this point. Evidently some politician or celebrity or rodeo star from somewhere is on the way to our little Shiprock, and that might create a traffic jam." He laughed. "I haven't heard any names yet. And we got a call about someone disturbing the peace and abandoning a fancy car out past the old Teec Nos Pos trading post. The fun never stops."

Chapter 3

Although he had invited his grandmother to join him, Droid had reconsidered. He'd tried to talk her out of coming earlier that morning. But Mrs. Melia Raymond would not be deterred. To his embarrassment his large, gray-haired shimásání stood next to him when the white van pulled up in the Shiprock grocery store parking lot, where his friend had dropped them off.

The van's door opened, and a woman in jeans and a sleeveless blouse climbed out. She had on a ball cap and straight blue hair that covered her ears and touched the tan skin at the top of her shoulders. She walked toward them.

"Hello there," she said. And then she tried a fairly good version of "Yá'át'ééh'."

Mrs. Raymond returned the greeting. Her grandson said "Howdy."

The blue-haired woman focused on the grandson. "You're Andrew, right? From yesterday."

He pushed his glasses up the bridge of his nose. "I go by Droid."

"So, ready to get clean? Ready for rehab and the counseling?"

"Yep. I'm all set."

She studied him. "I'm glad you called the number I gave you so I knew you were ready to get picked up. You're at least eighteen, right?"

Droid said nothing.

Mrs. Raymond realized that her grandson had ignored the question about age rather than lie to say he was older than his seventeen years, and the blue-haired woman didn't press him to answer. Instead, Blue handed him a clipboard with a paper form and a pen. Then she turned to Mrs. Raymond.

"Are you thinking about signing up for rehab, too? The more the merrier. I've got room in the van today."

"Tell me where he's going and what happens when he gets there."

Blue crinkled her nose in surprise. "We are helping people like him, people who want to get sober, join a program that will give them a safe place to sleep, eat, get some counseling, whatever else they need to fight their addiction."

Mrs. Raymond thought Blue sounded like she was reading a script. "Where is this place?"

"In Arizona."

"Window Rock?"

The woman laughed. "I wish. We're going all the way to Phoenix."

"How much does it cost?"

"Nothing. That's the beauty of it, you know? The government pays for everything. The folks in charge make sure of that." The woman stood a little straighter. "The government owes you natives, don't you think?"

Droid glanced up from the clipboard and nodded in agreement.

Mrs. Raymond looked at her handsome grandson. "So, drinking has a hold of you?"

"Yes, Shimásání. Drinking and weed." But she knew it already. She'd seen him high, noticed the slurred speech, seen the empties.

"Drinking, mostly. That's why I got in trouble after Mom died.

Why I can't run like I used to in track and cross country. I still run, b-but . . ." He took a deep breath. "Anyway, I wanna start fresh. Start over."

Mrs. Raymond knew about the drinking trouble and Droid's father's angry reaction to it. She'd had some bad days herself, after Droid's mother died. That's why Droid was staying with her some nights. And why she put the black purse with her money and the keys to her dead husband's car under the extra pillow next to her when she went to bed. Her arthritis pain medicine and what she took for blood pressure after her stroke went there too. She'd seen troubles like Droid's too often.

She was happy that he suddenly wanted help. But something about the blue-haired woman and the small white van bothered her. She didn't know exactly what, but something was off. She distrusted anything like this that seemed too good to be true.

She turned to Droid. "You need to stay here with me and your dad. You need a ceremony to make you strong."

"I'll do that when I get back, I promise. But I have to go now. It's not right for a man to be where I'm at, you know, with you always helping me with money and a place to stay and my dad telling me how I've disappointed him. I mean, I appreciate you, Shimásání, but things should be the other way around. Me helping you."

He stood a head taller than his grandmother now, but Mrs. Raymond outweighed him. He still had the lean frame of a runner. "I tried to stop drinking and getting high on my own, but that didn't work out. I've got friends here, you know, all of us caught in the same bad trap. That's why going away to get clean makes sense."

He looked at Blue. "I'll come back stronger, right?"

Blue said, "Get in. I have more pickups to make."

Mrs. Raymond gave the woman a hard look. "Wait. We're talking."

"I leave in five minutes." Blue climbed into the van and closed the door.

Droid spoke faster now. "Shimásání, I have to go. I saw one of my buddies die already. I know drinking will kill me. I'm scared to do this, to get in the van and go away, but I don't want to die drunk or be an adláanii." He stopped talking, and tears pooled in his dark eyes. "I don't want to embarrass you or the rest of my relatives. Besides, I got a sign."

She had known something was bothering him yesterday as soon as he returned from his run. He spent a long time in the shower, and then he was out all day. When he came back to her place, he wanted to talk. That was unusual for this quiet seventeen-year-old. She remembered every word.

"Grandma, I saw something terrible. It might have been a hallucination. Whatever. I have to get my act together. I have to stop drinking. I'm going to rehab."

"What did you see?" She had to ask him twice before he gave her even a hint.

"Something disgusting. I can't talk about it, but I know it was a sign." He stood and started to pace. "I took a shower to wash it away. After I left your house, I went out to meet my friends, and some older guys were there who had some beer. I drank with them, hoping to forget that image, but it still burns in my mind."

She waited for him to continue.

"We were talking, you know, messing around, and a white van just like this one stopped. The driver spoke to us, and that changed the way I thought about things."

Blue had told them about a free place to stay, free food, and rehab to help them stop drinking. The van was full of Navajos. The woman said she would be back in the supermarket parking lot the next morning for anyone who wanted free meals, a place to live, and rehab.

"The other guys still wanna party. But I'm ready to change." She remembered his hesitation and then the surge of confidence in his voice when he told her. "This opportunity sounds good. I have to get on the van tomorrow."

And now tomorrow was today, and the van had arrived for him.

Mrs. Raymond walked to the van door and motioned to the woman in the driver's seat. "Give me some of those papers. I'm going with him."

"OK." The driver handed her a clipboard. "You understand the program is for counseling, right? For people with drug and alcohol problems."

Mrs. Raymond nodded. She looked at the form, and it was just as she had suspected. She put her hand on Droid's arm. "Help me with this."

The stroke had damaged her vision. She could read the bigger letters without much trouble, and the standard print when she squinted, but even wearing her glasses, she couldn't make out the fine print. It looked like a lot of complicated mumbo jumbo.

"What does this mean?" She moved the clipboard toward him, and he glanced at it a few moments. Then he shrugged. "It's the rules for the rehab place. It says things like you won't sue nobody or be a badass. That's what it looks like to me."

She asked Droid more questions, and then she walked up to the van's door. Blue lowered the driver's window.

"We don't find the part about food and a place to stay here."

"Oh, don't worry about that." Blue looked at the clock on the dashboard. "You two coming or not? I need to get on the road."

Mrs. Raymond put her hands on her hips. "Those things need to be in the agreement if we are going. We can't ride in this van unless you can get that straightened out."

Blue frowned. Droid stared at the ground in embarrassment, but Mrs. Raymond didn't back down.

After a minute, Blue closed the van's window. They could see her doing something on her phone. Then she opened the door and spoke to Droid.

"You got a phone?"

"Yeah." His expression added that it was a really dumb question.

"I'll send you a text with the stuff your grandmother wants. Lodging while you're with us, treatment appointments, and three meals a day."

A moment later Droid's phone made a noise, and he held the screen toward her. "Here, Shimásání."

"Read it to me."

He cleared his throat. " 'Best Way Rehabilitation Center hereby agrees to provide food and lodging to you while you are in rehabilitation treatment for substance abuse.' And then it's signed by Beatrice Dottson, president, Best Way Rehabilitation Center."

Mrs. Raymond moved her chin up and down in subtle agreement. She felt proud of her tall, handsome grandson and proud of herself for getting the agreement. She would have preferred something on paper, but a note from the president sounded good. "You save that, OK?"

"Yes. For sure."

She found the place to sign, agreeing to counseling and addiction treatment at the Best Way Rehabilitation Center in Phoenix, Arizona.

She wasn't a drinker, but she liked the idea of counseling. When she and her helper, Darleen Manuelito, talked, Mrs. Raymond felt like she was a counselor for the young woman, and she thought Darleen's advice helped her, too. Darleen had mentioned that her sister was a police officer. Maybe that's why Darleen was so smart when it came to people.

Mrs. Raymond tapped on the open door to get Blue's attention. "Here it is. I'm ready now."

The woman's plump lips turned up into a shadow of a smile as she took the papers. "Great. Grab a seat. Let's go."

Droid slipped his phone into his pocket, and Mrs. Raymond motioned to him to climb in first. He headed to a pair of empty spots near the center of the van and put his backpack on the shelf over the seats. Mrs. Raymond sat next to the window. Their adventure was about to begin. She hoped the outcome would restore this young man she treasured to hózhó, that wonderful state of hope, joy, and balance in the face of life's challenges. And the counseling might even help her, too.

Chapter 4

When Chee didn't seem to have more to add, Bernie moved the phone conversation forward. "Can you tell me anything else about the captain's meeting?"

"Not much. The captain said the chief got the heads-up in a call from a special agent in Washington. The visitor is bringing a bunch of those security guys to Shiprock to provide protection. They want us to help."

"Wow." Bernie considered the information. "This must be a big-time government official. Did the captain give you any hints about who is on the way?"

"Nope, not a word. You know I like a challenge. We have a surprise guest coming to our slice of the nation, but no clue about who or when, except that it's someone important and soon. And all this before nine a.m."

"Yeah, Mama just had breakfast."

Chee sighed. "Sweetheart, I'm sorry you have to give up some of your day off for this."

"Oh, stuff happens. I'm sad about canceling my visit with

Leaphorn, but I like to be where the action is. I just hope I don't have to work all day. I need to spend some time with Mama."

Before he could stop himself, Chee said, "You need to spend time with me, too, you know. I miss you."

***

Bernie had started a load of laundry and was about to get ready for work when her phone rang again. As soon as she answered, she could tell that something had upset Darleen. She heard the worry in her sister's voice.

After a few pleasantries, Darleen got to the point. "I need your advice on something."

"You bet. Join us for dinner tonight?"

"I can't. Let's talk now, OK?"

"Sure, but I've got to get to work."

"I thought this was your day off." Darleen rushed. "This shouldn't take long. It's about—"

"Tell them I don't need any." Mama had heard the phone ring from where she sat at Bernie's kitchen table, and she started talking, too, in Navajo. "Tell them to stop bothering me." She raised her voice. "Daughter, you hear me? Listen to me."

"Hold on," Bernie said, both to Darleen on the phone and to their mother in person. She took a calming breath and walked toward Mama. Her mother did better at understanding when the person who was speaking faced her. Their physical presence helped focus her attention.

"Shimá, I need to talk to Sister for a little while." Bernie and Darleen always spoke to Mama in Navajo, Diné bizaad.

"She's here?"

"No, I'm talking to her on the phone. I'm going out to the deck for a moment. Why don't you sit on the couch and relax for a while?"

Mama nodded but stayed where she was. Bernie moved outside, where she could talk with privacy. "OK. I'm back. What's up?"

"How is Mama today?"

Bernie adjusted her chair so the morning sun could warm her back and sat down. "Oh, about the same, I guess."

"It's tough, right?"

She heard the empathy in Darleen's voice and nodded, even though Darleen couldn't see her. "Thank goodness for my husband. He's got more patience than I have."

Darleen laughed. "Ask Cheeseburger where I can get some of that." Cheeseburger was her special nickname for Chee. Mama had called him that, too, back when she remembered who he was.

"I would, but unfortunately, he's not here. He went in early again this morning. I don't think he's crazy about being a lieutenant." She was glad that he had awakened her so she could pray and run before he left. "What's up, Sister?"

"I'm worried about one of my elderlies, Mrs. Raymond. I'm talking to you from her house, and she's not here. She's always here, always has coffee for us, always has a story or two, and then she asks me about my plans. She wants me to come early, so I do." Darleen's words rushed out. "She hears me drive up, you know, and she's at the door.

"But today she didn't have the door open. I knocked and waited for her to come so we could start our visit. When she didn't show up, I knocked again and called for her. Nothing. So then I opened the door and went inside." Darleen took a breath. "Was that a bad thing, you know, like breaking and entering or trespassing?"

"No. Just tell me the rest."

"I wouldn't have come in without her permission, but I was worried that she might be hurt, you know, might have fallen or had another stroke or something. That's why I got the job, because she had a stroke. I stop by to check her blood pressure, make sure she's taking her meds, you know, because she's in our special program.

"I was a touch early, so I thought maybe she was still sleeping or something. But she never sleeps late. She tells me she's always up before the first bird sings. Anyway, she's not in the house, and there's no note or anything. It's totally unlike her to forget about our appointment. I don't know what to do next."

"What did you do before you called me?"

The phone was silent for a moment, and Bernie could practically hear her sister thinking. "I walked through the house, looking for her. I'm yelling, 'Mrs. R? Hello, it's Darleen.' Mrs. R is what I call her. But nothing. Then I went outside and searched and kept yelling her name. She never answered. She isn't here anywhere. You're a cop. What should I do?"

Bernie heard the anxiety in her sister's voice. Her memory flashed back to the time when Darleen thought their mother had disappeared and called in a panic, only to discover Mama at her neighbor Mrs. Darkwater's house.

"Are there any neighbors out there to check with?"

"Well, not close enough to walk to."

"Does Mrs. R have a car there?"

"Yes. Parked with the hood up, like always. She hasn't moved it."

"Does she live by herself?"

"She does now. Her oldest daughter and her son-in-law and her grandson used to live with her, but the daughter died last year, and the son-in-law moved to a new place. Her other daughter, Victoria, lives close to her, practically next door. I can walk there in about ten minutes."

"Maybe Mrs. Raymond went to visit Victoria. Did you check?"

"Not yet. I doubt that she's there, because she told me they don't get along." Darleen sighed. "I let Victoria know Mrs. R wasn't home before I called you. I texted—that's the way we always communicate. Victoria didn't respond, so I called her, but she didn't answer the phone either."

"What about the son-in-law? Maybe she went to see the grandson and his dad."

"Maybe." Darleen paused for a few beats. "They live somewhere around here, but I don't know where. I've never met them."

"Does your lady have other children?"

"Well, there's a son and a daughter-in-law living in Pennsylvania. I think it's sad, you know, that she has to live by herself. She's a strong-willed woman, outspoken and all that. But she misses the daughter who died. She told me that her birthday is coming up. The first one since her death."

"What about Mrs. Raymond's friends? Maybe someone took her out to breakfast." Bernie pictured Darleen's client having coffee with another lady somewhere, enjoying herself so much she forgot about the appointment.

"I didn't think of that. They come on days I'm not around, you know, so I haven't met them, but she talks about these other ladies quite a bit." Darleen's voice sounded a bit lighter. "I'll see if I can find their numbers. But could you check to see if Mrs. R has turned up anywhere, like the hospital, if she got hurt?"

"I can do that after you follow up with Victoria and the rest of your ideas. A lot of times people wander off and then come back. If Mrs. Raymond doesn't return and Victoria doesn't have any idea where she could be, call me again. We'll talk about the next step then. By the way, that notice for an elderly person is called a Silver Alert. We can work on that if we need to."

"Good."

"Even though you'd rather not do it, be sure to talk to Victoria, OK?"

"OK. I'm walking over there as soon as we hang up. Thanks. I feel better after talking to you."

Bernie heard the residual anxiety in Darleen's voice. "Hey," she said, "in the years I've been a cop, I've seen a lot of these cases work out on their own. I hope Mrs. Raymond will be back with a story about spending the morning with a friend or a clan sister."

Bernie was about to end the call when her sister surprised her.

"Sister, one more thing. I want you to know that I really appreciate you and Cheeseburger figuring out how Mama could live with you while I stay in her house. I feel like I've got my life back. Ahéhéé."

Chapter 5

The van rolled on through the New Mexico heat. Most of the other passengers were men, Mrs. Raymond noticed, and a few were people she'd seen before. No one looked as young as Droid; most were middle-aged and beyond and showed the damage that came from a hard life. There were a couple of other women. The vehicle had a sliding door like a minivan and, she estimated, could hold fifteen people.

The route from Shiprock to Gallup had taken them through familiar country. They had passed the settlements of Newcomb, Tohatchi, and Naschitti, and then on to the junction at Ya-ta-hey, with the untaken turn to Window Rock. Mrs. Raymond watched as they passed the businesses in Gamerco: feed stores, pawnshops, used car lots, the place where the huge Gallup flea market welcomed shoppers, and more.

The van quickly passed the junction for the road to Zuni Pueblo, and when she saw the sign, Mrs. Raymond touched her pocket for the little stone turtle she always kept with her. She didn't feel it, and that worried her. She had promised the Zuni friend who gave it to her that she'd keep it with her, but she must have left it at home.

Now they were on Interstate 40 headed west, new territory for her. The highway was filled with big trucks that made the van sway as they passed and lots of RVs, people on vacation. This was big country. She noticed a long train, a few range cows clustered near a gate in a fence, and a horse or two searching for something to eat in the sparse vegetation. A sign welcomed them to Arizona.

Droid had closed his eyes. The van headed on. It reminded Mrs. Raymond of a miniature bus with a sliding door.

After about an hour, the vehicle took an exit and turned in to a gas station that was also a convenience store. Sanders, Arizona. As they rolled to a stop, Mrs. Raymond noticed that the neon sign in the window advertised a popular brand of beer, the kind of beer her late husband loved.

She touched Droid's arm. "Do you have money?"

"Yes."

"Give it to me so you won't be tempted to buy beer." She held out her hand. "I'll keep it for you. If you need to buy something, let me know."

"But it's my money. I'm not a baby, Shimásání."

"You asked me to come with you, to help you have courage, remember?"

He took out his wallet. "OK, but I need some money for cigarettes and candy." He gave her two ten-dollar bills, a five, and two ones. He kept a five and a ten for himself.

"Cigarettes?" She frowned.

"I knew you wouldn't like it."

She didn't like it, but she didn't give him grief. One problem at a time was plenty.

Blue turned around from the driver's seat to look at the passengers. "Listen up. You all can get off and stretch your legs if you want. We're getting some new passengers. We'll be leaving in about twenty minutes."

Mrs. Raymond was glad for the break. She went to the ladies' room, and as she was washing her hands, someone she recognized from the van came in. The woman used a damp paper towel to wash her face, her neck, and then her arms. She wore three thin silver and turquoise bracelets on her left wrist, and her fingernails still had a bit of shiny red polish. She was somewhere between forty and fifty, or maybe younger. Mrs. Raymond had noticed that alcoholics aged more quickly.

Mrs. Raymond spoke to her. "What do you think of this trip?"

"I dunno. Why?"

"I hope the program will be good for my grandson. He's had some struggles."

The other woman laughed. "Me, too. That's why I started drinking." She tossed the paper towels toward the wastebasket and missed. "I guess booze will kill me one of these days. In the meantime, this might help. I've tried rehab before, but it never stuck. I figure this can't do me no harm."

Mrs. Raymond used her left hand, which she relied on more after the stroke, to pick up the towels from the floor by a dry edge and deposit them in the trash can. "What happens in these places?"

"It depends. They usually find someone to talk about the problems that come with drinking and drugs, you know? They tell you about AA. Some rehabs give you medicine to help with the DTs. Then they set you free." When the woman laughed, her turquoise earrings swung slightly with her hair. Her hair needed shampooing, Mrs. Raymond thought, but she kept her opinion to herself.

"Speaking of what's comin', I've got some joy juice. Want some?" She opened her purse, a large multicolored bag, and pulled out a bottle of something that looked like water. "You know, a last blast before we hit the pass. Getting sober is hard work, right? We need to fortify ourselves."

She unscrewed the cap and offered Mrs. Raymond the first shot.

"I don't drink. I'm here for my grandson."

"Oh." The woman took a swig. "Has he tried to get sober before?"

"He said he stopped drinking, but it didn't work."

"It's tough." She screwed the lid back on the bottle and hid it in her purse. "I coulda died in a car wreck last week. I think an angel or somethin' had my back. That's why I'm here. What happened with your grandson?"

"I don't know exactly. He said he saw something and he decided to get sober. He doesn't want to talk about it."

"Ask him. He'll feel better if he gets it off his chest."

They left the restroom together and headed into the convenience store that was part of the station. Mrs. Raymond noticed alcohol of various kinds for sale. This seemed like an odd stop for a van full of people with problems with alcohol.

She found Blue looking at sunglasses.

"It's time to go." Mrs. Raymond pointed to her watch. "Twenty minutes." She didn't believe in Indian time.

Blue nodded. "Yeah, but the men's room is having issues. See that line?"

Mrs. Raymond could see three men waiting. None of them was her grandson. "Where's Droid?"

"Who?"

Mrs. Raymond frowned. "Andrew. The tall one with glasses."

"Oh, right. I saw him outside with a cigarette."

Mrs. Raymond sighed. Her husband had smoked a pack a day or more until she shamed him into stopping. Then he died from a fall off a ladder. If she'd known he would be dead at age fifty-nine, she would have spent less time nagging him about smoking and drinking and more time enjoying his company.

"I have a question." She didn't wait for Blue to acknowledge that. "Why stop at a place that sells alcohol?"

"I don't decide where we stop for gas or to make pickups. The people who run the program set up the itinerary."

Mrs. Raymond went outside, and Droid walked up to her. They stood together in the parking lot.

"Shimásání," Droid said, "I don't think you should go with me to the rehab place. I'll call Dad to pick you up. I can do this journey on my own. I'm nearly a man. Next year, that's my last year of high school, you know?"

She smelled the cigarettes on him, and now alcohol, too, evidence of his youth and his weakness.

"Someone offered you a drink back there, and you said yes."

Droid didn't respond.

"So I'm staying with you. But even without that, I would have not gone back. I signed the papers."

Droid frowned, but Mrs. Raymond stood her ground. She had only promised to go with Droid to meet the van, but when the situation sounded suspicious, she knew she might have to go on the trip, too.

She let some time pass, then spoke quietly. "I'm an old lady now, and I've learned that talking about things that frighten me takes some of their power away. Tell me what you saw that scared you into getting in the van."

Droid glanced past her toward the traffic streaming by on the interstate, heading out across the open territory of Arizona. She gave him time to answer.

"A dead man. I saw a dead man. He had a nice hat and a silver ring." Droid paused, swallowed, and said the rest. "It looked like somebody beat him to death. I ran away as fast as I could."

"Where was he?"

"Behind the leetso fence. I was in the restricted area. Trespassing, you know? I had drunk too much the night before, way over my limit. Maybe I imagined the dead man. Maybe it was a sign saying that dude could be me. Whatever. I don't want to die like that."

She waited, and when he said nothing more, she told him what she thought. "Maybe you had a vision, but maybe there is a dead person out there. Maybe you didn't imagine it." She took a breath. "You need to call and tell the police what you found."

He flinched. "But . . ." And he fell silent.

"Think of it this way. If the person is real, that dead man's family is looking for him, worried about him. Your call will give them peace. What do you have to lose by making the call?"

"OK, here's the deal. What if the police think I'm a murderer after they trace my cell phone? Or what if they arrest me for trespassing?" He twisted a strand of hair as he spoke, and she could feel his worry.

She let some time go by before she responded. "You need to do the right thing, Shicheii. Once you do that, you'll feel better, free of that monster. Let the police deal with it. That's their job."

Mrs. Raymond had an idea.

"A person who helps me has a sister who works with the Navajo Police. She gave me the direct number for the police station one time when I was worried about something." Mrs. Raymond remembered the number and recited it. "Call them. They understand more about things that we shouldn't talk about. Things like dead people who might not be there."

Droid started to walk toward the store. "I need a cold drink." She must have made a face, because he added, "I mean water or juice or a soda or something."

"I'll go with you. I'd like one, too." She moved to his side. "What about that call? If you don't want to call the number I gave you, just use 911. The emergency number." Mrs. Raymond assumed that whoever answered the call would eventually get the message to whoever needed to know in Shiprock.

He stopped. "I don't like to think about what I saw, OK?

She understood.

They went back in the store. Mrs. Raymond noticed that two different men were in the restroom line. She moved to the refrigerated case where they stored the cold drinks, and considered what to buy. Her grandson looked at the display of snack food, then without selecting a bag of chips or a package of peanuts walked up to the sales counter. He spoke to the young cashier, and she said something to him and shook her head. He said something and then he handed her one of the bills from his wallet. The woman looked at the money, then moved the store telephone toward him.

Mrs. Raymond saw him pick up the phone and touch the screen. She couldn't hear what he said, but she read the relief in the way he held his body when he put the receiver down and left the store.

She paid for two drinks.

Outside, she handed Droid a large plastic bottle of sweet tea. "Does your father know about this trip?"

"No. I didn't want to tell him in case I couldn't do it. I don't want him to think I'm a loser."

She understood. "He'll be worried."

Droid sighed. "I'll text him."

"Take a picture of us for him so he'll know we're OK. He can show that to Victoria, too."

Droid had just finished sending the selfie when they saw Blue striding to the van with a white guy wearing shorts and three other people who looked like Navajos. Blue and the man in shorts, a small, thin bilagáana with a gold chain around his scrawny neck, climbed in first. Droid and Mrs. Raymond watched Gold Chain struggle to adjust the driver's seat. Then the van's door opened and the horn honked.

The three new passengers climbed aboard, and Mrs. Raymond, Droid, and the others did, too. They found their seats and settled in for another stretch of the trip. The cool air inside the van felt good.

Droid put his hand in the back pocket of his jeans and pulled out his phone before he sat down. "It's a long time until we get to Phoenix. I've got my music here. I don't wanna talk. You understand, right? It's nothing personal, but I have a lot to think about."

She nodded. The young man had never been much of a talker, and silence would serve him well.

Droid put something in each ear, leaned his head back against the seat, and closed his eyes.

Mrs. Raymond tapped him on the shoulder. "What is that?"

"What?"

"Those things in your ears."

"It's the way I can listen to the music. An earbud."

"Ear bug? That's a funny name."

'No, it's . . ." He stopped himself. "You're right. Ear bug is funny."

She leaned back and settled in for the long ride to come. Gold Chain was driving, and they were on the way again.

After a while Droid said, "Do you think I'll make it?"

"You have your mother's strength inside you. You can call on that strength when you need it. The challenge is difficult."

"OK."

Mrs. Raymond had never told him, her only grandchild, that his handsome face and cheerful disposition reminded her of his mother, her daughter who had died, and of her husband, the grandfather he had never met, the man she had also lost too soon. This boy gave her life meaning, and she would do whatever she could to support him.

Except for the two of them and the woman who had offered her a drink, the people on the journey treated each other like strangers. She remembered her husband's periods of quiet and his resolve each time he decided to stop drinking. She'd left him alone with his thoughts, and she wouldn't intrude on these folks, either. She wished them well.

She noticed that Droid had closed his eyes again as the van rolled on.

This was good, Mrs. Raymond thought. These people deserved another chance to be healthy, to help their families, to make amends for the damage that drinking had caused. Too much marijuana, naakai binát'oh, was bad, and other drugs were worse. As far as she could tell, Droid had only tried marijuana.

She picked up her purse from the floor near her feet, pulled out a paperback book, and opened it to a page she had marked with a downturned corner. She rarely had time to read, especially during the day; this road trip gave her that gift. The book was about the Navajo man who had gone with the bilagáana explorers to show some white people Na'nízhoozhí, the sacred rainbow bridge at Lake Powell. A good book to be reading now, she thought, when she was also on the move. But after just a few pages, her eyes grew heavy and she fell asleep.

Chapter 6

As usual, Lieutenant Jim Chee had arrived at the substation early. He greeted Sandra and found a note on his computer from Captain Texas Adakai, saying that he'd be in later and that the meeting with the chief was mandatory, all officers, no exceptions.

Chee had just poured himself his second cup of coffee when he ran into Officer Bigman.

"What is this morning's surprise meeting about? I heard the chief himself is coming up for it." It was rare for the chief of the Navajo Police to pay the Shiprock substation a visit.

"I don't know much," Chee said. "I just learned about it myself. It's something major, a big deal. I don't think the chief has stopped by here in years."

Bigman smiled. "I know. He's announcing that the number of officers will be doubled this year, and we all get more time off, too."

Chee smiled. "I bet someone from New Mexico's congressional delegation in Washington wants to let Navajos know how hard they are working for us."

Bigman rubbed his chin. "I heard a rumor that a high-powered somebody from the federal government decided to put Shiprock on the map by making a 'save the rattler' proclamation or something. That must be it."

Sandra buzzed Chee, and Bigman left the office so he could take the call. FBI agent Sage Johnson was on the phone. They chatted a moment, and then she got to business.

"Would you let the captain know I can't make it today?"

"Sure," he said. "Make it for what?"

"Sorry. Make it to the meeting. You know, the one about interagency cooperation for the big visit? My calendar is already packed, thanks to the DC office and all the extra excitement. And this is still a maybe— you know, a just-in-case. They won't say for sure that she's even coming."

"She?"

"The secretary, uh—" Johnson caught herself. "Um . . . just erase that."

Chee thought of how to play his cards. "No worries. The captain left me a note."

"This whole thing was supposed to be confidential until the secretary makes her final decision."

"That's right," Chee said. "But you know it's hard to keep a secret, especially when the word's already out to so many people. Captain Adakai has been closemouthed about it, but when he said the chief planned to come from Window Rock this morning for an all-hands-on-deck meeting, we got the idea that there must be some big shot on the way to warrant all this security."

"If the captain or the chief forget to mention it, the agency and I really appreciate how you guys are all in on this. You'll be a big part of keeping everyone safe, our main concern."

"Sure thing." Chee put aside his burning question. "The better you keep us in the loop, the better we can do our job. So tell me who's coming?"

She laughed. "No way. All will be revealed at your meeting with the chief."

Chapter 7

Mrs. Raymond read a while. When she glanced out the window, she saw the exit sign for Petrified Forest National Park. She had been there many years before. Her husband worked in Flagstaff then, and they had brought their two daughters along for that trip. She remembered the vivid colors of the sandstone: the pinks that turned to lavender, the deep purples, the huge expanses of red. Victoria had said that it made her think of blood that had turned into rocks. Her big sister, the one who was dead now, said no, it was a sunset that had settled on the earth.

She thought of another expanse of stone, El Malpais, the huge lava flow near Ramah. She remembered the old story she'd heard about how the lava was the petrified blood of a monster killed by the Hero Twins. She wondered why the twins, who killed so many monsters, had allowed certain monsters to survive, among them old age and death.

Mrs. Raymond didn't mind most of the changes that came with being old. She said "so what" to silver hair, a few more pounds, and an accumulation of wrinkles. She regretted that the stroke made it harder for her to see clearly, but she appreciated the greater confidence and the welcome inner peace that had come to her with aging. She had learned to let the criticism of people who judged her, people like her own daughter, roll away like water off a turtle's shell.

Not too far out from the park boundaries, the van stopped again in another tiny burg to pick up another passenger. Many of the riders went inside the convenience store there, but Mrs. Raymond stood outside in the shade. She watched Gold Chain put gas in the van while Blue looked for a squeegee to clean the windshield. The containers nearest the van were squeegee-less, but Mrs. Raymond saw one a few gas pumps away and gave it to Blue.

"Thanks. Tell me something, OK?"

Mrs. Raymond waited for the question.

"You're not a drunk, are you?"

Mrs. Raymond didn't answer.

Blue frowned. "If you're some kind of undercover cop, you know you have to tell me."

"I'm Droid's grandmother. I need to make sure he's OK."

Blue laughed and scrubbed a bit harder with the sponge side of the squeegee. "But there's something else bothering you, right? I mean, it's not just that young guy's drinking."

Mrs. Raymond had never been one to open her thoughts to others, not even family members. But she'd never been on a van headed to rehab either. She considered the situation for a while before she spoke.

"I have some trouble with my daughter. I thought talking to a person, a counselor, could help me figure out how to get her to behave."

Blue kept working on the sunbaked bugs. "When we get to Phoenix, you will have to say that you have a drug or alcohol problem that needs attention, and that's why you've come."

"I don't want to lie."

Blue put the squeegee back in the container. "From what I've seen, a lot of trouble is caused by booze or drugs or both. Maybe that's what wrong with your daughter. Just saying."

Mrs. Raymond knew Victoria liked to drink. "You're right about that. Part of my troubles do involve wine."

"You don't have to say everything, you know? That's not the same as lying. When they give you those forms, you can leave some lines blank. They aren't very particular about most things. The people who run the program get paid by the government, and the more people they bring in, the more money they get."

Blue's phone rang. She looked at it, then at Mrs. Raymond. "Gotta take this. Go get a snack or something. We probably won't stop again until we get to Holbrook."

Chapter 8

As sometimes happens even in the best of organizations, things were running late at the Shiprock police substation. Morning had almost slipped to afternoon, and Bernie was glad that Mrs. Bigman had agreed to stay with Mama as long as she was needed.

The officers assembled in the conference room were chatting among themselves or checking their cell phones. Bernie saw Captain Adakai and acknowledged him. The room was warmer than usual—it was summer, after all—and she noticed that the captain looked anxious and uncomfortable. There was no sign of the chief, and Chee was tied up on phone calls.

For the chief to drive to Shiprock for a meeting at the substation, whatever was going on must be a big deal. She'd heard a bunch of rumors since she came in. A free Taylor Swift concert was the one that made her grin.

Noticing Bigman leaning against the wall, she walked over to her clan brother.

"I hope Chee gets off the phone before Adakai goes ballistic," she whispered to Bigman. "The captain looks ultra stressed. I saw him pacing, and he even went outside for a cigarette."

"He smokes?" Bigman wiped the sweat from his brow with his shirtsleeve.

"I was surprised, too. He seemed embarrassed when I saw him. He told me he used to smoke before he got to Shiprock, but his wife finally nagged him into quitting. He said he wants to stop again, but he might wait until he gets the hang of the job."

"Quitting is tough, but worth it." Bigman exhaled slowly. "I stopped when we learned our baby was on the way. It was torture."

"I remember you were cranky."

"Cranky? That's not the half of it." Bigman grinned. "I was such a jerk that my wife almost left me. But I'm glad I stopped. I can breathe better now, and we're saving money."

They claimed some seats in the back row, and Roper Black joined them, sitting next to Manuelito. "Hey Bernie. I'm glad you found something to do on your day off."

"Yeah, thanks to you."

"Hey, I was just the messenger. Blame the captain."

Bernie smiled. "Well, it's a good thing that you and Bigman and the rest of this bunch are such fine company. Otherwise, I might get crabby."

Roper changed the subject. "I called Hannah on the drive here. She said she'd like to meet your mother. She's heard about her weaving."

For a moment Bernie wondered if she should explain that Mama's weaving days were lost in the fog that was suffocating her memory, but she held that thought to herself.

Finally they saw Captain Adakai step to the front of the room. The officers who were in their seats rose to their feet. The meeting room, which had been buzzing with conversation and an occasional guffaw, fell silent. Because attendance was mandatory, most of the seats were filled. The only empty places were at the front of the room, so stragglers—like Chee, when he finally showed up—would be obvious.

Adakai surveyed the assembly as the last of the officers settled in.

"Be seated but heads up, everyone. The chief will be pulling into the parking lot in about ten minutes. We'll get this show rolling shortly. Today's assignments are still on, by the way, and I expect everyone to hustle it up when we finish with this." Adakai sipped some water. "The chief will explain what's happening, and we will move forward from there."

Even from where she sat in the back, Bernie thought Adakai looked ill. She wondered if the boss was coming down with the flu, or if something about the chief's visit and the pending announcement was weighing on him.

The captain fiddled with his laptop for a moment while they waited, trying to set it up to project on the screen at the front of the room, then letting it go and leaving the room. Bernie watched for Chee, hoping he would arrive before the chief came in. She sent him a quick text:

Everything OK?

The message came back:

As OK as can be expected.

She knew that her husband had been itching to return to active police work, and that he had assigned himself an investigation. But it would not be wise to put that work ahead of a rare visit from the chief of police.

She heard a vehicle pull up and park, and a few minutes later the chief of the Navajo Nation Police Department walked into the substation. The captain was at his side—and, she was pleased to see, so was Lieutenant Jim Chee.

The officers stood in acknowledgment. Bernie had seen pictures of the chief but never met him. He looked like a marine who had served a few decades ago and could still hold his own. Not only did she admire the chief's apparent physical fitness; he also had a solid reputation as a leader who navigated both the long list of duties the job entailed and the politics that came with being chief.

"Good to see you all." The chief had a deep, resonating voice. "At ease, everyone. Take a seat."

Chee slipped into the front row and sat down. The chief exchanged a few quiet words with Adakai, and then the two walked together to the podium.

Captain Adakai fiddled with the microphone switch. When that didn't seem to work, he tapped it against the palm of his hand, creating screechy electronic feedback. The chief reached for the mic, played with the power switch for a moment, and then set the mic down. He gave the captain a look that said *Step aside.*

"Good morning." His voice boomed across the room. "The captain was going to introduce me, but there's no need for that. If you all don't know who I am, you don't belong in this room. " He paused a moment while the officers continued to settle in. "I'm sure some of you have heard already that we got big news, and we may have a huge job ahead of us if this comes to pass. So pay attention, and I'll entertain your questions when I finish."

The chief stepped out from behind the podium and walked to the center of the room, closer to the seated officers. "We may have company from Washington, DC. We are going to welcome the secretary of energy, Savanah Cooper. She will make her decision about including Shiprock in her itinerary tomorrow or the next day, and could be here the day after that.

"The Department of Energy's security plan for the secretary is based on what's happened elsewhere with these visits when she has stopped to speak in other communities around the country. But, as we know, the Navajo Nation is different than most of those elsewheres, right?"

The officers around Bernie nodded, and she realized she was nodding, too.

"Right?" The chief said it more loudly. "Yes, sir" came back as the response.

"Does anyone know what a visit like this means? Just call it out."

"Yes, sir," someone said. "Chaos all around."

Someone else piped up. "More work."

"And overtime, right?" a third voice added.

Bernie heard a few soft chuckles and saw the chief smile.

"You've got the basics. Sure, overtime is in the budget, and the captain will talk to you about the scheduling, but I want to delve into the chaos, so listen up. Chaos? Nope. No chaos. Our job is to do our utmost to prevent as much of that as possible. To do that, we have to anticipate the stuff that could kick us in the fanny and gear up for it. That's why I'm here, so hold on to your seats, people."

The chief studied his notes a moment, and from his posture, Bernie could tell he was ready to launch into the meat of the session. She glanced at the captain, who was seated at the table behind the chief. Adakai's eyes were closed, and his mouth hung slack and open, as if he were gasping for air. He looked tired and ill, she thought. And with what they all might be facing soon, this was a terrible time to get sick.

The chief cleared his throat. "First, some background. I probably don't need to tell you that the secretary of energy is the top government official to visit the Navajo Nation and New Mexico so far this year. The president of the United States himself selected her, and I consider this visit an honor, a responsibility, and an opportunity for us to show her both Navajo professionalism and Diné hospitality. No matter what your personal politics, I need everyone in this room to be at their best from the time she arrives on Navajo land until she leaves. Got it?"

"Yes, sir." The response was automatic.

The chief went on to add that either the Navajo Nation president or vice president, a slew of Navajo Tribal Council delegates, state officials from New Mexico and Arizona, San Juan County commissioners, and probably the mayor of Farmington would come to Shiprock to hear what she had to say. "I'm just speculating here, but I imagine that Farmington is chafed that the secretary picked Shiprock for her potential visit, instead of there."

Several officers smiled in agreement.

"If this turns out to be the secretary's only stop in New Mexico— and that's what it looks like now—plenty of other big shots might join her, like I said. No word yet from the governor of New Mexico or the New Mexico senatorial and congressional delegates in Washington. Even if they don't come, they'll probably send staff to represent them. But that's not everybody."

The chief took a long breath. "The secretary's office will alert the national media. They'll want lots of coverage on whatever she's doing here. We can expect Shiprock and the Navajo Nation to be in the public eye, with a flood of television crews, radio, internet, webcasts, YouTube, all that stuff."

He paused and took a sip from a water bottle he'd brought. Bernie noticed the official Navajo Nation seal, with its outer ring of black arrowheads, on the side.

"I see this as an opportunity for Navajos to shine. I see this visit—if it comes to pass, and it looks like it will—as a lot of work, but also a chance to show our strength. I see this visit as a challenge, but also as good news. Do you agree?"

The room took a second to respond. Then came "Yes, sir"—a bit half-hearted, Bernie thought.

"OK." The chief studied the room. "Now, I need to tell you about another complication. The secretary's positions are controversial. She's drawn a lot of detractors. The Department of Energy special agents who will be with her advised me that one of those groups may plan to disrupt her visit. They call themselves CUSP, Citizens United to Save the Planet. They tend to be most active around the summer solstice. If any of you have ever heard of them, raise your hands."

To her surprise, Roper Black's arm went up. From her seat at the back of the room, she could see that he was the only one who responded to the chief's question.

The chief seemed surprised, too. "Stand up, Officer. Identify yourself and tell us about your experience."

Roper hesitated, and Bernie read his embarrassment. Then he rose to his feet.

"Sir, I'm Officer Roper Black. I moved here from Utah. Some of my friends back there worked for a uranium operation. They said the mine received threatening phone calls from that group. The company doubled their security, but nothing came of it." Roper gained more confidence as he spoke. "They told me the group is intense, and run by a couple of crazies who think they have a direct line to God." He stopped. "Well, I'd call them crazies. People who don't believe in any kind of mining, drilling, stuff like that, you know? They called it the worst abuse of Mother Earth, and said they would die to stop the assault. But up there, that was just talk. Never actually did anything." Roper stopped.

The chief nodded to him. "Thank you."

Roper sat down, and the chief continued. "My information confirms what Officer Black said. Although this group has protested, they've never resorted to actual violence. The report I received from Washington about their presence here warned us to look out for the possibility of trouble if and when they show up. While the talk about CUSP and threats to the secretary could just be a rumor, it certainly adds a new wrinkle. I mention it so you'll keep your ears open and let the captain know if you hear anything."

The chief sipped his water again, looking more relaxed. "The captain will deal with the specifics of your assignments, so save your questions and complaints about that for him. If you have questions for me, please stand and identify yourself."

The room was silent as the officers considered the invitation and the possible risks involved. Finally a man in the middle of the room stood and identified himself. "Chief, if she's coming in a couple of days, do you know why we got such late notice?"

The chief chuckled. "Beats me. Ask the DOE security guys and let me know what they say. More questions?"

Roper stood. "I'm new here, so I might have missed this. But can you tell us why the secretary might be coming here? It's not like we get a lot of high ranking government visitors."

The chief seemed to have been expecting the question. "I haven't heard officially, but my sources think she wants to be in the shadow of Ship Rock to make some announcement about uranium." Bernie noticed that although the chief had grown up in Dinétah and knew the monstrous stories of leetso, he used the English word.

"Before you ask, I don't know if she could be announcing more funds for cleanup or additional compensation for miners, mill workers, and their families, or sharing her thoughts on the Grand Canyon uranium mine, or planning to stop here for something totally different. We shall see."

The room had grown respectfully silent.

"Officers, even if she is just coming for the weather and to take a look at Tsé Bit'a'í, we have the same job—to help ensure her safety as well as the safety of everyone who comes with her and comes to hear her."

Public safety was the baseline for the job. But Bernie knew that if Secretary Cooper was coming as a tourist, just for a look at Ship Rock, the Four Corners Monument, the Hubbell Trading Post, Canyon de Chelly, and maybe even Monument Valley, things would be different. The protestors might still come to the Shiprock area, but their presence and hers would draw little or no media attention. But if it was uranium bringing the secretary to town, the visit checked all the boxes for outsider disruption.

Someone asked how long the secretary would be in Shiprock.

"Another good question. At this point all I know is that she plans to confirm her visit in the next day or so, and that will probably include a suggested itinerary. If she comes, she will probably give a talk at the Shiprock Chapter House, and after that tour some of the uranium sites, but we won't see a proposed itinerary until the trip is confirmed."

Another officer raised a hand. "Sir, have you been involved in one of these Washington visits before?"

"No. Secretary Cooper is my first Washington VIP." The chief paused. "And from what I've learned so far, I'd say I hope she's my last."

Bernie noticed more smiles in the audience. The chief was doing a good job building comradery and setting a foundation for cooperation.

He looked at Adakai. "How about you, Captain?"

"Yep. Yes sir. I mean, no sir. I've never dealt with . . . ."

Adakai, who Bernie had never known to be at a loss for words, let the thought drift off.

The chief ignored the awkward moment. "Any more questions from you guys?"

No hands went up. "OK then. By the way, in addition to her DOE security detail from Washington, the New Mexico State Police and the county sheriff's department will be helping with traffic, security, and the rest. The captain will have those details as soon as I get them.

"I have one final thing to mention. Remember that our job is to protect not only the secretary but also everyone who wants to hear her. We need to make sure that all the people we serve are safe and that we stay safe, too, so we can go home to our families. We all know that our world has become more dangerous, so this might be a tough assignment, but I can see that everyone in this room is up for it."

The chief thanked them, picked up his fancy water bottle, and turned to Adakai. "I'll keep your captain informed of any new developments with the secretary's visit. He will talk to you about your assignments once the visit is a sure thing, answer those follow-up questions you couldn't think of before I left, and deal with the overtime compensation issue. And be sure to remember that he's the man in charge of complaints. Got that?"

He waited a moment for the chuckles to end. "So, look on the bright side. Before you know it, this whole thing will just be a memory. Thanks for your attention. I appreciate your service."

Everyone rose as the chief left the room.

A few minutes later, Adakai shuffled to where the chief had been standing, his shoulders slumped. "Take a twenty-minute break. Then I'll talk about specifics."

Chee smiled at Bernie and left with the crowd. When the room had almost emptied, she moved toward the captain. "Sir, I need to talk to you privately." She hated asking for special treatment, but she didn't see another solution. The other officers might be returning before she and the captain finished, and she didn't want any eavesdroppers.

"Right now? Really?"

"Yes, sir."

Adakai sighed. "In my office, Manuelito."

She followed him down the hall, silently rehearsing what she had to say. He took a few moments to seat himself in the chair behind his desk.

"OK. Get on with it. Say your piece."

"Sir, two things." She started with the easy one. "I wouldn't be surprised if the secretary said something about the proposed new Canadian uranium operation near Eastern Navajo, down by Church

Rock." The Navajo Nation had outlawed uranium mining on all tribal land in 2005. "If that's the case, it seems to me that's where she'll go after her talk here, and if anyone is going to protest, that's where they'll be. Are those officers in the loop?"

"They are. We know about that." Adakai took a shallow breath. "The chief and I heard that uranium story, too."

She forged ahead. "Sir, I'm dealing with some changes at home that make it impossible for me to work much overtime. I can't work extra hours or shifts on short notice because I'm caring for my mother." She swallowed. "In fact, I will be requesting a reduction in my hours until I—"

He cut her off. "You don't have a choice about the overtime in connection with the secretary's visit, Manuelito, so figure it out," he said, underlining each word. "As to your schedule, bring it up after we're done with this. I can't deal with you now. You're excused from the rest of the meeting. Chee can fill you in later. Go home and take care of your personal challenges so you can do your job." She heard the irritation in his voice.

"Yes, sir." Bernie looked at the captain a few moments longer than she would have if she hadn't been surprised and disappointed at his response to her request. She hadn't expected him to say, *"Get outa here and find yourself an attitude adjustment."*

"And tomorrow take care of that Teec Nos Pos noise complaint and the abandoned car. If you finish that, take some hours off to make up for the meeting today."

"Yes, sir."

After she left, Captain Texas Adakai closed his eyes and clutched his aching chest.

Chapter 9

Mrs. Raymond awoke when the van stopped. She looked out the window and she knew that they weren't in Holbrook yet. Gold Chain stayed in the driver's seat, keeping the engine running and the air-conditioning on, while Blue climbed out to talk to a man who looked to be in his thirties, standing in the shade of an anemic Siberian elm. She had noticed that there was one seat left, an empty space in the center of the three seats in the very back of the van. If this man joined them, the van would be full. Maybe then they could get to Phoenix more quickly, she hoped.

The guy wore old jeans, boots, and a black cowboy hat, and there was a black plastic garbage bag on the ground next to him. He looked Navajo, Mrs. Raymond thought, although he might be from another tribe, or more likely part Diné and part something else.

Through the window, she saw Blue give him the clipboard with the papers. From where she sat, she could see the man trying to fill out the forms, dropping the pen, picking it up with shaking fingers, while Blue waited, hands on her hips. Finally, she took the clipboard and motioned him up the steps.

Blue climbed into the van after him and made an announcement to all of the passengers: "There's some water bottles up here, if you'd like one." She had a nice deep voice that carried well. "I'll pass them back to you."

"What about food?" The question came from the man who just got into the van. "You told me we get meals."

"That's in Holbrook. Just sit tight."

The vehicle rolled forward, west and south through the landscape of new possibilities toward Phoenix.

Droid shifted in his seat. Mrs. Raymond was glad he was awake. Time to talk. She gently touched his arm, and he turned toward her, startled.

"Grandson, I have something to tell you."

He removed his ear bug. "Sorry. What did you say?"

"I am proud of you for getting on this van."

Droid kept his eyes low. A sign of respect, she told herself. But he frowned. "Grandma, speak English."

"No." She repeated it in Navajo. "Dooda." She shook her head. "No English for this. You need to listen to me now. You listen hard. I'm speaking from the heart, and this is the way my words come out.

"My husband, he struggled with the same nayee that wants to grab you, the very same monster. That man made his way free with two kinds of help." She thought of how to say what came next with respect. "He did like you are doing, but with AA. You know about that. Then we had a ceremony for him. And another. The nayee made him sick, made him a little crazy when it was leaving his body. That might happen to you, too. But then his spirit was free."

She stopped to gather her thoughts, wondering if she needed to add the vomiting, the shakes, the rages, the other troubles the monster of alcoholism had caused her husband. She decided she had said enough about that. It pleased her that Droid didn't interrupt.

Mrs. Raymond lowered her voice even more.

"The woman up there in that seat in front of you, I saw her take a bottle of liquor out of her purse. She offered some to me when we stopped. To stand straight, like my husband, people have to promise themselves to say no to everything with alcohol. They have to keep their promise. You already broke your promise once today. I smelled the beer. Are you ready to see this journey to the end?"

He looked up, shrugging. "What do you mean?"

"You know."

He studied the view out the van window for several minutes. "Yes. Well, I think so. I'm scared."

"Scared of what?"

He pursed his lips and exhaled.

"Scared I won't make it. Scared that I'm already an adláanii. I haven't had a real drink since I saw the dead man, if it really was a dead man and not a hallucination. I feel bad, Shimásání. My head hurts, and my insides are all screwy."

She stared straight ahead, so as not to embarrass him. "My husband, your grandfather, didn't have a nice van like this or people to help him. It was hard, but he did it. You have help to make this road easier."

When they got to Holbrook, Gold Chain pulled up to a fast-food place with a drive-through. Blue distributed the meals.

Mrs. Raymond thought the burger was delicious. It was bigger than she could finish, so she gave the rest to Droid. She pictured Darleen making her those healthy salads for lunch and cajoling her into eating them without much complaint. She liked that young woman and regretted that she hadn't told her not to come help today.

When they were done eating, she touched Droid on the elbow. "We need to call my daughter. I have to tell her something." Victoria, Droid's auntie or shimáyázhí, would not be happy to get the news. But Mrs. Raymond had to let her know that she couldn't stay with

Mr. Fluff that evening. Victoria's little dog got more attention than any person in her daughter's life.

"I'll try to reach her for you, but I have to tell you something. Auntie never answers my calls. I don't think she likes me."

Mrs. Raymond's eyes widened. "How does she know it's you?"

"The phone tells her my number. Because of that, when you call, she will think it's me."

He handed her the phone. "Go ahead. Try it."

Mrs. Raymond looked at the screen. "I don't know how this works. You do it."

Droid touched something on the screen.

"It's calling her now." He handed it to her. She held it to her cheek as she would have done with her house phone.

"Hold it like this, so you can hear if she answers." He moved one end of it closer to his ear, then handed it to her. She listened to it ringing, and then to Victoria's answering machine, with the curt message she'd heard before. *"Call back if it's important. Or leave a message if you have to, but I'm bad at checking."*

Mrs. Raymond looked puzzled. Droid took the phone and spoke. "Hello. It's Droid. Your mom wants to tell you something. Call us back, OK?" And then he pushed a button and the phone went black.

"You should get one of these phones, Grandma. They're handy."

"That's what everyone tells me." She patted his hand. "I like my old phone just fine."

Mrs. Raymond could hear a couple of men sitting behind her start to argue. The passenger across the aisle from her and Droid was fidgety. She'd seen all of that behavior and more before in her husband. He never got violent with her, but he would start pacing and muttering to himself. And when he left the house, she knew he'd gone to find a drink.

Droid was restless, too. She decided to try once more to get him to talk about why they were on the van. She asked the question gently and gave him time.

"Like I said, it's because of the dead man, Shimásání. I saw him, his nice hat, his silver ring." Droid swallowed, and said the rest. "It looked like somebody beat him to death. I ran away as fast as I could."

She waited for him to continue.

"Maybe it was a sign saying that dude could be me. Whatever. I don't want to die like that."

Droid stared at his shoes, the running shoes he had talked her into buying him that spring.

"You seem anxious."

"Well, if that was a real dead person, the police might track me because of my shoes, you know, my footprints. They could blame what happened on me. They do that on TV. I'm still scared. But I know I did the right thing."

Then he put in the earbuds.

Mrs. Raymond smiled. The stroke gave her trouble using her hand and arm, and now she took medicine for her blood pressure. But she was happy that her brain worked just fine when it came to saying what needed to be said.

She read for a while and noticed that Droid had fallen asleep. When he awoke, she made a sign for pulling something out of his ear, and he complied.

She got to the point. "I'm happy that you picked a good time to do this, to make this trip."

"Because I'm out of school for a few more weeks?" He laughed. "No, because there's record heat in Phoenix, right?"

"Don't interrupt me." Mrs. Raymond frowned at the bad manners. "The solstice will be here soon, bringing us the most light of the year. That is a time of change, a time of planning. It is a good time for you to make this change."

Droid waited to be sure she was done. "I didn't even think about that," he said. "Shimásání, I'm glad you told me about the solstice. That makes me feel more confident."

They rode in silence for a dozen miles or so, and then she said, "Use your phone for your auntie again."

Droid pulled out his phone and frowned at it. He pushed the buttons, waited, and when the phone started to ring, he put it in Mrs. Raymond's outstretched hand.

The phone went dark, and she passed it back. "I must have touched something. I broke it."

"It's OK. It's not you. Only one bar."

"Bar? What does that mean?"

"We can't call now. We can do it later, when we get to Phoenix."

She switched to Navajo, speaking slowly because she knew Droid didn't always understand. "You need to talk to your father, too."

Droid nodded. "Do you think he will be mad?"

She considered her son-in-law. "He will be pleased that you are doing this. And, maybe angry, too, because he worries about you, and you didn't tell him where we were going."

Droid stared at the back of the seat in front of him and said nothing.

"Tomorrow is your mother's birthday, and I know she would be proud and happy for you."

"I hope so. I miss her so much, and . . ."

She heard the tears in his voice, reached into her purse, and gave him a tissue without looking, to avoid adding to his embarrassment. She watched the scenery out the window—big trees now, and curving roads as the van entered a forest.

The van stopped once more for what Blue announced as the final place to get off the bus and do what they needed to do before they got to Phoenix. Mrs. Raymond noticed that this stop was even hotter than the last. Again, the place sold alcohol. Mrs. Raymond expected that some passengers would climb on with beer or whatever, and that Blue and Gold Chain would pretend not to notice.

She and Droid went into the store. She headed to one of the refrigerated cases where they stored the cold drinks. She considered what to buy, but saw nothing that appealed to her. Just looking at them was good enough.

When the van trip began again, she and Droid settled in for what Blue said was the last stretch to their destination. This time Mrs. Raymond found seats in the front, right behind the driver. When Droid sat next to her, he was smiling.

"I got you something." He pulled out a small yellow bag. "Sugar Babies. I know they're your favorites. It's a good thing they won't melt. They say it's really, really hot in Phoenix."

She smiled as he gave them to her. "Did you get something for yourself?"

"Yeah. Some special gum. It's supposed to help me stop smoking."

She would have told him to fight one monster at a time, but he hadn't asked.

Chapter 10

Chee walked to the captain's office and rapped on the open door.

He could see the man's back from where he stood. It looked like Adakai was staring out the window. But then Chee noticed that he was slumped in the chair. He knocked again. "Captain, it's Chee."

Adakai still didn't respond. Chee entered the office and walked toward the man.

"Captain?" Chee lightly touched the man's back, and Adakai raised his head. He had his left hand pressed against his chest and was using his right to keep himself from slipping out of the seat and onto the floor. With a single glance, Chee knew the situation was desperate.

"Hurts. Help me." Adakai's breath came in short gasps. "My heart."

Chee felt his own heart beating faster. He turned toward the hallway and yelled, "Sandra, call an ambulance for the captain! Tell them he thinks it's a heart attack."

"Yes, sir." Her voice was cold and professional.

Remembering his first aid training for situations like this, Chee leaned down to help the captain. Holding his own anxiety at bay, Chee quickly loosened the captain's tie and unbuttoned his shirt collar to make it easier for him to breathe. "Help is on the way, sir," he said, his voice low and steady. He sounded much calmer than he felt.

Then he yelled to Sandra again, "When you're done with that, bring the first aid kit. Quickly."

Chee could see the pain on Adakai's face. The man's voice was a whisper. "Call Brit."

When Sandra arrived with the first aid kit, Chee asked for aspirin, which she smoothly put into his waiting hand.

Chee stared into the captain's face and spoke firmly. "Open your mouth, sir. I have something that will help your heart." He tried to sound certain. "You need to chew this."

Adakai did as directed. Chee listened for the wail of the ambulance siren. He was grateful that the Shiprock hospital was only minutes away, unlike some places on the Navajo Nation were people had a long wait for emergency medical care.

He looked at Sandra. "Thanks. Now let Britany know." Chee knew Sandra had emergency contact numbers—wife, parents, siblings, or close friends—for everyone at the station, and she would be able to reach the chief's wife.

"Yes, sir. What should I say?"

"Tell her the captain had a medical incident, and we've called the ambulance."

By the time the ambulance arrived, word of the situation had spread. Several officers stood in the parking lot to watch, concern scoring their faces. The emergency crew sprang into action. Chee stayed close to Adakai, answering the lead EMT's questions as best he could until they had loaded the captain on the gurney and wheeled him into the ambulance. As it left the parking lot, lights flashing and siren wailing, Chee turned to the officers with the authority of the person in charge.

"I'll talk to the chief to let him know about the situation here, and we'll discuss tomorrow's assignments later. Do what you need to do to finish up today, and I'll let you know what's up as soon as I can."

Chee returned to his office and closed the door for privacy. He had met the chief of police a few times before that day's meeting and respected the man as a person who got things done.

The chief came on the line. "Lieutenant Chee? What's up?"

Chee got right to the point. "Sir, I've got some bad news. Captain Adakai is on his way to the ER."

"What happened?"

"I found him keeled over at his desk, complaining about chest pain. He just left the station in an ambulance."

"Oh." The chief let the silence sit a moment. "I'm sorry to hear it. The captain seemed off this morning. I shouldn't have been so hard on him."

Chee waited a moment to see if the chief had more to say. He did.

"Lieutenant, with Adakai out of commission for now, you'll be running the show at Shiprock, the go-to guy out there. I'll keep you updated about the trip and CUSP, same as I would Adakai. You'll let me know what's going on with him, right?"

"Yes, sir."

"I just heard that a few New Mexico legislators plan to be there for the secretary's talk. Maybe the person in charge of mining in New Mexico. The equivalent for the Navajo Nation will be on board, too. Quite a collection of local bigwigs."

"Anyone else from Washington?"

"I wouldn't rule it out." The chief sounded more serious now. "See what you can pick up about CUSP. We don't want anything happening that will put us in a bad light. The secretary and everyone who comes to see her need to be protected."

"Yes, sir. Any idea yet when she's coming?"

"No confirmations of anything. I heard that she has some family out this way and wants to roll that into the trip." The chief exhaled. "Another complication. Security staff will be traveling with the secretary, but if it looks like a protest actually is in the pipeline, I can send some officers from Window Rock to help."

The chief paused. "Did you and the captain have a chance to talk about assignments?"

"No, sir, but I can handle it. No worries. I'll set that up."

"Remember to let me know how the captain is doing." And then, to Chee's surprise, the chief gave him his cell number. "Call me, especially if Tex takes a turn for the worse."

Chee entered the chief's number into his contact list. He closed the reports he'd hoped to work on that day. He hated to set that research aside, but he decided it was more important to begin his online search on CUSP. When the substation got details of the secretary's visit, his time would be at a premium.

Chee learned that so far, the group the chief mentioned in the meeting that morning had attracted fewer than fifty followers, and their actions consisted of peaceful protests. Their presence had not been reported in New Mexico or on the Navajo Nation. Apart from their adding a bit to the traffic, he agreed with the chief. CUSP did not seem to pose a major threat.

Sandra came into the office a few moments later. "You might as well move in here," she said. "You know the captain's office is more comfortable, and his computer is newer. Make this as easy on yourself as you can. Sit down and relax a minute."

Chee smiled at Sandra, part dispatcher and part housemother.

"Sir, I called the captain's wife, and she's headed to the hospital. I asked her to let me know what was happening there so I could tell you, and you could . . . you know, figure things out. Britany sounded really upset." Sandra twisted the turquoise ring on the fourth finger of her left hand. "I'm worried about that man. He looked bad."

"You were a big help. Thank you. Can you let the officers know that we'll have a quick meeting in about fifteen minutes? I talked to the chief, and he told me to step in and take charge."

"Yes, sir." Sandra stepped toward the door, then turned back. "You're a good man, Jim Chee. Just between us, you should have been in charge here to start with."

***

In the conference room, the news about the captain's health had spread like a bad cold to those who had seen the man wheeled off. Chee explained what little he knew about Adakai's condition, adding that Mrs. Adakai had promised to keep them informed. He told them that the chief had assigned him to run the substation temporarily, eliciting several smiles and nods of approval.

"When we hear for sure that the secretary is coming, we've got two jobs: controlling traffic around the entrances and exits to the chapter house—or wherever she'll be speaking—and watching out for loonies. I'll show you what I'm thinking of in terms of the big picture."

Chee clicked a remote, and a moment later a map of the roads in the Shiprock area showed up on the screen that hung behind them. He used a laser to highlight the suggested road closures and detours. "We all know that our relatives don't like to be inconvenienced, especially by the government. We will use social media to alert everyone to expect extra traffic and delays, and give them a heads-up about the roads that will be blocked. This will be job number one once the visit is confirmed, and we know where and when the secretary will be speaking. I'll let you know your assignments as soon as I get an update from Window Rock headquarters about the status of the secretary's visit, her time of arrival, and the location for her talk."

The officers looked slightly bugged about the extra work, but not panicked.

"Any questions?"

There were none, probably because everyone had spent too long in meetings and wanted to get back to real police work. Chee felt the same. "Thanks. Do what you need to do today to clear the charts for tomorrow in case she shows up. I'll update you on the status of the captain's condition in the morning, unless he's feeling well enough to talk to you all himself."

Chapter 11

Because the solstice was approaching, the late afternoon sun was still high when the van hit traffic and rolled into Phoenix. The highway became a maze of connections, exits, offshoots, bridges, and construction sites cluttered with equipment. Blue steered through mergers and detours and the crowded, steady stream of traffic.

Mrs. Raymond felt a dull ache in the center of her back. She was stiff all over; she never sat this long at home. But she was also excited and happy and grew more so as the van moved off the freeway onto side streets. Finally they stopped in front of a tall hotel.

Blue turned toward the passengers. "Get whatever you brought and take it with you. If you leave anything here, it's gone. Head on inside. Someone will register you at the desk."

Droid started to stand, but Mrs. Raymond put her hand on his arm. "Wait."

He gave her a questioning look, but he sat down again. The other riders filed out, and they stalled to be the last ones off the van.

Blue and Gold Chain stood outside, watching the passengers walk through the sweltering parking lot and go inside the building. Droid was the second-to-last person off the van, followed by his grand-mother. Mrs. Raymond stopped in front of Blue.

"You remind me of my mother," Blue said. "I bet you have a question."

Mrs. Raymond nodded once. "How do we get in touch with you to get home?"

Blue frowned. "I only drive people here, not back. Ask about that inside, you know, after you guys have finished the program."

"How long will that be? Droid needs to get back to Shiprock for , , ." She started to say high school, but then remembered the fib. "For something in August."

Blue motioned toward the glass doors. "Ask them when you register."

Droid removed his earbuds. "It's hot out here. Let's go."

Mrs. Raymond frowned at him. "I was asking how long your program would be."

Droid looked at Blue. "Usually six weeks, right?"

"Hard to say."

"I have more questions," Mrs. Raymond said.

Blue made a face. "Make it quick. I need to get home."

"Do you take the van from here to New Mexico and the reservation every day?"

"Four days a week. You know somebody else who needs rebab?"

"I might." Mrs. Raymond didn't see the harm in a little fib. "Give me your phone number, OK?"

"Your boy has the number. That's how he let me know he was ready to come to the center."

Mrs. Raymond felt the heat from the paved parking lot seeping through the soles of her shoes. "Droid will call you when we are done. No reason you can't take me back."

Blue shook her head. "I told you I don't take people back."

"But you could. When I'm ready to head home, you or the man with the gold chain can give me a ride."

"It doesn't work like that." Blue took off the ball cap and rubbed her head. "Watch your back in there. They aren't used to people who ask questions. That might cause some, well, some hard feelings, if you get my drift."

"I have a sense that something is wrong here." Mrs. Raymond stood a little straighter. "There are places to stop for gas that don't sell alcohol. And it seems too easy to get on this van and go to rehab. I can see that some of these people won't stop drinking. I think that you understand all this, and that it makes you embarrassed."

Blue exhaled and turned away.

Gold Chain had stowed the extra water in the van and put whatever trash the passengers had left in a garbage bag. He disposed of that and then walked over to Blue. "Want me to give you a ride to your car?"

"Yeah."

Gold Chain climbed behind the wheel. Blue took the passenger seat and turned to Mrs. Raymond before she closed the door. "What I told you, that's just between us, OK? Take care of that kid."

Droid was waiting for his grandmother in the shade near the front door.

"Shimásání, I have an idea," he said. "Let's take our picture here, outside the hotel. This is the start of something great, you know?" He pulled out his phone and positioned it with the building in the background. "This will be the before shot."

"OK."

"I'll look kinda sad, you know. And we'll get that sign that says 'Broadway Manor' in the background, OK?"

Mrs. Raymond nodded. "That's a good idea."

"We can take the 'after' picture of us here, too—when we leave, you know? Then I'll be all smiley."

They posed, and Droid extended his arm with his phone to get the picture. He tried three times before he took a shot he liked.

Mrs. Raymond realized that maybe for once the cranky Victoria was right. Her daughter scolded her for worrying too much, over-thinking things. When Droid's treatment was over, they would figure out how to get home. No reason to worry about that now.

"I'm going inside to cool off but I want to send this picture to Dad. I'll send it with a note," Droid said.

"What will the note say?"

"I'll write something like, 'We made it to Phoenix. Don't worry.'"

Mrs. Raymond smiled, happy that Droid was acting more grown-up. She saw him fiddle with something on the phone. "My battery is dead but I'll send it later. He'll see that I'm OK."

***

It was deliciously cool inside Broadway Manor. Most of the people from the van were waiting to check in. The rest? She assumed they had gone to their rooms. Her grandson sprawled on a couch by the big glass front doors.

After all the enforced sitting on the bus, Mrs. Raymond decided to walk around the lobby. It felt good to move. After a while, she saw Droid leave the couch and join a group of other young men. Good, she thought, maybe they could encourage each other. In addition to the people from the van, there were others in the lobby. Many of them looked Navajo, she thought, or maybe Apache or some other kind of Indian.

She hadn't ever been in a rehab center, but she quickly decided that the hotel that Best Way Rehabilitation Center had taken for its base had seen better days. The walls of the old Broadway Manor needed painting, the threadbare carpet was stained in several places, and no one had washed the windows for quite a while. She hoped the room where she and Droid would be sleeping had received better care.

Mrs. Raymond watched the young woman at the big desk register people, noticing that as the last step, each person she registered received a small plastic bag. If they had a cell phone they put it inside. Then the young woman took the bag, wrote something on it, and put it in a box.

Mrs. Raymond quietly mentioned that to Droid, and he slipped his phone into a small pocket hidden inside his backpack.

When no one was left to check in besides the two of them, she motioned to Droid to join her. They quickly moved to the big desk where the woman in charge of registrations was waiting for them.

"Yá'át'ééh." Mrs. Raymond read the name on the woman's badge. "Heather, hello to you. This is my Droid." She motioned with a nod of her chin to the young man standing behind her.

Heather didn't say hello, or welcome, or anything like that, just asked for Mrs. Raymond's identification. Mrs. Raymond showed her the Navajo Nation ID card.

Heather examined the ID, looking puzzled. She typed something into her computer with long red fingernails.

"You aren't on our master list, but I have the forms you filled out before you got on the van. I can register you now. I need your driver's license."

Mrs. Raymond didn't respond.

The woman frowned and spoke louder. "I said, I need your license."

Droid recognized his grandmother's embarrassment and spoke to her softly. "Shimásání, I can help."

Mrs. Raymond said something in Navajo, and Droid responded.

"Ma'am, excuse me," he said, "I need to . . ."

"I was talking privately to this lady," Heather snapped at him. "Wait your turn."

"She's with me. My grandmother. We take care of each other. She doesn't drive." That wasn't exactly true. She did drive a little, but she'd never bothered to get a license.

"Well, that's what we use for ID," Heather hissed. And then she stared at them.

Mrs. Raymond frowned. "I didn't come all this way to be a driver. I gave you my official identification from the Navajo Nation. See, here's the American flag. And this is the Navajo Nation seal." She put her finger next to it. "Can you read English?" Mrs. Raymond shoved the card closer to Heather. "What's wrong with this?"

The woman gave them both a look of absolute disdain, then picked up the ID card, studied the information, and typed. She made a copy of the card and returned it to Mrs. Raymond without a word of thanks. Then she asked Droid for his license. She looked at it a moment and then at Droid.

Mrs. Raymond noticed Droid holding his breath. In New Mexico anyone under twenty-one receives a vertical driver's license. When they reach the state's legal drinking age, they can apply for the horizonal full-adult version. The different shapes make underage drinking easy to spot.

"It says your name is Andrew."

"Yes."

"She called you something else."

"She calls me Droid. That's a nickname."

Either Heather didn't know what the shape of the license meant, didn't bother to look at the birth date, or she just didn't care. Whatever the reason, Mrs. Raymond was grateful for it. Heather disappeared into the office behind the registration desk. They heard the hum of a printer.

"This is not what I expected." Droid spoke softly. "But it's awesome so far, right? I didn't think we'd be in a building all fancy. I met a guy just now, Diné like us. He said he could get me beer or whatever if I had some money. That was kinda strange, right?"

Mrs. Raymond suspected that Droid was thinking of how nice a cold beer would taste. "Who is he?"

"A bro from K-town. Warren something."

"K-town?"

"Sorry. Kayenta, Shimásání. And I told him no beer."

Heather came back with some printed pages. She handed Droid two sheets of paper. "Here are your appointments. You go on the van to the food stamp office tomorrow and then to the therapy center. Here's a key to the room. I assume you two are sharing?"

He nodded.

"The room number is here on the envelope. Don't lose it."

Heather turned away.

"Hey," Mrs. Raymond said. "Excuse me. I need a key, too, and my papers for the appointments."

The woman exhaled, did more tapping, and gave Mrs. Raymond a plastic key card.

"Where's the rest? My paper with the appointments."

"No appointments for you. You registered at the last minute. Check back in the morning."

Mrs. Raymond wasn't finished. "I have a question. I need to let my daughter know when our treatment will be done, so she won't be too upset. And I have a helper. That girl, she worries about me. What do I tell them?"

"I don't know. You'll have to ask Bea. The owner. Save your questions for her."

"Where is she?"

Heather shook her head. "I don't know. She'll be here later today or in the morning."

She gave them each a small plastic bag. "No phones allowed. Don't give me a hard time about this, OK? That's part of the contract you signed. Slip your phones in these, and use that marker to put your name and room number on the bag. We'll give it to you when you leave."

Mrs. Raymond handed the bag back to her. "I don't have a phone."

Heather looked skeptical. "Really?'

"I'm an old lady. If I need to call, I use the phone in the kitchen."

Heather turned to Droid. He patted his pockets, opened his backpack, and spent some time rummaging through it. "Wow. It's not here. I must have left it on the van."

Heather looked skeptical. "I'll have the driver check. If you don't turn it in, you're outa here. Got it?"

Droid nodded.

"Tonight is pizza dinner at six p.m." She stood. "The elevators are to the right."

Chapter 12

Discouragement and dead ends led Darleen to an unavoidable conclusion. It was time to talk to Victoria. She used the ten minutes it took to walk to Mrs. Raymond's daughter's house to plan what she had to say. She knocked on the front door, waited, and knocked again. It was 9:30 a.m. Surely Victoria wasn't still sleeping.

But she had been. Mrs. R's daughter opened the door with a scowl. She wore mismatched pajamas and her short, cropped black hair stuck out in odd places. Expecting the worst, Darleen jumped in to apologize before Victoria could lambaste her about her timing.

"I wouldn't have disturbed you, but I'm worried about your mother. I've been waiting at her house for an hour and she's not there. I went inside to make sure that she wasn't hurt." Or dead, Darleen thought, but she didn't say that. "Have you seen her?"

Victoria scoffed. "You're kidding? That's it? Jeez! I saw Mom when me and Mr. Fluff took her to dinner over there last night. She was as ornery as usual. Go back there and find some cleaning to do or dishes to wash while you're waiting for her. Check to see that she has enough vitamins or something. That's your job, right?"

Victoria leaned against the doorframe.

"My mother is a pain in the rear, you know? Today, you get a break from her complaining, but I'm not gonna pay you to do nothing."

Darleen sucked in a slow breath to calm her irritation. It was disrespectful for a child to criticize a mother. "I don't mind when she complains. I figure she's got a right to be grumpy if she needs to be, I mean, after that stroke and now having some trouble with her left hand and arm. And her eyes. She's not always cranky. I enjoy my time with her."

"Really?"

Darleen caught the sarcasm. "Yes. We've had some good conversations."

"I hope she's not sharing our dark secrets." Victoria smiled as though the comment were a joke but Darleen heard the overlay of anxiety. "What does she talk about?"

"She tells me about the old days, spending time with the sheep and dogs. Learning to ride a horse. Being mischievous. Sometimes she'll tell me funny stories about her husband. Things like that." More than once Mrs. Raymond had mentioned something about an ungrateful daughter. Darleen kept that to herself.

"All that nonsense. I know she makes half of it up." Victoria shook her head. "Get to work. Tell me when you leave." She went inside and closed the door.

Darleen slumped back to Mrs. Raymond's place, taking a short-cut through the field. She hadn't walked this way before.

An unusual rock caught her eye, and she bent to pick it up. But it wasn't just a rock. She held a small, carved stone, polished and shaped like a turtle, with bits of turquoise as its eyes.

Mrs. R had shown her the turtle on their first visit. "My good friend from Zuni gave me this," she'd said. Darleen remembered Mrs. Raymond extending the little carving toward her, the stone creature nestled among the wrinkles in the palm of her hand.

"It keeps me strong," Mrs. R had told her. "Here, hold it."

The fetish, warmed by the old woman's touch, felt smooth and surprisingly heavy.

"It protects me. Ch'eeh dighahii has perseverance, you know? That turtle, she keeps me going. My friend said a Zuni holy man blessed it for her, and the blessing comes to me."

Turtles didn't appeal to Darleen. Unlike her sister, she had never sought out the natural world. She'd seen her first and only live desert turtle, or maybe it was actually a tortoise, on one of the few occasions when she went camping. She found Mrs. R's little carving considerably more attractive than the odd-looking reptile itself.

"You know why these ch'eeh dighahii are sacred to us?" Mrs. Raymond had asked.

Darleen shook her head.

"Well, I'll tell you. Partly because they come from the water, which brings life. And also because they teach us about endurance and the value of not moving too fast. They carry their homes with them. That's what we did, too, with Hwéeldi. Our relatives who had to go there carried memories of home in their hearts. That's why we survived."

Hwéeldi, the place of suffering, and the Long Walk there and home again stayed in Diné memory like a deep scar. The Navajo had endured removal from their sacred land to a place of sad desperation, illness, starvation, and death and returned to their own territory five years later to grow in numbers and prosperity. Like the turtle, Darleen thought, they had carried their homes with them in their hearts during that terrible time.

As she reached Mrs. Raymond's front door, Darleen took another look at the carved turtle she'd found. It was about the size of a small, flattened plum. She let herself in, gave the turtle a gentle squeeze, and set it on the table inside. When Mrs. R returned, she would be happy to find it there.

As she drove home, Darleen tried to talk herself out of worrying. After all, Mrs. Raymond's own daughter wasn't worried, and she had known her mom her entire life.

But still Darleen worried. Her shift ended at noon. After so many lectures about driving while texting, she always called Bernie, not texted her, when she was in the car. Or waited to talk to her when they were together. This time she called, but Bernie didn't answer. Then she called Chee.

"I'm planning to see Mama today, but I'll be a little late."

"That's OK. Mrs. Bigman offered to stay all day."

Darleen planned to stop at the Chat and Chew first. "Should I bring Mama something to eat?"

"You know she loves milkshakes. Mrs. Bigman might like one, too."

"What's with Bernie? I tried calling her. No luck."

"Don't worry. Maybe she has her cell turned off. This was supposed to be her day off, so she might get home early."

"When did that ever happen?" Darleen knew about her sister's compulsion to do more than the job required.

"There's always a first time, right? Hold on."

Darleen heard the police radio in the background but couldn't make out the words. Then Chee was back.

"Bernie told me you were concerned about one of the elderlies you work with. Did that woman show up?"

"Not yet. I talked to Mrs. R's daughter about that situation, you know, as Bernie suggested. Victoria's not worried. She told me to chill."

"Good advice."

"Yeah. For you guys, too."

Darleen remembered Mrs. R's special turtle. Turtles, she figured, took life as it came and didn't jump to conclusions. They didn't jump at all. Turtle wisdom might be just what she needed.

A few minutes later, she pulled into a gas station along the main highway. A man she'd gone to high school with, Shorty Lee, ran the place. She went inside to give him cash for the pump, and he took a look out the door at her vehicle.

"Hey, Dee. What happened to your car?"

"What do you mean?"

"It looks like you gave it a bath or something." He chuckled. "I thought old road grease was the only thing holding it in one piece."

"Yeah, I had to stick the whole thing back together with chewing gum after Slim washed it."

"Slim? I thought you and that dude broke up."

"We did. We're taking another shot at it. How's life with you?"

"Not so good. My brother, you know, Clarence, the one with the limp? He hasn't been around for a couple of weeks. He kept talking about wanting to go to rehab. We think he went, because he hasn't been around. But he hasn't called us to come get him or nothin'. You think that means he's doin' good?"

Darleen shrugged. "I hope so. He'll let you know when he's ready to come home."

A few months after Mama moved in with Bernie, Darleen had stopped drinking, with Slim's encouragement and a nudge from Chee and her sister. She felt good, proud of herself instead of ashamed, happy instead of holding a dark secret. Now that she was sober, she appreciated the fact that the Navajo Nation allowed no alcohol sales on tribal land. It was easy enough, of course, to buy whatever you wanted in Gallup or Flagstaff or Farmington, or from bootleggers. Even so, she was glad that when she went in to pay for the gas, she saw sodas, bottled tea, energy drinks, and water on display, but not the beer she'd find off the reservation. On a warm day like this, with all the worry about Mrs. R, a cold beer would have tasted mighty, mighty fine. She appreciated the lack of temptation.

Darleen went out to pump the gas, glad she had enough money

for the fuel to get home and back, as well as to the college where she was training to be a nurse's aide, and to Bernie's place. She drove with all the windows open and the radio on, the music cheering her as she cruised toward Toadlena, the place where she'd lived her whole life except when she went to that art school for Indians in Santa Fe, the IAIA. The place where she began to realize that while art would always be part of her life, she could be an artist and also be something else that would bring a more reliable paycheck. In her dreams, she would figure out a way to do art as a living.

When Darleen pulled up to Mama's old house, Bidziil, Mrs. Darkwater's big black dog, rushed out to greet the car with a loud burst of barking and then came to the driver's door, wagging his tail. Mama's neighbor had to have some surgery, and Darleen had offered to feed Bidziil while Mrs. Darkwater stayed with her son to recover. It still seemed strange to be by herself at the house she and Mama had shared, but Darleen was adjusting. For the first time in her life, she lived alone.

She went inside and poured herself a glass of cold tea from the pitcher she'd made that morning. Still thinking about the beer and Mrs. Raymond and the disappearance of Clarence with the limp, she sat outside. Bidziil joined her for company. She noticed a lizard, one of those that looks like they're doing pushups when they get ready to run, and heard piñon jays squawking in the trees. Life was good.

June. Ya'iishjááshchilí. The month of the year's longest days with the solstice coming soon. It could be hot in Toadlena, but in the shade of the porch, Darleen found the warmth tolerable. As her home health aide job required, she wrote up her notes about the day—not much to say, since Mrs. R hadn't been there. She hoped that Mrs. Raymond was home safely now.

As much as she missed her mother, Darleen realized it was a huge relief not to worry about her every minute. She considered making a sandwich, then checking in with Slim and apologizing for ignoring him, and after that maybe checking up on Mrs. Darkwater before going to see Mama. But for a moment she relaxed, enjoying the quiet of the afternoon.

Then her phone chimed with a text. Bidziil, unused to the sound, perked up his ears.

Darleen put her tea glass down and rubbed the dog's broad head before she reached for the phone.

The message was from Victoria, Mrs. Raymond's daughter, but the text wasn't what she had expected.

Mom with grandson.

Then came a parade of frowning emojis.

Darleen preferred texts to phone calls, but she had too many questions to type. Victoria answered on the first ring and started complaining. "My mother. She is driving me nuts."

Darleen waited a beat. Victoria began to fill in the details without being prompted.

"She's off somewhere, and she didn't even let me know. The message came to Greg. I'm her daughter, for goodness' sake! He's not even a blood relative."

Greg. Darleen recognized the name. Mrs. R had mentioned her fondness for her former son-in-law, the man married to the daughter who died. The father of her grandson.

"Can you believe this? I only know Mom is with Droid because of a stupid photo and some dumb stuff Droid wrote."

Darleen was confused. "Droid?"

Victoria laughed. "That's what we call him. He started as Andrew, then Drew, and then it morphed into Droid because the kid liked to pretend he was a robot."

"Oh, the grandson. How old is he?" Darleen pictured an eight-year-old.

"He'll be a senior in high school."

"What did Droid's text say?"

"Something ridiculous. Hold on. I'll read it. He typed 'Hi. Don't worry, OK?' That's it."

"Where were they?"

"Oh, an old hotel or something. The photo looks like a parking lot. I'll send it to you."

Darleen envisioned a little shopping with grandma paying the bill, maybe lunch. "Well, it seems that your mom is safe. Maybe they're having some fun. I bet she will be home soon. I'm glad you let me know."

"You want to know what this is really about? It's about getting even with me. Here's the deal. This is the night Mom comes over and stays with Mr. Fluff. She gives him his shot, and I get to go dancing, party a little. If she doesn't get back in time, I'll have to change my plans. That's very inconsiderate."

Darleen knew a different side of Mrs. Raymond. "Did she try to call you?"

"That's another thing. She won't get a real phone. Droid called, just said she wanted to talk to me. I bet she came up with some weak excuse to disappoint me."

Darleen tried again. "Well, at least she's with her grandson. They can look out for each other."

"Seriously? You don't know that kid. The only time Droid wants to hang with his grandmother is when he needs money. With his mother dead, his grandma babies him. She was never that good to me."

Victoria switched from complaining about her mother and criticizing her nephew to some snide remarks about Greg and then other things that irritated her: her mother's friends, the dust on the road, the price of everything, and more. When she stopped for breath, Darleen ended the call with as much tact as she could muster.

She started to put the phone aside, then remembered the photo Victoria had sent and clicked it open. Mrs. R looked happy, but the young man next to her stared at the camera with vacant eyes. She'd seen that look before she got sober. Seen it in herself and her friends. Droid was dealing with a big trouble.

Darleen finished her iced tea, and decided it was time to get in her car and drive to see Mama in person. So what if Mama was out of sorts or gave her advice she didn't need? She could sit with her, hold her hand, maybe help her with dinner or even a shower. Maybe Bernie would be home and they could chat, share stories about Mama, and even laugh at some of the unexpected things she said and did.

She hoped Droid realized what a gift he had with the opportunity to know his amásání. And she hoped she was wrong about the big trouble.

She thought about Bernie as she climbed into her car. Maybe Bernie could give her some advice on Slim, too. Their relationship had been rocky over the last few weeks, but she attributed it to both of them working too much. Bernie worked harder than anyone she knew, and managed to keep her relationship with Chee strong. That was another thing she admired about her sister.

***

Bernie greeted her with a smile. Mama was in a good mood, although Darleen wasn't sure that their mother knew who she was. Mama shared a memory Darleen loved, the story of watching her mother weave and then the disaster of her first efforts at the loom. Mama laughed as she remembered it, as she always did. Then Darleen offered her a snack and Mama fell asleep watching TV.

Bernie used Darleen's visit to go for a run and was gone longer than Darleen expected.

"Good run?"

"Yes. I enjoyed it." Bernie sat to take off her running shoes.

"I was worried because you were gone so long."

"You worry too much. Are you still worried about Mrs. Raymond?"

"Well, I learned that she's with her grandson, a teenager. The guy even sent a picture of them in some parking lot." Darleen stopped. "You know, I'm still confused about all this. It's so out of character for the lady I know."

Bernie explained what the family should do to report Mrs. Raymond missing.

"Thanks, that helps." Darleen smiled. "I think the grandson stays at Mrs. R's house sometimes."

"But something else is bothering you too, right?"

"Slim. He can't find much time to spend with me. I can't even tell if he still loves me."

"Just call him," Bernie said. "If he's grading papers from his summer classes or working on lesson plans, he'll call you back."

"I don't want to seem too needy," Darleen said. "You know, like I'm desperate for love or something."

"You worry too much, Sister."

"Do you worry?"

Bernie laughed. "Sure I do. About you, about my husband, about what's going on at work, about Mama. A lot about Mama. But I try to turn worry into action."

"How?"

"For instance, some government official is planning a trip out here. When it happens, I'll have to work overtime. So, instead of worrying about Mama, I asked Mrs. Bigman if she could help. I told her I didn't know exactly when I might need her. And she said she'd stay flexible."

"Turn worry into action." Darleen stood to leave. "That's great advice. Instead of worrying about all my assignments, I'm going home to get to work on them."

Chapter 13

Mrs. Raymond would have preferred taking the stairs—those little moving elevator boxes made her uncomfortable—but she didn't see any, so she and Droid walked to the elevators. One had an out-of-order sign taped to the door. The other took forever to get to them. When it opened, the inside smelled of sweat. Droid pressed the button, and the elevator slowly creaked up to the third floor.

The room fit Mrs. Raymond's impression of the rest of the facility: shabby and neglected. It was furnished with twin beds covered with blue paisley bedspreads. The only window looked out onto a parking and another building. The air conditioner under the window filled the room with a noisy hum. She already missed her own sweet little house.

"Wow." Droid said. "We got our own AC. Sweet."

On the table between the two beds was an old-fashioned telephone, a boxy beige thing with white push-button numbers.

"I need to call my daughter again."

Droid had sprawled on the bed closest to the bathroom. Mrs. Raymond moved the ancient phone toward her.

"On that thing?" He smiled. "Yeah, that's smart. It won't be my number, so maybe she will answer it."

Mrs. Raymond picked up the receiver. No dial tone. She clicked on the plastic piece that she remembered sometimes brought a phone to life, but it remained deadly silent.

"It doesn't work. I'm glad you kept yours. Call her now." She realized that without Droid's phone, they would be cut off from their family until they could leave the hotel.

"We can call on my phone, but it needs to charge, you know. I forgot about that, and that takes a minute."

Droid scavenged a phone charger from the depths of his backpack and plugged it in to his cell phone.

"Good," Mrs. Raymond said. "But let's enjoy the peace and quiet for a while before dinner."

"Yeah, good idea. I don't want to call right now either." He stood. "I'm going downstairs. I need to walk round, check things out, a little, you know?"

"I know." She noticed that her grandson seemed itchy, bored, unsettled.

"You can call whenever you want. Auntie's number is in here. Swipe up and then put in my code." He rattled off the numbers and turned the cell phone toward her as he explained how to make the call. "Push this to call and use this button to hang up."

She nodded. "I'll see you for pizza." He needed something to distract him, Mrs. Raymond thought, something other than her encouragement and stories. And although she never would have said it to Droid, after all that time on the bus, she was happy to be alone.

She unloaded the little bag of necessities she had stowed in her purse when she realized Droid might need her help. In addition to her stone turtle, she had also left her pills behind. That was OK; she'd be home in a few days. Once she talked to her counselor about how to change Victoria's terrible behavior and made sure Droid's rehab program was working, she'd have Blue take her back where she belonged.

She took off her shoes, stretched out on the bed, appreciating how good it felt to not be moving or talking. When she woke up, she checked her watch. It was almost six, so she went down to the lobby. Droid hadn't come back to the room, but she wasn't worried.

A table had been arranged, with paper plates and napkins and several large pizzas in cardboard boxes. Mrs. Raymond strolled over to the pizza. She saw people she recognized from the van and other people, maybe thirty or so altogether. They mostly looked like Navajos. It was good they were here. Being in a safe place for a while would help them break free from whatever problems haunted them.

The pizza was plain cheese and lukewarm, but she took a slice anyway and grabbed a cup of coffee. After a sip, she added sugar and powdered milk and then sat on the couch.

She spotted Droid standing with some tough-looking older men. She caught his eye, and he came over to her.

"Shimásání, you make your call?"

"No, I fell asleep. I still need to apologize about Mr. Fluff. This is the night I take care of him so Victoria can go out."

"It's OK. She's . . . she's mean to you. I love you. I love my dad, too, but he doesn't get me the way you do."

She smelled something on his breath that wasn't coffee. "You've been drinking."

"Just a little to keep away the shakes. My last drink, I swear."

"Really?"

"I hope so. I wanna call Dad. Let him know what I'm up to. I'll go upstairs and get the phone. We'll call both of them now. There's lots of spots down here, no one will notice us."

Droid headed back to the room. Mrs. Raymond spotted the woman who had offered her a drink on the bus grabbing a can of cola from the cooler and a foam coffee cup. The woman poured some soda into the cup, then removed a bottle from her purse and emptied it into the cup, too. She gave Mrs. Raymond an air toast with the bottle before tossing it in the trash.

She watched Droid get off the elevator with the phone in his hand. He started to slip it into his pocket, but Heather appeared almost out of nowhere. Mrs. Raymond saw Droid go into the office and put his phone in one of those little bags.

After that, Droid told her he was staying in the lobby to play cards and tell the Navajo guy from Kayenta not to offer him beer. He'd see her later. Good, she thought, the card game might distract him from longing for a drink.

She used the plastic card to open the door to her and Droid's room, proud of herself for figuring it out on the second try, then turned on the light on the table next to her to read in bed. When her eyes grew heavy, she put on her nightgown and brushed her teeth. She looked at the watch her daughter, the one who died, had given her. It had a button that made the face glow at night. She was glad she had worn it.

She surprised herself by going right to sleep in the cool room with the noisy air conditioner. When she woke up later, she forgot where she was until she saw the glare from the streetlights through the thin shades. Her grandson's bed was still empty; she pictured him playing cards and making friends. The room was too cold now, so she put on her socks. In the morning, she would figure out how to work the cooling machine and ask the helpers for a blanket.

Chapter 14

When Sandra came into his office the next morning, Lieutenant Jim Chee thought she looked worried. And she was.

"I made a mistake yesterday," she said. "Around the time the captain went to the hospital, I answered a weird call. It didn't come in on the 911 line but on the regular non-emergency number. And it originated at a convenience store over the border in Arizona. Not even a place on the Navajo Nation. And the guy on the phone said he found a dead man. He sounded like a kid.

"With what happened to the captain, and the ambulance and calling Britany and all that, I just forgot about it."

She held the fingers of her right hand against her left palm and squeezed them as she spoke.

"But I saved the recording and something about it bugged me. I worried about it last night and I listened to it again just now. I'm sorry, but I should have told you yesterday. It might not be a prank."

"Yesterday was hard on all of us. You did your best." Chee said. "Tell me more. A child made the call that worried you?"

She spoke faster than usual. "I think a teenager or a tweener.

When I listened again this morning, the more he talked, the more it sounded to me like he was telling the truth. Not just messing with us. But I sure hope I'm wrong about that."

So, in his role as department leader, Chee quickly listened to the recorded call. He agreed that there might be some truth in it. He assigned Bigman the job of driving to the nuclear waste disposal site where the informant had claimed to have found the body. Bigman would verify the accuracy of that before they brought in the FBI—or, Chee hoped, Bigman would say the phone call had been a prank after all.

But unfortunately, Bigman discovered that the body was there, and dead as reported. In general, officers from the Navajo Police worked side by side with the FBI until it was determined that a death might involve a crime, and all murders were handled by the FBI. In the case of unattended deaths that weren't suspect—say, if someone froze or died from an obvious fall—the Navajo Police dealt with the case.

Bigman confirmed that the body was inside the restricted area where the caller had reported seeing it, inside the fence at the Shiprock Disposal Site, the old Navajo Mill uranium ore–processing facility. Not only was the fenced site well marked with NO TRESPASSING signs, the big yellow-and-black radioactive hazard warnings were easy to spot. It had taken Bigman a while to find the body, but once he saw the hat the caller had mentioned, it had become clear this wasn't a prank.

"And there's something weird about this, Lieutenant. You should come and see it before you call the feds. "

Chee quickly headed to the location Bigman described. After parking on the road behind Bigman's unit, he spotted the officer on the other side of what looked to Chee like a well-built chain link fence topped with razor wire. He saw no opening, official or otherwise.

"How did you get through that fence?"

Bigman pointed with his chin to a place a few yards away, where an animal had dug a hole near the base of the barrier. "I didn't see another way inside, so I crawled in down there. A lot safer than trying to climb over and back down again." He looked at the hole and laughed. "A tight squeeze, but I made it."

Nearly as tall as Chee and at least twenty pounds heavier, Bigman wasn't known for his agility. Chee gave him credit for solving the problem like a prairie dog.

"Tell me what you've discovered about the dead man before I go in there."

"OK. I can't see for sure if the guy is a Navajo, but probably not. I don't think I've spotted him around here. He looks like he got beaten really bad. About six feet, and I'd guess around one-eighty. He doesn't have a ring on his wedding finger, and his left hand looks damaged, like he was in a fistfight or something. I can't see his right hand; it's pinned under the body."

Bigman rubbed the sweat off his forehead. The morning was warm, and Chee figured the conversation was adding to the officer's discomfort.

"He's wearing black boots, a gray short-sleeved shirt, like a work shirt or something, and jeans," Bigman went on. "I wouldn't have found him except for the hat on his head."

Chee waited.

"It's light brown, a newish cowboy hat with a stamped silver hatband. The hat looks expensive. Custom-made or something, but the guy is wearing old jeans and a regular shirt. The hat's kinda sideways now, but it didn't come off his head. No fancy watch or jewelry I can see except for that silver ring. No cell phone, as far as I can tell, but it looks like he has a wallet in his back pocket. I took photos."

Bigman had a keen sense for details, a skill Chee valued. He was wondering if the man was done talking when Bigman answered the question he had been planning to ask.

"I'd say this guy has been dead a couple of days, anyway. That makes me wonder about the timing of the call to Sandra yesterday afternoon, you know."

"I'm curious about that, too. Maybe whoever dumped him had a twinge of conscience. Or it could have just been a weird coincidence, you know, somebody driving by and spotting it."

"No," Bigman said. "You can't see the man unless you're inside the fence, the forbidden territory. I had to look hard for him when I arrived, but now that I know where the body is, I can tell you where to look."

Chee waited.

"OK, if you glance out there to the right and ahead several hundred yards, you might notice something brown, something that looks out of place. See it?" Bigman turned toward the mesa and indicated the location with a nod of his chin. "That's the hat. If you look closely, you can see it. The weeds hide the body pretty well."

Chee saw the hat. "Anything else interesting?"

"Some tire tracks and a few shoe prints. I was checking the area to see if I'd missed something when I heard your unit." Bigman motioned to the hole beneath the fence. "You want to check the body for yourself?"

"Not really, but I need to. And I have to call Agent Johnson." Sage Johnson of the Farmington, New Mexico, office was the FBI agent Chee knew best. He thought she had adjusted well to life in northwestern New Mexico and to cases that brought her to the Navajo Nation. The Bureau had recently promoted her and given her additional supervisory authority.

Johnson sounded preoccupied when she answered. "So, where is this body?"

"You aren't going to like it."

"Tell me anyway."

He did.

"Seriously? *There?* That area is totally off-limits. How did you guys learn about this?"

Chee filled her in about the call to the Shiprock station. "The responding officer found the main gate locked and the entrance undisturbed. He's following the vehicle tracks near the dead man to find the point of entrance and exit. Before your crew gets here, we probably will have figured out how the vehicle got through the fence, so your guys can close the hole when they're done."

"Thanks."

"Sure. What's the ETA?"

"I'll leave in about fifteen minutes."

"You're coming yourself?" But because he knew her, he wasn't surprised.

"Sure thing. Me and the evidence response team. You know I wouldn't want to miss something like this. I'll see your guy when I get there. Is your officer someone I know?"

"Bigman will probably be here. I think you've met him. Call when you're close, and maybe we can tell you how to get to the body without crawling under the fence, like Bigman did."

After the call, Chee lowered himself onto his belly and inched his long, slim frame down onto the warm earth. It looked as though a coyote or another animal had created the hole, and Bigman had enlarged it. Chee pushed himself slowly through the opening beneath the fence, careful not to snag his uniform shirt or pants on the pointed wire. He felt grateful that, despite Bernie's skill at making those delicious peach pies he loved, he was still near his college weight. And grateful that the original hole maker hadn't put the entrance route too close to a cactus.

Chee stood, dusted himself off, and walked up to Bigman. They began to stroll toward the body together, moving into the wind through the tough native grass and those low-growing weeds with tiny sharp seeds that embedded themselves in a person's socks. Chee saw some fresh coyote droppings and the sticklike tracks of a bird.

"Here's the vehicle tracks." Bigman tapped his boot on the dry sand, and Chee looked toward the recent impressions. "I think they might have considered leaving the dead guy here, but then figured it was too close to the fence."

Bigman explained that he could see that the vehicle had taken the same route in and back out by the way the tracks overlapped. "I saw two sets of footprints near the dead guy. The first, waffle soles, looked like they came from a vehicle and then returned to it. The others looked like running shoes and I knew from the distance between the prints that whoever it was ran in here, then headed off in the opposite direction. I took photos. My guess is that the runner is the guy who called."

Chee thought for a moment. "How did the runner and the vehicle get inside the fence?"

"Good question." Bigman took off his hat and mopped away the sweat. "I don't know, but I'm going to check on that."

"Why do you think these tire tracks are from the vehicle that left the body?" Chee agreed but he wanted to hear Bigman's idea.

"Well sir, unless the guy in the running shoes carried the body in, it has to be. These are the only vehicle tracks I saw, and they stop near the dead man and then double back." Bigman paused and turned his face toward the mountains. "I've been with the dead man long enough. I'd like to figure out how they got him in here."

They agreed that the fact that the vehicle left the same way it came in could make finding the breach in the security fence easier. Even in the mid-June heat, walking along the tracks certainly would be a better method than driving off-road around miles of perimeter to check the fence for security.

"Go look for where the fence is down," Chee said. "I'll stay with the body, wait for the feds, and wait for you to let me know what you find."

Bigman nodded. "You can tell the agent that the main entrance gates are locked, and it looked to me like nobody had messed with them. I checked that out first. That's another reason we had to come in prairie-dog style." Bigman started to leave and then turned back. "If you lose sight of the hat, just follow my boot tracks to the body. I was careful not to step on any other prints out there."

Chee watched as Bigman trotted off alongside the vehicle tracks, noticing the spring in his step. Chee knew the feeling. Despite the uncomfortable presence of death, there was an intrinsic satisfaction that came with doing important work like this. Finding a body seemed like an odd way to get some peace, but the fact that this would not be his problem cheered him. This crime clearly would go to the FBI. He and Bigman might be asked a few questions, but then he could return to dealing with the logistics of a dignitary visiting Shiprock.

Chee stood a moment, collecting his thoughts, then followed Bigman's boot tracks to the body, noting how carefully the man had avoided the tire tracks or any other prints. As Bigman had said, the brown hat poking up though the tough native grama and rice grass showed the way. The silver band caught the morning sun.

The breeze had picked up, and Chee felt airborne dirt strike his skin as he walked toward the dead man.

The body lay next to a scrawny sagebrush, face up to the sun just as Bigman had found him. The wind had left a thin layer of sand that sparkled in the sunlight on the man's jeans and shirt and dusted his hat. His skin had a reddish tone, still apparent despite the gray hue of death. Chee determined with a glance that this was a sun-bronzed white man.

He moved in and squatted to study the body more closely. He noticed the ring on the man's left middle finger. It was a beautifully crafted silver turtle with turquoise in the center of its shell. He saw the sand that had settled onto the blondish hair of the dead man's forearms, onto his ring, and into the creases of his pants. Sand sparkled in the tooling on his expensive black boots.

The dead man probably weighed two hundred pounds. From the lack of blood and the way his body was positioned, it was clear that he had not been murdered here. His face looked battered, and the hand Chee could see had bloody knuckles. He deduced that the man had been in a fight. The hat looked as though someone had pushed it onto the dead man's head after the body had been dumped.

What had killed him?

Leetso—that was the word the man who made the call had said to Sandra. Leetso. But why leave the body here, where the government had buried radioactive waste from the nearby uranium mines and mills? Did the killer want the body to be found here? Certainly there were many remote, inaccessible spots that would have not involved breaking through a fence. Was the killer making some kind of statement?

Chee knew many people who considered leetso a nayee, or another of the monsters that interfered with human life. The relationship between uranium mining and the Navajo people was complicated and for the most part tragic, a story of cancer and miscarriage and desecration of the land and water.

Chee examined the vehicle tracks and the shoe prints in the sand. Whoever had lifted the body out of the vehicle wore larger-than-average shoes. He agreed with Bigman's assessment that the owner of the other prints hadn't helped move the dead man or come and left in the vehicle. A puzzle.

Chee studied the scene from a different angle. Tire tracks encircled the body, as if the person at the wheel knew exactly where the dead man should be left and wanted to create as little disruption to the natural environment here as possible. It was an odd combination, he thought. How many murderers were environmentally sensitive when they disposed of their victims?

He looked away from the scene, gathering his thoughts. The hot June air carried the whinny of a horse and the squeaky call of a desert bird he couldn't name. A large black beetle, the insect Chee called a stink bug, scurried toward a shady spot. He heard a faint rumble overhead, the wrong timbre to be thunder, and looked up to see a small plane, probably headed to Farmington. It reminded him of the big shot they were getting ready for.

Chee pulled out his mobile phone, took some pictures, and sent them to Agent Johnson. When he had done enough, he squeezed back under the fence and returned to his unit. It was a relief to know that he and Bigman could leave as soon as Johnson and her folks arrived at the scene. With Adakai out of service, he had a long to-do list for the pending visit.

A few minutes later, he saw Bigman approaching through the sage-and-rock landscape on the other side of the fence.

"Did you find the place where they broke through the fence?"

"Yes sir. I took some photos for the record, and I marked the spot with a red bandanna I had in my pocket. They cut through the wire and then pushed it back enough for the vehicle to enter. That was a tough job. I followed these tracks out of the secure area until they disappeared that way, on the road." Bigman jutted his chin toward the horizon. "I lost the other shoe tracks until I got back to the road. Then I found some on the shoulder. Looked like that person ran back to Shiprock."

Chee noticed that Bigman's words came slower than usual. The man looked exhausted and was sweating extensively.

"Good work." Chee motioned toward the dead person. "I took some shots of these tracks around the body, and especially the shoe prints that indicate that one man must have removed the body and then climbed back in the vehicle to drive away. With the wind picking up, this could all be gone in an hour."

"I agree." Bigman glanced toward the body then looked away. "Whoever did this drove something with high clearance—a truck or an SUV, maybe a four-wheeler. I saw some sagebrush bent and crushed, in and between the tire tracks, but they never got stuck, as far as I could see. These tires must have been new, sir. Johnson might find that interesting." Bigman squatted closer to the tracks and then stood. "Wow, I've got cramps in my legs."

"Good work, Officer. You sure did a lot of walking."

"I was jogging. I wanted to be done with it before it got too blazing hot out here." Bigman's face had grown pale beneath his hat.

Chee could tell that the heat clearly bothered the officer. And the day would only get hotter. "Officer, are you alright?"

"Yeah, I guess I should have stopped at my unit for water. I think I'm getting sunstroke or heatstroke or something. Kinda dizzy."

Chee spoke firmly. "Crawl back under the fence to your unit now. Turn on the air-conditioning, and drink some water. When you feel better, head back to the substation. I'll wait for Johnson and her crew."

Bigman frowned. "I can stay here. I'll be fine after I . . ." His voice trailed off.

Chee studied Bigman more closely. The man was shaking.

"That's an order, Officer," he said. "And pull over if you still feel dizzy or something. Got it?"

"Yes sir." Bigman exhaled.

Chee walked with Bigman to the hole under the fence and used his strength to raise the bottom wire a bit to make the entrance larger for the younger man's bulk. He was glad Bigman's unit was close by.

"Are you sure Johnson can find the rift in the fence?"

"She'll find it. I tied the bandanna on good. She can park there and walk in, but tell her our spot here is closer to the body, OK?"

"Sure." Chee watched Bigman climb in his unit, heard the engine start, and saw him drinking from an insulated water bottle. He trusted Bigman to wait until he felt well enough to drive to head back to the substation.

The June wind continued to blow, stronger now. Chee considered the victim's brown hat with its silver band. Another strong gust might carry it off.

He walked back to the body to secure the hat, slipping on the evidence-collection gloves he had stowed in his back pocket. He reached the site just as the wind took the hat off the dead man's head and planted it in the dirt several feet away. The head beneath it, covered in thick reddish-brown hair, began to collect the sparkling sand.

Chee snatched up the hat. He realized he had been holding his breath. Interesting, he thought, that after all his years in law enforcement, and all the dead people he had had to contend with, he still instinctively feared the dead.

He examined the cowboy hat again, remembering that often people with hats like that one put their names inside. He found no identification there, though, just an odd lump in the sweat band. On second look, he would have described the hat as middle-aged rather than new, but well cared for. The owner had worn it enough to give the hat some character, but it had a lot of life left in it. Kind of like himself, he hoped. He wondered again who the victim was, and why he had been murdered.

His long experience in police work had taught him not to remove anything from the crime scene. He thought about how to secure the hat so it wouldn't blow away in the wind. It already had sand on its brim, so he scooped more sand onto it. Then he scooted under the fence again to get an evidence bag, slipped back under, placed the hat inside, and weighed the evidence down with a big rock.

While he waited for Johnson, Chee focused on the beautiful stone profile of Ship Rock and the span of the Chuska Mountains. Ship Rock, he thought, was one of the most beautiful spots on the Navajo Nation if you liked the desert and thinking about the power of volcanos. Its stone bulk anchored him to this special place and reminded him of why his job mattered, of the long-held value of service to others among his people.

The warm wind had grown frisky enough now to kick up mini dust devils. The high-desert landscape offered countless empty places where a dead person might rot undiscovered for weeks or months, maybe forever. Why go to the trouble of breaching the fence around a nuclear waste storage site? Why would someone be jogging in this odd place? Had the phone call that led Bigman here come from someone who wanted the dead man to be discovered? There had to be a reason, but Chee decided he couldn't decode it without more information.

He was deep in thought, puzzling out these scenarios, when his phone buzzed, surprising him. The caller was Johnson.

"Hey, Agent. Are you close?"

"No. I'm not coming after all. Agent Dobbs will be out there. He ought to be arriving in about ten minutes, unless he gets lost."

"Dobbs?"

"He's here from Washington. He'll fill you in. You said the old waste site, right?"

In the background of Johnson's call, Chee heard vintage rock 'n' roll music.

"That's right. He'll see my unit along the road, so have him stop there. Is Dobbs alone?"

"No. His partner will be with him. Ginger Monahan. Did you find the breach in the fence?"

"Bigman did." Chee thought about it. "It took Bigman about a fifteen-minute walk to get from the body to the place where the vehicle came through. The body is over a little rise. Two or three minutes, or maybe five, from where my unit is parked. If they look for my unit, they can squeeze under the fence like I did. I'll be here to show them."

"Squeeze under the fence? On the ground in the dirt? I don't think Dobbs and Monahan will be crazy about that plan."

"If they aren't up for that, they can park on the road outside where the fence is down and come through the opening. Bigman marked it with a red bandanna. But they'll have to walk farther in the heat."

He remembered DC as hot in the summer. Maybe the agents were used to that. "The way Bigman and I got in is the closest to the body. I'll be here waiting."

"You know, this isn't my problem." Johnson chuckled. "Dobbs might call you for directions."

"Have you met these agents?"

"Never. I just found out they were here." Her voice had some surprise in it, and more than a touch of irritation.

"Did they come because of the secretary's visit?"

"I can't answer that."

"I'm disappointed that you aren't handling this." Chee knew Johnson was a total professional and easy to work with. He thought about the oddity of agents from Washington, possibly assigned to keep the secretary safe, coming to investigate the discovery of a body on the Navajo Nation.

"Yeah. Too bad the body turned up now. The secretary's visit and all the complications already have me tearing my hair out. I didn't need one more stinking thing to deal with, plus . . ." She stopped. "Sorry. Too much information."

"No reason to apologize. It's good to vent."

"I called the Office of the Medical Investigator, and the OMI unit is on the way."

As he waited for the agents and OMI to arrive, Chee watched the thin clouds assemble and drift apart again overhead. A raven scolded from a tree, then soared away from him in the blueness. He considered calling the hospital to check on Captain Adakai and then reconsidered. There was no reason to ask for more bad news. Trouble already had his address.

Chapter 15

After getting to the station, and learning that there was no news yet on the captain and that the details of the secretary's visit were still pending, Bernie started the workday with her assignment to investigate the noise complaint at Teec Nos Pos.

From her years on patrol, Bernie had a well-honed instinct for locating homes in remote spots on the Navajo Nation, places that lacked a marker on a computer map. She knew she'd eventually find the house, and then she and the man who lodged the complaint would talk for however long it took to get to the heart of the problem.

In the meantime, she used the solitude of her unit to return to hózhó. She had her trusty backpack with water, snacks, and a book in case the day gave her time to read. She focused on the road and felt her spirits begin to lift.

The Navajo Nation was changing. When Bernie first drove this road, she remembered, she'd had no cell phone service. But today, when Chee telephoned, her phone picked up without dropping the call. He told her about the body and that he had done some research into the national protest group that might be arriving because of the secretary.

"Have you found the car yet?" he asked.

"Not yet," Bernie said. "I'm still on the way to Teec. I think that car was probably stolen and dumped out there."

"Me, too," he said. "I mean, who do we know who drives a fancy sedan?"

"No one except city folks," she said. "Those cars need more clearance than there is on a lot of these roads. It's odd. But that makes this case more interesting. And the drive is nice."

"You might run into that mustang herd," Chee said. "There are a bunch of wild horses out that way."

"I hope I don't run into them. I'd rather just see them at a distance."

He chuckled, and Bernie heard a phone ringing in the background. "Gotta go," he said. "Take care of yourself. Stay safe."

Bernie admired the Chuska Mountains and a tower of white clouds, brilliant against the deep blue of the morning sky. She appreciated the quiet and the lack of traffic. Every time she drove this way, she marveled at the arrays of solar panels. They were proliferating faster than sheep. It was wonderful, she thought, that more families throughout the vast Navajo Nation could get electricity. And in territory blessed with an abundance of sunny days, using the sun for power made sense.

Officer Manuelito found the house of the man who made the call, parked her unit, and stretched a minute before she strolled over to meet the gentleman standing at the fence. He introduced himself with his clans, and then as the man who had made the noise complaint and reported the fancy car that seemed to have been left behind. When he finished, Bernie reciprocated with her clans and said she had a few questions.

He invited her to come inside his small, neatly kept home and gave her a glass of water. They chatted a moment, and then Bernie asked what she had to and took down his information about the disturbance and the car. He told her that there'd been excessive noise from a nearby building remodeling project for several nights, and that when he went to the site to complain, no one had responded.

"I guess they couldn't hear me over all that noise."

The interview took longer than she would have expected because his wife kept adding her information, a different version of the same story.

"See that roof over there?" He indicated the direction with a twitch of his lips. "That's where the noise is."

Bernie had been listening ever since she arrived. "I'm sorry, sir, but I don't hear it."

"The noise stopped yesterday. But the car was still there last time I looked."

When the man had answered her questions, she left to find the car that must have been stolen. It was hard to miss, a big, black, Mercedes-Benz sedan. A thin layer of dust confirmed the couple's observation that it had been parked sometime last week and hadn't moved since.

Bernie took a picture of the Nevada plates so she could check to see if the sedan had been stolen. Then she walked to the door of the building that had been the source of the noise. It looked like a workshop or an artist's studio but with a satellite dish mounted on the roof. She knocked. She waited and knocked again. When no one answered, she walked around the structure, hoping to find another door. The discarded construction material led her to assume the racket must have come from remodeling. She couldn't judge the extent of the work because most of the windows were covered with curtains, but she could peek in through a place where the drapes didn't quite meet. She saw lights on poles, a metal table with foam pads on top, lots of orange extension cords, and black boxes that looked like small suitcases.

The scene reminded her of a recording studio. She walked back to the abandoned car and wrote a note telling whoever owned the vehicle to call her or someone at the Shiprock station, or the Navajo Police would have it towed as an abandoned vehicle.

On the way home, she stopped at the Teec Nos Pos trading post and picked up her first Coke of the day, along with the news of the area. Evidently the driver of the Mercedes hadn't stopped for gas, and no one there could tell her who had moved into the old place and was remodeling.

That done, she parked her unit in the shade, kept the air-conditioning on, and wrote up a quick report. Then she radioed the station. Chee was out, but he had left a message for her to go home so she wouldn't be on overtime when the secretary arrived and things got busy.

It was a relief to have a short day, especially with the secretary's pending visit and a schedule of traffic duty looming on the horizon. If Darleen wasn't too busy with classes, maybe she'd stop by that afternoon and they could chat while they both kept an eye on Mama.

Chapter 16

The June sky had barely started to change from black to morning's gentle gray when Mrs. Raymond awoke again at Broadway Manor. After so many decades, her body was in the habit of greeting the day with a song and a gift of cornmeal to the holy people. She used to run, but that was before her hip started to protest, long before the stroke had compromised her balance.

In the dim light she slipped on her clothes. She had left her key card in the pocket of her blouse. Her purse with the sacred cornmeal was on the floor beside her bed.

She moved as quietly as she could toward the door, so she wouldn't awaken Droid. Light showed beneath the bathroom door, a sign that he was in there. She avoided the elevator and found the stairs, then discovered a side door in the hotel lobby that opened to the outside. She used a rock she saw nearby to keep it ajar until she got back.

The day was already hot. At home she would stand in the field near her house and sing out to the Chuska Mountains, or to Ship Rock itself, with the turtle for good company. Today, tall buildings shaped her view, and instead of birdsong she heard the roar of traffic, tires against the pavement.

It was early for people to be going to work, she thought, but she didn't know much about life in a city. She continued walking, softly singing her prayer as she went, until she found a little spot of nature in front of one of the buildings. When she got there, she tossed her cornmeal to the wind and let out her shout to let the holy people know that she was here for another day.

She returned to the hotel, put the rock that served as a door stop back where she'd found it, and took the stairs back to their little room. Droid's bed was made, she saw, and the light beneath the bathroom door was still on. She knocked on the door. "Everything OK with you?" No answer. She knocked again. "Droid?" She didn't want to intrude on his privacy, but what if he needed help? He hadn't locked the door, so she opened it.

The room was empty. Then she remembered that she had left the bathroom light on when she went to bed, to make it easier to find her way there if nature called. She thought about the situation as she took a moment to properly dress and comb her hair. She briefly entertained the idea that Droid had gotten up early and gone out to pray or to get some coffee. But no. When he shared her home, she was always the first one up. The only time Droid rose early was when his father called with work for him, or if he and one of his friends had made plans.

She knew that although her grandson was a good boy, he had been drinking too much ever since his mother died. Drinking and maybe drugs, too, although she didn't understand much about that. His father, suffocated by his own grief, didn't seem to notice. But she did and it had worried her for months.

Mrs. Raymond went to the lobby to see if Droid was there. The sunlight poured in through the dusty windows, and the smell of coffee momentarily cheered her. A small group of old men were sitting on the couches, both people and furniture looking worse for wear.

They gave her "Yá'át'ééh" a blank look, so she switched to English, wished them good morning, and asked if they had seen a young man with glasses in a gray T-shirt.

Two of the men shook their heads but the third man spoke.

"When I went out the back door for a smoke last night, I heard some men talking out by the street." He had a scar on his forehead just below a strand of dark hair that had drifted toward his eyes. "One of them had on a gray shirt, but, there's a lot of shirts like that. And those guys, well, they sounded kinda . . ." He moved a finger near his temple in a slow circle. "I didn't see him up close, so I don't know if that's the person you are looking for."

Mrs. Raymond felt colder despite the warmth in the room. "Besides the gray shirt, my grandson has one of those lopsided haircuts, you know, close cut on one side and long on the other." She called up his image in her mind. "And a silver earring, like an X. Does that sound like the person you saw?"

The man only shrugged.

She thanked them and went to the registration desk. No one was there, so she found a thin man with a black T-shirt that read SECURITY, someone she hadn't seen before.

"Excuse me."

The man looked up. "Yes?"

Mrs. Raymond asked the man if he spoke Navajo. When there was no response, she switched to English.

"I need some help. My grandson is here with me, but he didn't come back last night."

The man shook his head. "That's against the rules. No one leaves the facility without authorization."

Mrs. Raymond said nothing. The man went back to whatever he was typing, but she stayed standing at the desk.

After a few minutes, he looked up, a bit uneasy. "That happens sometimes. When he comes back, someone will have to talk to him."

Mrs. Raymond said nothing.

"He'll probably come back."

"Probably? Probably! That's not good enough." She glared at the guard. "He's never been in this town before. We have no relatives here."

"There's nothing I can do."

Mrs. Raymond spoke louder now. "His name is Andrew Morgan, but everyone calls him Droid. Write it down." Mrs. Raymond said it all again, more slowly and with emphasis. "What kind of security are you?"

The three older men stopped talking, and she could feel them staring at her.

Mrs. Raymond had more to say. "You people brought him here to help him. You need to do that."

The young man grabbed a pen, and Mrs. Raymond saw him making a note. "Wait over there, and I'll get someone to talk to you about this." Then he stood and went to the back room.

Mrs. Raymond got a cup of coffee from the big aluminum urn and a package of little doughnuts with powdered sugar from a box that had a few other sweet choices. She walked closer to the window to find a comfortable spot. The window needed washing, but she liked the light. Someone had spilled something on the first chair she saw, and it looked sticky. She selected a cleaner one and sat. She liked drinking her coffee by the window because she could easily watch for Droid's return.

Her worry simmered as she ate the mini doughnuts and as more people came into the lobby for coffee and to pick up something to eat from the box on the table. She recognized a few of them from the van.

She had almost finished her second cup of coffee when the idea came to her. She would call Darleen, the woman who came from the agency to help her. Darleen's sister was a cop, so she would know what to do. And since Victoria must be mad at her, Mrs. Raymond decided she needed to talk to Droid's dad. She would ask Heather or one of the security men to help with those calls.

A well-dressed, important-looking woman old enough to be Heather's mother walked to the registration desk. The security guy got up and spoke to her, then both stared at Mrs. Raymond and then looked away. The senior woman, who seemed to be in charge of the place, disappeared into the back office. A few minutes later she walked out again with a practiced smile. She headed directly for the quiet place where Mrs. Raymond had been waiting.

"Good morning. I hear that you have a problem. I'm Bea, and I'm here to help. Let's talk about this." She started to sit in the sticky chair.

"Wait." Mrs. Raymond pointed to the spill. "You don't want to get that on you. Someone should clean it up."

Bea remained standing. "I understand you're concerned about your grandson, and we'll get to that, but I want to talk to you about something else first."

"I need you to help find my grandson. His name is Andrew Morgan. He's somewhere out there." Mrs. Raymond motioned to the big glass doors with a jut of her chin.

"Yes, I'll get to that." Bea gave her a cold smile. "You aren't the kind of client we usually help. Tell me why you came in the first place."

"What's wrong with you? I told the girl this already yesterday." Mrs. Raymond's voice rose with anger. "I need to find my grandson. If that happens, then you can help me with my daughter. I need to fix her so she won't be so mean."

"Oh, I see. Is she a police officer?"

"No." Mrs. Raymond gave her a look that added *Dumb question.*

Bea relaxed. "Did she come with you and your grandson?"

"No. She's not here. Just like he's not here." Her tone dripped with scorn. "My daughter is back in Shiprock with her silly little dog."

"Well, if you want to feel better about all of this, you have come to the right place," Bea said. "We can connect you to the resources that offer the kind of help you need."

"What I need now is for you to find my grandson." Mrs. Raymond said each word slowly, as if she were speaking to a child. "What don't you understand about that? I need you to call my daughter and Andrew's father so they can help."

"I do understand, sweetie. But no calls, remember? That's part of the contract you signed. But I'll see what I can do. I'm sure your grandson is fine."

***

Bea understood her style of tough, hands-on management well enough to know that she shouldn't get personally involved with the day-to-day operations of the business. But when Martin, the supervisor at Broadway Manor, came down with COVID and then, instead of getting better, continued to fade, she stepped in to fill the slot until she could hire a competent replacement. In the meantime, with Heather's assistance, they kept the ball rolling.

As soon as Bea saw the elderly Navajo woman, she knew the driver had made a mistake and Heather had let it slide. This woman promised nothing but trouble. Bea went back to the registration desk. She was pleased to note that Heather had correctly scanned the information for Andrew Morgan and a Navajo registration card for Mrs. Raymond. With that, it would be easy enough to begin the process of signing them up for Arizona IDs they weren't entitled to so that the company could receive Medicaid reimbursements for benefits available to Indigenous people—benefits they never planned to deliver. The old woman might cause trouble, for sure, but she'd be out of there soon, on to a group home. And the fact that the state of Arizona couldn't keep up with the need for rehab services for people on Medicaid worked in the company's favor.

Bea called Megan, the blue-haired driver who made the New Mexico reservation runs, not caring that it was early. She asked her why she'd picked up such a problematic old woman.

"Hey, don't yell at me. I did everything by the book."

"By the book. Really?"

"What do you want from me, Bea? Yeah, really. I brought in a full van load. I don't get extra for that."

"Couldn't you see the old lady was nothing but a headache, for God's sake?"

"Don't yell at me. She signed the forms. I knew that the young guy with her wouldn't get in the van unless she came, too. I filled two seats. She told me she was having problems with her daughter because of drinking, so she'll qualify for something."

"I get it," Bea said. "But she's a stretch."

"So is the kid. I made sure that he signed off that he's eighteen. They're a package. I figured you would know how to deal with the old lady, and you'd like the money."

Bea ended the call. She checked the schedule in the computer. Heather had assigned Mrs. Raymond to the first group for therapy tomorrow.

She talked to the security guy again and he swore he hadn't seen anyone slip out. She told him to pay more attention or his job was on the line and he left looking somber.

But they always lost a few potential clients before they could get them registered for benefits. After that, it didn't matter because no one checked up on a bunch of homeless drunks.

Bea made herself a fresh latte from her new espresso machine and thought about the pushy old Navajo. What could that old lady do except complain? She added a spoonful of raw sugar and smiled. Each unexpected kink in the plan made her better at solving a new category of problems.

***

Mrs. Raymond was so angry she could feel her blood pound as she watched Bea head into the office. She had enough experience to know that Bea hadn't taken her complaint seriously. She would find her grandson herself, and after that they would tell the story of the white van to Darleen and her sister the policewoman. She decided to have another cup of coffee, even though it was bitter, while she considered what to do next.

A slim young man was refilling the pot. He wore dark-framed glasses and looked to be in his thirties. His name tag read WARREN. She remembered Droid saying that a guy named Warren had said he could get her grandson a beer if rehab got too hard.

She watched Warren working and then asked him in Navajo if he spoke Diné bizaad. He answered yes and introduced himself. She hadn't expected him to be so polite. She reciprocated and then said, "I see you need to work, but I am worried about someone you met who is missing. I'd like to talk to you."

Warren hesitated. "Are you Droid's shimásání?"

She nodded.

"I go on break at eleven. I can you meet there by that back door."

Warren looked nervous when she arrived. She followed him to an abandoned patio behind the building, a spot now used to store discarded furniture. Although the building provided shade, heat radiated up from the concrete. She saw some old chairs and a garbage can with a tray on the top with sand for cigarette butts.

"I noticed you two when you came in yesterday," he said in Navajo. "I usually don't see grandmothers here. And I thought the guy with you was too young."

"He's old enough to be in trouble with drinking." Mrs. Raymond had had time to think about what she wanted to say and how to say it. "My grandson didn't come back to our room last night. He told me he was coming down to the lobby to talk to some people and that me met a man from Kayenta who worked here named Warren. That's you."

Warren picked at a cuticle. "He didn't come back?"

"No." She had gone back to their room, thinking Droid might have returned while she was with the lady who would not help her. "No one slept in his bed. I am worried about him. I need to know what happened last night."

"I don't know." He clenched his hand into a ball. "I wasn't there."

"You know something that would help me find him." She waited for him to tell her, listening to the city noise beyond the patio walls. Someone was honking. A siren blared in the distance.

Warren shook his head. "I didn't see him after he left the building. I don't know what went down."

"You don't know, but you have an idea. Tell me so I can help him."

Warren put his hand on his chest, and Mrs. Raymond imagined that his jish hung there beneath his shirt. She thought of her missing turtle as she gave him time to come up with the words.

"Here goes." He exhaled a loud puff of breath. "Droid and I were talking down here last night. I had to work a double, so I was cleaning in the lobby. Lots of people can't sleep when they first come in. Droid told me he was trying to stop smoking, but he had the jitters. He didn't have any cigarettes, so I gave him one, and we came out here to smoke on my break. We hung out and talked about stuff, and then he asked me about something, and I turned him on to some guys."

He fell silent.

She looked at Warren a moment. "He asked you about something you don't want to talk about. Alcohol or drugs, or maybe how to find girls?"

"Ganja."

She felt oddly reassured. Marijuana—naakai binát'oh—caused trouble, but there were worse things. "Call those people and ask where my grandson is."

"No. It won't do any good." He shook his head, stressing the point. "Trust me on this. I know them."

"I have been wondering why you are working here. I think it is so you can make extra money with marijuana, or with booze, or maybe other drugs. I think the woman in charge doesn't know this."

"I needed a job, that's all." Warren said it in a way that confirmed that there was more to his story, but he wasn't sharing it. He looked at the old chairs and the garbage can for a moment. Then he took the phone from his pocket, tapped the screen a few times, held it to his ear, and, after a moment, handed it to her.

"This is Tommy. That's who Droid went to see."

To Mrs. Raymond's surprise, the voice over the phone was female. Tommy answered the phone with some swear words.

"Warren. What the f—"

"Yá'át'ééh." When there was no response, Mrs. Raymond said hello.

More swearing. "Who's this? Are you a cop?"

"No. A grandmother."

"What? How did you get Warren's phone?"

"Listen, lady. Please listen for one minute." And Mrs. Raymond explained as concisely as possible about Droid.

"Yeah, I saw him last night. Nice dude. We partied a little. He was doin' OK when he left. Flyin' high. Happy."

"Where did he go?"

"Just walked away. I figured he was going home."

"Home?" Mrs. Raymond spoke louder now. "No. You have to help me find him. He doesn't know Phoenix. He's never been out of New Mexico except for a couple of track meets. He's still in high school."

"Lady, chill. I didn't force the stuff on him. Leave me out of this."

"He's alone in this big town. What if you were in trouble?"

"I don't know where he went. That's the truth."

"Where did you last see him? Tell me that."

Tommy gave her the name of a building. "That's where we met. That's all I know."

"What time did—" But before Mrs. Raymond could even finish the question, Tommy hung up.

Chapter 17

Darleen slept until the early morning light woke her. She realized that she had been dreaming of turtles. In her sleep, the turtles had been hard at work with Mrs. R's help, planting a garden and bringing precious water to the seedlings. She awoke with the elderly woman on her mind.

Unlike Bernie, who had always been an early riser, Darleen wasn't usually a morning person. She knew that her sister made sure to start the day right by singing her prayers with corn pollen. So Darleen went outside and said her own prayer of thanksgiving to the Holy People for the gift of a new day and for a resolution to her worry about Mrs. Raymond. Then she added a note of gratitude for the miracle of coffee.

Before she left for a busy day, Darleen fed Mrs. Darkwater's dog and made sure his water dish on the porch was filled. She noticed some bird tracks in the dirt near his dish. Now that it was full again, it would be easier for the little chirpers to drink, too. Bidziil followed her as she dealt with her tasks. The dog must be lonely, she thought. They both missed Mrs. Darkwater. And she missed Mama, especially Mama when she'd been strong and happy.

Darleen texted a good-morning message to Slim, who had seemed preoccupied when they talked on the phone yesterday. When she asked what was bothering him, he had mentioned that he had too much to do. He told her he didn't feel like chatting and that he'd call back later. But he hadn't, and now she knew he was on the way to teach his summer classes.

She headed to campus. Her phone rang as she settled into the car. She didn't recognize the number, so she ignored the call and put the phone on mute.

The day was busy. Her classes—she had three—went well, and in the break between the second and third class she pulled out her phone to check for a text from Slim. Instead, she noticed two missed calls from Victoria. And then a text, call me, followed by half a dozen exclamation points.

Darleen went outside to use the phone.

"Finally." Victoria sounded hysterical. "I'm at the end of my rope. Mom didn't come home last night. I don't know what my mother is doing, but it's wrong. I'm furious with her. Can you talk to the police?"

"No." Darleen was glad that Bernie had talked to her about that. "My sister, the cop, said you are the one who needs to call."

"Why me?"

"The dispatcher will ask you what's your mom's birthday, what was she wearing when you saw her last, and stuff like that. And you are the person they should contact when they get news about her."

"News. Like she's dead or something?" Victoria fell silent for a few moments. "I don't like dealing with the police. You need to come over here and help me."

"I can't. I'm at school today."

"I'll pay you."

Darleen remembered something else. "Did Droid come home?"

"I don't know. His father and I don't talk much."

Darleen didn't like that answer. "Well, you should call him. If the boy is home, he ought to know where his grandmother is. If he's not there, maybe something happened to both of them. He can help you get more attention from the police."

"Are you trying to scare me? I'm already out of my mind." Darleen heard a new level of hysteria in Victoria's voice. "I'll call Greg. He needs to sort this out. His boy got my mother into this mess."

Darleen felt some relief. "Getting his help is a good idea."

"I'm glad it came to me." Victoria hung up without a goodbye.

Darleen went to her next class and then to the campus cantina and treated herself to an iced caramel mocha with two sugars. She found a table in the shade, sat with the laptop that the nursing program had provided for her, and forced herself to focus on schoolwork, avoiding the glittery temptation of social media and texts from her friends.

She'd almost finished both the mocha and the first of several assignments when she heard her phone chime with a text. She gave herself permission to yield to the distraction.

Mrs. Raymond's son-in-law Greg here. Call me pls, OK?

Darleen spent the next ten minutes wrapping up the assignment. Then she closed her computer and called Greg from her car, hoping for a quick confirmation that Mrs. R and the grandson were OK so she could head to Bernie's house to see Mama today before heading home.

"Hi." She introduced herself as Mrs. Raymond's health aide.

The voice was deep. "Hi. Victoria gave me your number. She told me you know someone at the police department who can help us find my son and his grandmother. I hope she got that straight."

"What's up?"

"Well, Andrew didn't come home last night, and he didn't answer the phone when I called. I'm worried."

Darleen heard some background noise, then Greg was back on

the call. "Victoria is demanding that I get the police involved. That photo Droid sent just made her mad. I don't want to panic, but I need to do the right thing. What do you think?"

"Did you talk to Droid when he sent the picture?"

"The photo of the two of them in that parking lot?" Greg didn't wait for her response. "No, I was at work. I called later, texted him. I wanted information—where they were, when they'd be back, what was going on, stuff like that. But no response. He ignored me."

"Did you have an argument or something?"

"No, but . . . No. No argument."

"But what?"

Greg hesitated. "Well, ever since his mother died, Droid's shut down. He's been spending more time away from home with his friends, and with his grandma. He says he's exercising a lot, helping one of his bros with chores, playing basketball, but I think alcohol is part of the picture. I told him he needed to get his act together. I felt that, besides losing his mother, I was losing him, too. He brushed me off."

Darleen waited to see what Greg would say next, but he stopped talking.

"Could he have stayed with a friend instead of coming home?"

"I called the ones I know. He's not there. My guess is that he and his grandmother drove off somewhere. Droid is always nagging to use her car. He just got his license. She lets him drive, but she always goes with him. My guess is that they went in it somewhere and broke down or something. That's why I want to get the police involved."

"Is it the gray sedan?"

"That's right."

"I saw it parked at Mrs. Raymond's house when I went to help her. She was gone, but her car was still here."

Darleen could hear Greg gasp over the phone. "Are you sure about that?"

"It's parked in the shade, and she left the hood open to help keep the packrats out. If I was there I could send you a photo, man."

She heard him sigh, and regretted her flippancy.

"Well, this takes my worry to a new level," he said. "I figured they'd driven somewhere, and, I don't know, maybe got lost or in a wreck or something. And that Droid was embarrassed, and that's why he didn't answer my calls."

"You should contact the police and mention that both of them are missing." Darleen gave Greg the phone number for the Shiprock station. "You'll probably talk to Sandra, the main dispatcher. Tell her that Darleen Manuelito told you to call, and then ask for Lieutenant Chee."

"OK. Thank you."

Darleen tried to focus on the next assignment, but her brain kept returning to the mystery of Mrs. R. Finally, she packed up her belongings and drove to see Mama.

The rest of the afternoon passed quickly because Mama was in good spirits. She'd just finished looking at some old photos with her mother when her phone buzzed with a text. She took time to read it when she saw it was from Greg.

Called the station. Chee unavailable. Left a message. Big time worried and thanks for your help

She texted back

Worried 2. Stay in touch.

She checked her phone for a text from Slim and found nothing. It was still early, she told herself; he was still in class, or busy with his own work. She didn't message him. She didn't want to seem too needy.

Chapter 18

Beatrice Marigold Flores never thought she'd stay in Phoenix after she got out of prison. Growing up here was bad enough, and now the town was too crowded, too noisy, too full of people who moved in from elsewhere and thought they knew everything. A city of millions, and it seemed to get bigger every day.

But then Bea met Robert Dottson and, as someone said, love changes everything. They married. More than physical attraction, she formed a partnership with a man who craved the finer things in life as much as she did. He wanted a red electric car and a house with a big garage where he could charge his new wheels before he went to the golf course. She wanted a swimming pool and a cruise to the Bahamas. Once they figured out how to make some real money, Phoenix's heat felt less oppressive, and she got used to the traffic.

The big idea came to her after Robert took a middle management job with Arizona Department of Health Services. He quickly realized that the department's system of so-called checks and balances was out of balance. Reimbursement for services provided for some clients had questionable oversight. The review for checking against possible fraud? Practically nonexistent. She and Robert talked about how they could make some money, but Bea was confused at first when he told her his plan. He started with an overview.

"There are lots of folks in Indian country who need rehab for alcohol and drugs. Thousands of eligible clients and not many services. The state of Arizona pays for this treatment with money from the feds. It pays big bucks, and there's almost no supervision. Programs that help Indians—excuse me, our Indigenous brothers and sisters—have amazingly few watchdogs, and there's a lot of unspent money waiting for someone to claim. That someone could be us."

She never forgot how smart Robert was. She had done her sentence for embezzlement, and with the spare time she had in prison, she'd pondered the mistakes she made that got her arrested and honed her accounting skills.

"Robert, get to the good part." She drummed her fingers on the tabletop. "Tell me the specifics of us getting rich, and how I fit in."

He explained the plan in detail and with gusto. They both assumed that the federal government was full of corruption from the top on down, so they'd really just be stealing from thieves. No shame in that. And everyone understood that most people who went to rehab didn't really get well. In addition to the down-and-out in Arizona, they could expand the operation to people from the reservations in neighboring New Mexico or elsewhere. They'd bring in the clients, give them a Phoenix group home address, which would get them Arizona IDs. That made them eligible for "services" that wouldn't be provided. Then Robert and Bea would pocket the Medicaid money that came from Arizona for treating these addicts.

Bea felt her heart beat a little faster. "I can help work out the details. You know the medical lingo, and I know how to find the billing codes to put into the system." She liked the idea more when he told her how much money the government paid for treatment. They would need vans and drivers to collect the clients and places to house the people they brought in. They could feed them with Arizona's food assistance programs, which the "clients" would qualify for with their fake IDs. Then Robert and Bea would bill the government for the broad menu of rehab services they never planned to offer.

Robert tossed out some other ideas, refining the scheme.

Bea remembered smiling as she listened to the plan for the lucrative con unfold.

She had no sympathy for any kind of addict. Her mother had checked out with booze and pills, and that had led to more family arguments and crises than she could remember, even if she wanted to. Mom was always criticizing her, telling her how worthless she was, how much grief she caused, how she'd regretted ever having a child.

But Bea had learned enough about alcoholics and drug addicts in prison to understand that they were not idiots. "What if someone complains they're not getting rehab services?" she asked.

"So what? We'll just give them a drink or another pill, and they'll forget about it. If someone gets seriously rowdy, we let him out on the street."

Bea approved. "Who would they complain to anyway? And who would believe them?"

He frowned, hesitating. "Well, some of these losers still have families, you know. We need to be shrewd about this."

Bea considered that. "What if my mom had told you she was going to rehab? Would you have believed her?"

"The first few times, maybe. After that, I would have been skeptical."

"And if she came home and said the sober house gave her the booze and pills, would you believe it?"

"Of course not."

"How about that?" She mussed his hair the way that pleased him. "We're onto something."

It took them a week to figure out the rest of the scam and then a few more days to fine-tune it. They started with one sober house, and after six months, they had added another three. The budget was complicated, with rent, salaries, cost of transportation, and at least a few days of food before the food stamps came through. The plan worked better when she found a run-down hotel they could lease as a staging area before shipping their "clients" off to the sober houses. The former Broadway Manor worked well as a receiving station until the Indians, and others they brought in, went to the sober homes. Bea set up a part-time office at the hotel so that she could keep an eye on the staff. When she divorced Robert, she began to spend more time there and noticed that her profits increased.

Before Robert and his new girlfriend moved to Las Vegas, Bea settled up with him fair and square. They knew each other too well to try and pull a fast one. She'd tolerated his philandering while she needed him because of his state job, but she was glad to be done with that. She had her system in place and her eyes on a second home in Malibu, solely for her own enjoyment.

Chapter 19

By the time the two East Coast FBI agents arrived to check on the body, Jim Chee was bored and annoyed at the wait. He alternated between waiting in his unit and pacing outside, where the summer wind scoured sand from the dirt road and drove the sharp particles against his pants and buffeted his face. Finally he saw a black sedan approach, moving fast toward where he was parked and creating long fantails of dust. The car stopped behind his patrol unit.

Two lean, well-groomed people got out and walked quickly toward where Chee waited. He greeted them and introduced himself, and they showed him their credentials. Agent Frank Dobbs was older than Chee, with more gray than brown in his hair. Agent Ginger Monahan was younger, probably in her late thirties, with deep-red lipstick that gave her a serious, slightly sinister look.

They were dressed for sidewalks, paved roads, and coffee stands. They looked out of place in the unforgiving high desert.

Chee wondered, again, what had brought them to New Mexico and the Navajo Nation. Was it a coincidence that they were covering this presumed murder? Obviously, they had arrived in the Shiprock area before Bigman found the body. He presumed their visit had something to do with the secretary of energy from Washington who was supposedly on her way. But they didn't mention why they had taken over what should have been Sage Johnson's case, and Chee didn't ask.

"Tell us about the body," Dobbs said. His partner nodded. Neither made any attempt at pleased-to-meet-you small talk.

Chee quickly reiterated the details of the discovery. Dobbs asked the expected questions: When had the call come in? Who made it? How had the caller discovered the dead man? When had an officer responded, and was the body as described? Had the first officer on the scene, or Chee himself, touched or moved anything? Monahan listened without a change in her stoic expression.

Chee elaborated when it came to the last question. "The victim had a hat that would have blown away in this wind before you got here. I secured it as evidence. You'll see it in the bag with the rock on the corner."

"Let's get to the body now," said Monahan.

Chee showed her the low spot where he and Bigman had squeezed under the fence. "This is the quickest way in."

Dobbs frowned. "You said Officer Bigman found a breach in the fence. The place they drove through? Where's that?" He turned away from Chee to glance out at the vast, open landscape. "The fence is intact here. I don't see anywhere it's compromised."

"You can't see the breach from here. You'll need to drive around the other way." Chee explained how Bigman had marked the opening.

"So the rift in the security fence was the point of entrance for the body dump," Monahan said. "Have I got that right?"

Chee shrugged. "The officer didn't discover any other damage along the perimeter, so that's what we think."

Dobbs nodded. "We'll drive over that way, look at the fence, and follow the tire track to the body. Meet us at the body, OK?"

Chee was tempted to tell the agents to watch where they walked and not to drive into the dump site. Instead, he kept his advice to himself, waiting until they drove off and allowing them some time to find the place where the wire had been cut and pulled back. Then he scooted beneath the fence to get inside again, grateful that his walk to the dead man would be short. He dusted off his pants and shirt and waited, feeling sunbaked and grumpy.

Finally he heard a car approach on the other side of the dump site. He couldn't see it or the breach in the fence from where he stood guarding the body. The agents kept the engine running awhile, and then the motor stopped. The day continued to grow warmer and by the time the two of them had hiked through the sagebrush, dirt, and cactus to the body, they looked hot and grumpy. Monahan removed her jacket and wiped the sweat off her forehead with a swipe of her shirtsleeve.

Chee watched the agents study the body and surroundings the same way he and Bigman had. Monahan paused at a place where the soil held shoe tracks with clarity. "Are these tracks yours?"

"That's right. Mine. Officer Bigman's are the soles with the circles." Chee tapped the ground next to one of Bigman's prints with the toe of his boot. "Like I said, he's the officer who responded to the call and found the body."

"He sounds like a good tracker."

Chee said, "Bigman is a fine cop. We took photos of the vehicle tracks around the body and leading to and away from it, as well as shoe prints that appear to lead to and from the vehicle, and a second set of shoe prints near the dead man."

"If the 911 call is traceable out here, we'll do that," Dobbs said.

"It wasn't 911. It came in on the regular line."

"Oh, that's right. That emergency system doesn't work out here on the edge on nowhere."

"Yes, it does." Chee's tone reflected his irritation. "We've had 911 service for a number of years. Navajo was the first tribe in the country with a special system that pinpoints the caller, whether over cell phone or landline."

Monahan said, "I'll get pictures of the body and the evidence here, then follow the tracks back to the fence. Nothing else of interest here, as far as I can tell." Chee heard a touch of Oklahoma in her voice. It reminded him of a person he had met when he went to Quantico for some special training, an enrolled Chickasaw with red hair like hers.

She took photos of the tire tracks and the footprints that were neither Chee's nor Bigman's, presumably made by whoever had called the station.

"It looks to me like one of these sets of prints belong to whoever dumped the body," she said. "You agree?"

"That's what Officer Bigman and I think, too," Chee said. "Yes. These are old, fainter. I can't tell how many people were in the vehicle that drove in here, but only one person got out. It looks to me like the exit was on the driver's side and he walked to the tailgate or the hatch of the vehicle and dumped the body. Then climbed in and drove away."

Monahan looked at the prints. "If that's the case, I'm surprised that the hat stayed on the dead guy's head."

"I doubt that it did. I think it came off and whoever dumped him here shoved it back on."

Dobbs looked at the scene from different perspectives while Chee watched.

"What about these other prints?"

"Judging by the length between them, this person was running. The soles look like my wife's joggers." Chee pointed in the direction from which the prints approached the body. "I think this person was jogging along, discovered the body, stopped, and then ran off that way, back toward the place where the fence is down."

"Interesting," Dobbs said.

"I think you're right," Monahan added.

The dead man remained as Bigman had found him. Without the

hat the sun hit his face. The man lay awkwardly skewed to his left side, as if someone had simply tossed him down. Chee notice a small red tattoo on his wrist. It looked like the man's nose had been broken and his mouth injured. He might have been handsome once.

When Monahan stepped away and began to focus on taking pictures of the footprints, Chee made a suggestion. "That right rear pocket has a wallet in it."

Dobbs called to his partner. "Done?"

"Almost."

Chee and Dobbs waited while Monahan photographed the hip pocket. Then she pulled on some evidence gloves, leaned over, and removed a slim brown leather billfold and a piece of paper shoved in next to it in the same pocket.

She opened the wallet and thumbed through the compartments. "No credit cards or ID. Ninety-two dollars in cash."

"What about the paper?" Dobbs asked.

"Give me a minute, OK?"

She unfolded the page and read silently. "It's about a solstice gathering to meditate about the future of Mother Earth. It's signed by Citizens United to Save the Planet, CUSP, not an individual. All it has for information is a phone number."

Dobbs slipped on his gloves, and Monahan handed the paper to him.

The flyer looked like a professional effort, printed in color, with the headline:

SOLSTICE MEDITATION IN INDIAN COUNTRY

And then, in smaller type:

Help heal Mother Earth in a place where uranium and other deadly evils lurk below ground

After Dobbs scanned the rest of the text, he turned his gaze toward his partner. They stood silently for a moment, then Dobbs showed the paper to Chee. "You know anything about this?"

Chee memorized the text and phone number.

"No, but people have been protesting against uranium for a long time out here. Our chief of police heard a rumor that this group might be coming our way."

He expected Dobbs to ask a question, but he didn't. Chee knew the Navajo activists focused on better compensation for those whose relatives had been sickened or died from their work in the uranium industry. But they weren't murderers, or folks who would be likely to organize a solstice meditation.

Dobbs walked to the other side of the body. "I've come across the group before. They staged some protests in California and Utah, then fell off the radar. Monahan, you know more about CUSP. Do you recognize the man?"

"No, but I need a closer look." She squatted close to the body. When she straightened up, her face was pale. The hot breeze had shifted toward them, and Chee noticed that it carried the stench of death. She left the question unanswered.

Dobbs looked at the body a moment longer, moving no closer. "We'll handle it from here, Chee. That's why the FBI is here. But be sure to let us know if you learn anything about CUSP, OK?"

Chee took a deep breath and regretted it because of the stench coming from the body. "What brought you so conveniently into the area for this case?"

Dobbs acted as though he hadn't heard Chee's question.

Monahan raised a well-groomed eyebrow. "I can't answer that. Next question."

"This country is full of places to hide a body. Why would some-one dump him here?"

Monahan shook her head, her chin-length hair catching the sun with its motion. "My take is that whoever did this is either unfamiliar with the other places you're thinking of, or wanted to make a statement. If it's a statement, I don't get it yet."

Dobbs looked toward the mountains and frowned. "Lieutenant, just so you understand, what we've got here isn't for public release. No media, got it? No TV. This never happened until we're ready to release something. Understand?"

Chee stared silently at Dobbs for a long moment. "If I see the TV crews pulling up, I'll refer them to you." Because most of the area's television news coverage came from Albuquerque, mentions of the Shiprock area were as rare as October rain unless something horrific happened. And even then, if reporters came from the main stations they faced a three-hour drive.

On the other hand, the discovery of a body inside a fenced area for nuclear waste would be news eventually. Certainly, the weekly *Navajo Times* might write a story. They did a good job of reporting on the reservation, and non-native news outlets often picked up their reporting.

Dobbs turned his back on the body, took a few steps, and pulled out a cell phone.

Chee started to move away, but Monahan stopped him. "Before you go, Lieutenant, what's your take on this?"

"I don't know enough yet to have an opinion."

She nodded. "What about the person who made that call?"

"It came from a convenience store in Arizona."

Dobbs cut in. "I just talked to Agent Johnson. She says the medical investigator and the removal team will be here shortly."

Chee had been around long enough to appreciate the finesse in using "shortly" as a measure of time. He knew the feds couldn't leave until the body was transported.

"Thanks for the tip about the billfold, Chee," said Monahan. "Good eye."

"You're welcome. And don't forget the hat."

"Hat?"

Chee indicated the brown hat in the large evidence bag anchored with the rocks. "I secured it so it wouldn't blow away. I noticed a small lump in the sweat band."

Dobbs said nothing.

Chee left them standing in the sun. He headed back to the station, relieved that the dead bilagáana would be in other hands, but curious about how a man with nice jewelry and a good hat had ended up in forbidden territory without any identification and with a flyer about a solstice meditation in his back pocket.

Chapter 20

Warren's face softened as he took the phone from Mrs. Raymond. "I didn't realize Droid was a kid. I'm so sorry."

"He's tall for his age, and he tries to act like a grown-up, but he doesn't know much yet. When he said he was coming for rehab, I was happy. But now . . ." Mrs. Raymond's throat tightened, choking off her words, and then came the pressure behind her eyes. It embarrassed her to cry, especially in front of a strange man, but her tears had their own agenda.

Warren stayed where he was until she had composed herself. "I know that building she mentioned," he said softly. "The one where she met Droid. I can tell you how to get there. But he won't be there now. Too hot. Maybe he came back here while we were talking."

They both knew that wasn't true.

"OK. Tell me about the building and there's something else you can do to help," Mrs. Raymond said. "I need you to get his phone out of the desk for me so I can call for help."

"That's impossible. They keep the office locked. I'd get fired.

There's a lot of surveillance around here. That's why I told you to come out here, so we could talk privately."

"I need to call my daughter. Just as I'm worried about Droid, she could be worried about me." She realized that even if she had relented to Victoria's pressure and gotten a cell phone, it would have been confiscated just as Droid's was. "I have her number in my head. Can you help me?"

She saw the worry leave Warren's face for a moment.

"I can call for you on my phone, but I can't do it now. I have to get back to work. Meet me here after dinner when I have another break." He gave her a time, then frowned. "You know, most people don't answer mobile phone calls from unknowns like me."

Mrs. Raymond sighed. "But we'll try."

They went through the unmarked door into the lobby, and she thanked him. She wished she had stored Darleen Manuelito's phone number in her head, too.

***

The old men were still in the lobby. The one with the scar motioned to her.

"You're the lady looking for the guy in the gray T-shirt, right? The kid with the weird haircut."

She nodded. "His name is Droid. But don't call him a kid."

"I thought of something else. You know those guys I mentioned?"

Mrs. Raymond remembered the conversation vividly, especially the idea that the people Droid was talking to might be crazy.

"Well, one of them, a girl, was speaking Indian, and Droid spoke it back to her. I've seen her when I was on the streets here."

Mrs. Raymond asked if he knew where the girl might be and he named some streets she had never heard of. It wasn't much, but it was a clue.

"Did you remember anything else?"

He laughed. "I remembered that I could use a drink."

She thanked him for the information, even though she wasn't sure what she'd do with it.

Trying to keep her hope alive and her fear at bay, she decided to go back upstairs and see if Droid was there. She didn't like waiting to make the call, but she could use the hours to think of something smarter than just walking around outside in the heat. Maybe, she thought, the counselor could help her with this problem, too. That reminded her that Heather hadn't given her any appointments. She'd deal with that later.

The room she and Droid shared was empty. She made a note of the clues the man had given her and then stretched out on the bed. She tried to get rid of her worry and disappointment. She closed her eyes and pictured herself at home, with Droid safely at her side, as she drifted off. In her dream, Darleen Manuelito was there, too. Darleen was showing Droid a game on her phone. She asked Darleen for her phone number, and Darleen said, "I wrote it down for you, remember? You put it in that little zipper pocket where you keep your change."

***

She woke up because the room, which had been too cold, was now too warm and too quiet. The air conditioner had stopped working, she realized, and she was hungry. A package of mini doughnuts didn't make a satisfying breakfast.

In the lobby, brown lunch bags had been set out on a table. She grabbed one for herself and one for Droid. The man supervising the table scowled. "Just one per person."

"I need one for my grandson."

The man gave her a hard look. "OK, but tell him next time he has to get his own."

"And the air conditioner in our room stopped working. Someone needs to fix it."

"Yeah, I'll add it to the list." His voice rang with sarcasm.

"Today." Mrs. Raymond didn't like being patronized. "It needs to be fixed today. Lodging is part of the contract we signed. That means we should be able to be in our room without sweating. Understand?"

The man shrugged. "Talk to Bea about that."

"I will." Mrs. Raymond glanced toward the office. The door was closed.

"She and Heather are out to lunch," the man said. "Chill down here."

Mrs. Raymond went up to her room and left Droid's lunch bag there in case he came back. Then she took her own lunch bag back down and out the secret back door, glad that Warren had shown her another way to escape. Inside the sack was a bottle of water, a small apple, and a white bread sandwich that, from the smear at the edge of the crust, looked like peanut butter and grape jelly.

Off the patio, another door led to a parking lot. She tried sitting on a bench near the parking lot entrance, but it was too hot to sit in the sun. The temperature had climbed from very hot to broiling, and it wasn't even noon. She needed shade.

She walked a little, searching for a place with trees. She finally found a shady spot near an intersection. Looking around, she noticed that the busier street was one the man had mentioned when he told her about the young woman who might be with Droid. After eating half of her sandwich, she walked some more.

The neighborhood changed quickly. In the very next block she saw more trash, more closed buildings, more unhoused people. The sight made her sad, and there was nothing and no one there to tell her about Droid.

Then she saw a man, perhaps in his forties, emerge from an alley. He looked like one of her cousins, so she spoke to him in Navajo. He answered in the same language, and she asked if he'd seen Droid. He shook his head, so she asked about the building Scar Man had mentioned. The man glanced up at her, confusion on his face. She offered him the apple from her lunch bag, and he looked at it as if he'd never seen one before.

It was too hot to go farther. Discouraged and sweaty, Mrs. Raymond walked back to Broadway Manor. In the lobby, she recognized people from yesterday's van ride. Heather, the woman from yesterday, stood with them.

Heather glowered at her. "About time you showed up. Where's the other one?" She glanced at her phone, which seemed to have a checklist. "Andrew Morgan. Your roommate."

Mrs. Raymond shook her head. "I don't know. I was just looking for him."

"Well, he'll have to join another session. We need to go."

"Where?"

"To sign up for benefits, so we can take you for treatment."

"No." Mrs. Raymond frowned. "You never gave me the schedule. I can't leave without him."

Heather opened the big glass lobby doors, stepped outside, and motioned the group to climb into the waiting van. Everyone did except for Mrs. Raymond.

"You're scheduled to leave now," Heather raised her voice. "Get in the van. We're going."

"No." Mrs. Raymond yelled toward Heather and van. "My grandson. He's lost in this big city because of your program. He could die in this heat. You need to help us. Call the police."

Heather walked back into the relative cool of the lobby where Mrs. Raymond stood at the open door. "Listen to me. If you don't come with us, you can't be in the program. That means you can't stay here at Broadway Manor. You'll be homeless. When your grandson comes back, he won't know how to find you. That won't help him, will it?"

Mrs. Raymond said nothing.

"That guy will come back whether you are here or not, right? You aren't some kinda human magnet, are you?"

Mrs. Raymond still hesitated. She didn't want to leave without Droid, but she knew she needed a place in this large, strange city where he could find her.

Heather kept talking. "Listen. When you signed up, you agreed to follow the rules. What good does it do for you both to be on the street?" The woman looked toward the parking lot. "The van's ready. Get in. Let's go."

Blue was behind the steering wheel again. She winked at Mrs. Raymond as she climbed on. "You did the right thing," she said, then lowered her voice. "If you see a therapist today, talk to her about your guy, OK?"

Mrs. Raymond nodded and took a seat in the front row. She wanted a good view through the windshield so she could look for Droid. She tried not to worry.

As they cruised along the broad streets of downtown Phoenix, Heather told them they were going to an office to sign up for benefits, which would pay for their rehabilitation, and for food stamps that the program could use for their meals.

"When we get to the agency offices, everyone stays in the van until I get things set. I'll do the talking. You'll need to fill out some forms, but it won't take long."

After that, Heather said, they would go to the therapy center, where everyone would get out, fill out more paperwork, and be given a counselor and assigned to a group. "The biggest rule, our number one, is to let me do the talking. I speak for the group, so keep your mouths shut. Remember that."

"What do you mean, assigned to a group?" Mrs. Raymond asked.

"A group for therapy. To talk about your problems with other people."

"I don't want to do that."

"Tell that to the therapist."

Blue parked in front of a nondescript building and kept the AC running while Heather went inside. Heather was back a few minutes later with another announcement. "Here are the forms. For your address, we used the rehab center, because that's where you live now. That's already filled in for you. Just print your name and age, fill out the rest, and sign."

The paperwork took a while because some of the passengers had trouble reading, but eventually everyone complied. Mrs. Raymond noted that the sheet made Best Way Rehabilitation Center the provider of service and the recipient of the client's benefits for the services received. That was OK with her. She'd never enjoyed dealing with money.

A heavyset man in a suit came to the van. He asked a couple of the passengers to rewrite their social security numbers because he couldn't read them.

When he picked up Mrs. Raymond's paperwork, the ID card on his lanyard dangled near her face. She read his name: Andrew Montoya. "Andrew is my grandson's name," she said. "Did you ever have a nickname?"

"Nope."

"Why not do this on computer?"

"Easier this way." He grinned at her. "You'd be smart not to ask so many questions."

After he took the forms and left the van, Blue drove to the next stop. Mrs. Raymond used the drive to think. She found some paper and a pen in her purse and wrote down Victoria's name and number and the phone number and address of Broadway Manor, where, according to the paperwork, she lived until she could get home again.

Then she remembered the dream. She looked in her coin purse, and sure enough, there was Darleen Manuelito's phone number. She added Darleen's name and number to her mental list of people she could contact. She would have added Droid's father, too, but she didn't know his phone number by heart. Droid always made the call.

At the next center, Mrs. Raymond noticed that Heather had a long white envelope with something Mrs. Raymond couldn't read typed on the outside. When they entered the building, Heather handed the envelope to the woman who came up to talk to her. The lady put it in her jacket pocket with a quick look around the room, as though something made her nervous.

Heather told the people in the van—there were eight of them—to go to the waiting area at the back of the large room and have a seat. Someone would meet them there to help with the registration.

To get to the waiting area, the group walked through the main office. Mrs. Raymond studied the staff who were assisting clients as she passed. One of the workers, a young woman with a round face who sat at a desk near the hall that led to the restroom and water cooler, looked like she could be Navajo. Mrs. Raymond noticed a slight resemblance to Darleen. The nameplate on her desk read GEORGIANA BLACKHORSE.

Because only one person was handling their paperwork—the woman Heather had given the envelope to—check-in moved slowly. Mrs. Raymond thought it was strange that they didn't use some of the workers in the other room, but it wasn't her problem. When Droid came back, the man at the desk at the hotel would tell him where she was. And she had left the sack with his lunch in the room.

Mrs. Raymond stood, and when Heather gave her a questioning look, she pointed toward the restroom sign with her chin. "Don't take long," Heather said. "There are only three of you left to check in."

From the restroom hallway, Mrs. Raymond could see Georgiana Blackhorse at work at her desk, with no one needing her attention standing nearby at the moment. She had to get word to Victoria and to Darleen. It was time to call the police and get them to help find Droid.

She boosted her confidence with a slow, deep breath. Then she walked toward the woman and hoped for the best.

Chapter 21

Chee radioed Sandra that he was headed back to the Shiprock station. "Anything I need to know?"

"Well, the chief called just to say he doesn't have a confirmation yet on the secretary's visit. And nothing yet from the hospital except Mrs. Adakai. The captain wants you to bring him his glasses. I said I could do it, but he said no, he wants to see you, too."

After that, Chee put all his questions about the body, about the two city agents, about the secretary's visit on hold and enjoyed the drive. He'd heard that some travelers, perhaps people like the new FBI folks, didn't see much to like in the town of Shiprock. They hadn't experienced the warmth of the people who called it home.

If you only saw the generic sprawl of fast-food restaurants, nondescript housing clusters, government buildings, and dusty unpaved roads, you could miss the beauty. You might not notice the blue of the Chuska and Carrizo Mountains, rising beyond the human settlement, a contrast in color to the warm tans and sage greens of this high desert country. You could even overlook the steady flow of the silvery

San Juan River through an aisle of cottonwood trees with leaves that shimmered in the wind.

However, it was impossible to miss the star of the show, the monolith of Ship Rock itself, icon of the southwestern landscape, a huge glorious remnant of the active volcanic field that had dominated the area when the earth was much younger. Yet Chee had met outsiders who simply called Tsé Bit'a'í "interesting."

As he drove, Chee let the peace of the landscape help soothe the upset that came with Dobbs's arrogance and the recent contact with death. He wondered why Agent Ginger Monahan didn't seem especially surprised to find an almost empty billfold in the back pocket of an unidentified dead man inside a fence around a uranium waste containment area. The agents knew more—a lot more—than they were saying.

The case was odd, but it wasn't his. He had enough on his plate. The captain's heart attack left him to contend with administrative duties he disliked and the turmoil the bigwig's visit would entail. The work he wanted to get back to waited on his desk. It would still be there when all this was done.

He considered Bernie's mother and the change Mama's residency had brought. Bernie had planned to talk to Adakai about reducing her scheduled shifts until they could find more help with Mama. If she had asked his advice, Chee would have told her to wait until after the secretary's visit was settled. But his sweet wife hadn't asked, and he'd quickly learned that she seldom welcomed unrequested advice. She hadn't mentioned the outcome, so perhaps the captain's heart attack had postponed that conversation.

When he got to the station, all was calm. Sandra gave him the captain's glasses and he headed to the hospital.

Chee had been to the Shiprock hospital far too often, dealing with medical emergencies. No matter how airy, bright, clean, and modern-looking, hospitals left him feeling uneasy. Early in his career, he'd almost been murdered in one by a hired killer. The hospital served the primarily Navajo population and non-natives who lived and worked in the area, and it had become an unavoidable presence in his life. Each visit reminded him of his uncle, the hatáálii, whom he and Bernie took away against the doctor's recommendation so he could die at home. And of visiting his mentor, Joe Leaphorn, in the ICU in Santa Fe after a vengeful person with a gun shot Leaphorn in the head and nearly killed him.

He parked in the spot reserved for law enforcement, wondering if stress over the secretary's still unfinalized visit was part of the reason Adakai had collapsed.

Chee walked into the hospital's chilled lobby and counted two men, a woman, and a gray-haired lady with two children all waiting to be seen in the emergency department. He bypassed them and headed directly to the staff member at the front desk. The woman recognized him and gave a just-a-minute signal while she finished a phone call.

"I bet you're here about Captain Adakai."

"How's he doing?"

She frowned. "You know I can't say much."

"I understand. If you tell me what room the captain is in, I'll just be a minute. Promise."

The woman nodded and gave Chee the number of Adakai's room. "He should be there now but they're doing a bunch of tests to decide what comes next."

The privacy curtain was partly open, and Chee could see the captain lying on his back, an oxygen cannula in his nose and some sort of monitor on his chest. "Captain?"

Britany appeared from the other side of the curtain. "Chee. Come on in."

There was no chair, so Chee stood at the foot of the bed. Adakai look pale and exhausted. "How are you doing, sir?"

The captain ignored the question. "Did you bring my glasses?"

Chee reached into his pocket and walked closer to hand them to Adakai.

"Just put them on that tray table. Thanks. I want you to keep things moving until I get back. OK?"

"Yes sir, you bet."

"And I need to give you a message for Manuelito, just in case something else goes wrong today."

Chee listened.

"Tell her I was rough on her on purpose, when she told me she couldn't work overtime because of her mom. She's got to decide what she wants to do. If she's in or out." Adakai's eyes fluttered shut and then opened again. "Sorry. They gave me something to help me relax, and it's starting to kick in. Tell Bernie I said she's a good cop. Tell her there's a lot of room for people in law enforcement where they don't have to risk their lives every single day. You know, where they can be of service without taking a chance at getting shot at. Regular nine-to-five jobs. So they can go home to the ones they care about at the end of the day without being exhausted."

Britany squeezed her husband's hand. "You should listen to your own advice, Tex. You've got to decide what matters more, your job or your health. Right, Lieutenant?"

Chee said, "Everyone at the station wishes you the best, sir."

The captain closed his eyes. The sound of the machines that monitored Adakai filled the silence. Britany held the captain's hand. Chee noticed the tears on her cheeks.

"Stay in touch, and good luck," she said.

"Same to you and the captain. Let Sandra know what's up, and if there's anything we can do."

"I will."

Chee walked out of the emergency wing quickly and headed to his unit. He welcomed the day's dry heat after the chill of air-conditioning. After a few minutes behind the wheel, he realized that the day was looking up. He was grateful for the captain's understanding of Bernie's situation. He hoped that Bernie would receive Adakai's compliment with an open heart.

Chapter 22

Mrs. Raymond had been watching the young woman she had singled out, waiting for the right time to approach her. The time was now.

"Yá'át'ééh, hatsóí ashkiígíí." Mrs. Raymond spoke more slowly than usual. She watched the young woman's face to see if she understood the greeting.

"Yá'át'ééh." Georgiana Blackhorse looked up from her computer monitor. Her darks eyes sparkled. She switched to English. "I haven't heard anyone speak my language in a long time, or address me as friend. What can I help you with, my grandmother?"

Mrs. Raymond had considered her approach and continued speaking in Diné bizaad. "I have a problem with one of my relatives. I think he is in trouble. And I think we made a mistake when we came to Phoenix on the white van." She watched the expression on the young woman's face to see if she comprehended.

"Ayóó anííníshní." Blackhorse switched to English and lowered her voice. "I'm sorry. My Navajo got rusty after shimásání died. But I certainly understand problems with relatives. Please call me Gigi."

Mrs. Raymond decided that a rusty comprehension of Navajo

was safer than English in case Heather showed up. She continued in Diné bizaad, speaking even more slowly. "Because of this trouble, I need someone to help me make a phone call, Georgiana Blackhorse who I will call Gigi. The people with the white van took our phone. Do you understand?"

"Aoo'. That was yes in Navajo, right?"

Mrs. Raymond nodded. "Can you do that?"

The young woman looked puzzled and relieved. "Only a phone call?"

Mrs. Raymond nodded.

"Yes, but I have to finish what I'm typing, and then we can talk." She paused, and then whispered, "Are you in danger?"

Mrs. Raymond didn't know if she was in danger or not. She lowered her voice. "It's my grandson. He's missing, lost in the big city. I'm worried." Noticing an empty water bottle on Gigi's desk, she gestured toward the water dispenser with her chin. "You need to fill up your bottle. We'll talk back there."

Then Mrs. Raymond walked away from the desk toward the hall with the water. She held her breath as she watched Gigi click on a few more keys, then rise, empty bottle in hand, and head into the hallway.

Mrs. Raymond knew she had limited time to explain what she needed, so to make sure the woman understood, she switched to English. She outlined the facts of Droid's disappearance and her unease with the rehab situation.

Gigi listened. "What a terrible thing. I've heard rumors about this."

"I wrote the numbers for you here. This is where I'm staying. My daughter Victoria, that's the second number, and this next person is—" She had extended the slip of paper toward the young woman, but quickly withdrew it and stopped talking when Gigi's expression changed.

Heather had appeared from around the corner. She saw them and stood with her feet slightly apart, shoulders back. "Mrs. Raymond, here you are! It's your turn. I told you we were on a tight schedule. Why can't you follow the rules? You're nothing but trouble."

Georgiana Blackhorse raised her eyebrows. "Don't be so rude. This lady and I have a mutual friend in Shiprock, and—"

"Don't you need to get back to work, honey?" Heather interrupted.

Blackhorse pressed her lips into a straight line. "I do. And you need to treat your elders with more respect." And then, to Mrs. Raymond's surprise, Gigi reached for her hand and took the paper with the phone numbers. "So nice to see you. Please tell your family hello for me." Gigi walked back to her desk. Mrs. Raymond hoped for the best and did what Heather wanted.

Next, the van took them to another office building. The people on the van were fidgety and grumpy. A couple of them had the shakes. One man's face was bright red. They needed something to help with the withdrawal symptoms.

Heather gave them instructions before they left the van to fill out more forms. Mrs. Raymond spoke up. "My husband who died was like some of these men. When he stopped drinking, the program gave him medicine to feel better. The people on this van are hurting. That's not right. What kind of program is this that promises to help and then lets people suffer? Something is wrong."

"Mrs. Raymond," Heather said, "the next stop is the counseling center. Talk to them about all this, OK? It's outa my hands. And I don't like complainers. Got it?"

Another woman said something in Navajo. Several people in the van laughed.

Heather bristled. "What did you say?"

"Oh, somethin' like I could sure use a beer and a buzz." But what she'd really said was ruder, funnier, and directed at Heather's attitude.

The afternoon was nearly gone when they made the final stop. The small sign on the door read INDIGENOUS ADDICTION SUPPORT. About time, Mrs. Raymond thought.

The therapy office matched what Mrs. Raymond had expected from watching people on television go into counseling. Everyone from the van came into the cool waiting room. This time, the form asked about their physical and mental health. Mrs. Raymond checked "No" and "Never" to some the questions, but "Yes" to feeling sad and worried. As Blue had suggested, she left some lines blank.

The question about why she wanted therapy had a space for "Other." She wrote: "To get my daughter to mind her own business." She could have figured out a better way to phrase it, but it was the truth.

Finally, the receptionist called Mrs. Raymond's name. An assistant walked down the hall with her to a spot where they checked her weight and her blood pressure. The woman asked what medicine she took, if she exercised, and other things like that and put it in a computer.

She waited alone in a little room for a while, glad that she could keep her clothes on, and then a man and woman came in. He introduced himself as a behavioral health specialist, and said he would be referring her to a group session after they chatted. The woman was a nurse's aide, but, Mrs. Raymond thought, not as friendly as Darleen.

"Why do you want to stop drinking?" he asked.

She didn't know what to say. Why had she bothered filling out the forms?

He kept talking. "I know that's a hard question, but motivation is an important key to sobriety. Take your time to think it over." He reached to the table and handed her a pamphlet. "This has some information that will help you on your journey."

She looked at it. The title was "Get Sober. Stay Sober." It made her mad.

"I'm not here to get sober. Why bother me with those questions if you don't read the answers? What's the point?"

"The point?" He gave her a look of disgust. "The point is to encourage people like you to give up denial and take full responsibility for your own behavior. When you come to realize how alcohol has stolen your best self, you will find the incentive to move ahead on the difficult road to change. And we're here to walk with you and help you along the way."

She sat up straighter. "OK. Find my grandson and get him to stop drinking. And then figure out what to do about my daughter. That's what I need help with."

The man patted her hand, the same way she patted Mr. Fluff's head. "We're on your team now." He rose. "The receptionist will give you your appointment schedule."

"No. Wait. I need to—"

But he'd turned his back on her and left the room.

The van grew noisier on the way back to Broadway Manor, as the restlessness of people who needed a drink increased. Mrs. Raymond tried to tune out the distractions and shake off her rage, so she could focus all her energy on finding Droid and getting home. Instead of help, the big city of Phoenix had put the boy she loved in more danger. She would figure out another way to help Droid. And before she could or anyone could help him, she had to find him.

She climbed off the van, full of discouragement. Inside the lobby, someone had set up a cooler with water, soft drinks, and, buried in the ice, cans of malt liquor.

She took a bottle of water and rode the warm, smelly elevator to their room.

It was exactly as she had left it, except even hotter. Droid's lunch bag still sat on the bedside table where she had placed it after she put his name on it. Her grandson, the joy of her life, was alone in a city of millions of people without his phone and with just a few dollars in his pocket.

***

Gigi made the call to Victoria right after Mrs. Raymond left with her mean-tempered escort. The old woman's sharp mind, quick tongue, and, more than any of that, overall warmth reminded Gigi of her own grandmother. And she had sensed that something suspicious was going on in the benefits office. Why was there a steady parade of people on the down and out, always handled by the same staff member in a private room?

Gigi listened to the phone ring, and finally she got a terse message. She recorded a voicemail.

"This is Georgiana Blackhorse from the Arizona Department of Health Services in Phoenix. Mrs. Raymond asked me to call this number and tell her daughter Victoria to contact her in Phoenix." And Gigi left the number of Broadway Manor on the machine.

Just as she was planning to call the next number, she got some emails and other messages she had to deal with. The office grew busy, and she focused on her job. She would call the second person later. The lady hadn't had time to give her the person's name, but she assumed it must be a relative.

Chapter 23

Because Slim was on her mind, Darleen picked up her phone from the table at Bernie's house when it buzzed. She had it on vibrate so the noise wouldn't awaken Mama, who had fallen asleep on the couch. She said hello before she realized the call came from a number she didn't recognize.

A human voice said hello back to her. "Mrs. Raymond asked me to call this number. This is Gigi Blackhorse. I'm sorry, but Mrs. Raymond didn't give me your name."

"It's Darleen." She felt her stomach tighten. "I've been worried about her. Is Mrs. R OK?"

"As far as I know. She asked me to call you and her daughter. She told me she was worried about her grandson. He's missing and I think she wants your help."

Darleen was confused. Weren't both grandson and grandma missing?

"Gigi, where are you and how do you know Mrs. Raymond?"

Mama, sitting on the couch next to her, put a finger on her lips and said, "Too noisy." Darleen took her cell phone into the kitchen.

"I'm in Phoenix. I don't really know her," Gigi said. "We talked for a few minutes when she came into the behavioral health services office with about ten other people and a caseworker. A lot of Navajos and other Indigenous have been here in the last month. Anyway, Mrs. Raymond could see I was Diné, so she came to my desk and asked me to make the calls for her. She was nervous, and before I could get much information, the caseworker started yelling that Mrs. Raymond had to finish her paperwork so the van could leave."

Darleen's brain swirled with too many questions and not enough answers. "Was there a young guy in the office with her, a teenager?"

"No." Gigi asked her own question. "Are you one of Mrs. Raymond's relatives?

Darleen explained their relationship. "You said Mrs. R wanted you to make a call to her daughter. Did you?"

"I think so. I dialed the number she gave me and got a weird voicemail. I left a message earlier this afternoon, but no one called back." Gigi paused. "I liked Mrs. Raymond. She made me homesick for my own shimásání. She didn't fit with that Best Way Rehab group."

"Rehab for people who've had strokes?" Darleen knew that the residual effects of the incident bothered Mrs. R.

"Not that kind of therapy. Best Way's clients have substance abuse issues. Alcohol and drugs. Hold on a minute, OK?" And when Gigi came back, she gave Darleen the phone number for Best Way Rehabilitation and the number where Mrs. Raymond said she could be reached

Darleen noticed that the area codes weren't New Mexico. "Where is this?"

"I don't know for sure, but somewhere in The Valley."

"The Valley?"

"Oh sorry. I guess you're not from here. I mean Phoenix. Valley of the Sun."

"Thanks. I appreciate—"

Gigi interrupted. "Mrs. Raymond is at Broadway Manor. That's the old hotel Best Way uses until they move the clients to sober homes, you know, like group homes for people in rehab."

After Gigi's call ended, Darleen stared at the phone. She dialed Best Way Rehab, got a generic message, and asked someone to call her. Then tried the number for Broadway Manor in Phoenix, but no one picked up. She called Bernie; again, no answer. Finally, she called Chee. Her brother-in-law could give her some sage advice that could maybe help her turn down the level of worry about Mrs. R.

Chapter 24

Mrs. Raymond went to her room in Broadway Manor feeling more discouraged and worried than she could ever remember. The day's heat and stress had left her exhausted, but when she lay down in the too-hot room, her mind raced. She had to find Droid. They had to go home. She remembered Warren's promise to meet her after dinner and call Victoria. That would help.

She ate the sandwich she'd saved for Droid and took a shower. The cool water revived her. She checked her watch and went down to the lobby.

Warren was taking out the trash. She walked toward him. "Need a hand with that?"

He motioned toward the door they had used to go outside for their previous conversation and then the nearest couch. "Please sit and wait for me there, OK? Right back."

So she waited, feeling nervous and unsettled. She tried to switch her thinking to what she would say to Victoria that would bring her to help. And while she was focused on that, she remembered that she also had Darleen's number. A fine idea came to her.

When Warren returned, he scanned the lobby, then opened the door to the dreary little patio and motioned to her to join him. The concrete had soaked up the day's sunshine, and the residual heat was intense. The young man looked tired, she thought, and no wonder, working a twelve-hour day.

"Mrs. Raymond, I can't make the call for you tonight. I had to take my break early because some new clients are coming in. And I haven't heard anything about Droid."

"Oh." She couldn't hide her disappointment.

"I'm sorry. If you want to look for him, don't go to that building Tommy mentioned. That's a waste of time. But I can give you some ideas. These are rough places, though. Someone should go with you."

"Just tell me," she snapped, and he mentioned three places that helped the homeless.

She listened closely. "OK. Now this. You know I don't have a phone, and the one in the room doesn't work. Teach me how to send a message on Droid's phone."

"What do you mean? A text?"

She nodded. Warren didn't respond immediately. "I don't mean to be discouraging, but Bea has never released a phone. Never ever. But we've never had anyone here like you." He took his own phone from his pocket and showed her how to find the contacts, type the message, and send. "You might have to play around with it a little, because his phone might be different than mine."

Mrs. Raymond thanked him. "I saw that the boss woman is in her office. I'll go and talk to her now before she leaves."

"Good luck."

At times like this, Mrs. Raymond was glad to be old. The experience she had accumulated gave her courage. She knocked on the doorframe, and Bea looked up.

"Hello, Mrs. Raymond."

"I need to talk about something important."

Bea sighed. "I don't know when your next appointments are. We're doing the best we can with the food and keeping the rooms cool. And I don't have any news about Andrew."

"He's out there, somewhere, alone in this big city. I have to find him. He has to come back here."

"There's really nothing you can do." Bea drummed her nails lightly on the desktop. "He knows where this place is. If he wants to be here, he'll come back."

"What if he can't?"

"Well, then I'm just stuck with you. You're more trouble than all the other people we're working with here, do you know that?"

"Yes. So, when my grandson comes back, we'll go home. I want out."

"Tomorrow." Bea said it confidently. "Tomorrow is a big day for your group. You all get to leave the hotel. You will head off in the morning. We've found a sober home for you and the others."

"What's that?"

"A house to share."

"Where is it?"

"Here in area. You'll see." Bea didn't tell her that she had purchased some houses in foreclosure that would serve as cheap places to warehouse the drunks.

"What about my grandson?"

"Sure, he'll join you if and when he comes back." Bea stood. "Time to lock up."

"Wait. I need our phone." And before Bea could explain why this was impossible, Mrs. Raymond laid out her story. Because it grew from the truth, she told it with her whole heart.

"Tomorrow would have been the birthday of my daughter who died, my grandson's mother. His phone has a picture of the three of us together, and she had a big smile. I just want to see that picture of her again."

"I'm sorry about your daughter, but I can't give you that phone." She motioned to a plastic bin on the shelf behind her. "No phones are returned until treatment is complete." Bea spoke as if she were sharing some regulation from the God of Rehab Services.

"You'd only be loaning it to me; I don't need to take it out of this room. I just want to look at my sweet girl, wish her happy birthday, you know? I miss her so much, and especially today. She would have been forty. Can you soften your heart?"

She saw Bea beginning to mellow, the line of her brow melting slightly. Her courage grew.

"What if someone who loved you very much had died, and you asked a stranger for one small thing, for the opportunity to see a picture of that person? Wouldn't you want that harmless little favor to be granted?"

"I don't know what I would do."

"Yes, you do. You know you would be kind." Mrs. Raymond looked at the plastic case with the phones. "The one with the blue cover and the orange sun. That's . . ." She started to say *Droid's*, but instead said *ours*. "I will look at it right here, say a little prayer in my heart, then you can put the phone back. One daughter doing a favor for one mother. That's all." She swallowed dramatically. "Sometimes, when I see her beautiful face, I start to weep. I miss her every single day." She sighed, folded her hands, and lowered her eyes even more. "Sometimes I wish I had been the one . . ."

Bea reached for the box with the phones, removed the lid, and grabbed the one with the sun on the cover. She set it on the table. "I'm leaving to get a drink of water. When I come back in about, uh, five minutes, I want to see that phone exactly where it is now, and I want you out of my office. And you must never mention this to anyone."

As soon as Bea left, Mrs. Raymond grabbed the phone. She remembered Droid's password. The phone opened to the picture of Droid and his mother. She nodded to it and struggled to see the icon for texts. Then she typed a message to Victoria and hit send. She saw "Dad" come up on a list in his phone and, hoping it was actually Droid's father, typed the same text again. She was slow on the tiny keyboard and hit some wrong keys, anxious that Bea might return before she finished.

Droid gone Phoenix Broadway Manor help us!

She pushed the button at the bottom of the screen to send it. She wished she could risk sending one to Darleen.

The sweet photograph of her dead daughter smiling with Droid next to her came back to life.

She was tempted to put the phone in her pocket, but instead she looked at the picture of her sweet girl and the grandson she loved one more time, wished her daughter a happy birthday, and wiped her eyes with the hem of her shirt. She left the phone where she'd promised, walked back into the lobby, and climbed the stairs to their room.

It would be a long time until morning. She rested and thought. When it got dark, she would go to the place the girl on the phone had told her about, she decided. Maybe Droid would go there again, looking for drugs or alcohol. If that didn't work, in the morning she would go to the places Warren had mentioned.

She left her room for the ground floor around nine p.m. She tried the side door she'd used before, but it was locked. Warren told her that sometimes the staff forgot to lock the big glass doors, so she walked right up to them and tried to leave that way. No luck.

The dark-haired man with a cap that read SECURITY sat behind a table with a small thermos and a cell phone that absorbed his attention.

Mrs. Raymond stared at him until he finally looked up.

"Unlock the door. I need to go out."

"No one leaves here. That's part of your agreement." He spoke as if he'd said that phrase dozens of times.

Mrs. Raymond raised her voice. "I have to find my grandson."

He studied her more closely. "Relax, lady." And then more softly, "I know where you can find some hooch."

"Hooch?" The word was unfamiliar to her.

"Juice, ya know. Beer or the hard stuff."

"No." Mrs. Raymond glared at the guy. "My grandson came with me. Now he's lost out there somewhere. Don't you understand?"

"Good luck to him, but no one leaves here tonight."

"Please help me." The words came to her with effort.

"No one leaves here tonight under my watch." The man said it again and then went back to his phone.

"When do you go home?"

"Seven a.m." He winked at her. "I have to open those doors then."

Mrs. Raymond knew the odds that Droid would be at the street corner then were slight to none, worse than tonight. She stayed where she was.

He looked up again after a few moments and shook his head.

"I can't. If anyone found out, I'd lose my job in a heartbeat. I've got a baby on the way, in addition to our twins. Have a drink, lady. It might calm you down."

Chapter 25

After Darleen got no answer at the number Gigi had given her to reach Mrs. Raymond, she knew she had to contact Greg. She kept the text short.

Mrs. R in trouble. Talk?

Greg called a few minutes later. He listened without interruption as Darleen told him of her conversation with Gigi.

He recapped what she'd said. "Droid wasn't there, and this lady told you Mrs. Raymond was worried about her grandson, right?"

"Yes."

"Give me Gigi's number? I want to talk to her about that rehab place. I can't reach Droid. I'm worried."

"Sure." Darleen recited it. "But before you call, I have a plan I need to tell you."

"What is it? Go ahead."

"I want to go Phoenix to find Mrs. R and Droid and bring them back here. That is, if they want to come."

"But you—"

"Wait." Darleen hated being interrupted. "Let me finish. When

I was at Mrs. Raymond's house, I noticed that all her medicine was there. Her joints will start to ache and swell without it. Even if she doesn't want to come home because of whatever the rehab is and because of Droid, she needs those meds. I don't understand why she had to go to Phoenix, but whatever therapy she's getting there, I'd like to help her find it here, or in Farmington or Cortez or even Gallup. Phoenix is too far away—six hours at least. I want to persuade her to come back so I can help her. I hope her grandson will come, too. I need to ask my sister if I can use her car because mine won't make it. I've left messages for her, so as soon as she calls me, I can work this out."

Darleen stopped for breath, and Greg jumped in.

"Did this Gigi say anything else about Droid?"

"No."

"And she said Mrs. Raymond was getting therapy? You sure about that?"

"Well, not exactly. Gigi met Mrs. Raymond when she came into the social service office to sign up for benefits. That's a little different, right?"

"Wait. Mrs. Raymond doesn't live in Arizona. She's a New Mexican, a Navajo Nation New Mexican like you and me. Why would she be applying for any kind of help in Arizona? I don't understand."

Even though Darleen had gone over the details, she had missed that problem.

"I'm worried about my son," Greg said. "He's just a kid, barely seventeen. Why did he go with her?"

Greg seemed to be waiting for an answer, so Darleen gave it a shot. "Maybe he wanted to help her. Or maybe he was looking for adventure, you know? Phoenix is a big city. A lot different than Farmington or Gallup."

"If he went to help her, why didn't he stay with his grandmother? He could have called me. His mother and I raised him better than that. His mother would be . . ." His voice dropped, and Darleen waited. She knew about grief.

But when Greg spoke again, she heard anger. "I'm driving to Phoenix today, as soon as I can get away from work, to search for him. I know Mrs. Raymond won't come back with us as long as he's out there, and I love her for that. I'll tell Victoria what's happening, and that she needs to come with me so we can get Mrs. R to come home, too."

Darleen knew he was right about Mrs. Raymond. "If Victoria can't help, count me in. It's a long drive to Phoenix, and it will be dark before you get there. Once you're in the city, it's impossible to pay attention to the traffic and look for someone like Droid at the same time."

"It sounds like you've been there."

"I spent a weekend. We went to the Heard Museum when they did the special Navajo fair." She'd gone with a boyfriend she met in art school in Santa Fe, a guy she'd hardly thought about since she fell for Slim. "I don't know it well, but I have a good sense of direction. We won't get lost."

"I haven't ever been there," he said. "I've never wanted to, until right now."

"I'd like to go with you, but no matter what, someone needs to take Mrs. R her medicine. I know where it is. I help her with that as part of my job."

"If Victoria won't make the trip, can you be ready to leave with me soon?"

"Yes."

"Can you drive an SUV?"

"I can drive anything. I'll go to Mrs. R's and get the medicine ready." She knew that Victoria couldn't do that job. "I'll meet you there, ready to go to Phoenix with you just in case."

After they hung up, Darleen noticed that she'd missed a call from Bernie, who'd left a voicemail.

"Hey sister, Chee and I have a change in plans. We've both got to work long days tomorrow. Mrs. Bigman offered to stay with Mama, so come if you want, but you're off the hook."

She had offered to help with their mother because Slim had a busy session of grading papers ahead of him, so Bernie's message was a relief. Now, all she had to do was pack a few things and leave food and water for Bidziil in case she made the trip with Greg. If Mama had been living with her, Darleen's plans would have been much more complicated. She knew Mama was safe.

As she pulled up to Mrs. Raymond's house, she noticed a newish SUV in the distance, parked in front of Victoria's home. It must be Greg's, she thought. He was wise to talk to Victoria face-to-face.

She let herself in, put the medicine in a bag, and noticed Mrs. R's turtle on the table, the little carving she'd found in the yard. She put that in a bag too, then went outside to wait, finding a spot where she could see the SUV and wait for Greg and Victoria. She'd ask Victoria to give the medicine and turtle to Mrs. R. Perhaps Victoria's presence in Phoenix would ease the tension between mother and daughter.

The door to Victoria's house opened, and a man wearing jeans and a sport shirt walked out alone and headed to the vehicle. He looked to be in his fifties, of average height, a few pounds overweight, with a buzz cut and some gray in his hair that matched the frames of his glasses.

Darleen could read the anger in his body language as he climbed into the SUV. In a few moments he pulled up at Mrs. Raymond's house. He rolled down the window and greeted her with "Yá'át'ééh," then gave the formal introduction with clans. She did the same, grateful for the respect he showed her.

"Do you have the medicine for Mrs. Raymond?"

"Right here." She raised the plastic bag.

He reached across the seat to open the passenger door. "Let's drive to Phoenix and find my son and his grandmother."

Darleen had been eager to go along when they talked on the phone, but now the idea of so many hours in the car with a man she didn't know made her a bit uneasy. She hesitated.

He read her discomfort. "I'd like you to call your sister the cop and I'll explain how all this is legit and how I need your help to find my boy and . . ." His voice broke, and he swallowed. ". . . and how if my son is hurt or worse, I don't wanna face it alone."

"I guess Victoria said no."

"She got a text from Droid's phone, asking for help. But she can't go to Phoenix because she has to take Mr. Fluff to the groomer in the morning." He curled his lip in disgust. "What kind of a woman picks a dog over her own mother and nephew? This weekend would have been my wife's birthday. Droid's mom, Victoria's sister, Mrs. R's younger daughter. I'm sorry to be so emotional, but, well, sometimes it gets to me."

Darleen called Bernie's cell and got no answer. She called Chee's cell phone. When he didn't pick up, she called the police station and spoke to Sandra. She explained the situation as simply as possible: She was driving to Phoenix with Mrs. Raymond's son-in-law to look for Mrs. R and her grandson. They were in his car.

"Give that to my sister and Chee, OK?"

"Darleen, honey. Phoenix in June sounds hot. Why are you going?"

"It's a long story and Bernie knows some of it already. Just let them know I'll be back in a day or two."

"Who are you going with?"

Darleen resented the questions. Sandra knew some of the decisions she'd made weren't ideal, but this was none of the dispatcher's business. "Hold on."

Darleen handed her phone to Greg. "This is the dispatcher at the station, and she thinks she's my auntie or something. Give her your phone number and the license plate of the car. Then let's go."

Greg took her phone, telling Sandra exactly what Darleen had asked and more. "Please tell Bernie that I appreciate Darleen's help to find my son and his grandmother, and I'll make sure she's back here safely."

Darleen tossed her bag with school work and overnight necessities in the back seat and added the sack with the turtle and Mrs. R's medicine to her purse. She smiled as she clicked her seat belt. She pictured putting the little turtle in Mrs. R's hand. She imagined the lady's joy that help had come to make sure her grandson was safe.

Chapter 26

For Jim Chee, one of the many complications of being the acting captain was that he had to set aside his work following up on a series of calls the station had received about homeless, down-and-out relatives. These people—mostly men, with a few women on the list—had been reported by concerned relatives as missing. This wave of concern left him feeling proud of the way the people he worked for cared for each other, and simultaneously sad and puzzled. At Chee's request, Captain Adakai had named him the point man on those cases.

Before he focused on scheduling staff for the pending Washington visit and other duties that came his way in Captain Adakai's absence, he found a few extra minutes to review his notes on those cases again.

Among the calls was one from a family he knew. He and one of the boys had played basketball together in high school, suiting up as proud St. Michael's Cardinals. The notes from the officer who took the assignment said that an uncle who lived with the family periodically hadn't shown up for a week. The report added that the man had been arrested several times for disturbing the peace and trespassing, "both the result of intoxication."

Chee called to see if Thomas Silver had shown up.

Voicemail picked up his call. Instead of the regular "Leave a message," Chee heard: "If you're calling about Thomas, he had someone let us know he's in a rehab. We look forward to seeing him soon." It was nice to get a bit of good news.

His spirits a bit lighter, Chee made his second call, this one to family he had met while volunteering last year at the Shiprock fair. A man with a gruff voice answered in Navajo, so Chee introduced himself first as a police lieutenant and then in the traditional way. The man responded appropriately.

"I'm doing a follow-up on a missing man, Daryl Scott. I understand he's one of your relatives."

"Not related to me, but my wife. Don't tell me you've found her no-good brother. Is he in alive?"

"We haven't located him, sir, and I was wondering if you've had any news."

The man guffawed. "That person brings shame to our family. If you find DS, tell him he needs to make things right with the little ones he has damaged by his drinking. With them, and with his sister and me. The only time we saw much of him was when he needed a meal, wanted money for booze, or came to tell us he was getting sober. That's all I can say about him. You're Lieutenant Chee, right?"

"That's me."

"So, Lieutenant, I heard there's a celebrity coming to Shiprock tomorrow, or maybe the next day or next week. Maybe some football star or a guy from the Olympics with a medal. You know about this, right, because the cops are involved. But then some guy at work said he had heard that it was just some windbag from Washington. Is that who it is?"

"Well, someone might be coming from Washington, yes, sir, but we don't have confirmation yet." Chee figured he could say that much without adding specifics.

"A government type, huh? Oh, shoot. I was hoping for LeBron James or even Tom Brady."

Chee smiled and ended the call. He looked at the those-who'd-gone-missing list one more time. He knew people came and went, and that adults had a right to chart their own course. But the number of calls caught his attention—it went well beyond normal. He found two cases where the files had been closed, and he gave those a closer look. In one instance, the man had returned. In the second, similar to the call he'd made earlier, the person who was missing had called, reassuring the family that he was OK. The rest remained open and unsolved.

Chee set the missing-persons list aside and focused on assignments for the possible Washington big-shot visit instead, trying to decide where the Navajo Police could be most effective and where it would be best to leave the area to the sheriff or even the state police.

Sandra buzzed him. "Lieutenant, there's a woman here who wants to talk to you about a missing person."

"Ask her to file a report." Chee was mildly irritated. Sandra knew the drill.

"She's done that. She's got some new information that she wants to give someone, and I know you're the guy in charge of the investigation." When Chee hesitated, she said, "She's the sister-in-law of the man at the garage who takes care of our vehicles."

"OK. I'll come out and talk to her. What's her name?"

Sandra took a moment. "Lantana Goodluck."

The woman was in her twenties, slim, dressed like a ranch woman, from her battered Stetson to her well-worn, pointy-toed boots. She wore a vintage squash blossom necklace that looked heavy and well-made. Dressed up, he assumed, for the visit to the police station.

"Miss Goodluck? Lieutenant Jim Chee. I only have a few minutes, but how can I help you?"

"It's about my brother, George Goodluck. I reported him missing, but we found him. He called our mother last night. That's why I came in. I need to tell you what happened to him." She pushed a strand of long black hair away from her eyes. "He would have come himself, but, well, he's not back to Shiprock yet."

Chee waited for the rest of the story.

"George told us he was sort of kidnapped. Those people said he was going to rehab, but they didn't give anybody any treatment, and they made it easy for the people there to party. They gave him drugs and booze and wouldn't let him call us or get out. It was supposed to be a rehab center, but it was a scam." Chee heard the energy from her anger as she spoke.

"Geoge said one guy died of an overdose. Can you imagine? An overdose in rehab. That's when he managed to get someone to call home." She stopped, her story told.

"Kidnapped?" Chee hadn't expected to hear that.

"Well . . ." She glanced at her the silver rings on her fingers. "Well, actually he agreed to go, but he got tricked. They took advantage of him. He told me he didn't have to pay for anything at first because he's an Indian. All he had to do was sign some papers. He said he didn't get any therapy. And when he asked about the programs to help him, you know, they just told him to shut up and gave him some beer."

"It sounds bad." Chee had heard a lot of strange stories around his job, but he had never heard one quite like this.

The woman nodded. "I'm here because he says there are other Diné people in the same boat. They got sold a bill of goods, lied to. I thought the police should know."

Chee asked if George had told her the name of the program or the people who had exploited him. He hadn't. She gave him her phone number as the best way to reach George.

"Our mom is picking him up in Phoenix the next day or two while I take care of the animals, but if you want, you could talk to him when he gets home, once he's over the DTs."

"He's living on the street now with a couple of his buddies. They didn't get clean either, but they figured out how to get away from the sober home. They feel safer." She leaned toward Chee. "Are you going to follow up on this?"

"Yes."

"People like George have enough struggles. It's not right to take advantage of them."

"Your brother is lucky that you and your mother care about him." Chee knew that many with George's problem had destroyed a treasure house of relationships.

"He helps us with the horses, works at the ranch when he can. He says all that helps him stay sober. I've been thinking that, you know, there might be some therapy that uses horses to help people get strong again. Do you know of anything like that?"

He shook his head. "No, but that's a great idea."

Back at the captain's desk, Chee jotted Lantana Goodluck's number on the desk pad and wrote "George Goodluck" next to it with a black marker. Working on that issue mattered to him more than the idea that some Washington hotshot needed extra protection because she planned to visit. But the secretary and those who came with her, or because of her visit, could all be in his jurisdiction soon.

He reviewed the information the chief had sent about the potential headache of the CUSP group and began a sketch of the assignment plan. Then Roper Black showed up with a question and an opinion.

"Lieutenant, I'm puzzled about something. Got a minute?"

"Not really, but go ahead."

Roper sat down. "Well, the idea of closing off some roads to keep these Washington visitors safe—I can't see how that makes sense. I mean, we work for the Navajos, right? Not the federal government. Why should our people be inconvenienced because of some visit we didn't ask for in the first place?"

"Good question. My best answer is that this is a trade-off. A few headaches for residents to make sure this visit goes well versus days of trouble from the feds if something bad happens while the secretary is here." Chee had another thought. "That's why I'm stationing our guys away from the central event, out where people might not know what the fuss is about. And then, if we're lucky, we will be done with this whole deal and can get back to business."

"Sir, have you heard why she's coming?"

"No. I don't even know when she's coming, or if she's coming. I'll let you know if you need to worry about it. Now get back to work."

Roper scowled, started to say something, reconsidered, and left.

The conversation worsened Chee's mood. Then Sandra buzzed that he had an incoming call from Britany Adakai, the captain's wife.

"You deal with her."

"I tried. I asked how he was doing, and she said better. But she insists on talking to you."

"OK. Put her through."

He took a breath and hoped the conversation would be short and offer some good news.

"Hello, Mrs. Adakai," he said, picking up her call. "How's the captain doing?"

"A little better, I guess. They want to keep him here for tests and more tests. He's not liking it, but they insist, and I know it's the right . . ."

Chee heard Adakai's voice in the background. "Brit, give me the phone."

She spoke over him. "The doctor is going to talk to us about what comes next, but he had a heart attack. I've had to take time off work, and the future could be more difficult than . . ."

"Brit! Stop it, for Pete's sake." The captain sounded weak. "Give me the phone."

There was a quiet moment, and then the man was on the line. "Chee, what's going on with the secretary?" Adakai sounded exhausted. "I ought to be back there instead of stuck in this place."

"Everything is under control, sir, but we still don't have a confirmed arrival or itinerary. I told the chief you might be out of commission for a while. We'll deal with whatever comes our way as smoothly as humanly possible."

"OK." Adakai sucked in a breath. "What about that body?"

"Last I heard, the feds were still working on IDing him and waiting for the OMI report on cause of death."

Adakai groaned.

"Don't worry about all this, sir. Just get better."

"Anything else going on?"

"Nothing much."

"Chee!"

Chee shared Roper Black's objection to the inconvenience of the secretary's visit, and told Adakai that Bernie had investigated the noise complaint and abandoned car.

"The plate was from a vehicle in a wrecking yard, so it's suspicious. We'll impound it. And I got a call about one of the missing persons. The woman who I talked to said her brother was coming home."

"Home! Speaking of that, I'm hoping to get out of here later today." The captain already sounded weaker than he had when the call started. "That is, if Brit is OK with me being around the house for a few days, complaining. I won't be cleared for the office until after the secretary has come and gone. Still waiting for more tests and to talk to the cardiologist about what the results mean." He exhaled. "Sorry about this, Chee, but keep up the good work."

"I will, sir."

"Get back to it. Thanks for taking charge of things, Lieutenant."

He finished up the most crucial duties, handled the unexpected, and headed home. The chief expected a date and itinerary from the secretary in the morning. A good dinner and a sound night's sleep would make everything look better.

Chapter 27

Darleen and Greg left Shiprock together, first cruising south on 491 south past the hogback and the looming mysterious lava formations that Darleen thought of as little siblings to the magnificent Ship Rock. They picked up Interstate 40 in Gallup and began to head west, driving into the strong light of the late afternoon light past signs announcing exit 311, for Petrified Forest National Park.

"I wonder what a petrified forest looks like." Darleen watched the exit grow closer. "Have you ever been there?"

"Nope." Greg signaled and pulled into the left lane to pass a Honda sedan. "I'd like to go someday. I think petrified wood is interesting, you know? But not this time of year. Too stinking hot."

"I'd like to see the forest sometime, too. What if the trees were still standing and the needles or leaves had turned to stone, too? Petrified Forest. The name makes me think of a movie where a monster, maybe a flame monster, shows up, and the trees are so frightened they just turn to stone. Then he can't burn them."

"Is that a real movie?"

"No. I just made it up."

"You're clever," he said. "Good imagination. Droid is like that, too. Got that from his mom."

Darleen adjusted the air-conditioning on her side of the SUV. The vehicle was too cool for her taste with the air on full blast. The thermometer on the dashboard said it was ninety outside. She was glad to be in Greg's newer vehicle.

"We could call it *Petrified in the Petrified Forest*. The hero is a shape-shifter made of water who drowns the flame monster."

"I like it." Greg sighed. "I'm petrified that something terrible has happened to Droid. If I lose him after losing his mother so quickly to cancer last year, my heart would turn to stone."

Darleen wondered how her heart and her brain would handle the grief when Mama died. She and Bernie had witnessed their mother's steady decline for several years. Like the years it took for wood to become rock, or the gentle force of raindrops steadily eroding a mountainside, losing Mama was a slow, ongoing process.

"Tell me about your wife. I'm sorry she died."

Greg was silent for a few moments. "She was my first love. We were married twenty years, and it wasn't long enough. I miss her smile, her warmth, her quirks. I think of her every day.

"We met when we were in high school and got married when she graduated from college in Durango. She taught first grade for a while, but quit teaching after Droid was born. When he started middle school, she was ready to get back to the classroom. Took some courses, filled out the employment applications, all that took a while. She got a good job offer and we celebrated. But when she went in for her work physical, something was wrong."

He shook his head, as if to dislodge what came next. "The doctors never said why she got cancer or how, but I blame leetso. The water, the soil, too much contamination from all the mining and milling.

I blame the work I did on the uranium cleanup, coming home with contamination."

Greg swallowed. "She fought like a badger to stay alive. Her dream was to make it until Andrew graduated from high school next year. The cancer advanced too quickly. She was a good woman, the love of my life. You would have liked her. Everyone did."

The drove along in silence for a few miles.

"What about you, Darleen? Are you married?"

"No. I have a boyfriend now I really like."

"What's his name?"

"He goes by Slim. He's a teacher, too, and he's teaching a summer class. He's passionate about his students. Worried about them. Spends a lot of extra time trying to get them to succeed."

"You really like him—is that the same as love?"

"Yeah, I guess." Darleen hadn't expected a conversation like this. "I think he means more to me than I mean to him." She remembered that she hadn't texted him that she was headed to Arizona. She pulled out her phone, typed the message, and hit send.

"You and your wife were lucky."

"Yes. You know, I was nervous about making a commitment before my wife and I got married, but it was the best thing I ever did. Our relationship flourished after that. Are you nervous, or is it Slim with the cold feet?"

"Maybe both of us." She fiddled again with the air-conditioning vents. "He's wrapped up in his job. I admire him for that. I mean, good teachers are special. But I wish he'd spend more time with me."

"And what about you really bugs him?"

"I guess the same stuff, you know?" She didn't want to get into her own faults. "I'm busy in school, at work, helping with my mother."

Greg passed a slow truck and then pulled back into the right lane. "It sounds like you're a lot alike."

"You're right about that. But the second thing that bothers me about Slim is that sometimes he goes quiet. I can't tell if he's mad at me, or what's up with him. I don't do that. If anything, I talk too much."

Greg sighed. "You know, my wife used to get upset with me over clamming up, too. I told her I was quiet because I was thinking. That's all. I teased her that she was smart enough to do the talking for both of us."

After an hour or so, Darleen took over the driving, grateful to be behind the wheel of such a smooth, powerful vehicle instead of Bernie's old Tercel. Or, even worse, her own car. It would be great to earn enough to get a good car, she thought. When and if she became a nurse, that might be possible.

They drove on, watching the sun set, admiring the crescent moon in a cloudless sky and the few stars poking through the blackness. It was only one day before the solstice, the longest day of the year, so it had taken a wonderfully long time for night to come.

"I considered coming to Phoenix on my own to find Mrs. R, but it's better for us to do this together."

"You and me? Like two of those detectives on TV?" She heard the smile in his voice.

"I'm serious," she said. "My brother-in-law—he's a cop, too—told me not to do this alone. He said something bad is happening to native people in Phoenix."

"I've got your back. And you've got mine, right? We're in this together."

"Right."

He sighed. "I just hope they're both OK. I'm glad you came with me, Darleen. It's nice to have someone to talk to."

"I'm glad I'm here, too," she said. "This is the perfect day for us to travel. The solstice will be here tomorrow and that's a big time for change."

After a while, Greg said, "I'd like to change my relationship with my son. He'll be a senior in high school, you know? Sort of our last chance to get things right before he's off on his own."

"I'm looking forward to meeting Droid," Darleen said. They turned off the interstate at Holbrook. Greg bought gasoline, and Darleen picked up some snacks and a couple of energy drinks, and then Greg went back to driving. They headed south on Arizona Highway 377. Traffic was light, and they cruised toward Phoenix.

Darleen tapped the screen in the SUV with the route map. "That's White Mountain Apache country coming up, and we drive through at least two areas of national forest land just off the road on the way to Payson. I bet it's beautiful."

"I'm not much in the mood for scenery. This whole thing is bizarre, you know? Why was Mrs. Raymond in Arizona at a benefits office, signing up for rehab? She's not a drinker. She's a tough lady, and she lets us know when something bothers her. I don't have anything against therapy—I mean, counseling helped me deal with the loss of my wife. But if she needed to talk to someone, why go to Phoenix?"

Darleen wrestled with the same question. "Mrs. Raymond talks about your son a lot. I think he's the reason she's in Phoenix." She added that she'd seen the improvised guest room.

"He likes spending time there but I worry that it's too much independence. A lot of guys Droid's age experiment with drinking and with whatever else is out there. I did some of that myself. But for most of them, their mother hasn't just died and their father hasn't sunk into depression." Greg sighed. "If I had been a better dad, we could have talked about this. About her. I failed him."

"You are a good dad. That's why we're making this trip. It's about second chances. I've made a bunch of mistakes already, and I haven't lived as long as you."

Greg chuckled. "We all hope that as we get older, we get smarter, but sometimes we just figure out new ways to screw up."

She opened a bag of chips and extended it toward Greg. He took some, steering with his left hand, and ate them quickly.

"Could you hand me one of those drinks?"

She did. "I'm up for more driving when you want to pull over. But first, I want to call my sister and her husband and let them know I'm OK, and if they have any ideas for us on how to find your son and his grandma."

"Take your time. I'm fine."

She tried Bernie's cell, and the call went directly to voicemail. She considered calling the landline, but Mama was probably asleep, and the phone might wake her. If Mama was awake, Bernie wouldn't be in the best state of mind to brainstorm.

She moved on to call Chee's mobile. More voicemail.

Then she thought of something else. Officer Bigman, their clan brother, might be able to give her some good advice. Because it was late, she sent a text.

? for you. Can U talk?

A few minutes later, the happy music of "Girls Just Wanna Have Fun," Darleen's ringtone of the moment, filled the car.

"Hey Miz D. What's up, buttercup?" Bigman was one of her favorite relatives. He seemed calm no matter what chaos surrounded him. "Tell me quick. I can't chat long. I'm working."

"I'm on the way to Phoenix."

"Phoenix? What's going on?"

Darleen explained briefly. "I'm putting us on speaker so Greg—he's the dad—can add something if he wants."

"You cops have experience finding missing people," Greg said. "Any hints?"

"Yes. Be careful in Phoenix," Bigman said. "Talk to the police there and ask them to help you. Something big is going on out there; lots of missing Navajos. Chee has been in charge of the investigation. Have you called him?"

"I tried him," Darleen said, "but I couldn't get through to him or Bernie. What's up with that?"

"Ah, they were working a big case. I'll ask them to call you."

And then, like a protective big brother, he added, "No risky stuff, you hear? I gotta go."

And before she could ask another question, he hung up.

Chapter 28

It was well after midnight when Darleen and Greg, with the help of energy drinks, pulled into downtown Phoenix. They used GPS to find Broadway Manor. They called the number Gigi had given Darleen for Mrs. Raymond from the old hotel's parking lot, and got the same cold-sounding electronic message they'd heard twice before on the long drive.

The lights were off and the doors were locked. So even though they were tired, they decided to search the area for Droid. They began with the streets closest to the hotel and circled out from there, Darleen driving slowly while Greg scanned the sidewalks and doorways for his son. The odds of finding him were slim, but it felt better to be doing something other than sitting in the car, waiting for the hotel to come to life.

They tried talking to people resting in abandoned spots along the city streets, rough-looking men and women who made Darleen nervous. She remembered Bigman's warning, but she realized that these homeless souls were also afraid of her and Greg. Many of them were awake, but when approached, they either wouldn't talk at all or said they knew nothing about Droid. The search stretched into a long, exhausting, and ultimately fruitless exercise.

And then, finally, they found Curtis, an unhoused Native man playing a harmonica in a storefront alcove. Greg described Droid, and when Curtis seemed open to helping them, they offered him the last of their drinks and a pack of trail mix in gratitude. He ate while they gave him more of the information that had led to their long drive.

"Broadway Manor? I was there a long time ago." Curtis snorted. "It's a terrible place, all right, but the group home they shipped me off to? Well, that dump was even worse." He described it with some choice swear words. "We were locked in. I had to crack a window to climb outa there. It's better here on the street, and that's not saying much. Sober home? It was a phony."

"Why did you have to leave the hotel?" Greg asked.

"They shipped us out. It's just a staging ground, kids. They bring us in from who knows where, sign us up as official Arizonans, and then it's back into the white van to some disgusting place where we're on our own. All the help for getting clean they promise? Forget about it. All those people want is the money they get from signing you up. They don't care about nothing or no one except raking in the dough."

Curtis stopped to sip his drink and looked at the two of them. "You're Navajos, right?"

They nodded.

"I'm Apache. San Carlos. I came to Farmington for an oil field job, got fired for drinking, lost my apartment, and kept drinking. When I got on that van, I figured salvation had rolled in my direction." He forced a laugh. "But I'm lucky. My sister said she'll bring me home when she takes her vacation next week. A lot of folks who rode the sober van here to get treatment can't get back home, you know? Back to where they belong. There's a song like that, right?"

"Right." Darleen had some change in the pocket of her shorts, and she gave it to Curtis.

He looked at the coins. "I wasn't asking, but thanks." He put the money in his pants pocket. "Good luck finding your relatives. There's a lady at The Beating Drum, that's a gift shop downtown. She knows a bunch of stuff about this bad medicine. She helps people."

Greg used his phone to get The Beating Drum's address, but it was far too early, of course, for the store to be open.

After finding a safe place to park near Broadway Manor, they slept fitfully in the car until the morning sun woke them. Then they headed to a twenty-four-hour diner that Darleen remembered passing, got some coffee, and drove back to Broadway Manor. This time there were a few more vehicles in the employee parking lot. The building had a paved half-circle driveway at the entrance, the kind where people leave their car while they check in. Darleen parked there, across from the front doors, and they both climbed out.

The doors were locked. They couldn't find a doorbell, so Darleen knocked. After a few moments a security guard came to the entrance. A plume of cooler air flowed out from the brightly lit room as he opened the door. Behind him, Darleen could see some shabby-looking furniture, and she caught a whiff of coffee.

The guard angled his body to block the doorway. "What?"

Greg took the lead. "Can you help us? We're looking for some lost relatives—a young man, my son, and his grandmother. We got a message that they were here."

"They're Navajo," Darleen added. "The lady is about my height and has gray hair. A big woman. And her grandson is with her."

"His name is Andrew Morgan," Greg said. "Goes by Droid. And the grandmother's last name is Raymond."

The guard looked tired. "No visitors allowed. Mrs. Raymond shouldn't even have told you they were here."

"We're not visitors. We're family." Greg included Darleen with a gesture.

The guard shrugged. "Bro, I don't make the rules. And there's no kids allowed in here. Come on, you two. I'll walk you to your car. It's the end of my shift anyway."

Darleen was tired and annoyed. "We're from New Mexico, Shiprock. We drove all night, and—" The guard winked at her. She stopped talking.

The guard stepped outside and pulled the door shut. He was thin and balding with a tattoo of an eagle on his arm. He seemed to relax as they moved away from the building. "We gotta avoid the cameras," he said, his voice just above a whisper. "Keep walking."

Darleen spotted the security cameras. Luckily, their vehicle was parked where it was surely out of range. The guard kept walking until he reached a red pickup at the far end of the lot.

"OK. I shouldn't have said nothin' about Mrs. Raymond. I could get fired for what I said already. Don't let on that you heard it from me. Deal?"

"Right," Darleen said.

"You bet," Greg chimed in.

"Those people they got in there come from wherever, and they talk to me, you know, because I'm there all night and they can't sleep. They come here with hope, but all they get is nothin'. Mrs. Raymond stands up for herself and for the young guy who came with her."

Greg leaned close to the guard. "What happened to that guy?"

"He got out and didn't come back. That's all I know."

"Someone mentioned that this place isn't really a rehab center," Darleen said. "Is that right?"

"They call themselves Best Way, but it's really No Way. They bring in people who want to get sober, you know, start fresh. Then most of them start jonesing for booze. There's medicine that helps with the shakes, but I've seen the guys who work the desk give 'em a beer to ease the pain. Or if it's drugs, some kinda pills. People get worse in here. One guy told me he got here thinking he would be able to talk to someone, you know, at least go to AA. When he griped, they gave him a twelve-pack and told him to shut up."

"Seriously?" Greg looked shocked.

"Then what happens to them?" Darleen asked.

The guard frowned. "I don't know for sure. They'll take these people to group homes tomorrow, and a new bunch will roll in."

"Is there someone in the building we can talk to so Mrs. Raymond can come home?"

"The boss shows up around nine. Heather comes in earlier to work the desk, but she doesn't have the power to do anything."

"What's the boss's name?"

"Bea. And she's got quite a stinger." When he laughed, Darleen noticed that his bottom teeth were crooked. "Don't get on her bad side. And you didn't hear any of this from me."

The guard climbed into his truck and drove off, and Darleen and Greg walked to their SUV in silence.

Finally, Greg spoke. "This is criminal."

"It's worse than I thought it would be." Darleen's worry came through in her tone.

The sun was up now, but Arizona didn't buy into daylight savings, so it was still far too early for Bea to arrive. But Darleen knew Mrs. Raymond would be awake.

Greg looked discouraged. "A new security guy will be on duty, but those people all have to be hard-nosed. We need a plan."

"Just what I was thinking," she said. "We might have to bend the rules so we can get Mrs. R out of here and keep looking for Droid."

They got into the SUV and sat waiting for inspiration, an employee they could sweet-talk, or some other opportunity. A delivery truck drove up to the building and turned down an alley between Broadway Manor and what looked like an office building next door.

Darleen leaned forward, watching the big truck disappear. "There must be a loading dock back there. Let's go."

Greg frowned. "Or we can wait until the boss comes, do it that way."

"I'm not good at waiting. If this doesn't work, we can talk to the boss at nine. What have we got to lose?"

"OK." Greg drove and reparked near the dock. He released his seat belt. "Listen, so we go together. We get into the building. Then what?"

"Well, Mrs. R probably won't be in the lobby, so we need to figure out where her room is. Then we get her, and the three of us leave as quick as we can."

Greg rubbed his chin. "The security guy might know her room number, or have it written down or something, but why would he tell us?"

Darleen reached in her purse and showed Greg the bottle of prescription pills. She slipped them into her pocket. "I'll say that I'm a nurse, and she needs these. When they tell me the room number, we'll get her and get outa there."

"What if someone asks how we got in?"

"I'll tell him the truth. Then I'll say I don't want her to die without her meds."

"That's a stretch."

"Not really. I don't want her to die and she does need her medicine. You have a better plan?" She waited.

"I guess not," he said finally. "I have to ask about Droid, about why they were such screwups they let an underage kid in there in the first place and then let him run away into the streets of Phoenix. I have to have some answers. Whoever is in charge of this mess needs to fix it. They should—"

Darleen held a finger across her lips. "Let's get Mrs. R out of there, and then she can help find Droid. The rest can come later."

He nodded. "Let's do this."

The delivery truck had backed up to the loading dock, and the dock's large roll-up door stood open. Greg and Darleen climbed up onto the concrete platform, relieved that the driver wasn't around. They walked through to an unlocked door into Broadway Manor's unkempt storage area, where cases of beer and boxes of cheap whiskey sat on the floor along with other supplies. Darleen slowed her pace. "Can you believe this? Just like the guard said."

"Walk faster. We've got to get Mrs. Raymond out of here."

Down a dimly lit passage they found another door. Darleen opened it and saw that it led to what she assumed was Broadway Manor's main lobby.

She closed it softly and spoke to Greg. "Are you ready? I don't wanna get busted."

"We'll be fine. Stay focused on the goal."

Darleen visualized going to Mrs. R's room and leading her safely out of the building.

Greg took a breath. "I'm so angry at the way these people abused my son, I could explode. So you do the talking, OK?"

Darleen smiled. "It's a deal."

They stepped into the hallway and walked to the hotel lobby. Some grizzled men sat on the couches, talking in low voices. They watched Darleen and Greg as they headed to the registration area. A woman in pink running shorts and a baggy T-shirt at the coffeepot ignored them.

A man with a black hat marked SECURITY in white letters sat at a table and fiddled with his phone. He looked up when they approached.

Darleen smiled at him. "Can you help me?"

He stayed focused on the little screen. "I know the coffee is too weak. If you don't like what's in the breakfast bag, it's not my problem either, girlie. Today is moving day anyway. Suck it up. No complaints."

"I'm not complaining. I have a question." Darleen worked at

staying polite. "I need to drop off some medicine to a lady who is here. It's important."

The man raised his eyebrows in surprise. "You're not the first drug dealer who's used that line. Talk to Heather." He waved toward the desk. "Over there at registration."

Heather seemed preoccupied with whatever had appeared on her computer monitor, but she looked up when the two approached.

"I have a question," Darleen said. "I hope you can help me."

The woman frowned. "Well, we told you all last night that the relocation vans won't leave until ten. Were you guys too drunk to listen?"

Darleen felt another flare of anger, but before she could respond, Greg spoke.

"We have some medicine to administer to Mrs. Raymond." He leaned toward her, reading the name on her ID. "What's her room number, Heather?"

Heather looked at them again, and a spark of realization flashed in her gray eyes. "You two don't belong in here." She stood. "No visitors allowed. Leave whatever it is with me and get out now, or I'm calling security."

"Listen a minute. Darleen is a nurse," Greg lied with conviction. "We're here because Mrs. Raymond asked us to come. She needs Darleen to administer her medicine."

"How did you even get in the building?"

Darleen followed Heather's gaze out the front windows to the parking lot. It pleased her to realize that Greg's SUV was around back, out of sight.

"All that matters is that I have to give her these pills and make sure she takes them immediately, or she could become seriously ill. She's past due for this medicine, and this is a dangerous situation." Darleen paused to give Heather her most somber look. "I know you don't want someone to be in serious medical distress. You don't want to have to call an ambulance, do you? Let us see Mrs. Raymond, and then we're out of here."

"Mrs. Raymond?" Heather stood. "I'm calling the boss."

Greg jumped in. "What if she has a heart attack or something while you're waiting for the boss to answer? She could die on your watch and . . ."

Heather sat down again. "What medicine? Why does she need it? Let me see it."

Darleen shook her head. "I can't share confidential client information. You've heard of HIPAA, right? But if her blood pressure gets too high without this prescription, she could have another stroke, develop vascular dementia, go blind, or even die. Mrs. Raymond has to take this as soon as possible. She's already missed some doses."

Now Heather looked nervous. "If Bea sees you here, I'm dead." But she pressed a few keys, and her monitor switched to what looked like a grid. She studied it a moment. "OK, I see what room she's in. Give the pills to me, and I'll—"

"No. Unless you're a registered nurse, that's against our code of ethics. I have to administer the medication to her myself."

They saw Heather hesitate. Greg jumped in.

"Tell us the room number. Or call her room and ask her to come down here."

"The phones are out of order."

"Then let Darleen take the medicine to her."

Heather looked at Greg. "You have to stay here. And if Bea comes in and tries to fire me, you get to explain all this and try to save my job."

"Of course," he said. "We just want to help an old lady. We don't want to get you in hot water. I can tell you're a decent person."

Heather looked at Darleen. "Room 310."

Darleen started to head toward the elevator.

"Take the stairs. Both elevators are broken." Heather pointed to the left. "Go that way." She turned to Greg. "Wait over there and look like you belong here in case the boss shows up."

*　*　*

Greg sat on an uncomfortable wooden chair in the lobby. After a few minutes, one of the men on the couch motioned him over with a look and a jut of the chin.

"We heard you talking about Mrs. Raymond. You really her family?" The man in the black ball cap seemed to speak for the group. He kept his voice low, even though Heather had disappeared into the back.

"I'm her son-in-law and the father of Andrew, her grandson."

The men took in the news. "So that's the skinny dude with glasses and the lopsided haircut who came with her? That old gal is worried about him, even went out looking for him when he first walked away."

"Any ideas where he could be?"

No one said anything at first. Then the man in the tan work shirt shook his head. "I'd help if I could, but I don't know the area. I'm not from here, man. I got on a van in Flagstaff."

Ball Cap rubbed his stubbly chin. "Like you heard Heather say, we leave here today. They're moving us into sober homes where they say we can start getting clean for real. That makes the old lady worry even more. Once we leave, it'll be harder for the kid to find her. Heather says the vans will take us out of this rat trap around ten o'clock." He switched to falsetto. "'Don't be late. You know the vans don't wait.'" Then, in his normal tone, "Heather says that like a broken record. Drives me nuts. Makes me itch."

"You're already nuts," someone said. "Booze fried your brain."

Greg sighed. "This is the wrong place for my son. I'm not surprised he ran away."

"If I was you," Ball Cap said, "I'd check shelters, soup kitchens, places for kids in danger. Even talk to the police. So far they fed us and signed us up for programs like they said, but I think the whole thing could be a scam. Something for nothin? Too good to be true."

Greg pulled out his phone. He wanted to make a note of Ball Cap's good ideas about where to look for Andrew, but before any of that, he wanted an update from Darleen.

Work Shirt spoke in a gruff whisper. "Put that away, man, or the guard will grab it. He don't know you aren't one of us."

Greg slipped the phone back into a pocket. He didn't want to waste energy on another confrontation.

A few moments later a well-dressed woman, perhaps in her fifties, entered the building after unlocking the big glass doors with a key she put back in her purse. Greg froze as she pranced by him, the heels of her strappy sandals clicking against the tile floor. She headed into the office. A moment later he heard her say, "Heather, I need you."

And then, with perfect timing, Darleen and Mrs. Raymond walked into the lobby, hand in hand. The elder woman's face brightened when she saw Greg.

"Shíyázhí. My son." Tears glistened in the woman's dark eyes. Greg put his hand on her shoulder, a touch he knew would not make Mrs. Raymond uncomfortable.

Darleen looked over at Heather's empty desk. "Let's get out of here while we can. We can slip out through the back."

"Wait." Greg stood. "The boss lady just came in, the woman who runs this place. How could she have kidnapped my boy? How could she let him disappear onto the streets of Phoenix? What kind of monster—"

"Later," Darleen said.

Greg could feel a blood vessel at his temple beginning to pulse. He shook his head. "I'm going into that office to give that woman a piece of my mind. I have to understand what happened here. How could they let Droid—"

"Hey, man," said Ball Cap. "Bea left the front door unlocked, and the security guy is in the john. You can have a come-to-Jesus with Bea later."

Darleen had begun to walk toward the front door. She turned back to Mrs. Raymond. "Let's go get Droid."

But Mrs. Raymond stopped and turned to Greg. "Shíyázhí, I'm angry, too. But I'm worried about my grandson. We need to find him quick. We need to do that now."

Ball Cap waved his hand back and forth, the classic *get going* sign. "The guard's coming."

Mrs. Raymond resumed her walk to the door. Darleen looked at Greg. "Stay and argue, if you have to. Mrs. R and I will start searching."

Greg paused a moment, then sped to the door and opened it for them. "We're partners, Darleen, remember?" He followed the women outside to the SUV.

Chapter 29

"Chee needs to talk to you," Sandra said when Bernie walked into the office.

Bernie waited for the explanation. Sandra's forehead wrinkled. "He'll tell you about it. He wants to see you as soon as you got in."

Bernie rapped on his office door. "Hey there. Happy solstice."

"Same to you. Have a seat."

She sat across the desk from him. It felt odd to have her husband as boss, but she hoped this was only temporary, until Adakai recovered.

"We got a call from the Yazzie house this morning, you know, the ones who host those revivals. The people they are hosting decided to build some kind of sweat lodge. When she and Mr. Yazzie told them they couldn't do that without a permit, they wouldn't stop. She and the mister wouldn't mind if it was safe, but they have their doubts. They want us to tell the folks to make sure it's safe or remove it. Or we evict them."

Bernie listened, knowing from Chee's tone there was more to come.

"She also mentioned an altercation out there between some of the attendees. That happened a few days ago, and everything has been quiet since then. She told them they need to behave or they're gone."

"What kind of altercation?"

"Mrs. Yazzie was vague on the details, but it was some sort of violent argument. In addition to checking out the sweat lodge, she wants us to warn them to behave. And evict them if you think they are serious troublemakers. Head that way and see what's up."

"I'll do it." She waited to see if he had another assignment.

"I saw your report on the noise complaint and the car with the stolen plates. That was a long trip for nothing, very exciting."

"Oh, I made some connections at the trading post. It was OK. Nice drive. Nice day. Saving my energy for the secretary's visit."

"The chief promised to get back to us today on that. I hope we don't have to hustle something up for tomorrow. Evidently the secretary doesn't announce her visits too far in advance for security reasons."

Before Chee ended the meeting, Bernie thought of something else. "Usually, the folks who go to those revival meetings at the Yazzie campground act civilized, or the guy in charge of keeping them on the Jesus Road gives them grief. Who's the preacher?"

"No preacher. This isn't the regular revival group. Mrs. Yazzie said this is an out of state crowd of white people who found them on the internet."

"I like the Yazzies. Nice folks. Too bad they have to deal with jerks this time. I'm on it." She paused. "Sorry, I meant to say 'Yes, sir, Lieutenant.' " She hoped he heard the smile in her voice.

Chee ignored the quip. "When Mrs. Yazzie called, she told Sandra she had a bad feeling about these guests, but her husband persuaded her to let them use the revival space. Sandra reminded me that Mrs. Yazzie is a hand trembler."

Bernie had heard that Mrs. Yazzie could diagnosis illness, find lost things, and sometimes anticipate disaster. When something seemed off to Mrs. Yazzie, it was wise to listen to her warning.

"Glad you said that. I'll ask her about her intuition and see if she can explain what bothers her besides the sweat lodge and the fighting, although that's bad in itself." Bernie had been a cop long enough to understand that each investigation took its own course. If it involved something beyond the expected nuts and bolts of a case, she could listen and do what needed to be done.

Chee smiled. "Take care of yourself. Stay safe."

Bernie headed toward the Yazzie place with a light heart. The drive to the remote ranch was beautiful, and a good antidote for her agitation about Mama, and the uncertainty of the secretary's visit, with the extra work it involved. She enjoyed driving the department's large Tahoe although she'd had to fiddle with the seat a bit to compensate for her lack of height. The car wasn't built for a woman who was barely five-foot-two.

She looked forward to a pleasant conversation with Mrs. Yazzie. The woman had a way of sizing up a situation that Bernie appreciated. She liked Mrs. Yazzie's husband, too, and the couple were raising a four-year-old that Mrs. Yazzie's clan sister had left with them. She radioed the station for the Yazzies' number to let them know she was on the way.

Sandra rattled it off. "When I called them, no one answered. Maybe they were outside working, where they couldn't hear the phone. It's a landline. Cell service is bad out there. Really spotty."

"Thanks for the warning."

Bernie tried the Yazzie number herself, but it rang without answer.

After a long drive, she saw the Yazzie gate. She turned down a dirt road marked with a handmade red sign: REVIVAL HERE. A flyer attached below it fluttered in the breeze, and she pulled over to read it.

SOLSTICE MEDITATION TO HEAL MOTHER EARTH.
ALL WELCOME. CHECK IN AHEAD

After about a mile, she came to the Yazzies' entrance gate, which the group had secured open. The road forked just past the gate, and

she saw another red REVIVAL HERE sign with two arrows, one pointing right to "parking and camping," the other directing vehicles to
check-in. She continued slowly down the washboard road past the
cars, pickups, vans, and campers in the parking lot and turned left
toward the check-in station.

As she drew closer, the Yazzie compound came into view. Bernie
could see the white tent the Yazzies had erected for the revival sessions. To the right of the tent, a small assembly of men and women
were working in the sun to build what looked like a badly designed
version of a sweat lodge, the source of the Yazzies' complaint. Other
people moved in and out of the white tent, perhaps setting up for a
group meeting. A few of them looked Indigenous, but probably not
Navajo. Most of the attendees here seemed to be men, and all of them
were strangers to her. Even though the day was still young, it was
warm for heavy work outside.

She passed a small group unloading boxes from a refashioned
school bus. They looked tired, she thought. One woman waved and
began to walk toward her unit.

Bernie stopped the SUV. From the look on the young woman's
face, something was wrong. She lowered the window. "Miss, can I
help you?"

The woman shook her head but leaned forward slightly. Bernie
saw part of a tattoo on her neck, something that resembled the curve
of a red circle, and fear in her green eyes.

"Be careful," the woman whispered, before quickly walking away.

Bernie rounded a corner and stopped. A large handmade STOP
FOR CHECK-IN HERE sign was blocking the entrance to the rest of the
Yazzies' compound.

A fit-looking, bearded man with a bald head walked toward her,
talking on his phone as he came. He wore boots, jeans, and a gray
T-shirt, and held a piece of paper in his hand.

Bernie lowered the window. "Yá'át'ééh. I'm Officer Bernadette

Manuelito. I need to get through here." Because of the vehicle's height, she could look him in the eye if she wanted.

He greeted her with a serious expression. "Whatever you said, back at you, Officer. On behalf of each person here, I want to say that we are honored to be on Navajo land, and we appreciate the struggle the Navajo people have made to protect their environment from devastation. We've been learning all we can about Navajo life and culture and the world of the spirit here and, well, good on you guys."

Bernie had no response, but the man didn't seem to expect one.

"What's your name, sir?"

"Call me Case." He extended his right hand toward the unit, but he made her uneasy, and she substituted a nod of her head for a handshake. "Pleased to meet you, Miss Bernadette."

Bernie bristled at the endearment. "Please call me Officer Manuelito and step back from my vehicle. I'm here to speak to Mrs. Yazzie. Remove the barrier, Case."

"I'll move it, but she's not there. She drove off." He ran his hand over his thick brown beard. "I'm one of the spokespeople for our chosen family here. Can I help you?"

"Mrs. Yazzie called the Navajo Police about some unapproved construction here, a sweat lodge that isn't allowed on the revival grounds. And she mentioned a violent argument among some of the guests. When dispatch tried to follow up, neither she nor Mr. Yazzie answered the phone. I'm here to check on their safety."

Bernie felt the bald man's eyes on her for a moment.

"Don't worry about Mrs. Yazzie. She told me she was going to see her sister. And Mr. Yazzie and Sam, their boy, are doing just fine. It's about time for their morning nap. That must be why he didn't answer the phone. Sorry you made a trip here for nothing." Case looked toward the Yazzie house and then away.

"Tell me about the fight."

Case seemed to expect the question. "A couple of men in the

family caused some commotion, but we handled it appropriately. All settled. But perhaps you have time to join our family here for the solstice meditation."

Bernie gave him a questioning look. The scene didn't look like a traditional family reunion. "Case, it sounds like you're the man in charge here, so I need to see your ID."

"I'm not the top dog, but yes, I help get things done." He pulled a wallet from his back pocket. "Here you go."

He pulled out a California driver's license, and while she took a picture of it for a background check, he moved the barrier to the edge of the road. Noting that Case's full name was Arthur Caseman, she handed the license back to him.

"What brought your group to the Navajo Nation?" she asked.

"In our community, we believe it is rude to turn down a chance to be helpful. We decided that this would be the ideal spot for our prayerful meditation to help the planet. We came here to the Navajo Nation to meditate and look for ways to be successful in our dedicated service of Mother Earth."

"I don't usually associate meditation with fistfights or building things that the hosts have not approved of." Bernie frowned. "Mr. Caseman, give me the details about what happened out here that disturbed Mrs. Yazzie."

"There's nothing much more to say. We worked it out with the Yazzies. You've made this trip for nothing."

She gave him a hard look. "Say it anyway."

Caseman gathered his thoughts. "I need to make a video of myself giving this explanation. Leader tells us to tape everything important that happens here so those who come after will have a record of these days." He reached for his phone. "Give me a minute to make sure the sound works right for both of our voices. And because the sun is so bright, I'll need to adjust the lighting to compensate for the intensity."

Bernie shook her head. "Look, I know you've got the right to video this, but let's keep it simple. I'd appreciate it if you'd tell me what happened as concisely as possible."

Case aimed the phone at his own face. Bernie assumed she was in the background. "Well, Officer, there was a fistfight a few days ago. Very inappropriate for a gathering to promote meditation and deep personal peace to heal our Mother Earth. Pat, a person who had not embraced these values, confronted Rollie, another member of our chosen family. Pat started an argument and that led to a fistfight over some issue that he decided could not be resolved without violence. But now, as you can see, peace is restored."

He raised his arms dramatically to motion toward the tent and the group building the odd sweat lodge. "As I said, mutual respect and peace have been restored, Officer, and we are preparing for the solstice." Caseman ended the video, but kept talking. "Do you know about the solstice?"

Before she could answer, he handed her a flyer from the check-in table.

A color photograph of the famous Sun Dagger at Chaco Canyon filled the center of the page. The picture captured the spectacular beam of sunlight that channeled through three large sandstone slabs to strike a spiral petroglyph. Centuries ago, the ancient ones who lived on the edge of what is now the Navajo Nation created this sacred marker to track, acknowledge, and welcome the solstice and equinox.

Chaco Canyon was honored as a UNESCO World Heritage Site in 1987, and the Sun Dagger drew so many thousands of visitors from around the globe that it had to be declared off-limits due to concerns about its preservation. In addition to the dagger, Bernie knew that Chaco has a pictograph that many people believe depicts the supernova of 1054 and a petroglyph that might be a tribute to the total solar eclipse of 1097. Nineteen tribes from New Mexico, Arizona, and Texas trace their ancestry to the people who lived there.

Case's flyer welcomed anyone interested in joining a solstice meditation to participate and bring their family and friends. In much smaller type, it said the event was a project of Citizens United to Save the Planet, with the capital letter of each word in bold type: CUSP.

Bernie recalled the name from the chief's talk. Mrs. Yazzie's complaint about the construction and the fight instantly carried more weight.

She decided to radio the CUSP to update into the station, then talk to Mr. Yazzie before looking at the sweat lodge. Because the Yazzies didn't allow it, the sweat lodge needed to go even if the construction wasn't as sloppy as Mrs. Yazzie believed. And if this group didn't follow the rules of the host, it would be up to her to evict them.

When she looked up, Caseman caught her eye.

"We are grateful to the Yazzies for sharing their beautiful place with us." He waved toward the mountains, and she noticed a small tattoo on his upper arm. Its tight spirals reminded her of a larger-than-life fingerprint and it reminded her of what she'd seen on the green-eyed woman's neck. "Any more questions for me?"

"Tell me about CUSP."

"You mean our family?"

She waited.

"Well, Officer, we are united by our work to save mother earth from the devastation of mining and other extraction. We come from all over to listen to the wise guidance of Leader, who instructs us in wisdom he receives from The Great Beyond."

Bernie pulled out a notebook and pen. "I need the names of the people involved in the fight."

"Pat and Rollie. I guess you weren't paying attention the first time I told you." Case smirked as he said it.

"I need their full legal names." She leaned on the word *full*. "I need to talk to them."

"In our family we go by first names, or chosen names, whatever the person wants to be called. Those original names don't matter here, so they just slip out of my aging brain." He rubbed a palm over his bald head from his forehead to the crease of his neck. "As far as talking to them, well, Pat isn't here, but I'll introduce you to Rollie. He's the big fellow over there." He motioned to a large man working on the construction project.

"Miss Bernadette, everything is fine here. Look at that photo of Chaco Canyon and let your heart rest. Join us for meditation this afternoon. And you should go to Chaco. It's a great place, you know, with lots of ruins, that sun dagger thing, and Fajita Butte."

"Again, call me Officer Manuelito." The classic mesa was known as Fajada Butte, named by the Spanish explorers for the dark bands of minerals in the sandstone. Caseman reminded her of other unpleasant men she'd known, people too full of their own bluster.

"I took that photo." Case put his finger on it for emphasis. "Quite the hike up there."

Bernie knew the park had closed that area to visitors several decades ago. "When did you get that shot?"

"Oh, a couple of years ago. At the solstice, obviously."

If he wasn't lying about being the photographer, he had trespassed into a protected zone. She trusted this man less the more he said.

"Please stand back. I'm driving up the road to talk to Mr. Yazzie and when I come back, have the legal names of those two men for me and be ready to show me the sweat lodge."

"Oh, that problem is all forgotten. We spoke to Mr. Yazzie about it. You know, men make the final call." Caseman waved at one of the workers, a gesture that said *Come over here*. "Talk to Rollie. He can set your heart to rest."

Chapter 30

As Rollie drew closer, Bernie saw fresh bruises on the large man's jaw, a blackened eye, and a swollen nose. A large woman with curly brown hair Bernie had noticed walked behind him. Bernie followed her training and instinct and stayed in her unit to speak with them.

Caseman watched them approach. "Officer Bernadette Manuelito, this one of our junior patriarchs, Rollie. And that's his woman, Alisa."

Rollie offered a handshake, but, noticing his swollen knuckles, Bernie nodded to him instead. Alisa stared at her shoes. "What happened to your hands and your face?"

"Oh, work-related injuries." He touched his swollen nose. "I'm glad I didn't break it."

"Work. Really? That's not what Case told me."

He laughed. "OK. I got in a fight. Is that what brings you here, little lady? No worries about that. It's history."

"I'm Officer Manuelito, and my job brings me here." Her voice carried irritation. "I explained it all to Mr. Caseman. I need to see your ID."

He looked surprised but pulled his driver's license out and handed it to her. Bernie took a picture. His full name was Rolland Chavez.

"What do you do here, Rollie?"

"Whatever Leader and Case want."

Caseman said, "Rollie and I share responsibility for the family's well-being, with Leader's guidance. I was about to tell Bernadette—oh excuse me, *Officer* Manuelito—that our meditations for Mother Earth could do away with the need for her job and bring us all into a healthier, calmer, more loving state." He smiled at Bernie the way an actor smiles for the camera. "Peace begins with each of us. After our meditation, we can take constructive action."

"Come to our gathering today, missy," Rollie chimed in. "Our spiritual path is of special benefit to women who feel overwhelmed by the world's demands. It will do your little heart good. Right, Alisa?"

"Rollie, call me Officer Manuelito." She put steel in her voice. "And my heart is the perfect size, and on its own spiritual path."

Alisa hadn't acknowledged Bernie or said a word since she'd arrived. Bernie turned to her and saw bruises the shape of fingertips on the woman's plump arm. Catching Bernie's gaze, she pulled her shirtsleeve down to hide the marks.

"Right?" Rollie's voice was almost a shout.

"Whatever you say." Alisa looked at Bernie again. "It's nice to live where women don't have so much on our shoulders. Where we don't have to make any decisions."

Alisa's demeanor and her words made Bernie both sad and suspicious.

"Alisa and I have some work to do at the sweat lodge," Rollie said. "Excuse us, Officer." He took a few steps away and then turned back. "See you at the meditation. I hope you change your mind. It works wonders for stress. Just give my license to Case when you're done here."

He walked away, and Caseman started to follow him.

"Case. Wait," Bernie said loudly and with authority. "Tell me why your group is here."

"Why?" He laughed at the question. "Why are any of us here on Mother Earth, Officer Manuelito? To leave our world better than we found it. Isn't that why you went to work in law enforcement?"

It was exactly the reason. "Why here, specifically? Why the Yazzie revival camp?"

"Well, it's beautiful and remote, a fine place for meditation, for creating new ideas."

Bernie looked at the high desert landscape framed by the mountains, at the big sky and the warm brown earth. Case was right about the beauty here. Her eyes settled on Ship Rock itself. According to sacred history, the diyin Diné, the holy people, used this rugged core of a volcano to help Navajo ancestors escape from monsters. And it was here, on Tsé Bit'a'í, that Monster Slayer killed the huge and terrible bird that was feeding the People to its young.

Caseman went on. "As you must know, this area, the Four Corners, also has its problems. The damage the extractive industry has done out here is heartbreaking. It's a travesty. Coal, oil, gas, and, worst of all, uranium. Uranium killed my own father. Cancer from exposure in the Moab mines. Nuclear waste plagues our poor earth today."

As Caseman expounded on the damage uranium mining had done to the Navajo people and their land, his voice drew the attention of the construction crew. The workers stood still, watching them.

Bernie interrupted the monologue. "Who is this leader you and Rollie mentioned?"

"Leader? Leader is our family patriarch. He rules and guides us and provides spiritual and all other direction he received from The Great Beyond."

"What's his real name? His full name?"

"Leader. That's what he tells us to call him and what he calls himself. If you want more details, you'll have to ask him."

"What's his background?"

"That's not for me to know or say. If you need more details, I can arrange an interview. He's involved in his morning meditation now, and then in listening for the word from The Great Beyond, but he will have time available later today or tomorrow."

Case paused. "Leader has never met Mrs. Yazzie or her husband. I handled all the details of setting up this solstice event. Any problems are my doing, so if you have any more questions about that, let me know. Otherwise, I need to get back to work."

"Don't forget that in addition to information on the leader here, I also need Pat's full name and Leader's full name. Their real names."

"Yes, ma'am—Officer. Whatever."

Chapter 31

An old turquoise pickup truck sat in front of the Yazzies' well-tended house, but Bernie noticed that Mrs. Yazzie's car was gone. Next to the home was the rounded shape of a hogan, the place for traditional Diné ceremonies. To the side was a barn and a corral with a few well-tended horses. Sunflowers bloomed here and there, along with several varieties of hardy native plants that stirred Bernie's love of botany.

Bernie parked her unit on the shady side of the Yazzie house, across from a sandy arroyo dotted with sagebrush. Her vehicle was protected from the sun by the shadow of the home, an important factor in the summer heat. Even though today was the solstice, the prediction was for more hot days for many weeks to come.

She left the motor running and the air conditioner on as she radioed the station. She checked in and Sandra said that Chee needed to talk to her. Then he was on the line.

She gave him a summary of the scene at the Yazzie revival camp and the fact that this group was CUSP. She told him what she'd learned of the fight, and that Arthur Caseman, the man who seemed to be partially in charge, said the person responsible for the disturbance had left and that she'd meet the other man, Rolland Chavez, known as Rollie. She rattled off the information from Rollie's license and gave him the data from Caseman's ID, too, so he could run a search for any outstanding warrants. "I'm going to take a look at the sweat lodge. Caseman told me Mr. Yazzie had approved the project."

"That's odd." Chee paraphrased what Mrs. Yazzie had said.

Bernie took a breath.

"Something is off about the scene here. I can't put my finger on it. Anyway, the place is calm now, and they are planning a major solstice meditation. Caseman gave me a flyer about it with an illegal picture he took of the sun dagger. This group is CUSP."

"Are you sure?"

"You bet." She laughed. "I didn't have to be much of a detective to figure it out. The flyer used the full name, Citizens United to Save the Planet. It's in small print, but the initials still spell CUSP. Case told me their head man, a guy he calls Leader, gets his instructions from The Great Beyond. That gives us something more than a fistfight to worry about."

"You're the one on-site. Give me your take on the situation. I want to make sure we stay on top of things out there. I can send Roper out there as backup."

"Not yet. I've run into a sexist, lying white guy who can't stop talking, a muscleman who was in a fight, and two women who seem intimidated. One of them warned me I was in danger. But so far, it's nothing I can't handle. I'm going to talk to Mr. Yazzie now, and if anything seems out of whack, I'll let you know."

Chee said, "I'm curious about Mrs. Yazzie's take on all this. She's a good judge of people. I can't believe she would let those guys stay at her place if she didn't trust them. Are you talking to her, too?"

"Probably not. Caseman said she left to visit her sister. That's another thing that seems odd. Why call us to come out and then leave before I arrive?"

"Did you hear any talk about mining?"

Bernie told him Caseman's story of his family and his statement about the harm to Mother Earth.

"Interesting," Chee said. "Word is that if Secretary Cooper comes, she might mention expanding uranium mining near the Navajo Nation under her supervision as secretary of energy."

Bernie waited for Chee to tell her about Adakai, but he didn't.

"How's the captain?" she asked.

"He has to have more tests. I saw him at the hospital. He wants to go home but his wife is worried."

"That stinks." She assumed Chee was about to end the call, but he surprised her.

"I'm worried about the captain. I never talked to him about special protection, about the ceremonies that help us with the things we have to face. I never asked if he had a medicine pouch."

"The captain knows the rez. He's a grown-up and he's a veteran cop." But Bernie understood Chee's concern about keeping the boss safe. They had both seen things happen that could not be easily explained without inserting at least a hint of the supernatural.

Bernie checked the time. "I'll deal with stuff here, get the full names of Leader and the men in the fight, and inspect the sweat lodge. Unless Mr. Yazzie wants to chat, I think I can be on the move in less than an hour."

"Let me know before you head off. Cell service is erratic out there."

"I'll radio you when I leave."

Bernie sat a few moments in the car before walking up to the Yazzie house. She thought about Darleen's missed call, wishing she had spoken to her sister when she had a cell signal. She hoped the woman Darleen had been worried about was home safely. Because it wasn't unusual for elderlies to walk off and grow confused, she realized that Mama's physical limitations were a blessing. She and Chee didn't worry about Mama wandering away. Oh well, she and Darleen could talk or text later. That gave her something she looked forward to. Darleen was always full of surprises.

As she walked toward the house to find Mr. Yazzie, she heard him call her name.

"Hello, Bernie. Sam and I are over here. We're in the corral." Mr. Yazzie sounded happy. "The boy and I are getting the horses ready for riding."

Bernie changed course. Spending a few minutes with Mr. Yazzie, his grandson, and the horses was sure to make the day better. She remembered that the Yazzies had built the corral against some sandstone cliffs. The natural rock walls kept the horses in and also gave them some shade in the afternoon. Noticing some caves in the stone above them, Bernie asked about them. She'd get to the sweat lodge and the rest of it next.

"There's a trail around back. Sprout and I go up there sometimes. It's cool and nice except for the critters who like it there." Sprout, Sam's nickname, suited the little boy.

"Critters? What is that, Shicheii?" He looked puzzled.

"Animals. They like those caves, too."

"They can hide there like I do, right?"

Mr. Yazzie had a bridle in one hand, and he hung it on the fence while he talked to Bernie. "In a few years we're going to start looking for a horse for Sprout."

"A pony." The boy smiled. "I'll call him Ponytail."

"That's a good name," she said. "Do you like to ride?"

"Sort of. I'm kinda scared."

Bernie remembered when she had first learned to ride. She missed having a horse, but with her job and Mama, there just wasn't time. And that was without factoring in the time she spent with Chee and Darleen. She knew she had to get to business, but time with a four-year-old was rare.

She squatted down to focus on the child. "What are the horses called?"

He told her the names. "My favorite one is Naabaahii. The black one."

"Do you know what that name means?"

The boy shook his head.

"Naabaahii, that's how we say warrior. That's a very good name."

"I want to be a warrior when I grow up. I'm already getting strong." Sam raised his arm and made a fist to show her his muscle. "Did you know that sometimes warriors have secret words?"

Bernie nodded. "Do you have one?"

He shook his head.

"If I could pick a secret word for you, do you know what it would be?"

"No."

"I think it would be Sprout, the name Shicheii calls you."

The boy looked serious. "OK. Don't tell anybody."

Mr. Yazzie smiled at Bernie. "I'm going to brush the mare, and then we need to go soon before it gets too hot. You can ride with us."

"I can't. But I have some questions for you."

"Oh, I see, You're here on business. I thought you came because of my handsome grandboy."

She smiled. "I came to make sure you were safe after Mrs. Yazzie called about a problem with your guests here." She didn't use the word *fight* in case it scared the child. "I wanted to make sure you were having a good day. And I was wondering if you gave the group permission to build a sweat lodge."

"No. They just did it. If they had asked, I would have said no." Mr. Yazzie thought for a moment. "And I would not have these meditation people back again because of what the wife told you."

"Do you have any records for the people who are here, with their real names. I need to check on someone."

"Mrs. Yazzie takes care of the visitors. The names must be in her computer, but I don't know a thing about that. Horses and boys, those are my specialties."

"One of your visitors told me Mrs. Yazzie left."

"That's right. She had a vision of evil here."

"I'm good with computers," Bernie said. "Would you mind if I took a look?"

The odds that the machine was powered up, and with the information she wanted on the screen, were slim, Bernie knew. But as long as she was there, it was worth a shot.

"Do whatever you need to," Mr. Yazzie said. "Unless she hid it, her computer is on the table in the living room. The password is *sprout*. Just go up to the house. It's open."

"I appreciate that. It's good to see you."

"I'm glad you came," he said. "Mrs. Yazzie wants to evict that group, but I told them they could stay at least through today because of their big meditation. But I told them they should not use that thing they built they call a sweat lodge. It's not safe. Not enough air gets in."

Sam had been staring at her uniform the entire visit. It was rude to stare, of course, but she took a moment and focused again on the boy.

"Have you met a police officer before?"

He shook his head. "Just you right now." He looked at her a moment. "Can I see your handcuffs?"

She showed him.

"For the bad guys, right?"

"Right. My job is to keep people like you and your grandparents safe. That way you don't have to think about bad guys."

He nodded. "Safe like a turtle in its shell." Bernie smiled at him, and he added, "Shicheii has a safe place in the house. He showed me."

"Oh."

"It's in the bedroom. Don't tell anybody."

She nodded.

"Maybe I can ride in your police car someday."

"I would like that." Bernie stood. "But now I have to get back to work."

Mr. Yazzie said, "I remembered that Mrs. Yazzie always prints out a list of people who are here in case of emergency. That should be on the table near the computer. If you don't find it, look in the drawer by the telephone. The folder that says 'Songs and Prayers.'"

"Songs and prayers?"

"That's right." Mr. Yazzie chuckled. "One of the groups we had in the past left it in the tent. Mrs. Yazzie needed a folder so she sticks her lists in there. She got rid of the songs but kept the prayers. She says if she ever has to call 911 for one of our revival visitors, prayers would come in handy."

Bernie walked to the Yazzie house for the list. She entered through the front door, stepped into the living room, then stopped. The table that served as Mrs. Yazzie's office had been overturned, papers strewn on the floor. She heard a noise and turned to see a man with a goatee jump out from behind the door. She got an unforgettable split-second glance at his ugly face as she reached for her weapon. Then the room went black.

Chapter 32

Sandra poked her head into Chee's office. "The chief is on the phone for you. I told him you were on another call, and he said to interrupt. Says it's urgent."

"Got it." Chee cut the conversation short. "Chief of police on the other line. I'll call you back."

The chief sounded tired. "I've got more information on that group Officer Manuelito went to check on. The FBI had them under surveillance, but they lost contact a few days ago. However, the feds think this group found out about the secretary's visit and might be planning some sort of disturbance. Manuelito's report helps."

Chee felt a surge of pride in his wife.

The chief was speaking faster now. "In the past, some CUSP members have threatened elected official and state and federal workers involved in the natural resources area. And, yes, the secretary of energy has been on their list. But it seemed to be just talk. All rants and no action, thank goodness. But that may have changed. The feds have asked us to keep an eye out for a man named James P. Sethley, who was part of this group at one time."

Chee waited for the chief to continue.

"Sethley worked as an informant for the FBI, feeding them information about CUSP. Rumor has it he was actually an FBI agent undercover, but you didn't hear that from me. Is Manuelito still at the revival grounds?"

"Yes sir, as far as I know."

"OK. I'm sending you the photo of Sethley." The chief paused for a moment. "Share it with Manuelito, and she can let us know if she saw the dude out there. Remind her that the feds are dealing with this because possible domestic terrorism is their jurisdiction. They will coordinate with Agent Johnson, and because Manuelito has been to their camp, Johnson might get her involved."

"Yes sir. In addition to the Feds, I'd like our officers to keep an eye on the Yazzie place, too. It can't hurt for us to pay attention to things out there. The Yazzies are good folks. I don't want any harm to come to them."

"I hear you. If Manuelito is still out there, tell her to keep her eyes open. Let me know if she picks up anything about a protest, demonstration, whatever. They could be dangerous. Be sure she has backup."

"Yes, sir."

"Thanks, Lieutenant. I appreciate you."

The kind words surprised Chee almost as much as the speedy arrival of the picture the chief had promised. It came before the chief ended the call.

Chee's stomach tightened when he saw it. "Sir, the photo just got here, and the man looks a lot like the dead guy at the uranium site. One of the two Washington-based agents who met me at the site seemed to recognize the body, although they were closemouthed about it. This means Bernie is in a bad situation out there. I'm sending backup now."

The chief grunted. "Sometimes the feds treat us like step-kids. I hate to be out of the loop on this. Especially a murder case."

Chee felt the same.

The chief said, "Before you go, the secretary's chief of staff asked me for a Navajo Police escort on her arrival at the venue. Play your cards right, and you could be her lead car." He chuckled, then turned serious. "Anything on the captain?"

"Nothing, sir."

"Let me know when you learn something. Even if it's bad, OK?"

"Yes, sir."

The call ended. Chee told Sandra to get Officer Manuelito on the radio. Sandra buzzed him a few minutes later.

"Sir, Manuelito didn't respond, so I tried her on the phone. She didn't pick that up, but service is marginal out toward the Yazzies' place."

"Keep trying, and let me know when you get through."

"Shall I call the Yazzie home phone?"

"I'll do it, just give me that number."

"I have it right here." Sandra recited it.

Chee felt the hot breath of worry on the back of his neck. The last time he'd spoken to Bernie, she'd just begun her investigation. He hoped she was on her way back to the station.

He told Sandra to send him calls that came from the chief or Bernie, and to hold the rest.

"What about Mrs. Adakai—do you want to talk to her about the captain's condition?"

"No." Good news or bad news, there was nothing he could do to help. "I'll get back to her when I can."

"Oh, I forgot to tell you. Darleen called, and—"

Chee, who never interrupted, interrupted. "Unless she was in an accident or something, tell me later." He saw Sandra's frown. "Can you handle all this?"

"Yes sir." But the tone of her voice didn't reflect deep confidence.

Chee knew that all of the other officers were too far away to reach the Yazzie place as quickly as he could. Bernie took precedence over the secretary's pending visit. He ran to his unit and dialed her cell phone as he started the engine. His call went straight to voicemail. He tried the number for the landline at the Yazzie place as he turned onto the highway. It rang unanswered.

Chapter 33

Chee gave Bernie another quick call from the road. She still didn't answer.

Cell service at the Yazzies was marginal, but she could have left there by now. He hoped she'd forgotten to radio in before she drove out of cell phone range. But she was a solid cop; that kind of mistake—and not responding to radio calls—wasn't like her.

A car parked along the dirt road about halfway to the Yazzie place caught his attention. Chee reluctantly pulled up behind it. He recognized the person in the vehicle, a woman in her late sixties, as Mrs. Jasmine Yazzie, the woman Bernie was coming to see. Mrs. Yazzie looked as he remembered her, hardy, lean, and fit with sunbaked skin the color of polished cedar.

He left the unit and Mrs. Yazzie climbed out from behind the steering wheel and stood in the sun to greet him.

"Yá'át'ééh, Lieutenant."

Chee returned the greeting. "Looks like you're having some trouble."

"Oh, my car is the one having trouble. I let it run out of gas. My sister is coming to help me."

Chee said, "An officer went to your compound after you called about a sweat lodge being built out there. When you weren't there, she was worried. Did you see her driving by?"

"She? Oh, you sent Bernie. I'm sorry, I didn't see her police car pass by on the road here, but I was reading. I might have dozed off for a minute." Mrs. Yazzie grew serious. "I'm worried about us, too. That's why I'm going to my sister's place. I am fearful of those people with Mr. Caseman."

Jasmine Yazzie was a respected ndiliihii who had worked with medicine people throughout the Navajo homeland. When a special lady was concerned about something, it got Chee's attention.

"When I was making bread this morning, I told my husband we should send Caseman and his people home before someone gets hurt. I told him to get them out of our place, but he said he already spent the money they paid us to buy hay and fencing. And he says we can't break the contract, but not to worry because it says Caseman has to pay for any damage and they'll leave after their big event today.

"But I'm not worried about the money."

"Tell me why you are worried." Chee wanted to hurry but he knew Mrs. Yazzie's information would be valuable for whatever he encountered at the revival grounds. He paused to learn what she had observed.

"I have a bad feeling about them being on our land. They aren't like the regular groups who come for revivals. They didn't even bring a band. And they keep asking me, Sam, and my husband to go to their meditation meetings." She paused. "Sam, he's our grandson, you know? Meditations? He's too little to do that, and the husband and I have our own beliefs. Like you, Lieutenant. Right?"

"Right."

Usually, when the Navajo Police sent an officer out to the Yazzie revivals, the situation involved someone attending the meeting who had prepared for the revival at home by drinking too many beers.

Chee had answered calls to investigate disturbances at a few of the revival sessions, but he had never come as an attendee.

Like Mrs. Yazzie, he preferred the old ways.

But as he saw more of humanities' foibles, he'd come to embrace the view that he could support whatever spiritual practice, or combination of practices, helped people live generously and with kindness toward their fellow humans. He had no gripes with the revivals as long as the people there behaved and respected the Yazzies' property and privacy.

Mrs. Yazzie wiped the sweat from her upper lip with the back of her hand. "I tried to get my husband out of there, too. I wanted him to come with me to my sister's house today and to bring Sam. I told him we had to get away from those people, to listen to my vision, especially because today is the solstice. But he promised the boy they would go out on the horses. So we had an argument. That man is stubborn."

Chee asked the question a different way. "What bothers you about that group?"

"Well, first of all, that sweat lodge is not right. They didn't ask us to build it, and they don't know what they're doing. It doesn't have enough ways for the air to get in. People could die in there."

Chee anxiously waited for the rest.

"And they don't respect their women and those women don't stand up for themselves. And the men? They act like that Mr. Caseman and Leader know everything. They don't ask enough questions." Her face had a sour look. "We're used to those Christian groups, you know, with lots of happy music. But these people are very serious."

Mrs. Yazzie looked at the mountains and the expansive deep-blue summer sky. "They don't seem to find any joy here. They focus on what's wrong with the world. I mean, why camp at our place if they don't like it?"

"I heard that Mr. Caseman is from California. How did he find out about you?"

She shrugged. "He told my husband that someone in their group had a vision of our ranch, the mountains, the revival tent, even our gate at the entrance. If you ask me, I think they saw our website. Mr. Caseman called me to ask if his group could come out and pray for peace around the time of the solstice. I said I would think about. Right then, my husband told me he had a vision, too. A vision that we could fix the fence and make the payment for our car."

"When was that?"

"That's another thing that bothered me. It was only last week. Wednesday. I remember because that day we also had a visit from a man who had a tumor. I told him what kind of a sing he needed. He couldn't afford to pay me right then, but he gave me some vegetables from his garden.

"Anyway, to make plans for thirty people at the last minute didn't seem right. I had my husband ask why they waited so long. He didn't tell Mr. Yazzie the truth."

"How do you know?"

"I just know. He said they had booked somewhere else, but the people they were dealing with had scheduled two groups for the same days, so they canceled on him."

It seemed logical to Chee. "Why would he lie about that?"

She shrugged. "Why do people lie about anything? Here's something else. I always get a list of the people in the group in case of emergency. We have the landline phone to call for help for them. He gave me just first names. I had to tell him they couldn't stay unless I knew who they all were. So, finally he did."

They heard the sound of an engine in the distance.

"That's my sister." Mrs. Yazzie stared down the road at a cloud of dust. Then she opened the back door of her stranded car and pulled out a brown grocery sack. "Here. Take this to your police station." Mrs. Yazzie handed him the bag. "You better go before Carla gets here. You know she likes to talk to you. Tell Bernie hello."

"Thank you. Call if you need anything, OK?"

She nodded and put her hand on her chest, where her jish was. "I know you are going there now. I don't like Caseman and those people. When I see them in my mind, I see death. I see heat and flames and death." She shook her head as if to shake away the nightmare vision. "Do you have your medicine to keep you safe?"

"I do."

"Good."

Chee hurried away with a growing list of questions for Mr. Caseman, the homemade presents in the sack, and a deep sense of unease. He hoped his instinct for danger was wrong, but he knew enough to trust it.

He put the bag on the passenger seat and turned his unit toward the Yazzie place and floored it.

He hadn't been to the revival grounds for several years, but far from being improved for visitors, the road was as bad as he remembered it, perhaps even worse. The parched landscape held life on pause in the June heat, waiting for the monsoon rains to bring the green.

An irresistible aroma had begun to fill his patrol unit. He could tell without opening the bag that Mrs. Yazzie had given him fry bread, freshly made in her own kitchen. He started to salivate. He reached in, grabbed the piece on top, as big as a dinner plate, pulled a bit free, and took a bite. He chewed slowly, savoring it as if it were his last meal.

Chee knew the arguments against fry bread. This was a food created in captivity and poverty, the nourishment of necessity that had become a traditional food for family gatherings and celebrations. Cooks made it from flour, baking powder, salt, lard, and nostalgia.

The U.S. government had given the People the ingredients during the Long Walk. When they returned to their homeland, the recipe for the puffy, chewy bread came with them and became comfort food for a hungry belly. Fry bread had been part of the cultural heritage of the Navajo and many other tribes for more than a century, despite its origins in hardship. At the moment, Chee needed all the comfort he could get.

If Chee didn't finish what was in the bag, Mrs. Yazzie's delicious gift could be topped with honey or powdered sugar or used as a platform for ground meat, onions, maybe some fresh green chile, chopped tomatoes, cheese, lettuce, and whatever else someone craved. The result was known as a Navajo taco.

He finished the still-warm bread one serving at a time, then wiped the oil from his fingers on the paper towels Mrs. Yazzie had graciously included. After that, he focused on driving.

Chapter 34

Chee worried about Bernie as he dodged potholes and found the right speed to cruise over the washboard roads out to the Yazzies. The route didn't lend itself to driving fast, even in one of the department's rugged SUVs. And he'd selected the better of two routes; the other way in was even rougher.

Chee followed the fence line, roller-coastering down some dry arroyos and back up again. After another fifteen minutes he drove through the Yazzies' entrance gate and saw the first red arrow with REVIVAL printed in big block letters at the fork in the road, and turned left. He turned again at the second marked junction, and that gave him his first glimpse of the Yazzie compound: a large white tent, where the meeting would be held, and beyond that, the family house, corrals, and hogan.

As he got closer, he spotted a dozen or so vehicles—pickups, SUVs, a few sedans, and, parked away from the others, a fancy-looking motor home. There was no sign of the green-and-white Navajo Police Tahoe that Bernie drove; he told himself she must have left for the station and taken the other road. But he kept looking.

He had the photo of the dead man on his unit's computer, along with a surprising update on the secretary's visit, which, due to a family emergency, had moved from "pending" to "potential."

Based on what Bernie had said earlier, Chee planned to interview Arthur Caseman as the group's spokesperson, but he also wanted to nose around a bit, hoping he could learn something from unofficial sources.

He drove past an unstaffed table beneath a canopy with a sign that read CHECK-IN HERE and drove toward the white tent. He parked his unit near what looked like a poorly made copy of a Navajo sweat lodge and walked over to take a closer look.

Larger than the lodges he was used to, the building had a make-shift roof of dry logs and branches. Instead of traditional blankets to cover the entrance, this place had a small wooden door. He saw no building permit. No wonder Mrs. Yazzie considered it unsafe. He agreed. The people inside could die from lack of oxygen; the odd door might leave them trapped inside. Or the structure could catch fire.

He approached a group of five men and women who were hauling away the construction debris. They fell silent and looked understand-ably nervous about the appearance of the policeman in their midst.

"Yá'át'ééh'. Hello. I'm looking for a man named James Sethley. We had a report that he was a member of this group. Do any of you know him?"

A tall, sunburned fellow with a ponytail, wearing a T-shirt with the sleeves cut off, turned to him. "Nope. That name isn't familiar. We're all well acquainted here, and no one by the name of Sethley is part of our family."

The four others nodded in agreement.

It surprised Chee that the name of the dead man meant nothing to them. "OK. Thanks. I need to speak with the person in charge here, your leader, about him and about this sweat lodge. It isn't safe."

The workers froze as if he had sworn at them. No one spoke.

Chee noted their reaction. "I think the person I want is Mr. Caseman. Does anyone have an idea of where I can find him?"

He watched the group relax, tension draining away as quickly as air escaping from a balloon. The man with the sunburn nodded, and Chee caught a glimpse of a red tattoo on his neck. "Try the tent."

"What does he look like?"

"He is bald and has a brown beard." A man with sunglasses said. "If Case isn't there, go to the Temple."

"The temple?"

"The Temple of Righteousness, that's what we call it. Over there."

Chee followed the man's glance and spotted the deluxe motor home. "Thanks. When are you doing the sweat?"

The man answered quickly. "The women will begin theirs later today, and we men tonight, and then every night until Leader says it is time to leave. Come join us. Everyone is welcome to help heal our Mother Earth."

Chee didn't see the connection, but withheld comment. "How long will your group be here at the Yazzies' place?"

"We'll leave when our job is done. We will stay and work for healing the earth until our message is received."

That could be a very long time, Chee thought, and these folks didn't know that Mrs. Yazzie was about to ring the exit bell. "I understand Mr. Caseman is top dog here. Is that right?"

The man shook his head quickly. "He's not the patriarch. Case tells us what the 'top dog,' as you say, wants from us. And Leader's messages come from The Great Beyond."

"Do you think Leader can answer my questions about Sethley?"

The man shrugged and went back to work.

Rather than ask more questions that probably wouldn't lead to any information, Chee walked toward the tent. He had been in it before on calls out here, but this time it looked slightly different. It was empty of the chairs he was used to seeing at revival meetings but held the usual assembly of speakers, microphones, and other electronics, all powered by a generator. In front, an elevated platform awaited a band, a choir, and the speaker/preacher who would address the people in attendance. The current setup also had big screens for video projections. He saw a few people working quietly, but no one with a brown beard.

Chee walked toward the RV, clearly the most expensive vehicle at the compound. It was a fancy, rugged-looking, gray-and-black rig that resembled a trim, well-designed box with doors and an extended awning on a heavy-duty truck chassis. He saw a vintage turquoise pickup truck parked behind the motor home.

The windows in the RV stood open, and as he got closer, Chee could hear voices raised in a heated discussion. Two men were involved, and as he drew nearer, he could distinguish the words.

A higher voice said, "Don't be ridiculous. This is what we came for. You knew it from the beginning."

The other said, "No. Not this way. I don't mean to sound disrespectful, but this is not what we talked about. It's not what we agreed to, sir." Chee heard the emphasis on *not*. The voice sounded rough and gravelly.

"Well, so what? Plans change. Chill, Rollie, you'll get over it. You sound like a fool."

And then came a smoother male voice. "We agreed to serve you and the cause. That's what matters. My brother Rollie seems to have forgotten that."

"Shut up, Case. I can speak for myself. I'm full on for the cause, but the method seems extreme."

Chee rapped on the motor home door. "Navajo Police." He gave his name, then moved away from the door to stand out of the bright sun in the awning's shade. "I need to talk with Mr. Caseman."

A tall bald man opened the door and trotted down the metal steps from the RV onto the sandy earth. "May I help you?" His was the smoother voice Chee had heard.

"Mr. Caseman?"

"That's me. I go by Case." He stroked his beard." At your service."

Chee introduced himself. "I'm looking for information about one of your members, James P. Sethley."

"Who?"

Chee repeated the name.

Caseman's brow wrinkled. "Hmm. James P. Sethley? Never heard of him."

Chee could tell that Caseman was lying; he'd answered too quickly. "Take a moment to think about it. Are you sure?"

"Well, you know, we all go by one name here, because we are family. And each of us decides what they want to be called. Simpler that way. Why are you looking for him?"

"Police business."

"Of course. What I meant to ask is, why are you looking for him here?"

Chee shook his head. "I'm not at liberty to discuss that. Have you seen one of our officers here? Officer Manuelito?"

"Officer Bernadette? Oh, she must have left." Caseman tugged at his beard. "Lieutenant, I'm afraid you made the drive out here for nothing. Even if I knew who Sethley was and his whereabouts, I couldn't tell you. We have a policy about protecting the privacy of our family members."

Chee stood a bit straighter. "Groups with policies like that look attractive to people with something to hide. Why the secrecy?"

"Lieutenant, that's easy to explain. Our meditation retreats are sanctuaries for everyone. No government interference, no ex-wives or lawyers, no bill collectors. People here are sovereign citizens. After all the BS you Navajos have put up with over the years, our attitude shouldn't seem odd to you."

Caseman extended his arms, and as the sleeve of his red windbreaker rode up, Chee noticed a tattoo on his forearm, a circle with lines inside. Something about it was familiar, but he couldn't quite place it.

"I'd like to tell you more about our group, Chee, talk to you about the value of our meditations, the role of the solstice as a time of change. About what we believe and how we want to leave the world better than we found it. It's no coincidence that you are here on the longest day of the year."

"All that information could be helpful. I'm going to record this conversation." Chee turned on his phone. "Start with your group's official name."

Caseman smiled broadly. "I'll tape this, too. Let's go to the tent, get out of the sun." The man obviously relished the attention. If he'd been a bird, he would have puffed out his chest.

"No. Start talking."

Case pulled out his cell phone and pushed several places on the screen.

"Officially, we are Citizens United to Save the Planet, unofficially known as CUSP. I'm one of the patriarchs of the group, and often our spokesman. If you knew more about us, Lieutenant, you wouldn't suspect one of our members of being involved in what you call police business. The best place to start understanding us is at our meditation this afternoon." He sounded like a salesman making a pitch.

Chee said, "Your group has been involved in demonstrations against mining of various kinds in other parts of the country. We want to be prepared in case a similar demonstration here leads to violence. Recently we've learned that your group might have information about the man I mentioned, a man the Navajo Police found dead."

Case frowned. "If that's the Sethley dude you mentioned, I told you he's not part of us."

Chee nodded. "You must have a record of who's in your group. I know Mrs. Yazzie requires that. Show me the list and I'm on my way, except for an inspection of that sweat lodge. It looks dangerous."

Caseman, to Chee's surprise, switched course. "Well, yes. I have that list somewhere, but it isn't easy to access. I can get it for you, but I wouldn't be able to do that until tomorrow evening at the soonest. Today is filled with our solstice events."

Chee had been a cop long enough to recognize stonewalling. "Don't bother. I'll get the list from Mrs. Yazzie, and leave it to you to tell me why you're lying about this. For now, let's go check on the sweat lodge Mrs. Yazzie complained about. You know, the one your crew is building. I will need to see a permit for it. That should be posted."

Caseman shifted his weight from the toes of his boots to the heels. "A permit? No one told us we needed a permit for the lodge. It's on private land, only for the use of our family. I promise you it is totally safe for the function it will serve today and for the next bit of time until we're done here. Save yourself some trouble, Lieutenant. Just call Mrs. Yazzie when you get back to the office. She can confirm that the lodge is as safe as it needs to be. Have her check on that Sethley guy who you think is on our list. Or, if you don't trust her, she can send it in over the computer."

Trust was the issue here, but it didn't involve Mrs. Yazzie.

"Mr. Caseman, tell me about Officer Manuelito's visit."

"That cute little Bernadette asked some questions and then went to the Yazzie house. She is probably waiting for you in Shiprock, looking forward to her next assignment." Case winked.

Chee's jaw tightened. "Don't disrespect her. When did she leave?"

Caseman lowered his voice. "I don't know. Between us, Lieutenant, she's overconfident. She's doing a man's job, and someone should rein her in a bit. A lot of women get uppity. I'm sure you've noticed that work like you and I do is best left in strong male hands, not given to the ladies."

Case paused, inviting a response.

Chee had to swallow his anger. He wanted to tell Caseman he was a jerk in language strong enough to match the rage he felt at the man's blatant misogyny. Instead he said, "Manuelito is one of our top-rated officers. Being female gives her an advantage in many situations."

"Ah, you're sweet on her, aren't you?" Caseman chuckled. "That's another reason you should come to our meditation. It helps calm the passions."

"What did Office Manuelito have to say about the sweat lodge?"

"Nothing. If she'd come to inspect it, that must have slipped her mind. You know how forgetful women can be." Caseman gave Chee a practiced smile. "My invitation is heartfelt. You could even talk to us about some Navajo spiritual practices. Our family would like that. Join us?"

"I'd never be part of any group that demeans women."

"Suit yourself, Lieutenant."

Chee began to walk to his unit, but Caseman called to him. "Before you go, tell me something. When is the secretary arriving?"

"Secretary?" Chee turned, giving himself a moment to think. The question caught him off guard.

"You know who I mean. Secretary of Energy Savanah Cooper. That woman who works for the president. When does she get here?"

"Why do you ask?"

"Oh, we heard a rumor that she was on the way."

"I heard that, too." Chee wanted to draw the man out. "Do you think it's true?"

"It makes sense that she'd plan a visit close to the solstice. You're an Indian, my friend, so you've noticed that nature grows uneasy around this special day. Painful things can happen as the sun moves into position, especially here on a part of our sacred planet that has been wounded by the search for uranium, the greed for coal, oil, natural gas, and other precious elements that should have been left in the ground. The solstice is a powerful time for change. And this is a powerful place for change to begin. So, I know Savanah Cooper will be here for it. I believe she is coming today, and her visit will not be what she expected. The scent of change is in the air."

"Change from what to what? What kind of change are you talking about?"

"Huge change. Dramatic change. That's the ultimate goal of our meditation, and of the sweat lodge sessions. You're a Navajo as well as a policeman, right? You should understand this." Caseman leaned on the *should* and Chee heard the derision. "We are working for the good of Mother Earth. We welcome you to be part of us, but if you decline, I'd advise you to keep out of our business."

Chee heard the message behind Caseman's rant. "It sounds like you just threatened a police officer."

Caseman took a step back toward the motor home. "I'd never do that, Lieutenant. I'm so sorry that you misunderstood. I've had some experience with the unexpected, and I would hate to see anyone hurt unnecessarily. But do what you will. I have to make a call and then I'll meet you at the sweat lodge for your inspection."

As he walked to his unit, to calm his own worry, Chee tried to picture Bernie back at the station, writing her report about the Teec Nos Pos incident, checking to see if any other information had turned up about the black Mercedes. But he knew it wasn't like her to be out of touch. On top of that, he was concerned that the man knew that the secretary was coming, but not surprised. It seemed like the word was out everywhere.

Back in the SUV, he radioed Sandra.

"Tell Officer Black I need him for backup ASAP."

"Yes sir. I have some messages. Do you want them?"

"Go ahead. Make it quick."

"First, the chief's assistant said he had some information on the other case you've been working on, Mr. Goodluck and the rest. An officer from Phoenix will contact you."

"OK."

"Mrs. Adakai called to say the captain is in surgery. And no, I haven't heard the details." Sandra softened her tone. "I'll follow up on it."

"Anything else?"

"You wanna hear about Darleen?"

"Did it sound like an emergency?"

"Not exactly. Well, maybe sort of."

Chee sighed. "Go ahead."

"She asked me to tell you and Bernie that she's in Phoenix with a man named Greg Morgan."

Darleen never failed to surprise him. The news left him momentarily speechless.

"What did Bernie say? Never mind. Let me talk to Manuelito."

"She's not here, Sir. I haven't seen her since she left for the Yazzie place. I thought she was out there with you. She has not been in contact for quite a while. Darleen said she couldn't reach her on the phone."

Chee ended the call and his worry rose another notch. He called Bernie on the radio again with no response. Then he tried Officer Roper Black.

Roper answered quickly. "I got the message and I'm on my way, sir, but I'm about an hour out."

"OK. Get here ASAP."

"Yes sir."

Chee parked at the sweat lodge. The afternoon had grown warmer, and men had removed their shirts to work in pants or shorts. Their skin, which ranged in shades from ebony to deep brown to pinkish tan, glistened with perspiration. He noticed that each of the men had a tattoo similar to Caseman's: a red circle with lines inside, a hand-drawn spiral. There were a few women on the ten-person crew. Like the men, they looked hot and tired, but they all wore pants and long-sleeved shirts.

The crew stopped and watched him approach. He called out to introduced himself. Most of the group simply stared at him.

A worker in a blue hat walked toward Chee. "Welcome, but we can't talk now. The lodge has to be finished for a big event this afternoon, a sweat for the women coinciding with our central meditation. Perhaps you can join the men for a purifying sweat."

Chee said, "The Yazzies are worried that this structure isn't safe."

"Are you an inspector?"

"I've been in a lot of sweat lodges. I know the basics. I can tell by looking that there isn't enough ventilation—that doorway is far too small. And that door to close it off is dangerous. Someone could get overheated and die before they could leave. I'd never go into a lodge like this. And no one here should either."

The worker said. "We do what Leader tells us. Questioning his wisdom brings punishment for our disrespect. If you don't think this is safe, tell him, not us."

An older man on the crew joined the conversation. "Safe? Lieutenant, few things are safe on the road to peace and freedom, and the journey is long and treacherous. But in the knowledge we gain, we are strong, better able to set worldly concerns aside."

A taller man said, "Leader says we shall walk through the unbearable heat, the women leading the way, but the reward is infinite glory in honoring The Great Beyond."

A few others chimed in with "Amen."

Chee had heard enough. "Tell me where to find Leader." He asked in a tone that expected an answer

A couple of the workers glanced in the direction of the motor home.

Chee walked to his unit and drove through the sagebrush, making his own trail back to the place where he had first talked to Caseman. If the group was focused on making the earth a better place, Caseman would cooperate in shutting down the sweat lodge and the proposed sweat ceremony. The man might be an arrogant blowhard, but surely he wouldn't want people in his family to get hurt.

As he drove, he looked for Bernie's unit, but saw nothing helpful or promising. He glanced at the Yazzie home quickly, but it wasn't there.

At the motor home, he knocked again, and paced while he watched for someone to answer. Waiting always made him nervous, and the closed blinds prevented him from knowing who was inside.

Caseman opened the door. Chee stood prepared for conflict if it came. "Your sweat lodge is a disaster, a genuine hazard. People could die in there. You have to close it to all users."

"Oh, that's terrible." But he didn't sound surprised.

"And Officer Manuelito is missing. This was her last known destination."

Caseman frowned. "That's awful news. I'm shocked to hear that about the sweat lodge. Tell us how we can help with your dear officer. Should we organize a search party for her? Come inside, Lieutenant. I'll introduce you to Leader, my boss and the gentleman in charge, and our brother Rollie."

An invitation to the inner sanctum was the next best thing to a search warrant. He drew his Glock as he stepped into the RV, both hands pointing his gun into the interior.

Chapter 35

Greg was driving, with Mrs. R in the passenger seat and Darleen in the back. Darleen half expected someone to chase after them, but no one appeared. As they had both anticipated, Mrs. Raymond began to take charge.

"I talked to a man at that hotel," she said, "and he gave me some places where the one we need to find might be. That's where we're going first." She had seemed tired—more than tired, exhausted—when Darleen first went to her room. But now the Mrs. R Darleen knew was back.

"Of course," Darleen said. "But before that, here are your pills." She handed them to Mrs. R, along with an unopened bottle of water she'd stowed in the back seat. "Greg and I need some breakfast and some coffee. Doesn't that sound good to you?"

"No time for that. You two listen to me now." Mrs. Raymond sounded like a stern teacher. "We need to go to look for the boy, and I know where to go."

"Drive-up coffee and a doughnut or something," said Greg. "As we head over there, you can tell us why you and my son ended up in a lousy hotel, so far from home."

Mrs. Raymond shook her head. "I don't want to talk so much. What matters is the boy. I will tell you about places he could be."

As she spoke, Greg turned up the AC. It wasn't even midmorning, but the car's exterior thermometer already registered ninety-six. "Did your friend at the hotel tell you about The Beating Drum?"

"Yes."

"It's closest to here. I'll drive there first after coffee, while you help Darleen locate the other spots you know of. She can use her phone."

Darleen showed Mrs. R the phone screen and clicked on an app. "This can find those places the man you spoke to told you about. Tell me the names, and I'll put them in."

Mrs. Raymond gave Darleen a list of half a dozen locations in the order in which Warren had given them, as the most likely places to find Droid or news of him. As Darleen put them in the phone's navigation system, she appreciated Mrs. Raymond's sharp memory and her mind for detail. She thought again about Mama and how much she had changed.

"That's all," Mrs. Raymond said. "You were right that coffee would be good. And a chocolate doughnut."

After that, they drove to The Beating Drum. The shop was in an older brick building that faced a busy street. Although there was an OPEN sign in the window, the lights were off, and it was clear that no one was inside. As Greg pulled into a parking spot in front, they saw a young woman with long black hair standing near the door.

He lowered his window. "Miss, do you know when that shop opens?"

The woman turned toward them. "Soon, I hope. She told me to be here at nine, and it's after that."

Darleen approached the young woman, introduced herself, and told her about Droid.

"What does he look like?"

Darleen realized she'd never seen Droid in person, but she remembered the photo that Mrs. R had on her dresser and described the image. Going by the laundry in the guest room, she added that he was tall and lean.

"How old?"

"Around seventeen."

"Oh right, that guy," the girl said. "I saw him yesterday."

Darleen felt a surge of hope. "Do you know where he is now?"

She shook her head. "He looked bad, strung out. Kinda desperate."

"Why did he come here?"

"He didn't tell me." The girl shook her head. "But Mrs. Sandler, the lady who runs the shop, helps people who need a hand up. Lots of our Native relatives are in his shoes."

Darleen walked back to the car and through the open window told Greg and Mrs. R that Droid had been there. "The woman I talked to said he needed help. It's time to call the police."

Greg nodded. But Mrs. Raymond shook her head. "These city police might not be kind to him. He's a good boy. He won't cause trouble."

"He already has caused trouble," Greg said. "That's why we're here."

He climbed into the back seat to make the call while Darleen drove. She used the navigation to head for the next place on Mrs. R's list, a community outreach kitchen. Greg's phone was loud enough for Darleen to follow the phone conversation. After some transfers, he told the person on the phone Andrew Morgan's birthday, hair and eye color, height, and weight. He mentioned the glasses and the fancy haircut. Then he stopped.

"Shimá, what was he wearing?"

"Jeans and a gray T-shirt."

Darleen heard some *uh-huh*s and "Yes" and "That's about it" from Greg. He ended the call just as they reached the next destination, a church-run food distribution point. The people waiting outside in the warm morning were mostly adult men, with a few women and young children added to the mix. Darleen parked.

"What did the police say?" she asked.

"The person who answered the phone forwarded the call to someone else, who handed me off to the missing persons bureau," Greg said. "They took my number. Said they'd call if they heard anything. We're lucky he's only seventeen."

Mrs. Raymond shook her head. "No. If he was older, he might have more sense. He might know better how to get around in a city like this. Or not to run off in the first place."

"What I mean is that once a person becomes an adult, they have a right to stop contacting their family without the police getting involved. As a minor, he'll get some attention." Greg opened the car door. "I'll go in and see if he's there, or if anyone has seen him."

"I'm coming, too," Mrs. Raymond said.

Darleen considered the situation. "I'll wait in case he walks past or something. And I need to call my sister and my mother."

Greg nodded. "Can you call Victoria, too? She might be worried."

"You or Mrs. R should call her. She might not pick up my call. I don't think she likes me."

He laughed. "OK, I'll call her. But just so you know, she doesn't like me either. She doesn't like anybody very much, right, Shimá?"

Mrs. Raymond hesitated. "I told the people at the hotel that Victoria was why I came, you know? When the lady driving the van talked about therapy, well, I thought maybe some therapy would help me figure out how to get her to change."

That said, she headed toward the waiting line, and Greg followed.

Darleen called Bernie first and got the quick message that her call didn't go through. She tried the home landline next and talked to Mrs. Bigman, who said Mama was OK and that Bernie and Chee were at work. Darleen heard the child crying in the background and cut the call short.

She was considering calling Chee when Greg came back to the SUV with Mrs. R in tow. They looked worried. Before Darleen could ask what had happened, Mrs. Raymond said, "They say someone who might have been Droid was here and got in an argument with somebody." For the first time since they'd started the search, she sounded discouraged. "They say he ran off. They say he was drunk."

Greg picked up the narrative. "The kitchen director told me Droid had breakfast here yesterday and that she'd talked to him about a youth shelter, and he seemed interested. She gave me the address."

Darleen didn't know if she should celebrate the fact that they had another solid lead, or lament the fact that Droid had been in a fight and was still on the run. She put on a brave face for them. "A youth shelter sounds good."

"It's the best we can hope for." He opened the back door. "You keep driving, OK? I wanna make some more calls."

Mrs. Raymond settled into the car again without another word.

Darleen navigated with the GPS, and they heard Greg on the phone in the back seat, leaving a message on one phone and then a second, and finally leaving another message, for Victoria.

It was close to noon now, and the thermometer on the SUV's dashboard read 105. The streets had plenty of cars but very few people. The ones Darleen saw were waiting at bus stops, walking from cars to buildings, or sweating on street corners, holding up cardboard signs.

The shelter was hard to find. Darleen parked in the only space not marked STAFF or RESERVED.

"I'm going in." Mrs. R unfastened her seat belt. "You come, too."

Greg opened the back door. "Of course. If he's here, we'll talk to him together."

Darleen had no desire to intrude on this family reunion if, in fact, the missing young man had made his way to this safe haven. She waited in the car and hoped for the best.

She saw Greg ring the bell, wait, and push the button a second time. Then he was talking to the door and she realized the building must have an intercom. After a few moments, he and Mrs. Raymond headed back to the air-conditioned car. She claimed the front seat.

"He's here," Mrs. Raymond told her. "But the lady in charge won't let us come in to get him."

Greg looked angry. "Even though he's a minor, they're leaving it to Droid to decide what he wants to do."

Mrs. Raymond took a deep breath and readjusted herself so she could see both Greg and Darleen. A lecture was coming.

"I have something to say. That one is unhappy. He misses his mother, but he's too young to have the strength he needs to fight that monster. That's why he's drinking. That's why he got on that van, and that's why I came with him. It was not right for him to stay at that hotel. That program was fake."

Greg sighed. "I can find treatment for him somewhere if he needs it. My son comes home with us. Period. That's why we came to Phoenix, right? To get him and his grandma and bring them back where they belong. We lost his mother. We can't lose him, too. If I have to call the police again, I will."

"You expect too much of my grandson," Mrs. Raymond said. "He's a good boy, becoming a good man. But he has a tender heart." She stopped, and when she spoke again, her voice had a softness Darleen hadn't heard before. "A tender heart, like your wife, his mother, my baby daughter, who meant more to me than my own self. He wants to shake off the monster that holds him now. You have to let him stand strong. His mother would want that." She paused briefly. "My son, you and your son need to heal together, to lean on each other. To put down sadness and pick up hope."

They were quiet for a long moment. Then Mrs. Raymond said, "My daughter liked to smoke, same as my husband. I told her no, but she'd sneak cigarettes. She laughed when I caught her, scolded her. I worried about that because of cancer, you know, lood doo na'ziihii. She said she'd stop if she had a baby. Then she told me the little one was on the way, and she did what she promised. But then she started up again after he was born. I should have—" She stopped, and they heard the catch in her voice.

"Does Droid ever talk about his mom?" Darleen asked.

Mrs. R shook her head.

"Not to me either." Greg pressed his folded hands together. "I guess he follows my example. Push sadness away. Don't be weak. In the old days, people never talked about the dead, you know."

His phone rang, with a chime that reminded Darleen of her microwave.

"It's them." He motioned toward the center with his chin. "They must have talked to Droid."

He exhaled and answered "Yes" and "Oh," and then listened for several moments. And then "I understand. I'll tell her."

He put the phone on his leg, face down. "Droid said he wants to see his grandmother. The lady said he wants to apologize for worrying you."

Mrs. R nodded, undid her seat belt, and started to open the car door. "Ask someone at the shelter to call us when you are done, OK?"

She put her hand on Greg's hand. "Shíyázhí, thank you for finding us."

"Take this with you." Darleen reached into her pocket and handed Mrs. R the turtle fetish she had found.

Mrs. Raymond smiled. "Ahéhéé. I've been missing this one." She closed her fingers tightly around the little carving. "Turtle wisdom."

They watched her approach the shelter's entrance, push the button, speak to a woman who came to the door, and then walk inside.

Greg climbed into the passenger seat. "That's the third time today she's called me her son. She never did that before." Darleen heard the emotion in his voice.

"I'm sorry my son didn't want to see me." His voice trailed off for a moment. "But at least we are working together to help him back to hózhó."

Chapter 36

When Bernie came to, the first thing she noticed was that her head hurt. She opened her eyes, saw what looked like the inside of a car, and quickly squeezed her eyelids shut again to keep out the painful light. Gradually, she realized that she was slumped against the center console of her SUV. She pushed herself to sitting and realized that the windshield was broken and the hood crumpled, and that the vehicle rested at an odd angle in an arroyo with a large boulder blocking the way forward.

Why had she crashed into this gully? She closed her eyes again, and then the scene in the Yazzie house came back to her: the unexpected mess of papers on the floor, the quick glimpse of a man with a goatee, her attempt to draw her weapon, and then the crushing weight of his blow.

What was she doing in her unit? She didn't remember driving away?

Bernie checked for her weapon. The Glock was there. She pushed herself to sitting, noting that the key fob was in her pocket. She checked to see if the car would start. No luck.

Then she tried the radio and, to her surprise, it worked.

"Bernie!" Sandra answered. "Oh my gosh. We've been worried about you."

"I'm OK." She had a headache from the blow on the head, but no need to mention that. "I need to talk to Chee."

"He wants to talk to you, too. He's at the Yazzie revival camp."

"I'm here, too. Can you reach him?"

"No. He's away from his unit."

"Who's in charge?"

"Bigman."

"Put him on."

Bigman answered quickly. "What's up?"

"Bad business at the Yazzies' place. The group they booked is CUSP, the cult the chief talked about tied to mining protests. One of them attacked me." She described Goatee and what he had done. "My vehicle is disabled and in an arroyo."

"Are you injured?"

She ignored the question. "I think the person who assaulted me was going through the Yazzies' private papers. I just had a quick glance, but I think their business laptop is gone. The computer might have information about CUSP."

Bigman told her Chee had already asked for backup and that the San Juan County Sheriff's department would get involved, too. "Roper should be there soon . . ." Bigman took a breath. "I'll call Agent Johnson and fill her in."

"What's up with Chee?"

"I don't know. We haven't heard from him in a while. He went there because the dead guy turned out to be an FBI informant. Can you let him know that we just learned that the FBI has identified Sethley as the brother of Secretary Cooper. And she's postponed her trip indefinitely."

"That's big news. Anything else?"

"Go get 'em, Bernie."

She opened the car door and climbed out of the steep arroyo. She ached, but nothing was broken. She knew she was lucky the man hadn't killed her.

Then she heard the crying. At first, she thought it was an animal. But she listened more closely and changed her mind.

"Sam? Mr. Yazzie?"

No answer, but the noise stopped.

"It's Officer Bernie. Do you need some help?"

She heard another sob. The noise wasn't coming from the barn, the last place she had seen them. The horses were still in the corral so she knew the two hadn't left for their ride.

Bernie spotted a trail up the hillside that lead to the sandstone caves Mr. Yazzie had mentioned. She climbed up past several switchbacks, calling for the Yazzies as she went. The trail gave her a bird's-eye view of the revival site. The construction activity at the sweat lodge had stopped, and from that vantage point she could hear soft, soothing music carried from the white tent by the breeze.

"Sam? Mr. Yazzie?"

As she paused to catch her breath, she saw two black SUVs and a black pickup with something in the bed leaving the compound. They were followed by a Navajo Police unit. Seeing that she had one bar of service, she sent a text to Bigman.

Just saw an NPD unit leave the Yazzies. Was that Chee?

Bigman responded: Haven't heard from him.

They both knew Chee would have radioed his location.

Bernie felt her stomach tighten. She typed: Something's wrong.

He responded: Yeah. Black on the way.

Bernie took a breath.

Units might be FBI, Bigman texted. Checking with Johnson.

She thought about what she had just seen. Bigman might be right. If the SUVs were FBI, that pickup could be an unmarked San Juan

County sheriff's vehicle.

But what about the Navajo Police unit?

Something about the new black SUVs that drove away stirred a memory. She closed her eyes to recall it, and in a moment her first sight of the vehicles flashed into her brain. They had seemed out of place among the more modest cars, much-used trucks, and old vans in the CUSP lot she had driven past on her way in.

She called out again. "Let me know where you are so I can help."

"OK." It was Sam's voice.

She continued up the trail and, to her relief, found the child beneath an overhang.

She squatted down to talk to him at his level for a few moments. The child seemed fine. "Let's go now."

Sam crawled out and hugged her pant leg. "But Shicheii didn't come to find me yet. He told me to go outside and hide. He would come to find me."

She'd never interviewed a four-year-old but she knew she had to ask questions without scaring the child. But before she thought of what to ask he said, "I saw your car crash."

"Oh. Tell me about that."

Sam nodded. "It went way down there. The man got out and ran away."

Bernie pictured Goatee shoving her limp body into the seat.

"What did the man look like?"

"He looked mean." The boy shrugged. "Shicheii was talking to him when I went to hide."

"Where did the man go?"

"I don't know. That way." Sam turned toward the road that led away from the Yazzie house.

Bernie took his hand and they went down the path back to the Yazzie house. She began to weave the elements of a plan. Return the child to Mr. Yazzie and try again to get the list that must be tied to the fight and the murder; find the dangerous man who hurt her before he injured someone else; check on the sweat lodge and make sure none of these visitors get hurt in there. And, as quickly as possible, get back up out there.

The boy broke her concentration and she heard the worry in his voice. "Shicheii always finds me. But he didn't. Why?"

"I don't know."

"Maybe he forgot."

Maybe, she thought, but highly unlikely.

Bernie wanted to change the subject. She spotted a little reddish stone, flat on the bottom with some small protuberances on the side, and handed it to Sam.

"What does this look like?"

He studied it. "A turtle?"

"A turtle. Ch'eeh dighahii. A turtle takes its home with it. If something tries to hurt it, it hides in the shell until the threat disappears. I think that's what your grandfather would do, if that mean man tried to hurt him."

The boy nodded.

"That place where I found you, that was like a shell, too."

He looked at the cliffs that surrounded them on three sides. "Here, too, right? This is our big shell."

She had planned to ask Sam to wait on the porch while she went inside, but it wasn't necessary. Mr. Yazzie meet them at the door. She could see from the way he limped and the pain in his eyes that his encounter with Goatee had been violent. But he smiled at Sam and welcomed them in. He sent the boy to wash his hands and told her what had happened.

"After you left the corral, I watched for you to drive away, but you didn't so I figured you hadn't found the list that Mrs. Yazzie left. I came to check. Sam came with me."

Mr. Yazzie said Goatee was inside the house. Goatee ordered him to hand over the keys to the turquoise truck, and Mrs. Yazzie's laptop and records. At that point, Mr. Yazzie told the boy to hide and that he'd find him when the man left.

"I told him no one drove my truck except me and I didn't know anything about the computer. I yelled at him to get out of my house.

"I hung the keys to the truck on that board by the front door and Goatee saw them there. I knew he was going to take them, so I tried to block his way. Goatee shoved me and I fell. I got up and started yelling for him to leave. He punched me in the face and kicked me when I went down again. I think he broke some ribs. I found a place to hide."

"Did he say why he needed your truck?"

"No. But for the computer, he said Caseman had accidentally given Mrs. Yazzie the wrong names for some of the people here and they wanted to change it for her. He said they wanted to make her life easier. The man lied real good." Mr. Yazzie gently ran his hands over his battered face. "I should have done what Mrs. Yazzie said and never let those people in here."

"Did he take the computer?"

"I don't think so. I remembered that Mrs. Yazzie hid it when she left. I don't know where it is. She doesn't want anyone walking off with it."

"That means he might come back and look for it again. Do you have a gun?"

"A rifle and a handgun for coyotes." Mr. Yazzie looked at her a moment. "Get that man who hurt us."

When the boy came back from the bathroom, Mr. Yazzie talked to him about staying safe. The injuries the man had suffered, she knew, raised his anxiety for the boy, but he spoke about it in a way that didn't seem to worry the child.

"You did a good job of paying attention." Bernie gave the boy a gentle look. "Now tell me what you're going to do."

"Whatever Shicheii says. And be quiet if he asks me to hide."

"That's great. Do you remember our secret word?"

"Sprout."

"What will you do when I or another policeman says your name?"

"If you say Sprout, I'll say here I am!" He yelled it out.

"What if someone says Sam? Or is anyone hiding here? What will you do?"

"Be quiet. That not the secret word."

"What if that person pretends to be your friend or even a policeman?"

Sam shook his head and put a finger across his lips.

"I know you will be brave for your grandfather."

Sam nodded. "What does brave mean?"

"Brave means doing the right thing even if you're scared."

"I'm not scared."

It was a lot to ask of a four-year-old. She hoped all Mr. Yazzie's fretting was for nothing.

***

Even though Bernie had never learned to weave well, the lessons Mama shared at the loom taught the value of patience. Waiting wasn't Bernie's strong suit, but she could do it when she had to, and this was one of those times.

She walked away from the Yazzie home to meet Roper. She wanted to talk to him before he reached the compound. Finally she saw his Navajo Police unit in the distance on the dirt road heading toward the revival grounds. She stood where Roper Black was sure to see her.

The SUV approached in a cloud of dust, then stopped. Roper lowered the window. "Good to see you. You OK?"

"Fine." Bernie started with the immediate issue. "I saw two black SUVs, a pickup, and one of our units heading away from here. Did you pass them on your way in?"

Roper looked surprised. "No. They must have turned at the junction. What's going on? You look like someone hit you."

"I'm OK. Radio the station to send out a BOLO for Chee's vehicle and the SUVs. They are Cadillac Escalades, new ones with New Mexico plates—the yellow-and-red design. I couldn't read the numbers."

"One big question is where is Jim? Where is Chee?"

He called in the be-on-the-lookout, and Bernie climbed into the SUV and told Roper about the CUSP situation.

Roper shared his news. "The secretary isn't coming."

"Yeah, Bigman told me."

"I'm glad. We've got our hands full with this mess."

He kept his eyes on the challenge of the road. "You OK, Bernie? It looks like someone beat on you."

"A guy with a goatee."

"We'll get him," Roper said. "How many people are at the compound?"

Bernie cleared her throat. "I'd guess around 30."

After the short parade of suspicious vehicles, not a car or truck had left or entered the compound except for Roper's police unit. The hot June air seemed unnaturally still, not even graced with birdsong.

Roper handed her a bottle of water.

"Ahéhéé."

"What are we getting into, Manuelito?" She heard nerves in the rookie's voice.

"Good question. I came out here because of a disturbing-the-peace complaint about a fistfight, and an unauthorized sweat lodge. Now it's assault on a police officer and a civilian, a suspicious death of one of the cult members, theft of Mr. Yazzie's pickup, and at least attempted burglary based on the condition of the Yazzie house."

"This cult stuff freaks me out. The word in Utah was that these CUSP folks are wackos who get directions from The Great Beyond."

"The people I met here who aren't in charge seem fearful, intimidated, a bit cowed. But not crazy except for Caseman, or violent except for the man who attacked me."

"Cowed?"

"You know, timid. Like people who have been threatened, demeaned, abused."

"What about weapons?" Roper asked.

"I didn't find anyone who was armed. I think the man who attacked me had a gun, but I only saw him for a second before I went down. I don't know what's in the RV."

"Bernie, you ever shot anybody?"

She sighed. "Yes. I would have died otherwise. I didn't like doing it, but I'm glad I could."

"I never have. I never want to. Does that make me a bad cop?"

"No, not at all," she said. "I hope you never have to fire your weapon except in target practice."

They came to the fork in the road and the abandoned registration table. Roper slowed the vehicle. He looked puzzled. "Which way?"

"Left. Head that way."

They could see the sun's glare reflecting off the windows of the CUSP vehicles in the parking lot as they drew closer.

Bernie explained where the CUSP motor home was, and they saw the tent and the sweat lodge the cult had built. She pointed back at the Yazzie home and corral at the end of the road.

"What's the plan?" Roper asked.

Bernie had been thinking about it. "Come with me and we'll start at the tent to look for Chee and if he's not there we'll check the motor home. I need to get to the sweat lodge, too, and make sure they aren't using it until it's been inspected. We'll both be on the lookout for Goatee and arrest him if he shows up."

"I hope that the FBI shows up soon, if they aren't here already," Roper said.

Bernie took another sip from the water bottle. She didn't see any sign that the FBI agents were on the scene but she didn't mention that to Black.

Bernie remembered Caseman saying something about a meditation. Roper continued toward the sweat lodge and the big white tent.

They looked for Chee's police unit and Bernie wasn't surprised when they didn't spot it. They also saw nothing that made them think the FBI had already arrived.

"We're on our own, Roper," Bernie said. "The unit I saw leaving here must have been Chee's."

"And you're sure he wasn't driving?"

"I'm sure. Chee's a tall, slim guy. The guy behind the wheel was short and stocky." She knew the man she loved was in big trouble: held hostage, incapacitated, or dead somewhere in the compound. Maybe he or his body was in that police vehicle. She tried to come up with a more hopeful scenario, and failed.

Roper drove skillfully and fast and kept his thoughts to himself.

"Stop here, near that tent." She turned worry into action. "That's where the meditation meeting will be. Let's go."

Roper parked. "OK. Let's do this."

Chapter 37

As Bernie approached the tent, her hand on her Glock, she heard soothing, generic music coming through the fabric and the hum of portable fans moving the air inside. Except for that, the day was as quiet as a schoolroom on a Sunday. It was as if the June heat had sucked up the comforting sounds of birds and the familiar whisper of the dry wind.

Then a male voice began speaking in a hypnotic drone, repeating the same words over and over again. It sounded like a recording. *"Now is the time. This is our calling. We go forth without hesitation to save our mother planet. We are chosen by The Great Beyond to do this work and we do it with gratitude."*

Bernie continued toward the gathering, reassured by the fact that no one came out to confront her.

When she looked in through the open tent flap, she saw people sitting calmly or lying on their backs. They seemed to have their eyes closed. Chee wasn't there. Neither was Caseman. She noticed Alisa, the large woman with the curly hair she had met when she first encountered the group. Unlike the others, Alisa wasn't sitting.

She looked as though she was about to leave. Bernie stared until she caught Alisa's eye, then motioned to her with a jerk of her chin. Alisa complied, quietly moving away from the meditation assembly to where Bernie stood just outside the tent.

"Where's Lieutenant Chee, the other officer who came out here?"

The woman looked puzzled for a moment, then pointed toward the gray-and-black motor home. "Probably there. That's where Leader stays." She spoke even more softly. "Something big is coming down and women are showing the way. It's important. Come with me to the sweat lodge."

"What's happening?"

Alisa sucked in a breath and blew it out again. "Leader calls it 'Heat, Fire, and the Earth's Rebirth.' Only chosen women are allowed." Her big hand reached toward Bernie's shoulder. "You are welcome. We have to leave now for the sweat lodge."

Bernie stepped away. She looked at the woman and remembered the bruise she'd seen , the dark purple marks that looked like the place someone's hand had squeezed her arm painfully hard.

"Alisa, 'Heat, Fire, and the Earth's Rebirth?' What does that mean?"

"I don't know."

Bernie sensed that Alisa was telling the truth and that something else was going on, too.

"Leader and Caseman have been teaching us about the planet's struggle, how the solstice is the perfect time to sacrifice for change." Alisa pursed her lips. "They selected me to assist with the first group of women to gather in the sweat lodge to meditate and to help Case when he comes to make the video. We know our prayers for Mother Earth demand maximum effort. We lead the way, to sacrifice for the good of our mother. To transform our lives as a prayer."

"I have to find Chee," Bernie said. "Then I'll go to the sweat lodge."

"Promise?"

"Yes."

"OK." Alisa gave her the hint of a smile. "See you there."

Bernie headed toward the motor home, thinking of Chee, forcing herself to picture him unharmed. The five minutes it took her to run there seemed like an eternity. She offered a silent prayer for protection, then rapped on the door.

"Navajo Police. Open up," she said, and waited.

Hearing nothing, she put her left hand on the door and raised her Glock. She pushed the door open and looked and listened, staying outside. The space was quiet, except for the buzzing of the refrigerator and the soft hum of the air-conditioning.

"Anyone here?" she called again, giving her name. Someone had lowered the blinds, but the bright June sun would not be deterred, and a subtle glow filled the space. The driver's area and a small kitchen and dining area were empty. In the dim light, she walked to the back, into the bedroom area.

Chee was lying awkwardly on the couch, eyes shut, duct tape on his mouth and more tape securing his legs and arms.

"Chee!"

She yelled his name as she rushed to him.

His chest rose and fell with each breath and there were no signs of blood, but he didn't respond to her voice. She put her hand on his arm and said his usually unspoken Navajo name. His eyes stayed closed and he didn't stir. Her worry growing, she shook him gently, and then again more forcefully.

"It's Bernie. Look at me. Chee?"

He groaned.

"I'm going to rip off the tape over your mouth." Bernie winced as she did it, knowing it would hurt. He groaned with pain. When she saw him working his wrists against the tape, she pulled out her knife to cut him free.

Finally, he opened his precious eyes and seemed surprised and then grateful. She felt relief course through her body. Pale and exhausted, he moved his arms slowly to rub his wrists as she cut through the tape on his ankles.

"Where am I?" He spoke just above a whisper, trying to sit up.

She told him. "Lie still a moment. Just take it easy. Then we'll talk."

Chee squeezed her hand. Bernie didn't want to push him, even though she knew they had to get out of there.

"You talk," he said.

"I'm glad I found you. I thought you might be dead."

"My chest aches like a fifteen-hundred-pound bull fell on it. They must have drugged me. Room is spinning."

"Who's they?"

"Leader. The boss. White man in his sixties. And Caseman."

Chee put his hand on the back of his neck and grimaced.

"Take it easy." She brought him some water, and with her encouragement he sat up. He looked intently at her. "What happened to you?" He struggled for words. "I thought you might be dead, too."

Bernie realized the encounter with Goatee had left its marks. "I ran into some trouble. I'll tell you about that later. I'm fine and Roper's here for backup. Why are you in here?"

"I came to the Yazzie place when we didn't hear from you and when the chief sent a photo of the dead man. He was an informant and the secretary's bother. His body was in bad shape, but one of the FBI people. . . ."

Bernie noticed that he gasped for breath. "Rest a minute. Take your time."

But Chee spoke faster.

"I came to the RV to ask for help to find you, and tell them that they couldn't use that sweat lodge. I met Leader and a big man named Rollie. Caseman told me he was leaving to organize a search party, but he lied about that. Rollie and another guy I hadn't seen, a man he called Victor, a guy with a black beard, grabbed me. They smashed me down in a chair. The man with the beard took my weapon and taped my arm and legs. Caseman came back with a camera to video what they called my interview. But before Caseman could start the questions, Leader began talking.

"He gave me a lecture about the evils of uranium, oil, gas, and coal. Then it got weirder."

He rubbed his wrists a moment.

"Leader started to brag about Sethley, but he called him Pat, and how they had timed their trip here, the meditation session, and the sweat lodge ceremony all to coincide with the secretary's visit. He called it a plan inspired by The Great Beyond. I tried to push Leader into saying more about that, and when I got tough, I felt something like a wasp sting on my neck.

"It must have been a syringe with some type of sedative. After that, Rollie and Victor left. I was surprised," he said. "I thought they would shoot me. But Caseman began asking me for details about the secretary's visit. The drug, whatever it was, loosened my tongue, but I had no information for them."

Even though it was cool in the building, droplets of sweat were running from Chee's temples. Bernie looked at his neck and saw a red welt.

"Finally, Leader said they would leave me here for Victor. They didn't spell out what Victor would do, but I wasn't looking forward to it. Meanwhile, the drug was numbing my brain, my whole body."

Bernie remembered a critical point. "Did you know the secretary cancelled the trip?"

Chee looked surprised. "No, I didn't and I'm glad I didn't. Leader said they would hold her hostage until the government agreed to ban all mining of any kind. They planned to coerce her into making videos supporting their cause."

Chee's mention of videos reminded her of Alisa and the women in the sweat lodge. "Chee, are you strong enough to walk?"

"Maybe." He attempted to stand, began to shake, and sat down again.

"Wait. Get your strength back."

Chee nodded.

"Did you ask how they planned to kidnap the secretary?"

"Leader bragged that they had two SUVs and a truck loaded with rocks and bags of fertilizer they'd mislabeled. They would crash the truck into one of the vehicles traveling with the secretary and block the highway. When her driver stopped, men in the black cars were going to approach the secretary, pretending to be security guys. Leader said their SUVs look the same as the ones the security detail drives and the guys would be dressed like agents."

Bernie realized that description matched three of the vehicles she'd seen leaving the compound. And Chee's unit would give the convoy extra credibility.

"After that, they were going to take her somewhere to make a video saying that forms of mining and extraction had to cease to protect the earth, and if the president didn't sign an order, she'd be killed. And that the CUSP family would all be meditating and doing a sweat to encourage the president to do the right thing."

"That's crazy."

"Leader said The Great Beyond told him this was the way to save the planet. But money from the family members' bank accounts is what bought this fancy motor home. The rest of the CUSP people are out there in tents or sleeping in their vehicles." Chee cringed as he sat straighter.

"Someone planned to video all this and use a satellite dish to create live feeds to national media along with the secretary's statement."

Bernie could tell Chee was recovering because his speech was better and his color almost normal.

She said, "I have to go to the sweat lodge. Something is happening there."

Chee sat straighter. "Let's get out of here. They took my gun, but I have a backup weapon in my unit."

Bernie helped him stand. "Your unit is gone. I saw it leave the Yazzie compound along with the SUVs and a pickup with something heavy in the back. It's good that word of the secretary's cancellation didn't reach them."

Chee patted his front pockets and confirmed that the key was gone. "They killed Sethley before he could let them know she wasn't coming. Leader knew the feds were on to him. He said it didn't matter because the wheels of change were in motion."

Bernie handed him some water. "Drink this."

Chee grabbed the bottle. "Fill me in while we go to the tent. Leader said they had a special video for the family to watch to give them courage for the days ahead. Something bad is going down and while you're at the sweat lodge I'll try to stop it."

"Where are Caseman and Leader?" She studied him as he stood and they started to walk.

"I don't know for sure. Maybe at the big meditation. Or probably they were in that group you saw with the pickup and the SUVs. I noticed someone driving off in Mr. Yazzie's old truck. Was that what you saw?"

"No. This was a new, Ford F-150. Roper asked for a BOLO on those vehicles." Bernie stood a bit straighter. "You have to talk reason into the CUSP members assembled in the tent, make them realize that they don't want to be part of this crazy plan and that Leader is misusing them and their money. They can find saner ways to make things better."

"I'd like to do that, but I don't see how." Chee's walk grew more solid as they neared the tent. "It might be impossible to shift the course of this river, to persuade them that Leader and Caseman are wrong."

"These people are here because they felt a need for something spiritual, and they want to make a difference," Bernie said. "They've been intimidated and mislead, but that doesn't mean they support kidnapping and murder."

"I hope they're ready to move out from under Leader's thumb."

"All you can do is give it your best. You're a man of the spirit. Leader betrayed them. That's clear to us, and you can make it clear to them."

Bernie studied the tent and the sweat lodge beyond it. "One of the women told me that part of the plan involves heat and fire and a group of women in the sweat lodge. She said they'd be praying until Leader told them to stop. I want to make sure those women are safe. But I'll walk with you to the tent. You're still shaking."

"I'm feeling better," he said. "It helps to think of what I'll say to the people in there."

They continued without talking. She noticed that Chee was sweating more than the warm day warranted.

"Are you nervous?"

He nodded. "I don't have experience working with a group like this."

"Remember that these people are basically good. They want a better world, the same as you and I do."

"I can keep it simple. Stress that one of our main jobs as five-fingered creatures is to respect each other and the earth. Help them chant. Pray with them in a positive way and encourage them to chart a new course."

She squeezed his hand. "You are a powerful force."

They found Roper standing just outside the tent. He nodded to acknowledge them.

"Lieutenant, you don't look so good. You OK?"

"Getting there."

Roper gave Chee the backup service weapon he kept in his unit. "I thought you might be a little short, so I brought you this." Then he turned to Bernie. "Where's that Goatee guy you warned me about? Let's find him."

* * *

The vibe in the tent was different from the peaceful calm Bernie had seen earlier that afternoon. The soft, generic meditation music had stopped, and perhaps a third of the people in the tent were standing and talking to each other rather than sitting on their mats or lying in a meditative pose. They looked worried.

Only the sonorous male voice could be heard. From one of the open front corners of the tent, they could see a huge screen with a video image of the old man who was speaking.

Bernie said, "Who is that?'

"It's Leader," Chee said. "The guru who left me for dead."

He turned to Roper. "Look for the source of that noise and shut it off. Keep your eyes out for the man with a black goatee. And be careful."

Leader's recorded voice was hypnotically monotone: *"Follow your hearts, my people. Do what you know is right. Do what you have to. Make the sacrifice, embrace the purifying heat and you will be rewarded. Women are leading the way, and more will follow."*

The recording stopped.

Chee stood with his eyes closed for a moment, and then, still outside the tent, where he couldn't be seen, he started to sing. The rich, rhythmic notes were more than music; they were a prayer strengthened by repetition.

Bernie recognized the chant from ceremonies she had attended for friends and relatives in need of healing. She remembered what Caseman had told her about why they had come to the Navajo Nation. Perhaps inadvertently, he had primed his followers to be receptive to Navajo healing. She hoped that was the case.

Bernie touched Chee's arm and spoke softly. "Good luck. I'm going to the sweat lodge."

***

Chee continued to chant as he walked through the open side of the tent and into the group of people who had assembled for the meditation.

Chee's song resonated in the tent now, although the audio of Leader's voice had returned and now boomed from the speakers. The eyes of the assembly were on the images that flashed on the screen. Chee knew he could not gain the group's full attention until Leader's message was silenced. Roper had to shut off the power.

The pictures and the audio looped into a new cadence. Over and over again, Leader was repeating, "*We dedicate ourselves for Mother Earth. We do what must be done. We surmount those who would harm our precious earth.*"

On the screen, instead of soothing shots of mountain waterfalls and hummingbirds, Chee saw a swift montage of disturbing pictures. An open pit mine and the scar it made on the landscape. The image shifted to the Black Mesa coal-mining operation, and then to the orange sludge released from the Gold King mine, which had contaminated and poisoned water in the sacred San Juan River. The video showed farms decimated by drought, towering dust storms, and finally, uranium mines and the land poisoned by their abandoned waste products. All the time, the music grew more ominous.

Leader's voice came on again: "*Who will stop this curse? We will. Our sacrifice can heal the earth. We will pray and meditate until the deed is done.*"

Chee kept chanting as he watched Roper study the AV system's complicated mess of wires and cords. He saw Roper walk out of the tent and turn off the generator. The power died.

As quickly as a nightmare ends with awakening, the images disappeared and Leader's droning voice fell silent. The muscular man at the control board had his back to Chee. When he turned, Chee saw his black goatee. The man trotted outside to check on the nonfunctioning generator. Judging from Roper's quick response, he recognized Victor, too. Roper sprang into action. Chee watched his fellow officer wrestle the man to the ground and handcuff him.

Chee spoke into the sudden silence. "Dear people, we all know what's wrong but kidnapping and threats aren't the solution. Change is possible, but not through violence. Please join in. Chant with me now."

Before he started singing once more, Bernie spoke softly into his ear. "I got a text that the FBI just arrived. They are securing the site so no one can leave. I'm going to the sweat lodge."

Chapter 38

Bernie raced off through the afternoon heat to the sweat lodge, relieved that only one task lay before her. As she neared the structure the CUSP people had built, she noticed no one in sight. In her experience, at least one person would remain outside the lodge to make sure no one intruded on the participants and in case someone in the lodge needed assistance.

Instead, she saw women's clothes folded in separate piles, shoes next to them. From the array, she realized there must be at least eight people inside. And she saw no source of cooling water to revive the participants.

The small entrance to the lodge was sealed, not with loosely hung blankets as was Navajo custom, but with a solid door. Bernie could see the latch on from the outside. What had these people been thinking? The only way the people inside could leave was if someone standing outside opened the door for them. So, even before she unlatched and opened the door, she knew that what lay before her would be bad news. And it was worse than she imagined.

If this had been a Navajo sweat such as those in which Bernie

herself had participated, or even another purposeful cleansing ceremony, she would never have disrupted it. Certainly she never would
have taken her weapon into this space. But a Navajo sweat was a volun-
tary practice intended to cleanse body and spirit, reinforcing the idea
of community support for a return to wholeness. Based on what she'd
seen at CUSP, she knew this pseudo sweat lodge was a political statement, a disturbing hybrid, distorting something that could nurture the
spirit to serve one man's desperate plan to draw attention to his cause.

When she opened the door, the odor of human sweat met her on
the flow of escaping heat. Squatting down to peer into the humid,
dark space, over a tinny recording of a repetitive chant, she heard
women moaning and gasping for breath. Over the heat radiating from
red-hot rocks and the steam from the water sprinkled on them, she
smelled woodsmoke.

The lodge was a death trap.

The lack of ventilation she'd noticed when she first saw the building provided just enough oxygen to keep a fire going, and the tightly
closed door contained the steam and smoke. How long had these
women been here? Who was stoking the fire and pouring water on
hot rocks to make a hot place even hotter? This sweat lodge was an
execution chamber. The women in here could die.

Bernie focused on the recording coming from inside the lodge.
As in the tent, Leader's deep voice droned over and over again: "*We
sacrifice ourselves for Mother Earth. We do what must be done. We surmount our fear in the heat of transformation.*"

Bernie took a deep breath of fresh air and pulled out her flashlight. She already had her weapon in hand. Then she yelled into the
lodge, "I'm a police officer. Everyone in there, out right now! Crawl
toward my voice, the light, the open door. Your lives depend on it."

She heard whimpering and moaning, but no one came forward.
She yelled again. This time she heard a woman's faint "Can't move.
We need help."

Bernie lowered herself to hands and knees and crawled into the space to avoid the smoke. In the dim light that came through the entrance and with the help of her flashlight, she saw women in their undergarments, their skin aglow with sweat. The flashlight's beam showed her that their wrists and ankles were bound with tape, just as Chee's had been.

Setting aside her growing sense of horror, she got to work. She had to act fast before someone died.

She could only save one woman at a time, she realized. She began with the slim young woman closest to the open door, to create a clearer path for the others. The oppressive heat in the cave-like space made her hands so sweaty that she struggled to keep a grip on the woman's muscular arms. As Bernie moved her inch by inch toward the opening, the woman grunted and tried to help. When they reached a space near the door where the air was slightly cooler, Bernie took out her knife to cut the restraints, but the woman pulled away.

"I can wriggle myself outside. Save the others."

Bernie watched the woman roll onto her belly and crawl forward, using knees and elbows, before she collapsed onto the dirt. She coughed. "Sorry. Nothing to eat for the last three days . . ."

Bernie put her face close to the struggling woman's ear. "You're almost there. Keep moving."

But the woman's eyes closed. Even though her own lungs ached from the smoke, Bernie eased the woman onto her back and started pulling her out. She knew there was no point in freeing the woman's hands until they were both in the fresh air. Breathing became a conscious effort.

As they reached the stronger light of the doorway, Bernie noticed a spiral tattoo on the woman's neck. She pulled the woman free, and in the fresher air she began to revive. Bernie felt better, too. She stood and looked for water, for the woman and for herself.

Someone behind her was calling her name. "Bernie? Officer Manuelito?"

She recognized the voice. "Alisa. This is bad. These women could suffocate. Help me get them out."

"I know what to do." Alisa came closer. "I'll do just as Leader asked of us. I gave you a chance to join us, but now I'll help you die."

She pushed Bernie hard, forcing her off balance and into the open door of the sweat lodge. At the last moment Bernie used her boot to keep the door open, then grabbed for it, pushing hard against Alisa's weight and catching her by surprise. Alisa took a few steps away from the door, and Bernie scrambled out of the sweat lodge and threw herself against the larger woman. The impact brought Alisa to the ground on her back.

Bernie leaped to her feet and drew her weapon.

"Alisa, stop this. Listen to me. You're—" But before Bernie could finish, Alisa grabbed Bernie's left leg to pull her down. Bernie jerked free and stumbled backward, crashing into the building with her right shoulder with an impact hard enough to make her weapon slip from her sweaty hand. Agile for a woman of her weight, Alisa was now standing. She reached for Bernie's hair and shoved her left hand into her face.

Bernie was quick. She grabbed the arm to pull her face free and twisted skin, fat, and muscle with all her strength.

Alisa loosened her grip on Bernie's hair just enough for Bernie to grab the woman's throat and press to cut off her breath. She pushed Alisa against the wall of the sweat lodge and felt her weaken. Then with a groan, Alisa leaned forward, using her head for a hard blow to Bernie's collarbone. She gripped Bernie's shirt and tried again to force her toward the open door of the sweat lodge. They struggled, sweaty and panting. Finally, Bernie kicked Alisa hard, a strong shot to the knee. Alisa fell again. Bernie heard the thud as the woman's skull hit the ground. Alisa moaned, and then the big woman fell silent.

Bernie retrieved her weapon. She knew she would have used it if it hadn't slipped out of her grasp, but she was glad she hadn't fired. She handcuffed Alisa and left her where she lay.

Taking a few deep breaths, she assessed the damage the fight had caused her. She could deal with it later. Women could be dying in the claustrophobic heat. She noticed that the woman she'd rescued sitting against the wall, which caught some shade. Bernie used her knife to cut through the woman's bonds.

"Thanks," the woman said. "Save the others."

Bernie went into the sweat lodge and quickly killed the fire. She pulled the next woman free, then struggled back for a third woman. This one was heavier. Bernie worked hard to drag her outside, and each breath now came with effort. When that woman was finally free, Bernie rolled on her back, gasping to put as much air as she could into her hard-pushed lungs.

She closed her eyes to settle her spirit, noticing the cooling air against her sweaty skin. She knew she would go back inside, help the others, and do what she could for Alisa. But for a few stolen moments, she waited for her heart to slow and the pounding of blood in her veins to quiet.

Was that water she felt flowing over the tops of her pant legs, soaking through to her hot skin? She came back into her body and opened her eyes. The first woman she had pulled to safety was standing next to her with a garden hose. She was young and fit-looking and gave Bernie a huge smile as she spoke.

"Here." She handed Bernie the hose. "Drink."

Bernie put the water on her face and let some flow into her mouth.

"I'm Uliana Belkina. You saved my life."

"You have a beautiful name."

"Thank you. We have to get my friends out of there."

Bernie looked at the woman more closely and recognized her green eyes. This was the person who had told her to be careful when she first arrived.

"Let's get back to it," she said.

Helping the exhausted women was easier as a two-person task. Together they moved them, one by one, outside into the shade and freed their hands and feet. Without their long-sleeved shirts and pants, Bernie could see that many of the woman had bruises in various stages of healing. Clothes could conceal the physical damage, but Bernie knew dealing with the psychological wound would be more difficult.

After everyone was out, Bernie attended to Alisa. She removed the shoes from the woman's swollen feet, both for comfort and to discourage her from walking away. The shoulder she had injured in the fight must be painful; Bernie could see that it was dislocated.

"Alisa, would you like help to sit up?"

"Leave me alone." Alisa glared at both of them, grimacing as she eased her way to a seated position by herself. She cursed Bernie and then turned to Uliana. "And you? Traitor! We were sisters for righteousness. You know what Leader said: 'Only sacred heat and the word from The Great Beyond can save us from eternal darkness, and by our endless prayer we help save the earth.' He told us to stay in the sweat lodge as the true test of our commitment."

"Stay until we die?" Uliana glanced at the clear blue sky and the mountains. "No. That was idiocy. Insane garbage. Leader and Case betrayed us. Why did we allow it? Leader dehumanized us, denying us our full names. I'm reclaiming mine. Uliana Belkina." She emphasized the last word. "Sure, the environment is in bad shape. But our deaths would only have added to the terrific toll of violence. I want no part of that. Do you?"

Alisa cursed her again. "You're evil. Leader knew we all are evil. That's why he had us bind our hands and feet. In case we weren't strong enough to stay in the heat. To feel the fire."

"No. Everything Case and Leader said was a pack of lies." Uliana said again. "I think they brainwashed us. They're the ones who deserve to rot in the dark place. Not us."

"Shut up!" Alisa yelled. "That cop has perverted you. She's going to hell, too, along with everyone who doesn't follow Leader's way to The Great Beyond."

"How is it that you know so much about hell?" Bernie said. "I think you've had a sample of it here."

Uliana turned to Bernie. "So, where is Case? Where's Leader?"

"I don't know exactly, but the FBI is here, and those guys are on their radar."

Uliana nodded. "Tell them to look in the RV. They call it the Temple of Righteousness. It's where Leader and Caseman punish women who don't follow the rules. They video the punishment and show it to everyone in the tent to keep us scared."

Bernie felt a chill. "What about men who . . ."

"They suffer, too. We had to watch the video of what happened to Pat. We all respected him. Case had made him assistant producer for the videos. He was a good guy. But Leader found out that he was the brother of the woman who is the secretary of energy. Pat didn't deny it. He said his sister wanted to help heal the earth, too, but she also understood that the world needed the resources that came from mining. He urged Leader and Case to rethink their craziness."

Uliana spoke like someone who had been keeping a terrible secret and finally had permission to set it loose. Her words tumbled out.

"Leader went off the rails and started preaching about how women like Pat's sister were weak and easily turned toward evil, and how it was a disgrace to have a female in that position. Pat defended his sister—he even said she was doing a wonderful job. Then he announced that he would leave our chosen family if Case and Leader couldn't tone down the rhetoric. Pat tried to get away without more conflict, but Leader told him he was an apostate and had to suffer the consequences."

Uliana's green eyes began to fill with tears, and she stopped talking.

"What consequences?"

"Men who step out of line have to fight. Case picks the opponent. It's usually Rollie. The worse their sin, the worse the fight. Pat had to fight to the death but Rollie wouldn't do that so Victor came in. We had to watch."

Bernie gave Uliana time to collect her emotions. Then she asked, "What happened to the body?"

Uliana shrugged. "They dumped it somewhere."

Bernie checked on the women they'd rescued, encouraged them to dress, and told them that the FBI would want to interview each of them.

"Sisters," Alisa yelled, "don't believe anything she says! She's one of them, not one of us."

Bernie sat down next to Alisa and spoke softly. "You were Rollie's partner, right?"

"Why should I tell you anything?"

"Because I can tell you're a leader here. That's why Caseman gave you the big sweat lodge assignment."

"Case told me to keep the fire going inside so the heat would purify us. He told me to watch, and when most of the women fell asleep, I should go in myself and close the door. Then he would come and make sure our sacrifice was complete.

"With the door closed, no one could leave. Case would make the video of our great sacrifice, and then set the flames to consume our bodies. Didn't you see the wood piled near the lodge and the gas can?" And now, rather than anger, Bernie heard pain in Alisa's words. "Leader is a man of deep wisdom, a person far greater than the rest of us. Why didn't you let me do what I should have done? We've lost the chance for a better life through sacrifice."

"No." Uliana frowned. "We never agreed to die. Only to pray in the sweat lodge. To pray for restoration of the earth. We all want to help Mother Earth grow healthy. But at the cost of our own lives?

Think about that, Alisa. Those men took advantage of us and they took our money, too."

"She's right," Bernie said.

Alisa readjusted herself against the building and winced in pain again. "All you cops are part of the conspiracy. You work with the dark forces that want to take away our freedoms."

Bernie shook her head. "No one needs to take your freedom, Alisa. You gave it away."

Bernie turned away. Time to check on Chee. And maybe head for home before too much longer.

Uliana got Bernie's attention. "Before you go, the oldest lady in our family wants to talk to you."

Bernie squatted next to her. "Officer, thank you. I have kidney problems, and I thought I would die in there. I told Caseman that when he picked me for the first group, but he said I should be an example. You probably think we're all crazy, but the planet is in such a discouraging state, it made us feel better to think this protest might get the powerful forces in Washington to put an end to mining. Starting with uranium."

"I understand. Rest now. Give your body and your brain and emotions time to settle. You'll find safer ways to put your ideas to action."

Chapter 39

Officer Manuelito's phone chimed. She pulled it out, surprised that it worked, and saw that a text from Sage Johnson had somehow managed to get through the dead zone.

Johnson had kept the message simple: U @ Yazzie revival camp?

Instead of texting, Bernie tried a call. Johnson answered and Bernie gave her an update. She explained about the traumatized women and how she had handcuffed Alisa after the assault.

"Several of the people I pulled out of the sweat lodge may need medical attention."

"An ambulance is on the way," Johnson said. "This is a disaster. The secretary's brother, James P. Sethley, known as Pat to CUSP, died because someone figured out he was spying for the FBI. According to Dobbs and Monahan, he never delivered his final packet of information about CUSP's financial dealings and its plan for the secretary. That's enough to send the people in charge here to prison for a long time. That's why I'm here."

Bernie knew there were also other reasons for Pat's death but that could come later. "What about Caseman and Leader? Have you arrested them?"

Johnson's voice had the hint of a smile. "Not yet. We believe they are among the people in the convoy that included Chee's stolen unit. No one is talking, of course, but they all had those red spiral tattoos." Johnson exhaled. "What's that about?"

"I think it's a version of a famous petroglyph at Chaco Canyon. The basis for the Sun Dagger solstice marker." Bernie took a breath. "It's appropriate for CUSP not only because they plan their big events around the solstice, but also because the land around Chaco Canyon is disputed territory for oil and gas extraction. Next to uranium mining, that's what has CUSP upset."

Bernie looked around. "Have you seen Chee?"

"I noticed him heading toward that motor home. That's my next stop as soon as I get things organized here." Johnson glanced toward the RV and then back to Bernie. "That new officer, Roper Black, flagged me down right before I texted you. He had a man in custody, a guy with a goatee. Roper said he's Victor Graystone. He told me Victor had assaulted you and Mr. Yazzie. Are you OK?"

"More or less. I'm going to check on Mr. Yazzie and then I'll meet you at the motor home."

***

No one responded when Bernie knocked on the Yazzies' front door, and the house was locked, as she would have recommended. But when she went around back she found the kitchen door open. "Mr. Yazzie? It's Bernie."

No response.

"Mr. Yazzie?"

More silence. She stepped inside. Bernie remembered Mrs. Yazzie and her husband as meticulous housekeepers. Now the place was a mess. Rugs were crumpled, furniture shoved out of place, and toy trucks and books for beginning readers dumped on the floor. Even the bedroom showed signs of disruption. The double bed was unmade, and the blanket and pillow someone had placed on the floor were disturbed. Dresser drawers hung open, the clothes that had been inside now on the floor.

This must have been the work of Goatee, she thought, or disruptions caused by someone else who worked for Caseman. She knew why they had come back and she worried for Mr. Yazzie and the boy.

She searched the house and found no invader and no Yazzies. Maybe they were outside with the horses. Mr. Yazzie couldn't ride with his broken rib, but maybe they had hidden in the barn. She had turned to leave through the back door, but then from somewhere near the bedroom, she heard a moan and thought of Mr. Yazzie's injury. She went back to the bedroom. No one was there. She looked in the bathroom and it was empty, too. Mr. Yazzie wasn't there.

She turned to leave when she heard the sound again. This time, she followed it to a solid wall covered with wood paneling. Odd.

"Mr. Yazzie?" She spoke to the wall in Navajo to make the message more convincing. "Sir, it's Bernie Manuelito. You in there? Is the boy with you?"

She put her ear to the wall and heard something moving. There must be a way to get inside, a secret passage somewhere. Bernie looked at the wall closely and then used her hands to examine it, but found no obvious entrance.

"Mr. Yazzie, it's safe now. I'll help you out, but I can't find any opening in the wall. Tell me how."

Nothing.

She felt along the wall again, finding no door or hinges. Then she remembered the popsicle, and the code word. They had used the boy's name.

"Sam?"

Nothing.

Then it came to her. "Sprout?"

A small voice said, "Here I am." It came from behind the solid wall. She remembered that someone had mentioned a secret hiding place.

"I'm glad you are there. Is your grandfather OK?"

"He's sleeping. I tried to wake him up. But I couldn't."

"Sam, how did you get in that hiding place?"

"Shicheii said we should be in here and opened the door. But now he is sleeping."

"Sam, can you open the door?"

"No. I don't know how."

Bernie tried to visualize the secret door. It must have some sort of hardware.

"Do you see the door handle?"

"No." Then the boy started to cry. "Shicheii, wake up." The child's crying grew louder, loud enough to disturb a sleeping man. But Bernie heard nothing from Mr. Yazzie. She feared the worst. If she had to, she could find tool and break through the wall, but she'd try to work with Sam first.

"Remember when we talked about turtles, and how they are safe in their shell?"

"Uh-huh."

"So that place where you and Shicheii are now, that's like your own shell. You are safe in there, right?"

"I want out."

"Yes, so you will get to be a clever turtle. You know something else about turtles?"

Bernie waited while he thought.

"They go slow."

"Right. They go slow, and they figure things out. Can you do that just like a turtle would?"

"Yes."

"So, go slow and look around in your shell very carefully. Look at the walls, and see if there is anything special."

She heard the boy moving inside the secret closet.

"I see a little hole. It's round."

Bernie tried to visualize what he was looking at. She leaned back against the wall, and it shifted slightly. That gave her an idea.

"Can you reach the hole?"

"No."

Bernie thought a moment. "Why not?"

"I'm too little."

"What if you stood up?"

More noise, and then, "Should I put my finger in there?"

"Yes."

"I'm scared." She heard him whimpering. "What if there's a spider in the hole?"

"Take a deep breath. Then blow in the hole. Blow really hard with all your air."

She heard him do it.

"Good. I'm glad you are brave so you can put your finger in the hole."

"What does brave mean again?"

"It's doing the right thing even though you're scared. Because you are brave, you will put your finger in the hole."

"I did it!"

"Now push to the side to open the door for your grandfather."

"What side?"

"You can figure out the way that's easiest. Give it a try."

She noticed the wall moving ever so slightly.

"You did it. Can you push again?"

"It hurts my finger."

"Try another finger."

"This is hard."

"I'm glad you are so brave."

After his third try, Bernie was able to shove the toe of her boot into the small opening, She slid the wall a bit more, making enough space for her hand to slip between the wall and the edge of the door and push it open.

The space that concealed the boy and the man was larger than she expected, and very warm.

She gave the child a hug. "You did well. I'm proud of you."

Mr. Yazzie sat on the floor, his legs straight in front of him, his back against the wall. His head had slumped against his chest, which rose and fell with his breath.

Bernie put her hand on his arm and he opened his eyes. After the flow of fresh air from the rest of the house began to revive him, she asked the first question. "What happened?"

"The man with the beard came back for the laptop. Sam was very brave. We'll talk later."

"Did he get the computer?"

"No. Mrs. Yazzie hid it in here. It's on that shelf in a bag that says *Christmas.*"

Bernie called Agent Johnson on her cell in the hopes that both cell phones might still work, and they did. She explained the situation at the Yazzie house, and learned that the paramedics who were assessing the debilitated women would come for Mr. Yazzie.

"I'd like your insights and help over here," Johnson said. "Chee's, too. Is he with you?"

"No," Bernie said. "CUSP headquarters is that fancy RV. I'm sure that's where he is."

Johnson said, "That's where I'm headed now. Evidently someone made videos of the daily life of the CUSP group. Sethley sent some to his contacts in Washington. I bet the group kept records of all that in there."

Bernie knew Case had recorded Chee's assault; that would be important evidence. "I'll meet you there," she said.

"I'll be a minute. We're finishing interviews with these cult members about the murder and the plan to kidnap the secretary. Everyone we talked to agrees that Caseman presented the secretary to them as evil. An evil to be eliminated for the good of the planet."

After the call, Bernie explained to Mr. Yazzie that the medics were coming to evaluate him and see what came next. She was talking to him when Officer Black arrived.

"Hey," Bernie said. "What's the story on Goatee?"

"I turned him over to the FBI. They had a warrant for him on a gun charge, so the assault on you and Mr. Yazzie will be added to the list." He told her that when he left the tent, Chee's chanting had already started to calm the cult members.

Bernie motioned to Roper to join her in the other room. She told him that Mr. Yazzie might need to go to the hospital. And that she wanted to go to the motor home to meet Chee.

"I'll wait for the ambulance. What about the boy?" Black answered his own question. "I'll call Mrs. Yazzie at her sister's house so Sam can go there. I know where Mrs. Yazzie's sister lives and it's on my way to the station."

"Good plan."

Bernie saw Roper sit on the floor next to Sam in the secret closet. After a moment he said, "I heard that you would like to hear the siren in my police car."

The boy nodded.

"I could take you for a ride and turn on the siren. We could go to your grandmother's sister's house. Your grandmother is there and she wants to see you. Does your grandfather agree?"

Mr. Yazzie nodded. "That's a great plan."

Bernie said she would see them again soon and headed to the RV.

***

At CUSP headquarters, the FBI believed the RV could contain the master list with the full names and financial information for members of the cult. The records might tie them to what Johnson had mentioned earlier: violent disruptions and criminal offenses in other communities around the United States and unsolved incidents of serious vandalism, destruction of public property, and more.

Bernie wanted to see justice for these men, especially after what she'd found in the sweat lodge. With all the talk of heat and fire, she wondered if Caseman's plan included setting the RV ablaze.

The door to the motor home was open, and she could hear noise from inside. She drew her Glock and announced herself.

"Bernie," Chee responded, "it's OK. Come on in." His voice had a surprising calmness to it. "Rollie and I are figuring things out."

"What?"

Bernie saw Chee seated next to the huge handcuffed man at the kitchen table in the motor home. She felt some of her tension drain away. Chee looked better. He was sorting through a collection of zip drives on the tabletop.

Chee saw the expression on her face.

"We're trying to find a copy of the video of Pat's fight, and the one that talks about their plans for the secretary."

"Case always made a backup copy on a flash drive in case the file got corrupted or something. He dated each thumb drive and wrote a little description."

"See this?" Chee said.

In tiny black script she read day/month/year and then *sweat lodge*.

"Some of these are instructions for the family," Rollie said. "But I know they also recorded finances and made a video with Caseman and Leader, talking about how the secretary's visit would help save Mother Earth. The videos must be here somewhere."

Bernie noticed that Rollie seemed less boisterous than when she had met him earlier that day. "I hear that you fought Pat."

He looked away, and when he turned back, she saw the grief in his eyes. "I liked the guy. I wouldn't have laid a hand on him, but Leader and Caseman threatened to have Victor hurt me if I refused to fight. So I slugged him a few times and he got some licks in, but then I stepped away. They wanted a fight to the death. I couldn't take his life. They turned him over to Victor, and after Pat died, Victor hurt me pretty bad. If I refused orders again, they said I'd be dead for insubordination."

Rollie shifted on the bench. "Ever since they told me that being the punisher was my job in the family, I've been trying to find a way out. I was glad when you showed up, and then the lieutenant. But every time I could have talked to one of you, you know, asked for help, something happened.

"I had to get over here and find the video of the murder. I knew you and Lieutenant Chee had figured out that something was wrong before the FBI showed up and hauled me away."

Chee kept his eyes on the thumb drives. "What do they do with the money the members pay them?"

"Oh, they are buying a place in the mountains where we can all live, farm, raise animals, and help restore the planet firsthand."

"When will that happen?"

"I don't know. They don't give us project reports on that dream. Some of the money goes for food and shelter, or actions like this one. Leader says he invests in research on alternative energy like wind, solar, and geothermal, so mining can stop. And then he helps with groups that focus on population control, healthier farming, saving the rain forest, stuff like that."

"They are lying," Bernie said. "CUSP is evil."

Chee said, "I'd like to see those records and so would the FBI."

"Sure," Rollie said. "There's got to be a copy of those reports here somewhere, too. Case is obsessed with recording everything."

Bernie continued to watch for Johnson. Despite Rollie's new congeniality, she was glad to see him cuffed.

"Do they make financial reports to the family?"

Rollie raised his eyebrows. "No, ma'am—Officer. The family trusts them."

Chee jumped in. "If the financial reports are here, I bet they show that the men in charge have been stealing from the membership, using the money to pad their own bank accounts."

"No." Rollie's eyes opened wider. "Case is like a brother to me. And Leader, well . . ."

Bernie heard the hint of doubt. "Rollie, these are the men who threatened to kill you if you didn't kill a man you liked. They hurt women. And they wanted you to kill Lieutenant Chee, right?"

He nodded.

Bernie heard a vehicle roll up outside. Her adrenaline raced as she went to the window. It was Agent Johnson in a dusty SUV. Then she saw a black sedan that looked more like a typical FBI vehicle and a man in a suit climbed out.

The FBI agents came inside.

Chee introduced Bernie to Agent Dobbs and explained why he had arrested Rollie and read him his rights. "What's all that on the table?" Dobbs asked.

"Evidence," Chee explained.

Dobbs picked up a flash drive. "Evidence of what?"

"Well, probably Pat's murder, financial shenanigans, the plot to attack the secretary, and the decision to put women in the sweat lodge as a sacrifice."

Johnson, usually calm, looked annoyed.

"Pat. James P. Sethley. P as in Patrick or Patricio. The reason you and Monahan came out here. The guy with the hat and the turtle ring. The secretary's brother."

Johnson turned to Rollie.

"What do you know about James P. Sethley?" she asked.

"We called him Pat, and he was the assistant producer here. He helped me and Case with the videos. Until Chee told me, I didn't know his full name. I'll never forget the date of the fight, and that's what I wanted to find. But it's not here."

"So you assumed Sethley's murder would be on one of these?" Johnson's disbelief came through in her tone. "Why do that?"

"To keep the rest of the family obedient." Rollie said. "If it happened to Pat, it could happen to anybody. I'm sure it was videoed."

"What else might be missing?" Johnson said.

"It's hard to say for sure," Rollie said, "but I know the camera was running when they drugged and questioned Chee. I doubt that Caseman had time to copy that one. It's probably still on his phone or the computer."

Bernie frowned. "*Questioned* isn't the right word, is it? He was assaulted by Caseman and Leader . . ."

"Tell me about that," Johnson said.

Chee explained. "Leader wanted to have me killed, the same as Sethley, but Caseman intervened. Their discussion got heated. Case was recording the whole time. The video will be proof of assault on a police officer and the secretary kidnapping plan."

He turned to Dobbs. "You aren't here by coincidence. What's your connection to CUSP and the secretary?"

The agent hesitated until Johnson nodded to him. "Go ahead. Tell him while I take Rollie to the tent for processing." And they left.

"Sethley worked for us out of Washington, at least at first," he said. "We think Caseman and Leader got to him. We hadn't heard from him for a while, and with the secretary's visit, we worried that maybe he'd give CUSP too much information about her." Dobbs paused.

"Caseman takes pride in his documentary videos, but he's no fool. He's probably deleted that incriminating recording of your assault. I'm surprised any of these copies are here. Surprised and relieved. They'll help with the case against CUSP."

"Rollie said one of his jobs was to back up everything on Case's phone and computer," Chee said.

Dobbs's phone buzzed, and he glanced at it, then picked up a call. Bernie and Chee watched his face change as he listened, from neutral, to surprised, to angry. All he said was "OK." And then "Thanks for letting me know."

He shook his head. "That was Agent Monahan. When they stopped the black SUVs, the Navajo cop car, and the truck, the men in them starting shooting. One of our agents was wounded. Two of the CUSP men are dead. They arrested major players in the cult, but none of them is Leader or Caseman."

"We had a report that Leader drove a black Mercedes," said Dobbs. "Have either of you seen it?"

"I don't remember seeing a car like that parked here when I came in," Chee said.

Bernie spoke up. "I saw an abandoned car that turned out to be a Mercedes at Teec Nos Pos parked outside a building where some noisy construction was going on. Someone called to let us know. He thought it seemed suspicious. When I ran the check, it turned out the plates on it were stolen. Caseman and Leader had something going there."

Johnson returned a few minutes later, looking unhappy. "Agents have been searching the compound, but there's no sign of Caseman or Leader." She glanced at the tent and then turned her gaze to the sweat lodge. "Whatever they planned at Teec Nos Pos with Leader's Mercedes was connected to all of this."

"How are you going to apprehend Caseman and Leader?" Bernie wanted specifics.

"We've got roadblocks up, and people watching for them at the airports. We're asking everyone here if any vehicles are missing. So far, we've come up empty, but some of these people are still true believers."

Johnson turned to Bernie. "I heard about what happened to your unit. Let me know if you need a ride. You, too, Chee."

Chee looked puzzled.

"I'll go back to the Yazzie place to take another look at it." Bernie remembered the damage to the hood and that it wouldn't start. "Maybe it's not as hopeless as I first thought."

"Thanks for everything," said Johnson. "You and Chee will have to provide some testimony in this case. But at least you don't have to worry about the secretary's visit."

Chee looked exhausted, and Bernie realized she was tired, too. It was time to go.

Dobbs announced that he was done. "Sethley was a good man. I knew and respected him—that's one reason I wanted to be here when I heard he was in trouble. I'm sorry he's dead, but what he shared with us over the months . . ." Dobbs stopped, and Bernie read the emotion in his face. "He might have saved his sister's life. That's a memorable legacy. But now that this is over, there's another thing that brought me here."

Chee glanced out the window. "I know it's not the landscape. You're a city guy, right? You aren't crazy about all this open country."

"I'm not fond of the scenery, but I admire you Navajos. You've got determination. You don't give up. Years ago, as a dumb beginner, I worked a case out here with a smart detective. Joe Leaphorn. Have you two heard of him?"

"Yeah. Good man." Chee kept a straight face. Dobbs obviously didn't know that Leaphorn had been his boss and remained his mentor.

"I figured as long as I was out this way, I'd look him up. Do you guys know how I can reach him?"

Dobbs left with Leaphorn's phone numbers, and Bernie and Chee walked back to the Yazzie house to check on her department-issued SUV. She told Chee what had happened.

"At first, I was puzzled about how I could have been in an accident and not remembered. But then I flashed on the guy with the goatee and I realized why my head hurt.

"He's known as Victor. He must have carried you to the car after he knocked you out, then tried to drive away to hide the vehicle but got it stuck in the sand. It won't be hard to rock the car out of here if we can get it running." Chee raised the damaged hood and fiddled around with something. "Try starting it now. I reconnected the battery."

She pushed the ignition and the engine came to life.

"Thanks," she said.

"You would have noticed that battery issue and fixed it yourself, but I'm glad I could help."

"I've had enough excitement." He heard the exhaustion in her voice. "Let's check on Mr. Yazzie and go home."

Chee nodded. "Mrs. Yazzie warned me to expect the unexpected. Today lived up to that—losing you, you finding me, chanting with a bunch of misguided white people."

Bernie said, "There's been so much unexpected, we must be done with it."

Chapter 40

Mr. Yazzie had been transported in the ambulance and Sam was safe with Roper and heading to his grandmother. Bernie and Chee made sure things were secure before they left the house. Agent Johnson confirmed that Alisa had also gone to the hospital in cuffs, along with some of the other women that Bernie and Uliana Belkina had rescued. Alisa had been arrested and was under guard. Several of the women cult members had given statements about the abuse they suffered from Caseman and Leader.

"It's been a long day. Let's make sure the horses are OK and go home," Bernie said.

"Sure," he said. "But I'd like to sit here a minute first and be grateful we survived."

The Yazzie home phone rang, and Bernie picked up. The caller was Darleen.

"Oh, thank goodness you finally answered. I was worried about you and Cheeseburger. It's not like you guys to be out of touch. Sandra gave me this number. What's going on?"

"Oh, lots of stuff." The question caught Bernie off guard. Where to start? "It's complicated. But nothing to worry about now." She wanted to hear Darleen's story, not narrate her own. "What's up with you?"

"Well, that's why I called. We've got a situation here, and I need your help."

Bernie felt her heart sink. She noticed that the Yazzies' landline had a speaker function and pressed it so Chee could hear, too.

"Darleen, are you with Mama?"

"No. Remember, I told you I was going to Phoenix with Greg, Mrs. R's son-in-law?"

"What? You didn't tell me."

"Oh, maybe I told Chee. I know I told Bigman and Sandra."

"Phoenix! Chee's here, too. Talk to both of us." Bernie felt her heart beat faster. "What happened?"

"I called to tell you everything. Be patient, OK?" Darleen spoke more slowly. "Mrs. R and her grandson got caught up in something that's wrong, you know, really bad. And they aren't the only ones. And yes, we did call the police. And we found Mrs. R and Droid."

"Droid? What?" Darleen knew how to drive her crazy.

"His real name is Andrew, but they call him Droid, and he's seventeen. He shouldn't even have been allowed to get on the van."

"Wait, I'm not following this," Bernie said.

Chee leaned closer. "Give us the details from the start, OK?"

Darleen laid it out, and they asked a litany of questions.

Chee frowned at the phone. "Mrs. Raymond and her grandson and the people there with them aren't the only ones tricked by these scammers. I've heard from other families whose relatives have disappeared. Your friends got caught in a huge scheme. Big sums of federal Medicaid money are involved in this sleazy operation. We are working with Phoenix area law enforcement to help bring these relatives back home but there are a lot of complications to this."

"I'm glad something's happening," Darleen said. "Some of the people Greg and I saw are in bad shape."

"You need to be careful. These scammers are dangerous." Chee decided to give Darleen more information. "We're working with a group called Rainbow Bridge. My contact in Phoenix is Sergeant Chandler. I'm going to tell him what you told me so he can get to the hotel right away, before those people are dispersed. I know that his team will want to talk to Mrs. Raymond and her grandson, and probably you and the boy's father. And the woman from the agency who made the call for Mrs. Raymond."

Darleen found the number for Gigi and gave it to Chee. "She's afraid she might lose her job because of helping Mrs. R, so she called me on her cell. I'll tell the sergeant everything I saw, and I'm sure Greg will help, too. He's really angry about all this."

"A lot of us are. Keep your phone turned on for Chandler. And give yourself some credit. You did a good thing."

Bernie jumped in. "Sister, you and the people with you need to get out of there. Like Chee said, there's a lot of money involved in this scam, and money can make some people vicious."

"I get it. You don't have to . . ." The frustration in Darleen's voice said the rest.

"I can't help it," Bernie said. "I know too much about how bad people can be."

"I worry about you, too," Darleen said. "I promise I'll be careful." Then she asked, "How is Mama doing? I've been thinking of her all day today. I called but only spoke to Mrs. Bigman."

"She's fine." As Bernie said it, she realized that that was just an assumption. She hadn't spoken to Mrs. Bigman to get a report.

"Let Mama know I miss her. Don't forget to tell her that today is the solstice."

"I will," Bernie said.

Chee went to the living room to call the Phoenix PD. When Chandler answered, Chee put the call on speaker. "Another officer on my team, Bernadette Manuelito, is here with me."

"Hey, Manuelito. Welcome." The voice on the phone sounded energized. "The information we might get from those latest Shiprock victims will help break a case we've been working for months. It's not just one bad player. The problem is wide and deep." He explained how the scam worked, with details that matched what Darleen had said. "The whole thing is a huge, cruel con job. If the victims want out, sometimes they have to break a window or something to escape. Sometimes they die from liver failure or get stranded here in The Valley with no way home."

Bernie said, "I've heard that they even take advantage of children and elderly women."

"Whoever they can find. One kid they had signed up for alcoholism treatment was only six." Chandler's tone grew lighter. "It's great to have the Navajo Police Department in the loop, to help figure out how to get these folks home."

"I agree," Chee said. "But we have to find them first."

"Transportation back to the Navajo Nation should have been included in the treatment contracts, right?" Bernie said.

She heard a siren in the background, and Chandler spoke more loudly. "Those contracts are nothing but a bunch of broken promises. The case Chee just told me about is rare, you know, with a friend or relative able to help. A lot of these folk have lost their connections with their kinfolks. You've both seen that."

"When are you going to talk to Mrs. Raymond and her grandson? My sister is with them, and she's eager to get back here."

"Let me have the numbers, and I'll make the calls. We want to close down these places, ASAP."

"When someone contacts the elderly lady, face-to-face would be better. She could be embarrassed." Bernie thought about how to phrase what came next. "That's probably true for many of these folks, and some of them will be more comfortable speaking in Navajo. Do you have any Navajos on your team who can do these interviews?"

"Not right now. I have an idea I want to follow up on when I get more info. I'll call Chee, OK?"

"Sure," Chee said. "We are wrapping up some loose ends on a case we just handed over to the FBI."

When the call ended, they went to check on the horses. Bernie filled the water trough while Chee put alfalfa in the feed bins and securely closed the corral gate. She saw the bridle Mr. Yazzie had hoped to use for the horseback ride with Sam that never happened.

Bernie and Chee went back to the house for a drink of water before they left. They heard the Yazzies' phone ringing. Chee picked it up. It was Chandler.

"Not much cell service out there. Glad I got you. Manuelito still there?

"I'm here," she said.

"I'll be quick. Can you two come to Phoenix? You guys could really help with the questions. My boss talked to your chief, and they're fine with Navajo PD coming out this way for a few days to bail us out of this crisis."

Chee and Bernie glanced at each other, momentarily speechless.

"Both of us?" Chee asked.

"That's what I'd like. You both speak Navajo, and you're both cops, so you know the rules when it comes to interviews. We can pay for a flight into Phoenix for you, and a van, or even two, for you to use to drive back to the Navajo Nation with folks who want to return."

"When?" Bernie asked.

"I'm working on that."

Chee said. "It's been a long, long day and the captain is out so I'm running the office. Let me think about it."

"I second that thinking part," Bernie said. "I'll let you know."

"You guys are our first choices," Chandler said. "The extent of the fraud and human trafficking means that a whole range of law enforcement will be sorting things out. We need to get this rolling. Let me know." He ended the call.

They looked at each other. "We've got a lot to think about," she said.

He gave Bernie a thumbs-up. "Let's go, Officer. We can think in the car."

"OK, Captain. You're the boss."

* * *

Jim Chee was glad to be with Bernie, glad that the day was done, glad that he was still alive and that his smart wife had survived the attempt on her life. Bernie told him she had a headache and he expected that both of them would be sore, at the very least, for the next few days.

When they drove near the white tent they noticed FBI vehicles still there, agents talking with the cult members. One of the men Chee had seen in the tent waved to them as they drew close, and then walked over to Bernie's damaged vehicle.

"Officers, I want to say thanks. We were headed in the wrong direction. You brought us back. That was powerful chanting." The man gave him a soft smile. "We heard what had happened to Officer Manuelito and to Mr. Yazzie. On behalf of all the good people in our family, I apologize. What happened to Caseman and Leader?"

"I haven't heard." And even if he had heard, Chee knew it wasn't his place to share the information.

"You probably don't know about our money either, do you?"

"That's right, but Rollie is under arrest and talking with the FBI."

"Rollie?" The man stood a bit straighter. "Poor Rollie. Being required to kill a man or die. He always spoke up for the family. Bless him for standing tall even against The Great Beyond."

Chee said, "The Great Beyond? Do you believe that Leader was getting special messages?"

The man shook his head. "No. Not anymore. We all were tricked and cheated while Leader and Caseman took our money. But that's done now. You guys be safe getting out of here."

Bernie said, "Have you thought about what's next?"

He nodded. "We're leaving together, caravanning as soon as the FBI says we can go. Heading to Chaco Canyon even though the solstice is over. We've got a lot of thinking to do. Thinking and grieving, I guess. The loss of our friend Pat, the loss of trust in people we believed in." His voice choked with emotion. "Uliana and the other women are providing excellent leadership. We're going to reach out to Pat's sister, the secretary, with our condolences. We might even form a new group in his honor to work on environmental issues. But no violence. And no demeaning anyone."

"Good luck with everything," Chee said.

Bernie drove. When they finally had a phone signal, Chee used her phone to call Mrs. Bigman to check on Mama.

Mama's companion answered at the first ring. "Bernie? Thank goodness. I heard about the fiasco with the secretary's visit. Is everything OK?"

"It's Chee, but Bernie is here, too. I don't have my phone, so I'm using hers. Hold on." He put the call on speaker.

"I asked Bigman what was going on. It sounds like a mess. I bet you two are ready to come home."

"More than ready," Bernie said.

Mrs. Bigman said, "Hold on. Your mother has been asking to talk to you all afternoon." And then Mama was on the phone.

Over the past few months, talking to her mother when they weren't together had become more of a challenge. She didn't know if Mama couldn't hear well or if she wasn't able to concentrate, but telephone conversations often led to frustration.

"Mama, it's Bernie. I hope you are having a good day."

"Bernie! My daughter! I thought you were dead."

Bernie took a calming breath. "Not dead yet, but I am really tired." She laughed to lighten her heart. "I'll see you soon. I'm heading for home."

But she'd forgotten that hearing the word *home* now made Mama upset. "I need to go home," Mama said, and then said it twice more. "You come and get me. I want to sleep in my own bed. You take me home now."

"I'll be there as soon as I can." Bernie knew that arguing and explaining made no difference.

"If you are really my daughter, you should be here already. This is wrong. I raised you better. And where is the other one?"

Bernie knew she meant Darleen. "She's working, Mama. I'm working, too. We will be with you soon. We love you."

Her mother made a rude noise.

"Mama, I'm doing my best. I can't—" A wave of overwhelming sadness choked her voice.

Chee gently reached for the phone. "Hello, my mother-in-law. I want to thank you for all the kindness you extended to me and to your daughter. Do you remember our wedding?"

Mama didn't respond.

"I will never forget how much happiness was in the hogan. You have helped me move forward as a husband." He went on speaking to Mama in Navajo, slowly, clearly, and with patience and compassion.

Mama, as was her long-hewn habit, neither acknowledged him nor asked him to stop. When he thought he had said enough, he fell silent.

They wondered if Mama would speak.

Then she said, "May you walk in beauty. Come and see me. You should come to see this old lady." She said it again, and said nothing more.

"We will," Chee said, and he ended the call.

They cruised without words until up ahead they saw the Yazzie family's turquoise pickup, pulled onto the side of the road.

Everything about the situation yelled danger.

Chapter 41

Leader and Caseman had congratulated themselves. Stealing the turquoise truck had worked like a charm. Caseman knew it helped that he was about the same size as Mr. Yazzie, and had put on the battered straw hat the old man left in the truck. Leader slumped down in the passenger seat so the deputies couldn't spot him. They planned well, leaving right after the convoy that would capture the secretary.

They were gone long before the sheriff's deputies who would come to the Yazzie place to help the FBI and those Navajo cops. Neighbors in this part of the Navajo Nation had seen the Yazzies driving the turquoise truck for at least a decade, marveling that even a quirky old codger would drive a vehicle like that.

Still, out of caution, they followed Caseman's plan and took a seldom used back road, a short cut that forked to Shiprock or their destination, Teec Nos Pos.

When they got to a place where his cell phone worked, Caseman would call Rollie and learn exactly what had happened at the compound after he and Leader left. But because Leader always knew best, he assumed that the plan had unfolded perfectly. The women would have sacrificed themselves, and Alisa would have videoed the scene. After the Navajo cop died of an overdose, Victor would have disposed of him and the video, as required.

The videos they had left behind would be their legacy, watched and rewatched, spreading their message and their total devotion to the cause and The Great Beyond. After today, there could be no doubt that CUSP would pull out all stops to save the planet.

Earlier that day Rollie had loaded the bags of fertilizer they'd purchased in the back of the black pickup truck, making sure the fake TOXIC and FLAMMABLE labels were clearly visible. Leader had decided to overrule Victor's plan of dumping the fertilizer onto the highway. That would take too long. Instead, the driver, a family member who pledged to die for Mother Earth, would ram the loaded truck into one of the Secret Service vehicles accompanying the secretary. When they got out to examine the damage, they'd see the timer Case had rigged to look enough like a detonator that the FBI would go into high alert because of a possible explosion.

Meanwhile, their people impersonating a security team would have taken advantage of the confusion to grab the secretary and take her in one of the big black cars to the recording studio they had built beyond Teec Nos Pos. Leader had left his new Mercedes at the studio for a getaway.

But one thing had been out of their control. They learned too late from the men in the convoy that Secretary Cooper had cancelled her visit. It was too late to abort the operation, but he'd learned from it. Next time, they'd be smarter. Caseman thought about what came next as he steered the old truck along the endless dirt road. They were heading to swap the truck for Leader's Mercedes and then drive to the Durango airport.

It was warm in the truck. Caseman removed his red windbreaker, steering with one hand. A question still nagged him.

"Sir, may I ask you something?"

Leader, sitting in the passenger seat, turned his body toward Caseman. "Go ahead."

"I'm not questioning your wisdom, but why did all this matter to you so much? I mean, finding the Yazzie property, setting things up for the solstice, arranging for our core group to be here, building the sweat lodge, distributing the flyers. That was a huge amount of work. Wouldn't it have been easier to have captured the secretary at her home in Virginia?"

Caseman listened for Leader's reaction and heard nothing, so he continued. "I am in awe of your ability to receive direction from The Great Beyond, but I am having difficulty seeing the endgame. And I'd be grateful if you could help me understand."

Leader sat back in the seat. "Hey, give me that jacket. I need it for as a pillow."

Caseman kept his eyes on the road as he handed it to Leader and heard the man readjust himself.

"Case, the idea came to me when I learned who the new secretary of energy would be. A woman in that position?" He made a rude noise. "That appointment was the last straw. I knew we had to make our presence known, share our thoughts on the planet's salvation."

Caseman understood that women were the weaker sex, and that this had been the way of the world for most of history. Just consider the story of Adam and Eve. But there must be more to it. Leader hadn't answered his questions.

"Sir, why did the plan involve this remote place and the solstice? I don't get the connection."

"That's because you're an idiot. This is the perfect setting. We have Indians, uranium, and the secretary: that adds up to national public-ity. And, as the cherry on the sundae, everything converges around the solstice, the great time of longest light and great awakening."

Caseman swerved to avoid a pothole in the road. He knew Leader wasn't a man for details. The man's mind, when faced with a complicated issue, boiled it down to the simplest point. Leader liked pictures; that explained his love of video. And that was another passion that tied them together.

Leader talked on in a monologue Case had heard before. "Restricting access to some of the world's largest mining deposits, as the Navajo Nation has done, is part of keeping the planet healthy. And what better time to explain this to the secretary and world than now? What better place than here?"

"Sir, I agree, of course. But what do we do after we get to the studio, remove what we need, and take the Mercedes to the airport?"

"Drive, Case. Just drive. Leave the thinking to me. All will be revealed."

Leader's attitude got on Case's nerves, a sign of his own personal weakness. He knew there was no point in arguing. One of his goals in meditation was to set aside anger, but he was failing at that today. He had done a lot of research in an attempt to link the vast uranium deposits on the Navajo Nation to Leader's place of deadly meditation in the sweat lodge. His brain failed to cough up a connection. Darkness and light? The darkness of the damage uranium caused to those who had brought it up from the dark underground and milled it in the light.

Leader interrupted his thoughts. "Hey, did you take care of those video copies?"

"Yes, sir. I left some for the agents to see to understand our goals. I secured all the originals at the studio for us to collect before going to the airport."

"You destroyed the bad ones?"

"Of course, sir."

But Caseman knew there were three thumb drives Leader wanted erased that he hadn't dealt with. One captured the glorious meeting in which Leader disclosed their plan for the secretary, the marathon meditations and the prayers to exhaustion or beyond in the sweat lodge.

Because his search of the motor home headquarters had been thorough, Caseman figured Pat had hidden that thumb drive somewhere.

Caseman would never have given Pat the position of assistant producer because there was something suspicious about him, but he agreed with Leader that the man was smarter than Rollie or even Victor, their bearded assistant.

Pat had access to all the video and backups, reviewing them to make sure Case's edited copies showed the family in the best light and did the job well. But after Pat moved to that position of authority, they had to call off several demonstrations to protect Mother Earth because security in those venues had unexpectedly been enhanced. Case puzzled over how word of their plans could have moved outside the family. Pat seemed to be the only logical suspect.

Even so, the man would be alive if he hadn't criticized Leader's view that a woman should never have been named secretary of energy and talked about leaving the family. After he died, they searched his pockets to make sure he hadn't taken any thumb drives with him before Victor took the body away. Nothing to worry about, Case told himself.

And the other missing drive, the one on which he had recorded Leader ordering Pat's own death, Case had secured in the zip pocket of his own red windbreaker, now serving as Leader's pillow. He assumed Leader would want it destroyed, but he had erred on the side of caution. If Leader turned on him, as he had on Pat, Caseman saw that video as insurance.

Caseman wanted to get to the studio, trade the ugly truck for Leader's Mercedes, and speed to the airport. Things would be OK. They would regroup and continue the fight. Secretary Cooper would schedule more visits, and their plan to use her as a hostage to save the planet could be tweaked.

Leader had fallen silent, eyes closed, breathing steadily. He must be meditating, Case realized, using his fine mind to come up with the next step in the plan.

Caseman slowed as the road grew worse. He would rather be driving his own air-conditioned van. A lean coyote trotted into the road and Caseman swerved. The old truck rammed into a deep pothole.

"Watch where you're going, numbskull. You practically knocked my teeth out."

Caseman spoke up before he could stop himself. "I'm doing my best, sir."

"Your best needs work, Case. Pick up the speed and get this junk heap moving. And drive over there, where the road is smoother."

"Yes, sir, as soon as I can. The sand is deep there, and this truck's tires are nearly bald. At the top of the next ridge there should be—"

"Don't question me. Do it now."

Caseman steered for the smooth sand as ordered. The rear wheels spun themselves into a deep hole and sunk deeper when he tried rocking back and forth to get the truck out. To his amazement, Leader said nothing for a long time until Case finally suggested that his boss move behind the wheel while he got out of the truck to push.

"See that vehicle approaching back there with the lights flashing?" Leader said. "It's too far away yet to hear the siren, but I imagine it's wailing."

Caseman had been too busy with the immediate situation to notice.

"It's a Navajo Police SUV."

And with that, Leader slipped on the red windbreaker, opened the passenger door, and began to run down the wash. Caseman studied the situation for a split second, then began his stress reduction meditation. The hour of reckoning was here.

***

Bernie and Chee pulled up next to the turquoise pickup. The driver sat quietly but the passenger door hung open. They left her battered

SUV unit, guns drawn. Chee approached on the driver's side. Bernie walked toward the open passenger door.

Chee did the yelling. "Whoever is in that truck, get out now with your hands over your head."

The driver's door opened, and Caseman emerged.

"No one else in there." Bernie shouted the information, then handcuffed Caseman without any resistance while Chee held him at gunpoint.

"Where's the person who was in the truck with you?" Chee asked. "It was Leader, right?"

"Leader, yes. He took off down the wash." Caseman's voice was surprisingly calm. "He saw you coming and he ran off as soon as I stopped."

Bernie gave Chee a quick glance and decided she felt better than her husband did. "I'll do it." She ran in the direction Caseman indicated, following the footprints in the sand.

Chee searched Caseman's pockets for weapons, confiscated his cell phone, and secured him in the back of the unit.

Chee glanced down the wash where Bernie had gone. He didn't see her returning, and he was glad there had been no gunfire. At least not yet. He raced after her.

***

A regular routine of running kept Bernie sane and fit, so despite the heat, Leader's head start, and her own rough day, she began to catch up with him. Within a few minutes she was close enough that she knew the man could hear her. When she yelled at him to stop, he didn't, but he was running erratically, weaving from side to side. Then she watched him collapse heavily onto the sandy arroyo. She called to him again as she ran in his direction. There was no response.

By the time she reached him, he was lying face down, still as death, crumpled into the wash. She pulled her gun and squatted next to him. She could hear him panting for breath as she cuffed him. She hesitated, then touched his chubby neck, searching for a pulse, and found the faintest of flutters under a sweaty red tattoo that matched the others she had seen. She patted him down for weapons.

Despite the heat, he was wearing a red windbreaker. She pulled the fabric of the jacket free from beneath the man's bulk and felt something in the pocket. She ran her hand over the shape. It was small and flat. Assuming that it was one of the missing flash drives, she left it in place for the FBI.

"Chee!" she yelled as loud as she could.

"Bernie!" She saw him running toward her.

"I've got Leader. I'm OK." She stood up straight and felt the tension in her body relax. She knew there were lots of loose ends for the FBI agents to tie up. Sorting out the details might be harder if Leader died. Or perhaps his absence would free Caseman to tell the truth.

Chee pulled up next to her, gasping for breath.

"Take it easy," she said. "You were half dead earlier today, remember? Chill, OK. We've got this."

He smiled at her.

She pulled out her phone and, with the faintest of signals, dialed 911 for an ambulance. Then she called Agent Johnson, gave her a quick summary, and learned that an agent from the Yazzie investigation would be there soon to take charge of both suspects.

She took a deep breath of the high desert summer air. "Did you notice the tattoos the CUSP people have?"

"Yes. The solstice marker at Chaco Canyon." Chee smiled. "And that's today. And it's not over yet."

While Bernie waited with Leader, Chee walked back to search the stolen truck, finding only Mr. Yazzie's hat.

Caseman sat where Chee had planted him, eyes closed.

"Caseman, Rollie told us there are videos of Sethley's death, the plan to kidnap the secretary, the meditation marathon, and the sweat lodge prayers. Where are the thumb drives?"

Caseman shook his head. "Leader knows everything. I'm just the guy who takes his orders."

"I don't believe you. You're in on all this."

"I don't care what you think. All of us are just puppets. Servants of The Great Beyond."

Chapter 42

Darleen and Greg waited outside in the car for Mrs. Raymond. Greg kept the engine running for the air-conditioning to combat the searing heat, amplified by the pavement of the youth center's parking lot. Darleen told him about her call to Bernie and how her sister had urged her to talk to the Phoenix police. She had given Darleen's number to an investigator named Chandler who promised to call.

Time dragged on, and the call didn't come. Mrs. R stayed in the building. Greg got out, paced in the heat for a minute or two, made a call, and then came back. "I phoned the shelter here and they said Mrs. Raymond and Droid are talking and they will let me know if he wants to see me. Let's go to that crummy hotel. I need to give that owner a piece of my mind."

Darleen shook her head. "That situation is dangerous."

"That's right. They put my son and his grandmother in danger. It's just pure luck that we found Droid. They need to understand that this is unacceptable."

"Chandler will be calling to talk to us about the situation. Let's wait and see what he has to say."

Greg shook his head. "If someone actually calls from the police, they can reach me over there. And you can stay in the car if you don't want to raise hell. Or you can get out now and wait here."

"Going back there is a terrible idea."

Greg clicked on his seat belt and stared at her. "But you're in the driver's seat, so it looks like you're coming."

She sighed. "We're partners, remember? But now my job is to keep you from doing something you'll regret. You can't talk to Droid or bring him home if you're in jail for assault."

She saw the anger in his face, but he said nothing.

"Why don't you practice what you plan to tell Bea on me? You know, get out the most important stuff before the security guy comes over."

"OK." Greg took a deep breath. "What kind of underhanded operation are you running here? My boy should have never been allowed to get on that van. And his grandmother! What kind of treatment did you think she needed? You're pure evil. Aren't you ashamed of yourself for taking advantage of people like the ones who are here, and—"

"You're yelling," Darleen interrupted. "The security guy will strong-arm you and throw you out. Maybe he'll call the cops."

"But—"

"Hear me out. I want to find out why they took Mrs. R and what's behind all this, too. It bothers me. A lot. But calling Bea names will get you nowhere, except maybe arrested."

"I have to tell her what a rotten thing she's done. You aren't going to change my mind."

"Well, at least don't shout at her. I don't want to drive back to Shiprock by myself." She clearly remembered Bernie's closing words. *Don't get injured or arrested as part of this. These people are dangerous. Don't do anything stupid.*

They pulled into the Broadway Manor parking lot and found a spot. A white van was parked near the front doors. A woman with blue hair stood beside it, looking toward the lobby. A smallish man sat behind the steering wheel.

Greg leaped out of the car and yelled at the white van. "Hey! Are you the ones who kidnapped my son?"

The woman looked at him in surprise. The man turned toward Greg's voice, and Darleen saw his gold chain when it caught the light.

Greg kept moving toward the van.

"Get outa here!" the man shouted. "Private property."

"You're the ones, right?" Greg kept yelling. The woman stiffened and glared. The man slid from behind the steering wheel, preparing to leave the van. Darleen hoped they wouldn't get into a fistfight.

The blue-haired woman ignored Greg and headed toward the hotel. Darleen figured she was summoning the security guard.

The lobby doors opened, and a group of people began to walk toward the van. Some looked like Navajos, and all of them seemed weather-worn and desperate—the same look she found on the faces of people at the community kitchen.

Greg stopped yelling and headed for the open entrance doors.

"Hey! You can't go in there." Gold Chain was quicker than he looked and stronger, too. He trotted up behind Greg, lunged, and tackled him onto the parking lot asphalt. Darleen rushed to help, but Greg had already pushed himself to standing. His nose was bleeding.

"Keep an eye on the transports while I deal with this," Blue shouted at Gold Chain. She frowned at Darleen. "Your boyfriend is an idiot."

"He's not my boyfriend."

"Why are you causing trouble?" Blue squinted at her.

"We want some answers about a couple of people who came here from Shiprock, an old lady and a young guy. They are our relatives."

Blue lowered her voice. "I saw the lady yesterday. She's OK. The kid wasn't here for the appointment run. I don't know anything else."

"You know more than you're saying." Greg turned away from

the women toward Broadway Manor. "Something stinks about this. What happened to my boy is criminal."

Darleen and Blue watched as he dodged the crowd and attempted to push his way through to the lobby. Several of the people boarding the bus stepped aside for him. Then the security guard they had run into earlier appeared and blocked the entrance.

"Residents only."

"Get outa my way. I have to talk to the boss."

"Leave. Now." The guard was in Greg's face.

Greg took a small step back, and Darleen saw his body tense. "Chill," she called to him as she trotted to his side. "Remember why we're here. Remember Droid." When she reached him, she put a hand on his arm.

Greg stepped back.

When the guard left, Blue said to them, "Get over there in the shade and I'll talk to you for a minute. Hold on until we get the van loaded."

When the van was full, Blue kept her word.

"Look, I like that old gal, and the kid had good manners. Respectful. So listen to me. I know Bea won't help you, and she will turn nasty. She's strictly business. She's got money and connections. You two shouldn't be here."

Greg exhaled. "I don't . . . What's Bea's last name?"

Blue told them, and then moved toward the van. The engine was running.

"Where are you taking those people?" Darleen asked.

"They call it a sober house."

Darleen heard something in the woman's voice. "Where is it?"

Blue hesitated, then mentioned an address.

Greg looked at the locked doors of Broadway Manor again. "How do I reach the witch who runs this place?"

"You don't, unless you're dumber than this melting asphalt."

Darleen had another idea. She focused on Blue. "I can tell you have a conscience. Do you want to help stop this scam?"

Blue ran her fingers through her hair, then pulled a phone from her pocket. "Give me your number, missy. I can't talk now. I can't get fired until I have another job."

When they did a quick phone bump, Darleen noticed a missed call.

Blue climbed in the van and drove away. Greg's nose had started bleeding again. Darleen opened the car's back door, offered him some tissues, and persuaded him to lie on his back in the back seat until the nosebleed stopped. She started the engine for the air-conditioning and then pressed the number for the missed call.

The male voice on the other end of the line answered, "Sergeant Chandler. Is this Darleen Manuelito?"

"Yes."

"Great. Thanks for calling. The Navajo Police gave me your information. I have a bunch of questions for you, and the two people I think you are with. Can we find a time to talk?"

"I'm happy to do that, but I'll have to call you back"

Chandler had a deep, reassuring voice. "Sure. How long will you be in Phoenix?"

"I don't know yet. It depends on Greg, the man I came out here with, and the people we need to bring back to New Mexico."

Chandler offered to buy them lunch in half an hour.

"Lunch sounds great. Hold on. You need to talk to Greg."

She filled him in briefly and then handed him the phone. Greg explained his and Mrs. Raymond's situation and the issue with Droid. Then they drove back to the place where they had left Mrs. R.

For some reason, Darleen assumed that Mrs. R would be standing by the entrance, but of course she wasn't. Even if she and Droid had finished their conversation, it was too hot to wait outside. Because Greg was Droid's dad, Darleen expected him to check on them, but he didn't even unfasten his seat belt.

"Do you want me to ask about Droid?"

"Yeah. I acted like a jerk back there. I'm glad Droid didn't see it. I'm not surprised he doesn't want to talk to me."

"Your son must still be missing his mother," she said. "He's young. Give him time. Give yourself time, too."

He offered her the hint of a smile. "You're pretty wise for a wannabe nurse."

She walked to the door and pushed the intercom, introduced herself. After a few moments, the voice that came from the box asked if Andrew's father was with her.

"Yes. He's in the car."

"Andrew and the counselor would like him to come in."

Darleen went back to the car, delivered the message, and saw the relief on Greg's face. After he left, she called Chandler and explained the situation. Not only did he suggest a nearby place for lunch, he offered to pick her up.

"I'm in a white Toyota. You'll recognize me because I'm in shorts and a Hawaiian shirt. And because I'll roll down the window so you can see me, even though its one-ten out here."

"You'll recognize me because I'm a gorgeous Navajo wearing a blue-and-white T-shirt from the San Juan County health fair."

"You a doctor or something?"

"Just a something at this point." She laughed. "A tired something."

"We'll make this quick and painless. I really appreciate your help."

She texted Greg about the plan before she left.

The restaurant Chandler picked was quiet. He ordered a burger and she picked a salad. His questions honed in on what Darleen had observed at Broadway Manor. He recorded the conversation and also took some notes. She told him what Blue had said about the sober houses and gave him Blue's number and the address she'd mentioned, with the warning that she was nervous about getting fired.

"Tell me more about the woman in charge. You said her name was Bea, right?"

"Right." She gave him the other information Blue had shared.

"What does she look like?"

Darleen started to describe Bea and then came up with a better idea. She had a notebook and a pencil in her purse. "Give me a minute, and I'll make you a sketch."

She took her time to get it right, then handed the paper to him. "She has pale eyes, kind of a gray blue. Dark blond hair."

"Wow. I recognize her. She's been on our radar for a year with a different name." He grinned and tapped the picture. "You're good at this."

"Thanks. I love art, and people's faces interest me because they are so uniquely different."

Chandler finished his iced tea. "I remember some posters we got from a retired detective, another Navajo, Joe Leaphorn. Do you know about those? They were part of the Missing and Murdered Indigenous Women project. The art on them was first rate."

Darleen grinned. "I worked with Lieutenant Leaphorn on MMIW. It was tough to make sketches. Some of those women had been gone for a while. I had to look at the photos and figure how they might have aged."

"That was genius. You have real talent."

Darleen studied what was left of her salad. She wasn't used to receiving compliments.

Chandler asked a few more questions and thanked her for her help. At his insistence, she was about to order dessert when her phone buzzed with a text from Greg:

Need to stay here tonight at least to make sure Droid's OK. Sorry for the change, partner. More later. Getting hotel.

She didn't say anything, but Chandler must have read her expression.

"Bad news?"

Darleen thought about what to say. "It's actually good news, but inconvenient for me. Greg and Mrs. Raymond have to hang here longer than we planned because of Greg's son, Andrew."

Chandler wiped his mouth with a napkin. "I bet they were your ticket home, right?"

"Yes, I'm ready to get back to Shiprock for my job and school on Monday. But we came in Greg's car, so I'm stuck here until he's ready to go."

"Maybe not. Before you and I met, I asked Officer Manuelito to help transport a group of Navajos who were caught up in this fake sobriety scheme and want to get home. She's your sister, right?"

"Right."

"So she might solve your problem and give you a ride."

"I'll talk to her about that." Darleen wished she'd brought another change of clothes, her sketchbook, and other things to help her adjust to this sudden development. Some extra cash would be nice, too. Maybe Chee or Bernie could make sure that Mrs. Darkwater's dog had enough food and water. And Mama, poor Mama, might think she'd been abandoned. But so it was.

Chandler thanked Darleen again for the drawing and her information. "Where can I drop you off?"

"I guess at the youth shelter where you picked me up. I'll settle in there while Greg and Mrs. Raymond get things figured out. I still have a key to the car."

"I've got a better idea. Why not wait at the public library? It's not far from the youth shelter, and much more comfortable than a car in a hot parking lot." Chandler nodded, pleased with his suggestion. "They're open late today. Air-conditioned. Good books, free WiFi, a place to charge your phone."

"Sounds good, but I need to stop at the shelter, get my homework out of the car, leave Greg the key, and tell him where I'll be."

"Of course. We'll go there first."

Chandler's kindness reminded her of the way Chee and her sister dealt with people.

As they drove, Chandler shared an idea with her. "Here's something to think about. Maricopa County just got a juicy grant to hire an artist or two to work with us on all kinds of drawings. Suspects, kidnapped children, elders who wandered off and might be in danger. Assignments like that. Would you consider a job with us?"

Darleen sucked in a breath and grinned. "Gosh. I don't know what to say."

"Say yes!" He added an exclamation point with his voice. "At least yes, you'll think about it. This is a chance to use your skills and do some good. Phoenix is a fine place to live. My family and I love it here, especially in the winter, and I know you'd like it, too. The department would help you find an apartment."

The offer stunned her. "I . . . I . . . I'm flattered, but . . ."

"Read the posting about the position. You'd have a leg up because you've worked with police before. I'd be your supervisor and I know we'd get along great."

Darleen nodded. She felt as though she were getting solid advice from a wise uncle.

After stopping at the shelter, Chandler let her out in front of the largest library she had ever seen. Darleen took out her phone to put it on mute before she went inside. She found three missed calls from Slim, but no voicemails. Slim, the patient man who put up with her moods and even Mama's bad days, had finally had too much. The man she loved and had treated badly was so furious with her he wouldn't even leave a grumpy message.

She called him. When he didn't answer, she tried to explain what had happened to his voicemail. She sped through the beginning. "Now I'm stuck in Phoenix. I got myself into a big mess. I can't blame you for being mad at me, but don't give up on me. You're the best man I've ever . . ." She wanted to say more, but her voice clogged up.

She went into the library, noting that it was named after Burton Barr. She'd never heard of him, so she distracted herself by reading the plaque that explained what an important man he was. He must have been special, she thought, to have such a fine five-story library named for him. The building had three elevators and a giant staircase. Maybe Phoenix wasn't so bad.

Darleen rode to the fifth floor. It was filled with people young and old, using the computers. She tried to force herself to study. She'd removed her books and laptop from her bag, but instead of school, she kept thinking about the missed calls from Slim.

After half an hour of schoolwork, she logged on to her email. There was the job description Chandler had talked about. The starting salary was three times more than she was making as a health aide on the Navajo Nation. No college degree was required to start, but the program would pay for her to go to school.

She texted Chandler to thank him, and texted Bernie a situation update and asked about a ride home. When she'd done all the classwork she could stand, Darleen worked on the sketch she was making for Slim, a drawing of the old car he'd been restoring. She finished it and then went back downstairs and stood in the lobby. She had to make another call, so she dialed the number. She expected it to go to voicemail, but this time Victoria answered.

"Darleen! I've been thinking about you. Mother isn't back yet, and I'm really worried."

Darleen quickly walked outside and found some shade so she could talk.

"Mrs. R is safe. It's complicated, but—" But Darleen didn't finish her thought. Victoria was sobbing.

Finally, the woman calmed down enough to talk. "Oh, honey, thank you for telling me. I've been so stressed. You know Mom and I have our differences, but I can't help loving her. I miss her like crazy. Why don't you come over and have a cold drink and tell me what's going on."

"I can't. I'm in Phoenix."

Before Darleen could explain, Victoria took over. "Greg told me that he was going. Something about Droid and his grandma, and you'd offered to help. Gosh, you did it! When are you coming back?"

"Well, that's another reason I was calling. I might need a ride to Shiprock."

The phone went quiet for a few moments, and Darleen waited.

"You're asking me to drive all that way?"

"It would be great if you would. And you could see your mother, too, and your nephew. Mrs. R wants to stay until they know for sure what's happening with Droid."

"Are you—" Darleen heard Victoria bite off the rest. "Let me think about it. I'll let you know if I can, but there's Mr. Fluff. He gets carsick. Tell Mom hey for me." And the line went dead.

Darleen went back into the library and tried to cheer up.

Chapter 43

Organizing the details of the Navajo Police Department's Rainbow Bridge trip to rescue the displaced tribal members required considerable effort, but the chief and his staff focused on it and got it done quickly. Because many of the Navajo people Chandler had contacted were from the Shiprock district, it made sense for Bernie to be the contact. Chee confirmed that the plan made sense.

Bernie went out to the deck and sat with Mama while she called her sister. Darleen had texted that she needed a ride home.

Her call went to voicemail, but a few minutes later Darleen called back.

"Hi."

"Hi." Darleen sounded far away.

"I'll talk to you about the ride in a minute, but Mama and I are sitting here listening to the river. Would you like to say hello to her?"

"Of course."

Bernie heard the eagerness in her sister's voice. She gave Mama's arm a gentle touch.

"Your other daughter wants to talk to you."

Mama opened her eyes. "Oh, where is she?"

"Here, on the phone."

Bernie handed the phone to Mama and switched it to speaker so they both could hear.

"Hello, Mama."

"Oh, where you are? I've been missing you."

"I've been missing you, too, Shimá. How is today going for you?"

"I am an old person now. Did you know that?"

"Yes. And did you know that I love you more than ever?" Darleen seemed to choke on the words.

"That's good." Mama then stared at the phone in silence

Bernie took the phone back. "Our mother was snoozing on the couch when I called you."

"It's OK. I know how she is. You sound tired, too."

Bernie left the comment sit unanswered. "So, you need a ride home?"

Darleen hesitated. "I think so. Greg and Mrs. R are figuring things out. They're in a motel tonight, and they say I can crash there, too. But I want to get home. I wasn't prepared for staying overnight, so I didn't bring a change of clothes. I should have thought this through better. I didn't even tell Slim."

"Why not?" Bernie wondered how that relationship was going, or if it was over.

"Dumb, I know. I didn't want to bother him because he had all those papers to grade for his summer school kids, and he's taking that class to renew his accreditation."

"Sounds like he's been ignoring you."

"And I've been ignoring him back, but not because I don't care about him. I didn't tell him because I didn't want him to waste time worrying about me."

"He called here last night, wondering if you'd come by to see Mama, and asked if I had seen you. I told him that you'd left me a message about going to Phoenix, but that was all I knew. He sounded sad that you hadn't talked to him. He's a good guy. If I were you, I'd be nice to him."

Bernie heard some sniffling, the kind that came with unfallen tears.

"He called me three times but didn't leave a message. I texted him a couple hours ago, apologized, and said I was stuck in Phoenix. Nothing. I guess he's done with me."

Then Darleen said, "Don't worry about this. I'll figure it out. I think I left enough food and water for Bidziil, but could you ask Chee to check on him?"

"Sure." Dogs made Bernie nervous.

Mama poked at Bernie. "Get off the phone. Tell them we don't want any."

"In a minute, Mama."

Darleen said, "Sergeant Chandler told me you might be coming to Phoenix to pick up some Navajos."

"Yes, that's why I called. I'm leaving in the next day or two, as soon as we get the final details worked out. I'll have to stay in Phoenix as long as it takes to gather up the Navajo people who were trapped in this scheme. I was hoping you could spend more time with Mama while I'm gone."

"I'd be glad to, if I can get back to Shiprock."

Bernie said, "Chandler mentioned that you were a big help. He thinks Broadway Manor can be closed permanently. They have an arrest warrant for the woman who ran it. She was involved in a number of other scams that brought Navajos, Apaches, even native people from outside the Southwest, to Phoenix. She used several different names for herself and the organizations she started. Other crooks running similar scams did the same thing."

"Why be so mean?"

"Chandler says it was about money. When he questioned her earlier, she tried to pin the whole thing on her ex-husband."

Darleen paused. "If it doesn't work out with Greg, can I get a ride back with you and the ones you're picking up?"

"I hope so, but I can't say for sure until I clear it with the chief. Worse comes to worst, I'll buy you a bus ticket. Don't worry. I'll make sure you get home soon."

She heard Darleen's deep sigh. "All of this is my own fault. Chee or you, or maybe both of you, thought this was a bad idea."

"We were wrong. You and Greg found Mrs. Raymond and that young man against the odds in such a huge city. You did a lot of good. Don't be hard on yourself. Do you have enough money for the next few days?"

"I'll get by. Don't worry about me."

After the call ended, Bernie sat quietly with Mama, listening to the river's song. She tried to put aside the images of the women in that terrible fake sweat lodge and the look of fear on the little boy's face as they helped his grandfather. She remembered a happier sight—the relief in Chee's eyes when she found him in the motor home.

What she had seen at the Yazzie place would be hard to forget, but Uliana's courage, Sam's bravery, and Mr. Yazzie's clear thinking helped restore her faith in human goodness.

She felt Mama flinch, and came back to reality.

"Mama, are you OK?"

"Yes. I was late bringing the sheep in." Her mother patted her hand. "You stay with me now."

"I will. Let's go inside and have some tea."

"Where?"

"Right in there. Come. I'll show you."

Mama's moods were transient these days, and Bernie was grateful for this calm in the late afternoon. Fatigue settled over them both like an irresistibly soft blanket. Bernie helped Mama stretch out for a nap. She needed to stretch out on the couch and close her eyes, too.

As she was leaving the room, Mama reached for her hand. "Do you have children?"

"No, not yet."

"You know how to help people. You would be a good mother."

***

Chee got a phone call from Agent Johnson with news of the case they were hoping for. She told Bernie that Leader would live and both he and Caseman were in custody along with Rollie and Victor. Johnson was pleased with the investigation and the evidence they had helped the FBI find.

He joined Bernie on the deck. The day had finally cooled a bit.

"What was the point of all that drama at the Yazzie place?" Bernie asked. "What did any of this have to do with uranium and the Navajo Nation?"

"When I took Caseman to jail, he couldn't stop talking. He explained that Leader told him he was drawn to the Navajo Nation because of our isolation, and our history with uranium and coal mining. He called it a shameful legacy. CUSP had been tracking the secretary's events, and knew she was coming this way before the chief did.

"Remember the thumb drives we were looking for? The one with the video of the plans for the sweat lodge deaths and of Sethley's murder?"

"Of course." Bernie said. "Did they turn up?"

"Johnson said they found one in the red jacket labeled *Pat*. It shows Leader and Caseman threatening Rollie unless he fights to the death, and then a man with a goatee killing Pat. They found a second thumb drive in Caseman's pants pocket and it had plans for the secretary's kidnapping. And they also retrieved a third thumb drive with something unexpected on it."

"Tell me."

Chee grinned. "Dobbs found it but I'm taking the credit. When I put the dead man's hat in the evidence bag, I saw an odd lump in the sweat band. I mentioned it to Dobbs when I gave him the bag. I asked him to let me know about it. Well, he pulled out a thumb drive hidden in there, and he and Agent Johnson took a look. Sethley had all the files about the group's financials. The people who got defrauded might get some of their money back."

Bernie took a moment to absorb the news. "Those CUSP guys let their egos do them in."

She told him about the call from Darleen. "She's annoyed with herself for getting into another jam, but she'll be fine. Let's call it a day, handsome."

He nodded. "What about Mama? I'll sleep on the couch here to make sure she's OK."

Bernie grinned. "I talked to Mrs. Bigman about how we worry at night. She left us a gift. It's a monitor she used for her little one. She doesn't need it any more so I set it up in our old bedroom. If Mama, needs something, we can take care of it. We can sleep together in the trailer."

"You are brilliant as well as beautiful. I've missed cuddling up with you."

Chee gave her a kiss.

Chapter 44

After talking to Bernie, Darleen called Slim again, and got a robot message that his phone was "out of the service area," whatever that meant. She texted Greg, asking for an update on Droid. And maybe, she thought, he could lend her the money for bus fare home.

Darleen went back inside the beautiful library and used the free internet to check the bus schedule. She studied a little more, and charged her phone with the library's electricity. She found a book with an interesting cover in the giveaway pile and put it in her purse. The library would close in half an hour. Then, if she hadn't heard from Greg, she'd walk back to the youth shelter and wait.

She took another look at the job listing Chandler had sent. It cheered her a bit that he appreciated her talent. But Phoenix? So far from Mama and Bernie and Chee. And maybe, if Slim got over being mad at her, they could at least be friends.

Phoenix?

Part of her brain kept whispering, *You know you love to draw. What's really there for you on the rez?*

But what about her new dream of being a nurse? Could she take nursing classes in Phoenix while she worked with Chandler? She would consider it later, she told herself. She was too tired to think straight.

Her phone, which she'd muted as a good library guest, told her it was 114 degrees outside. Before she could slip it back in her pocket, it buzzed.

Slim wrote: Where are you?

She texted back: Phoenix Main Library. Long story. Let's talk please.

She added a praying hands emoji.

You have to leave the building to take a call, right?

Right. Hot out there

Slim wrote: OK Give me 15 minutes

She sent back a thumbs-up emoji. Then she logged out of the library's computer, gathered her stuff, and rode the elevator to the main floor. After she talked to Slim, she could get in touch with Greg again. No buses left for Gallup or Farmington until the morning. She'd ask if she could stay with him and Mrs. R overnight.

Darleen waited for fourteen nervous minutes, then walked through the big doors and found a spot in the shade where she could take Slim's call. The heat hadn't relented, but that didn't matter. She'd stay there as long as she had to, apologize for not telling him she was leaving town and for not taking his calls, and try not to cry when he broke up with her.

She looked at the phone, waiting for it to ring

Then she felt someone standing beside her. The librarian had cautioned her about homeless people, so she turned, expecting a request for money.

"Hey there, gorgeous." Slim smiled at her. "I've been missing you."

"Oh. How . . ." And she felt the rush of tears.

He put a finger across her lips. "You sister told me you were in Phoenix and you mentioned the Barr library in your first text. It's too hot to stand out here. We'll have a lot of time to talk on the way home."

And then Slim draped his arm over her shoulders, and they walked to his car.

***

Joe Leaphorn, retired Navajo Police lieutenant and detective, looked across the restaurant table at Jim Chee. "I hear that now you're filling in as captain at the Shiprock station."

"We don't know when Captain Adakai will be well enough to come back to work."

"When or if," Leaphorn said. "Good job on Operation Rainbow Bridge. I figure you're up for a commendation and a promotion."

"We brought home quite a few relatives." Chee sipped his coffee, ready to change the subject. "If Adakai can't come back, the chief has talked to me about taking charge in Shiprock. More pay, less risk. But I don't know if I'm ready to totally give up being in the field."

"I get that. That's why I never did it. I mean run the department." Leaphorn stirred a bit of sugar into his coffee. "But we both understand that good leadership is important. I hope you realize it's an honor to be considered. Captain Jim Chee."

Chee shook his head. "I'm thinking about it."

They sat absorbed in their thoughts while the server brought breakfast.

Leaphorn spread some jelly on his toast. "I'm glad you have a day off. I heard about that cult. Tough case. When I encountered that level of violence, it left me shaken."

"That's how I feel, and Bernie had it bad, too."

"Where's Bernie? I thought your wife could join us."

"She wanted to, but she had a date with a four-year-old. She's at the Yazzie place checking on Mr. Yazzie and his grandson."

"Spending a day with a kid, huh? You understand what that could lead to."

Chee laughed. "I hope so."

***

Bernie had found that in the days following the CUSP case her thoughts returned to the Yazzie family, especially to the little boy. She missed him.

So while Chee caught up with their mentor, she drove her Tercel back to the Yazzie place. It lifted her spirits to discover that the dangerous sweat lodge was gone, the motor home headquarters towed away, and the first summer rains had begun to green up the vegetation. She steered toward the corral, where she saw Mr. Yazzie unloading some hay from the back of his turquoise truck. She lowered the car window and, as sign of respect, waited for his acknowledgment before she climbed out.

Mr. Yazzie's face lit up as he walked toward her. "Yá'át'ééh, hatsóí ashkiígíí. I didn't recognize you in that old car. And no uniform today either. Welcome."

She got out and saw Sam shyly standing behind his grandfather. "A friendly visit today. Hastiin, how have you been?"

"I'm healing and the Sprout has been a big help. But we haven't gone horseback riding." Mr. Yazzie moved his hand to his ribs. "Still too tender. The boy is disappointed."

Sam patted his grandfather's leg. "It's OK."

Bernie squatted to be on the boy's level. "I have an idea. Maybe we could ride together today."

"Can I, Shicheii?"

Mr. Yazzie saddled Naabaahii and off they went riding double. Bernie rode the horse toward the sandstone cliffs at a comfortable walk. Sprout leaned into her and sighed. "I'm glad to see you."

"I glad to be here with you, too."

With the warm comfort of the horse beneath her and the plea-sure of the boy's company, Bernie felt herself begin to relax. As they headed away from the place where bad things had happened, Sam shifted against her. "Do you have kids?"

"No," Bernie said. Not yet. But maybe someday.

When she got home, she stood on the deck with her good hus-band, listening to the soothing song of the San Juan River. Chee squeezed her hand.

"I told you that the chief wants me to apply for Adakai's job. Well, what we saw with the CUSP case made me realize that I have skills that haven't been put to use in planning, organizing, training, hiring, reading people and situations. Becoming captain could be a positive thing. I'm open to it."

Bernie gave the idea time to settle. "The evil I saw with that case disturbed me, too. I've decided to step back a little, take a break. I know Mama is going to need more care and it's already a challenge juggling my job, Mrs. Bigman's availability, and Darleen's schedule. Now that Slim is back in her life and she's thinking of moving to Phoenix, Sister will be less available."

Bernie looked at the old cottonwoods. "I'm ready for a big change, but it will be a big change for you, too. My idea involves more than helping with Mama."

She saw the look of attention on his face.

"I loved being with Sprout today. It helped me realize that I'd like us to . . ." She felt the tears building and told him what was in her heart.

He gently placed his hand on her cheek and whispered her name.

"Your idea is perfect. We're both ready now." And he pulled her into a warm embrace.

GLOSSARY

Adláanii: Drunkard
Ahéhéé: Thank you
Amásání: Maternal grandmother
Aoo': Yes
Ayóó aníínishní: I'm sorry
Bidziil: The strong one
Bilagáana: White person
Ch'eeh dighahii: Turtle
Diné: The People, the Navajo word for the Navajo people
Diné bizaad: Navajo Language
Diyin Diné: The Holy People of the Navajo
Dooda: No
Hastiin: Title of respect for an older man
Hatááłii: Medicine man, healer
Hatsóí ashkiígíí: Granddaughter
Hózhó: A state of peace, balance, beauty, and harmony
Hwéeldi: The place of suffering. Fort Sumner, the internment
  camp at the end of The Long Walk
Jish: Small pouch worn for protection usually made of deer

skin. Usually contains a few items that have totemic, spiritual, and ceremonial value.

Leetso: Uranium, "yellow dirt."

Lood doo na'ziihii: Cancer. Literally, the wound that never heals

Naabaahii: Warrior

Na'nízhoozhí: The sacred rainbow bridge at Lake Powell

Naakai binát'oh: Marijuana

Nayee: Monster, something that interferes with a successful life

Shicheii: My maternal grandfather or daughter's son

Shideezhí: My younger sister

Shimá: Mother. Also a term of respect for a woman

Shimásání: Maternal grandmother

Shimáyazhí: Maternal aunt, literally "little mother"

Shíyázhí: Endearing term for a son

Ta'cheeh: Sweat Lodge

T'iis nazbas: Circle of Cottonwood trees, Navajo for Teec Nos Pos, a settlement about 30 miles northwest of the town of Shiprock, NM

Tsé Bit'a'í: Ship Rock, the geological feature

Yá'át'ééh: Hello, it is good

Yá'át'ééh, hatsóí ashkiígíí: Hello, my friend

Ya'iishjááshchilí: The month of June

AUTHOR'S NOTE AND ACKNOWLEDGMENTS

Unlike my other novels, which began with a location on the Navajo Nation as their inspiration, this book started with an idea. The seed came from a real-life tragedy—the kidnapping and exploitation of Navajos and other Indigenous people by unscrupulous operators of fake drug and alcohol rehabilitation centers in Arizona. The scheme primarily preyed on people enrolled in the American Indian Health Program, among them many Diné. The Navajo Nation's Operation Rainbow Bridge team believe up to 8,000 men and women from the Navajo Nation may have been tricked by these fake programs. Then they were abandoned in Phoenix and its suburbs.

This massive Medicaid fraud probably started around 2019 and had two groups of victims. The first? The addicts who were promised treatment for substance abuse disorders but instead received substandard care or no care at all. Some were given addictive drugs and alcohol to keep them complacent while fraudsters continued billing for phony treatment. These victims were carried off the reservation in white vans with the hope of coming home sober. Some of them died instead.

The second group of victims is the United States taxpayers who were bilked of more than $2 billion. When Arizona Attorney General Kris Mayes announced the discovery of the Medicaid scam, she called it "one of the biggest scandals in Arizona history." In one case, Mayes said, Medicaid was billed for more than thirteen hours a day for alcohol rehabilitation services for a four-year-old child. As I write this, Arizona authorities have issued forty-five indictments in the investigation, including one against two men for thirty counts of fraud amounting to more than $9.4 million. Arizona has suspended more than 300 fake providers and assisted 10,000 or more victims of the scam.

In late June 2024, the United States Attorney General announced criminal charges against seven defendants in connection with Medicare and Medicaid fraud against the Arizona Health Care Cost Containment System. Brian Driscoll, acting special agent in charge of the FBI's Phoenix Field Office, said, "Fraud against government funded health care systems not only costs taxpayers billions each year, but as we've seen in Arizona, deprives critical care and benefits for our most vulnerable populations."

When these scams were discovered, the phony sober houses closed, leaving their residents without food, housing, or even a way back home. The Navajo Nation established Operation Rainbow Bridge to reunite the Diné people affected by the scam with family if they wished. Navajo police officers went to Phoenix to help the victimized people.

The other story in *Shadow of the Solstice* grew from the legacy of exploitation of the valuable underground resources found on the Navajo Nation. The riches include large deposits of uranium, coal, oil, and natural gas. The Nation has benefitted from and suffered damaging consequences as a result. Among all of these gifts of nature, the Diné have an especially troubled history with uranium mining.

Beginning in the 1940s, the Navajo Nation leased land to U.S. companies for uranium extraction and milling as part of the defense effort for World War II and beyond. In addition to serving bravely in the armed forces, many Navajos worked as miners and in the uranium mills. Often families would move with these workers to uranium camps and nearby towns. Some miners constructed homes with uranium-rich rocks from the mine debris or used water collected from the mines in their homes, unaware that these practices left them contaminated with radiation.

In 1950, the U.S. Public Health Service began to investigate the effects of radiation on the human body, enrolling more than 4,000 miners in a study without their consent. The government learned that exposure radiation had negative heath consequences, but neglected to effectively share the information with Navajo uranium workers and their families. When most uranium mines shut down in the 1970s due to a drop in uranium prices, mining companies left Navajo land abruptly. Piles of radioactive waste and open mines remained. In 2024, there were between 500 and 1,000 abandoned uranium mines and milling sites on the Navajo Nation.

Many Navajos learned about uranium's dangerous, long-reaching effects from tragic firsthand experience. A terrible legacy of disease and suffering is the apparent result of the exceptionally high level of uranium exposure among Navajo Nation residents. Birth defects, infertility, diabetes, kidney failure, hypertension, lung disease, and several kinds of cancer are among the health issues for the miners and their families. The problems continue.

In 2005, the Navajo Nation banned all uranium mining across its sprawling, ore-rich land. By then, nearly 30 million tons of the radioactive ore had been extracted. The tribe began regulating the transportation of uranium ore across its land in 2012. The route brought ore from a mine near the Grand Canyon to the only operating conventional uranium mill in the country, the White Mesa

Uranium Mill in southeast Utah. The route passes through both Ute Mountain Ute and Navajo lands.

In 2024, Navajo President Buu Nygren issued an executive order temporarily banning the transport of uranium ore across the Navajo Nation without the tribe's consent. Nygren signed the order after trucks had already carried an estimated fifty tons of uranium ore through tribal land in one day. The Navajo Nation now has tougher laws calling for better notice of uranium ore shipments across tribal land and requiring transport fees and emergency preparedness plans.

The uranium waste site in *Shadow of the Solstice* is loosely based on the Shiprock Disposal Site, which sits a mile south of the town of Shiprock. The site is a former uranium and vanadium ore-processing facility built and operated from 1954 until 1968. In 1983, the U.S. Department of Energy (DOE) and the Navajo Nation entered into an agreement for site cleanup. By September 1986, all tailings and associated materials were encapsulated in a disposal cell built on top of the existing tailings piles. This was not an easy job: the cell contains approximately 2.5 million tons of residual radioactive waste.

The site is monitored, managed, maintained, and inspected by DOE's Office of Legacy Management. The office conducts annual inspections and tests groundwater to verify that the disposal cell is leak free. For the purposes of my story, I made the place where the body is discovered different than the real site.

And here are a few words about the summer solstice—the longest day of the year. The celestial event marks the astronomical beginning of summer, although in the sunny Southwest, where I live, the solstice is preceded by a parade of hot, dry days.

The summer solstice occurs when one of Earth's poles tilts toward the sun at its most extreme angle. The date changes a bit but is always around June 21. The name *solstice* comes from two Latin words: *sol* for sun and *sistere* meaning to stand still. At the summer solstice, the sun reaches its highest point in the sky.

Solstices have been celebrated world-wide for thousands of years. The Diné term for this event, Jóhonaa'éí T'áá' Nídeesdzá, can be translated as "in the summer the sun travels back." Many view the solstice as a time for contemplation and change, and an opportunity to consider the wonders of our beautiful world.

Chaco Canyon, a UNESCO World Heritage site in northwestern New Mexico on the edge of the Navajo Nation, offers a variety of public education events connected to the solstice. When the sun rises on the summer solstice in this remote place, the morning rays will shine directly through a window on the northeast side of a kiva, or ceremonial chamber, to illuminate a niche in the opposite wall. The Chacoan people, ancestors of today's Pueblo Indians, were keen observers of the sky. In addition to the famous sun dagger petroglyph mentioned in the novel, they created other architectural features to document specific solar events.

This book would not be here without the superb help of editor Miranda Ottewell, whose bright mind and sharp eyes made this novel so much better. A thousand thank-yous.

As always, deepest appreciation to my talented beta readers: David Greenberg, Gail Greenberg, Benita Budd, and Lucy Moore. An extra tip of the hat to Dave Tedlock who in addition to reading the unedited manuscript helped me handle problems concerning the structure and content of this book with skill and insight. He also brought me coffee.

Big thanks to my editor, Sarah Stein, assistant editor Jackie Quaranto, and Nikki Baldauf and her staff for their help with the manuscript. As always, I appreciate the good work of Rachel Elinsky and Tom Hopke for their assistance with promotions and publicity.

Arin McKenna is a whiz at helping me on my website and social media.

The name of one of the characters here, Uliana Belkina, came from Robert and Nataliia Elliott. The Elliotts were the high bidders in an auction to benefit ReadWest, and their generosity gave them the opportunity to create the name for a character. Uliana is the Elliotts' granddaughter, and I'm sure she will be as smart and kind as the character named for her. Or even more so. ReadWest Adult Literacy Center is a New Mexico nonprofit 501(c)3 that has helped adults with low literacy for more than thirty-five years. They specialize in reading, writing, high school equivalency programs, computer literacy, and financial literacy.

I am grateful to the men and women who work in law enforcement for the Navajo Nation and with other agencies that help keep us safe. I deeply appreciate the booksellers who have cheered for me, recommended my books to customers, and hosted events either live or electronically. I owe a huge debt of gratitude to public libraries for extending to me the honor of speaking about my work to their constituencies. I appreciate the ongoing support of my all readers, and hold my fans close to my heart. A warm thank-you to you, one and all.

ABOUT THE AUTHOR

ANNE HILLERMAN is the bestselling author of the Leaphorn, Chee & Manuelito mysteries. She is also an executive producer of the *Dark Winds* television series on AMC based on her and her father Tony Hillerman's Navajo detective stories. When Anne's not working, she loves to walk with her dogs, read, cook, travel, and enjoy the night sky. She lives in Santa Fe, New Mexico, and Tucson, Arizona.